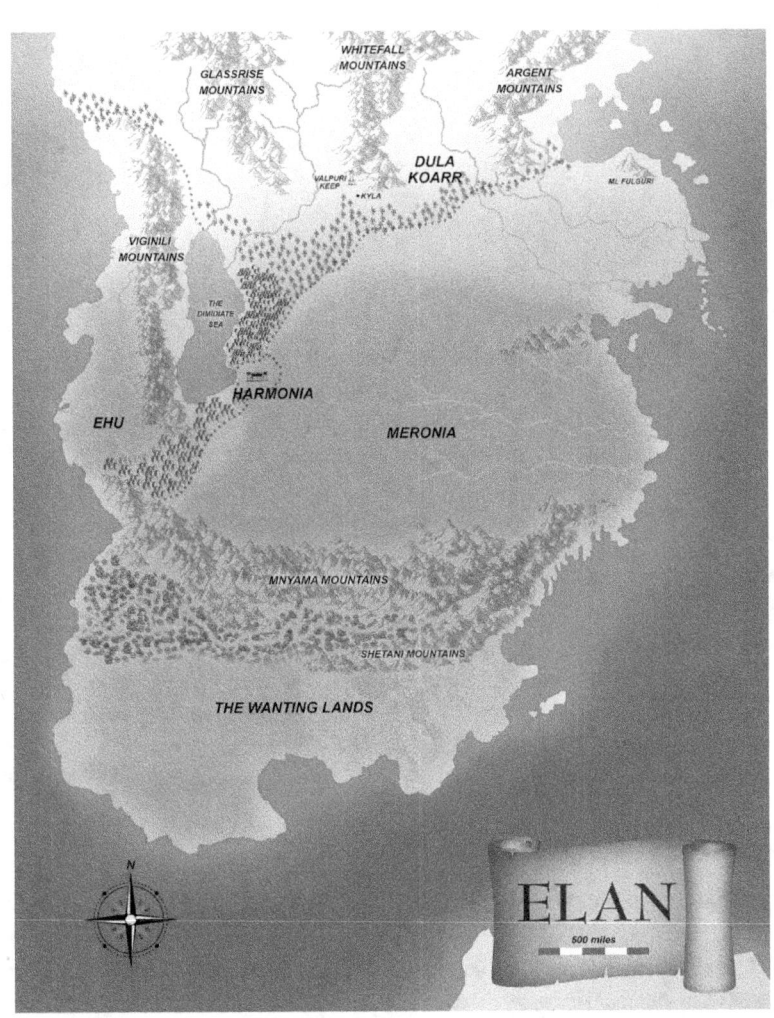

Published by Pandahead Publishing a division of Pandahead Productions. Pandahead Publishing and the pandahead logo are trademark of Pandahead Productions.

Book design by Pandahead Productions

Cover and map illustrations by Brett Brooks

Please visit www.championsofelan.com

The publisher is not responsible for websites (or their content) that are not owned by the publisher.

ISBN: 978-0-9723710-9-4

DEDICATION

I have had a lot of help with this book. People who have given me their time and effort to help this be the best book it can be at this time. So, with that said, I want to thank Mike Morrey, Katherine Anderson-Davilla, and Joni Lauri for all of their contributions to the end product.

And a special thanks to my amazing wife, Allyson. Your continued support keeps me going.

-Brett Brooks

THE CHAMPIONS OF ELAN

CHILD OF SHADOWS

CHAPTER
ONE

THE COLD

At first, it was nothing more than a shadow on the snow—a patch of low light. After it moved, it revealed itself as an animal. And after that first revelation passed, she became something uniquely her own.

Renarde took another four steps in the snow. Prancing, high steps as she sunk to almost mid-thigh in the drifts. The silver of her coat picked up the lightness of her surroundings, making only her dark chest and belly, and the tips of her tail and ears to stand out. Her ears swiveled, finding a direction for her to turn, and she followed them slowly. Eventually, she stood perfectly still, waiting….

With a sudden burst, she leapt high into the air and came down face first into a snowbank, leaving only her butt, tail, and legs sticking straight up out of the snow.

For a moment, she didn't move. And then a wiggle. And a twist. Then she pulled herself back, stepping up out of the snowbank, her face plastered with the soft white fluff. She shook her head viciously, throwing snow in every direction.

"Huh. I was sure that it was there," she stated with a frown. She turned her head to the left and then right, her ears twisting and tail twitching. Her eyes narrowed into slits of blue steel. "You may have won this round, but this isn't over."

With a short hop, she turned to her right and started walking, roughly northeast, bobbing her head to an unheard tune.

For the past two months Renarde had been walking north, looking for…something. She wasn't exactly sure what it was, but she was reasonably sure that she would know when she found it. At least that was her plan. It wasn't exactly cleared when she left Harmonia—at least she didn't remember it being cleared. Thibaan said a whole bunch of things, but it eventually just evolved down to her staring at her and nodding.

The one thing that she did remember was that she was the first to leave. Thibaan, Porter, and Altair were still in Harmonia as far as she knew, but they all wanted to have a plan and some concept of what they…yadda, yadda, yadda. It all became a drone at some point in her head. How could they plan for so long with the world out here calling to them?

She spun around, her head high and her eyes darting left and right.

"I don't know how everyone could stay behind. There are so many new things out here." She mused aloud. "Harmonia was amazing, sure, with its people and everything, and the goddesses and the castle and all, but this…this is living. Being able to just run and discover and find new and interesting things to see.

"Like all those dark green trees with the odd, pokey green needle-like leaf things. And the big birds that keep following me everywhere I go. And the wolves. There sure are a lot of wolves. And even those odd lights waving through the occasional night sky like…colorful ribbons stretching to some hidden present or something."

She took a deep breath of the cool air and trotted along, doing a remarkable job of staying on top of the snow.

"Of course there is plenty to smell and taste, too. True, most of it is the strong smell coming from those trees, but I like that smell, so…okay."

Her ears swiveled about, twitching every now and then.

"Oh, and all of those neat sounds." She pointed randomly as she spoke. "The cry of those strange birds. The howls of the wolves. The whistle of the wind off of the mountains and the snow. The clash of steel and cries of battle."

She stopped herself and turned her head to the side. Her ears continued to twist and turn, searching for something.

"Okay, that's not normal."

With a short hop she began to run, dropping down to all fours and scurrying across the top of the snow. Her tail weaved and bobbed behind her as she dropped her head down and rushed as fast as the terrain allowed towards the sound growing louder with each step.

Her speed increased when she reached the edge of the woods and a break in the snow. Racing along the forest floor she dodged and darted between trees, her long, lithe body a silver streak against the dull color.

It only took a minute or so until the sound was very close. She slowed down, slinking her way up the rise and behind a tree to glance down at the source of the commotion.

Below her four people were locked in battle. Three men, each clad in a black jacket with one red sleeve, circled around a solitary woman. Her face was hidden from view by a large hood, but she wore a tan coat and pants. All of them were carrying swords.

"Come with us, woman, and we will not harm you," one of them stated loudly. "We will take you by force if needed."

"No," the cloaked woman growled. "You won't."

She spun and lunged towards one of the men, who raised his sword to deflect her strike. The force of her blow was enough to lurch him to the side off balance, which gave her time to turn and deal with his onrushing companion.

With a quick spin, she rolled past him, heading towards the third member of his party. She feigned an overhead strike and turned the blade to attach his exposed side. It struck soundly, tearing into the coat, hunting for the flesh below.

A quick kick sent him backwards, reaching for his side, and she turned to face both men coming towards her once more. Pressing forward, she angled her own sword to meet steel, and then cut across to force the other blade back. She turned and drove her blade up, pushing back her foe who barely deflected it aside with his own weapon. Before he could respond, she turned back to the other man and lunged the blade forward, causing him to lurch back in a desperate attempt to avoid impalement.

The two men circled back together while the woman stepped back to gather herself for another round.

"You can't win," one of the men said with a ragged breath.

"Really? It seems to me I'm doing a pretty good job of it so far," she answered.

She heard the crunch of snow behind her a moment too late. From the corner of her eye as she turned her head she saw the third man's figure looming, sword high and prepared to strike her down. Dropping down, she rolled to one knee, raising her blade above her head to hopefully stop the blow that seemed poised to take her life—which never struck.

The man's arm was stopped. It hung in mid-swing, held by a silver arm and black hand covered in fur.

"You are the good guy, right?" Renarde asked her. "I mean, normally if it's three against one, the one is the good guy, right?"

The man pulled away, staggering backwards. Renarde glanced over to see the other men fumbling over themselves as they retreated as well. The woman fell back to the ground.

"Demons!" one of the men yelled. "The woman is consorting with demons! She's a witch!"

They gathered together, swords pointing towards Renarde.

"Demons? Oh, come on!" She rolled her eyes. "Seriously? Do you guys not have a better first response than that? Seriously, do I look like a demon?" She took her hands and motioned down along her body.

"Do not think this demon will save you, witch! We will bring as many as we need!" The men slowly began to walk backwards, holding their weapon before them defensively. "We will find you again!"

Four more steps backwards and they turned and ran, sprinting away from Renarde as fast as their legs could manage.

"Hey!" she shouted after them. "Hey, we never cleared up that whole demon thing! I'm not a demon! Hey!" They didn't slow down, and were quickly lost from view in the dense copse of trees.

Renarde shook her head and turned back to the woman. "Can you believe that they—WOAH!"

Leaping backwards, Renarde barely avoided the woman's sword as it tried to slash her in two. Immediately she dropped down onto all fours and lowered herself to the ground, tail twitching behind her.

"You won't take me either, demon. I don't know who summoned you here, but I will not—"

"Hey, hey, hey!" Renarde raised up slightly. "I just went through that whole demon thing with—"

The woman lunged forward, driving the point of her sword at Renarde. Faster than the cloaked figure could follow, Renarde leapt up and twisted her body, grabbing the woman's hand as she landed. With one flick of her wrist, Renarde dislodged her opponent's grip and let the sword fall down into her other waiting hand. With a single spring, she launched backwards and landed ten feet away, holding the sword.

"Would you stop trying to stab me!" She drove the sword into the ground by her feet. "You're making me feel unwelcome—and I'm a really fun person!"

"I will not surrender to you!" the woman spat as she pulled two knives from beneath her jacket.

"Okay. I'm good with that. Wasn't asking you to surrender, honestly," she said. "And how many pointy things are you carrying, anyway?"

"Enough." The woman ran forward, slashing back and forth with both arms. Renarde stepped backwards carefully, making sure to stay just out of reach of her assault.

"You know, I'm starting to question that whole 'come in to save the outnumbered woman' thing that I did." Every swipe of the woman's blades found nothing but air.

With a growl of frustration, the woman flung both knives out simultaneously. Renarde spun once in a perfect pirouette, stopping once again to face the woman—holding both of her knives. She tossed them both over her shoulder.

"Look, would you stop…" her voice trailed off as the woman grasped the sword from the ground once again. Renarde took in a long, deep breath and held it as she pulled her hand down across her muzzle.

Carefully, the woman stalked towards Renarde.

"Okay, look," Renarde said flatly, "let's say you swing that at me again. What do you think is going to happen? I'm probably going to take it away from you—again. And then, just so you know, if you pull any more knives or anything on me," Renarde lowered her head, bared her teeth, and growled, "I'm probably going to get a little upset and stick that thing up your butt!"

The woman hesitated.

"Okay, now...." Renarde stood back up straight and smiled, still showing a little fang. "Hi."

"What manner of beast are you?" the woman asked.

"Okay, okay, that's a little better." Renarde's tail began to sway behind her again. "Not really polite, but better." She took a step forward. The woman took a half-step back. "I'm Renarde."

"What is that?" she asked, her voice still carrying an edge.

Renarde glanced to her left and then to her right. "I...don't understand the question. What what is what?"

The woman stood up, and stuck the sword into the ground at her side. Her hands raised up to the hood covering her face and slowly pulled it back driving off embedded flakes of snow from the cloth's surface. Frazzled red hair hung to the side of an attractive face, freckles running from one cheek across the bridge of her nose to the other cheek. Fierce brown eyes stared out from a tired, sunken expression.

"What is a renarde?" she asked. "You say you aren't a demon, but... Explain yourself."

"A Renarde is me. I'm a Renarde. That's my name," she pointed to herself and smiled.

Her eyes trailed over the strange woman. Her mind tried to reconcile silver and black fur over an obviously female humanoid body, along with a muzzle and ears on her face, as well as a bushy tail behind her. "You're a fox—but not a real one."

"Hey! I'm real!" Renarde shouted, laying her ears flat.

"Okay, let's get right to the point: are you here to harm me?" the woman asked.

"What? No. I just saved you," she answered. "Well, helped save you. You were actually doing pretty good on your own until that one guy kinda snuck up behind you and was about to whack you over the head. Good thing I was here. Actually, I was over there watching the fight. Not the whole fight, though, I came in at the point where—"

"Stop!" she interrupted, raising her hand. "Next question: are you a demon?"

Renarde's jaw dropped open. She raised an open hand, palm up. "Really? Really?" She shook her head in a short, sharp motion. "No. No, I am not. And I think I'll make up a sign to take with me that says 'Not a Demon!' to show people."

"Who sent you? Why are you here?" she asked. "And what exactly are you?"

The other hand came up to join the first, and Renarde lolled her head to one side, closing one eye. "Okay, that's a trickier question—or set of three questions, actually. Do you want me to answer them in order or in level of importance?"

"Do you ever get tired of talking nonsense!" the woman shouted, grabbing her sword from the ground once more.

"Um…no?" Renarde answered. "I guess it really depends on what you consider nonsense, though. I don't think that what I'm saying is nonsense at all. It's really more of a series of statements in response to your questions and actions. I personally feel that—"

The woman turned and began to walk away.

"Hey! Where are you going?" Falling to all fours, Renarde began to bounce along with the woman at a distance.

"Away." She kept walking determinedly.

"Why? I told you I wasn't going to hurt you," Renarde said as they wound their way through the trees.

"Those men will come back. They weren't lying. I can't stay here." Her voice stayed crisp and dry in the cold air. "And you won't be done talking before they return."

"Really?" Renarde popped her head up, shifting slightly right and then left as she tried to peer around the trees through the forest. "I don't see them. How long before they get back?"

"I'm guessing tomorrow some time," she said.

Renarde stopped and stood up. "Hey!"

The woman didn't stop, continuing on her roughly western course. After only a moment's hesitation, Renarde fell back in, this time walking along on two legs.

"Another question, hopefully a short answer one: are you a curse sent here to torment me?" For a moment, her eyes darted over to look at Renarde. It was a look sharp enough to make Renarde recoil briefly.

"Wow. Um, no. I don't even know what you are talking about," she answered.

A snort of laughter came from the woman. "I understand that feeling."

They walked in silence for a few seconds, until the lingering absence of sound began to wear on Renarde. "You know, I'm starting to think that you don't like me."

The woman spun around, bringing her sword up level to Renarde's eyes and pointed at the fox woman standing several feet away. "I don't know you. I don't know what you are. I don't know why you are here. And right now, I don't have time to wait to get answers to those questions." She lowered the sword and stared at her. "I don't trust you."

"Oh," Renarde answered with a blink. She looked down at the ground, her lips curling down with her eyes as she took a deep breath. Suddenly she brought her head back up with a huge smile on her face. "I can fix that! We just have to spend a lot more time together!"

The woman held Renarde's view, no expression cracking through her face. Without a word, she turned and began to walk away.

"Ooh, where are we going?" Renarde bounced along after her.

"We're not," she growled.

"Really? It seems like we're going somewhere."

"WE are not. I am. YOU are going away," she shot a look of daggers at the fox woman.

"Oh, no. Don't worry about that. I won't leave. It's okay," she reassured the woman.

A deep rumble rose up from the core of the woman, forming faint words that were carried away on the wind. Her feet stomped across the frozen bed of the forest, heading out towards open snow.

"You know, I have really, really good ears," Renarde said. "I heard that, and it's not true, actually. I have the same number as any other person."

"Go away," she said. Renarde trotted along behind her.

They broke out of the tree line and stepped onto the open plain, and the deep snow that awaited them there. The woman glanced up at the sun, shielding her eyes with the back of her hand.

"About four hours to dark," she muttered. "I'll have to hurry."

Renarde appeared beside her, glancing up at the sun herself. "Yep, that's about right." She looked over at the woman. "Don't like walking at night?"

The woman dropped her gaze back forward, and smacked her lips once. "You're not going away, are you?"

"Oh, heck no! I'm here to help!" Renarde nodded vigorously.

"Why aren't you going away?" she mumbled, pulling her hood back up over her head.

"Well...." Renarde dropped down to all fours and scurried out on top of the snow, turning around to look at her. "To be honest, you're the first person I've met up here who hasn't run away screaming. It's nice to have someone to talk to."

A sound of resolute determination—or perhaps just utter frustration, the two sound very similar—came from underneath the hood. With a crunch under her foot, the woman stepped into the snow, sinking down to mid-calf.

"So, uh," Renarde stepped along, her feet occasionally breaking the crisp white surface, "is it okay if I ask your name?"

A deep grunt was her only answer.

"I'll take that as a yes," Renarde smiled. "So, what's your name?"

No answer came. She just kept on walking forward, step after step sinking into the snow. Renarde stayed ahead of her, smiling back brightly.

The woman sighed. "Sigrid."

Renarde positively beamed at the word. "Hi, Sigrid! I'm Renarde!" The woman grumbled again. "Oh yeah, you already knew that, didn't you?"

Sigrid walked on, and Renarde followed her—a few steps ahead.

. . . .

Most of them huddled around the fire. It was large enough to be a beacon—or to warm a group of thirty soldiers. Even so, most of them were still wrapped tightly in coats and blankets to shield against the wind, while also stepping back and forth to keep their blood flowing.

He stayed apart.

A thick, black fur covered his shoulders and fell down his back. Several large patches lay empty on it, while over the majority of it the fur was matted down and oily. A single large tear ran along the right side of the ill-fitting cape, beginning two-thirds of the way down and following down to the end of the material. Simple rope tied it across his chest, revealing the majority of a dingy black metal that covered his torso.

He sat alone, resting on the stump of the tree helping to feed the fire keeping others warm. Again and again his hand rubbed across the edge of his axe, gliding against the flat of the blade and pushing outward. From time to time he would pull his hand back, reach into a pouch carried around his waist, and return with a reddish powder in his palm, beginning the routine over again.

When the three men rushed past him, he didn't even move.

"Captain!" the first man said breathlessly. "Captain Valpuri, we encountered her again."

A figure standing by the fire turned at their words. A woman with a long braid of blond hair trailing down her back. She rose up straight, pulling back her shoulders.

"And?" she asked coldly.

They all slowed to a walk, stepping closer to her and saluting. After a quick glance around, they continued speaking in lowered voices.

"She got away, ma'am," he said.

The captain sighed visibly. "Did you at least get her name this time?"

They glanced nervously at each other. "No, ma'am."

Slowly, she raised her left hand to the bridge of her nose and softly pinched the space between her closed eyes as she rubbed gently. Without opening her eyes, she continued to speak. "Did you find her, or did she find you?"

"Sort of…both," he said.

"Both?" She opened her eyes and looked at all three men. "Care to elaborate?"

A quick glance at his companions, and the man spoke again. "We were on outer patrol—"

"As ordered!" a second man added.

"Yes, as ordered, we were on outer patrol, just watching out for anything unusual," he continued.

"We heard a noise," the third one stated.

"Right, we heard a noise. Like someone chopping wood for a fire. So, we went to see what it was—"

"And there was no one there," the third one said.

"There was no one visible," he corrected. "Apparently the woman heard us approaching and cleared out. We saw the wood, though, and the chips where she had been chopping it."

"If no one was there, how do you know for certain it was her?" Captain Valpuri asked.

"Well, um…." The man rubbed the back of his head.

"She came up behind us," the second stepped in. "If we hadn't heard her at the last minute, she would have gotten at least one of us."

"We did hear her, though!" the first man jumped back in.

"Yeah, I was able to turn on her and block her attack. She wasn't going to get the best of us!" the third man proclaimed proudly. The first man winced at his choice of words.

The woman stood there with her back to the fire, creating a silhouette of flame around her. Her tongue barely parted her lips as it ran across the edge of her teeth.

"Then how did she escape?" she asked.

"I…I beg your pardon?" the third man asked.

"If she didn't get the best of you, then why isn't she here? Why didn't you bring her back?" Her hands snaked around to clasp together at the small of her back. "I assume you bested her, since you said she didn't best you, which means you must have been joking when you told me she got away. So, where is she? I can't wait to meet her."

"It isn't like that, ma'am. We—"

"You were beaten by one woman. I understand you are incompetent, but there must be a limit to it, certainly. Three of you, supposedly trained soldier's in my sister's forces, were beaten by a single woman who has been stalking us for weeks. We've seen her several times, but have only had contact with her twice. The first time I understand, since it was a lone soldier, but you are three—THREE—men, and she is just one—"

"She wasn't alone," the first man interrupted quickly.

Her head turned to him. "What? Who was with her?"

"I'm…not even sure it was a who," the man mumbled.

The captain shook her head, mouthing unspoken words for a moment. "What? What do you mean by that?"

"It was a beast, ma'am," the third man said.

"I've never seen anything like it," the second one added.

"A beast? An animal, you mean? Like what? A bear? A wolf?" She looked from one man to the next.

"Yes," one answered.

"No," another contradicted.

Behind her back, Captain Valpuri's hands flexed open and closed. "I would appreciate a concise answer, gentlemen." Her eyes locked with the first man, the original speaker for the group. "Describe what you saw."

"Um, well, she stood about," he raised his hand to the height of his shoulder, "about this tall, and she—"

"Not the woman, the beast," the Captain's voice tightened.

He swallowed. "I am talking about the beast, ma'am. It looked like a woman. Part woman, part beast. A fox, I think."

She stared at him, silently, until he felt his throat go dry. "I beg your pardon?"

"It was a creature that looked like a woman…and a fox. She stood like a woman, had the…figure of a woman, but had fur, ears, and the face and tail of a fox."

She turned her head slightly. "Fur, ears, a tail and face of a fox?" She nodded. "And did you even consider that she might just be wearing a fur coat?"

"She wasn't wearing a fur coat," he answered. "She…. You would just have to see her, ma'am. I don't think that she's…human."

"What are you suggesting, soldier?" She stepped up to him.

"I…." He looked around, again, making sure no one else was listening. "I think she was a demon. That woman, she's…she's a witch."

The eyebrow raised up above the captain's right eye. "A what?"

"A witch, ma'am. A witch who has conjured a demon," he explained. She looked to the other men, who nodded slowly in agreement.

She took a deep breath, narrowing her eyes. "Are you suggesting that this woman, who has been following us for weeks now, is somehow connected to something…out of a story we tell CHILDREN?!"

"I'm sorry, Captain, but…yes." He swallowed back his fear.

Her body rose up and swelled—and then slowly relaxed. "I'm sorry, soldier, but I don't believe there are such things as demons. And I'm fairly certain that woman is no witch! Do you have any other, more reasonable explanations as to what happened and why she escaped? Or should I just assume that you came up with this ridiculous story to hide your own incompetence?"

He opened his mouth, waiting for the right words, but before they found a way out, a huge hand fell upon his shoulder, shocking everything back inside. He twisted around to see the man in the matted fur cape towering over him.

"Tell me about this...demon."

•   •   •   •   •   •   •

"So, what do you like for breakfast?"

Sigrid stared out at the snow, surveying the land they had just covered. Many deep footsteps lined their way back over the hills and well beyond. Turning, she looked ahead at the virgin snow waiting for her.

"Are you even paying attention to me?" Renarde bounded up past her, jumping up to the top of the stone outcropping where they had stopped.

"No, I'm not," she answered. Shielding her eyes, she looked towards the horizon, then turned a full circle, keeping her eyes on the distance. A thin line of trees extended to the West as far as she could see.

"I like eggs," Renarde told her. "Pretty much any way you can serve them. And pretty much any kind of egg." She stopped and scratched her chin. "Come to think of it, I don't think I've ever had an egg that I didn't like."

"Wonderful. Maybe you should go find some," Sigrid suggested casually.

"Well, after we make camp, maybe." She walked over to Sigrid and stared out over her shoulder. "We are going to make camp, right? That's why you stopped here, isn't it?"

"No," she said flatly, only glancing over her shoulder. "I mean, yes, eventually I'll make camp, but not here."

"What's wrong with here?" Renarde looked around at the terrain. A large, flat stone surface, with a few stones that jutted high above the ground. "It looks defensible, and there is high ground to watch from, and the rock provides a nice break from the wind."

Sigrid slowly turned and looked at the fox woman with wide eyes.

"What?" Renarde pulled back. "I'm just saying."

"I…didn't think you would think about that sort of thing," she admitted.

"Huh? Why not? I mean, I am pretty capable you know." She pushed out her chest, ears tall, tail high and swaying behind her.

"All right then," she pointed back the way we came, "what's wrong with that to prevent us from stopping?"

"Oh, that's easy: you left tracks behind. Easy for them to follow us." She nodded smugly.

"Yes, I did. Not everyone can walk on snow, after all," she muttered before raising her voice to normal levels. "We can't stay here because they'll be behind us. Three, maybe four hours. The sun will set in about an hour, but I don't think that will stop them."

"Which is why we should stay here." In two leaps, Renarde vaulted herself to the top of the rocky outcropping. "We're safe up here."

"Not from arrows or spears," Sigrid stated.

"Those guys didn't have bows or spears. Just swords." Renarde dropped down to sit on the rock, letting her legs dangle over the side towards Sigrid.

"The three you saw didn't, no." She took a deep breath and let it out slowly. "The wind will cover the tracks, but it will take several hours."

"Three I saw? How many people are after you?"

"I'm not sure. At least thirty, but I don't want to get too close to make sure." She walked over to the new snow, and nodded resolutely.

"Thirty?" Renarde's voice was right next to her, causing Sigrid to turn suddenly.

"Stop being so quiet! You startled me," she grumbled.

"What the heck did you do?" Renarde had a huge grin on her face and was actually bouncing on the balls of her feet.

"I think I can make that tree line in about an hour," she said aloud, ignoring Renarde again. "And if I'm lucky…."

She took a step off of the rocks and into the snow, leaving a deep impression. Each step after left an equally deep imprint into the snow.

"You know, they're still going to be able to follow you," Renarde stated, casually walking out onto the snowdrift beside her.

"Exactly," she stated.

Renarde walked along beside her, staring down curiously and silently. Step after step she followed along, watching wordlessly. After five minutes, Sigrid turned and glared at her.

"What? What? You're just staring! I never thought I would say this, but…what are you thinking?"

Renarde twisted her mouth. "Your feet must be getting really cold."

Sigrid blinked. "What? That's it? My feet?"

"Well, yeah. You seem to get mad when I talk about stuff like that, so I thought I would just walk with you for a while." She shrugged.

With a deep breath and resolve, Sigrid answered slowly, "Yes, my feet are cold. That's because they are deep in snow. You wouldn't know that since you don't seem to be able to sink into the snow at all."

"Oh, I can sink into the snow. That's no problem, either," she said with a smile. "I just have to put my feet down a little harder."

"You can?" Sigrid raised an eyebrow.

"Sure. Why wouldn't I? It's actually a lot harder to walk on top of the snow than it is to sink into it."

Sigrid closed her eyes for a moment. When she opened them again, she did something very difficult—she smiled. "Renarme—"

"Renarde," she corrected.

"Right, Renarde, can I get you to do me a huge favor?" Her voice was calm and soft.

"You sound funny."

She kept up her practice of ignoring her. "Since you are so fast, do you think that you could run ahead, just like I'm doing, leaving deep footprints, and then run back here on top of the snow?"

Renarde glanced up to her left. "Yeah, I could do that." She nodded. "But it'll look different. I don't have boots like you do."

"Good point," she mumbled and grit her teeth. "I can solve that."

She began to step backwards, putting her boot in each footstep exactly as she had stepped out, until she once more stood on the stone. Renarde casually sauntered back beside her. Sitting down, she removed first her left and then her right boot, leaving her feet clad in only stockings. She held up the boots towards Renarde.

"Here, put these on," she ordered.

"What? But that will leave your feet all cold and stuff," she answered. "I mean really, really cold."

"I'll be all right. I just need you to walk all the way over to those trees, leaving clear footprints. Can you do that?" She pointed to her planned destination.

Renarde followed the indicated direction. "Yeah, that's easy." She looked back at Sigrid. "Why?"

"So they'll follow you—or hopefully, they'll be thinking they are following me, actually." Sigrid pulled a scarf from beneath her coat and began to wrap it around her feet. "And when you get there, come back this direction—on top of the snow. It's very important that you don't leave any tracks back."

"Oh! You want them to think that you're over there!" Her mouth hung open briefly. "Wait, where are you really going to be?"

Still wrapping one foot up in the scarf, she pointed over her shoulder back the way they came.

"Uh, won't that put you closer to them?" Renarde asked. "Not trying to be obvious or anything, but still...."

"No, you're right." She glanced up at the fox woman with a smirk. "And with luck they'll be well past me by morning."

"Ooooohhh." Renarde nodded. For a while, actually. "Yeah, I still think you're going right back to the people you're running from."

"Can you just do this for me?" She barked.

"Sure." Renarde shrugged. "Give me about fifteen minutes, and I'll be back."

"You're going to have to walk on only two legs," she reminded her.

"Oh yeah. All right, make it half an hour, then." Renarde plopped down beside Sigrid and began to pull on one of the boots. Sigrid pulled out one of her knives and cut the scarf in two, and began to wrap the other foot.

"I'll wait a half hour. If you aren't back by then, I'll have to start tracking back over my path again," Sigrid stated.

Renarde giggled, causing Sigrid to glance over at her.

"What?" Sigrid asked.

"You like me," Renarde said.

"What? Where the hell do you get that idea? I never said anything like that!" Sigrid's face scrunched up further with every word.

Slowly, Renarde held up a fur-covered boot. "Um, you gave me your shoes?" Her head shimmied slightly as she waited. "Shoes?" She repeated.

"Boots. Yes, I know. That's so you can—"

"Lead them away, yeah I know. Which means you trust me to actually do that. Which means you must like me enough to trust me." She wiggled the boot again. "You gave me your shoes."

"I'm desperate," Sigrid clarified.

"You like me," Renarde said confidently, pulling on the boot she was displaying. "I'm likable."

"I've only known you for a few hours. I don't like you. I just…."
She shook her head. "Just go do this, okay?"

"You bet!" She jumped up and rushed to the edge of the stone.
"I'm excited. You're the first friend I've had since I left the
goddesses at their castle! I'll be back soon!"

With a grace that defied description, Renarde pranced through
the existing steps and continued on past them with ease, racing
out into the snow away from Sigrid, who sat still watching her
run.

"Since she left the who where?" Her jaw fell slack.

• • • • • • •

He walked cautiously through the area examining everything he
could see, which wasn't much in the quickly fading light.

"This is where they were? You are certain?" His voice rumbled
and rasped, like the sound of a snake crawling through dried
leaves.

"Yes, I'm sure of it. I know this is where we fought." The man
replied nervously.

Unlike his companions, the larger man wasn't dressed in a black
coat with one red sleeve. He still wore the furred cape and black
metal armor. Thick boots crunched against the forest floor, as his
eyes scanned in front of him carefully.

"And where was she? The demon?" he asked.

"I…I think over here," he muttered.

A half dozen other men stood around them at a distance,
watching the area for anything approaching. A cascade of motion
seemed to pass through them as one of them shifted their weight
back and forth, stopping just in time for another to pick up the
nervous energy.

The large man crouched down, running his fingers along the ground. He slowly pushed a single digit down into the earth.

"Did...did you find something, Mr. Hjalmar, sir?" The man swallowed.

His hand pulled back slowly, his fingers rubbing together gently. His head lowered down, lying almost flat against the ground.

"Mr. Hjalmar?" The man's body bent slightly at the waist as he turned his head to the same angle as the larger man.

"No," the larger man said slowly. "Not mister, just Hjalmar."

"Oh, uh, yes...sir," he winced at that last word.

"She didn't leave much of a print," he said as he stood, wiping his hands clean of dirt. "Though that might be wiped away because of your fight." Hjalmar pointed to the ground. "Did you put your sword in the ground here?"

"No. No, none of us did," the man answered.

"And you say the demon didn't have any weapons," he stated.

"Not that we saw, no. The demon did move quietly. She was on us before we knew she was there."

"Did she fly?" Hjalmar asked.

"No. She didn't have wings at all. As I told the captain, she looked like...a fox."

"Despite appearances, some demons can still fly, boy," his eyes trailed off with his voice. He took a few steps forward. "They went that way."

"A good place to start in the morning, then," the man said.

Hjalmar turned around and stared at him. The man felt his heart rise into his throat and his stomach fall out. Each step towards him took more moisture from the man's mouth, until it was barren by the time Hjalmar stood over him.

"There is no morning, boy. There is now. We'll be following this trail tonight, and I expect you to be right there beside me, since you are the…expert…in the situation. Don't you agree?" There was no wondering in his question.

"Of course, sir. I…I agree completely."

"Good." He turned and began to walk the direction indicated.

"But, how are we going to track them in the darkness?" The man's voice cracked as he spoke.

Hjalmar stopped. The only movement coming from him was the swell of his body as he filled his lungs deeply. For several moments he did nothing more.

"Come here, boy." His voice rumbled.

"Sir?" He took a step backwards.

"Stop calling me that!" He didn't turn. "Now, I said to come up here!"

He stopped himself. Swallowing hard, he began to step forward once again. The few feet he walked took him far longer than the time that passed, until he was standing beside and just behind Hjalmar.

"What's that?" Hjalmar pointed to the horizon.

"It's…the sun," he answered.

"And that puts out light to see by, doesn't it?" He turned his head to look down at him finally.

"Y-yes," he stammered.

"And what is that man holding?" Hjalmar pointed to one of the others nearby.

"Torches," he answered.

"And those put out light, don't they?" His eyes were dark and expressionless.

"Yes." He nodded.

"Then why are you worried about darkness?" Hjalmar asked.

"I…I…." The man looked down at the ground. "I'm scared. I don't want to face the demon, especially not in the darkness."

He closed his eyes, waiting for what he was sure to come. In his mind he was thanking his parents, his friends, and his loved ones for their time. A deep part of him wondered what the next life would hold, unsure of anything beyond his current existence. Every muscle in his body clenched tightly and froze in the cold air.

And nothing happened.

"First smart thing you've said since we got here," Hjalmar stated.

The man opened his eyes and saw Hjalmar stepping ahead of him once again, heading towards the open snow.

"Y-you aren't scared?" the man asked.

"Only a fool isn't scared, boy," he said. "That isn't the point."

He stumbled along, catching up to the larger man quickly. "I… what is the point, then? If that isn't too stupid to ask."

Hjalmar shook his head. "To find out, boy. To find out."

He stepped clear of the woods and stood at the edge of the snow.

"To find out what?" the man whispered as he stepped up to Hjalmar.

• • • • • • •

She pulled the woven branches over the front of the opening, sealing them both inside. The confines were small, worked into a large crook at the base of a tree to provide extra protection from the elements. Night could lower the temperature up to fifteen or twenty degrees, making it potentially lethal. Sigrid was far too familiar with the temperature and the means to protect herself, though lately she had been alone for these things.

"This is cozy," Renarde said, turning around in place. Sigrid was amazed she could do it at all, let alone do it so effortlessly without destroying the makeshift shelter.

"Don't do that," Sigrid fussed. "I don't want to rebuild this thing tonight."

Renarde stopped and looked at her, a huge smile across her muzzle, her teeth almost glowing in the near non-existent light. "I'm not gonna break it. I like it in here. Like I said, it's cozy."

"Not on purpose, I know…I guess. You might have an accident, though. Be careful." Sigrid scooted her way back, leaning up against the tree and folding her arms across her chest. Almost immediately, she felt a warm body pressing up against her. Her head slowly turned to look at the top of Renarde's head pressing itself into the crook of her neck.

"What are you doing?" Sigrid asked with a flat tone to her voice and wide eyes.

"Snuggling," Renarde answered. To seemingly illustrate her words, she shimmied her whole body closer.

"Why?" she asked with the same level sound.

"Why not? Besides, it's better than just sitting here not snuggling," Renarde stated. She took a deep breath, and Sigrid would swear that she heard a purr from her.

"I don't know if I'm comfortable with this," Sigrid admitted.

Sitting back, Renarde stared at her in shock. She shook her head very slightly and then spoke. "But…but I'm warm and fuzzy. It's cold outside. How can you not want warm and fuzzy when it's cold?"

"It's not the warm…fuzzy problem," Sigrid stated.

"Oh, good!" She plopped back against her instantly.

"That wasn't telling you to go back." Sigrid gently pushed her away once more.

Renarde frowned. "Well, what's wrong, then?"

"I just…." She shook her head. "Look, it's been a long day."

"Oh, yeah, I can totally see that," Renarde agreed. "Is that a normal day for you?"

For a moment, only silence answered. A heavy sigh preceded her response.

"You said something earlier about a goddess and a castle." Sigrid changed the subject. "What did you mean?"

"Uh, well, that I came here from the goddess's castle?" Renarde stated.

Another sigh. "Well, tell me about it. It'll help me relax."

"Oh, I can do that," Renarde shuffled in place, sitting up slightly and looking at Sigrid in the darkness. "Okay, so basically, it's like this….

"Altair and I—Altair is an eagle guy, kinda grouchy—anyway he and I were sent down from the goddess's domains above the world to prepare their castle. I met Porter, who is a totally cuddly bear, and Thibaan who…" her voice trailed off, wistfully. "I like Thibaan."

She shook her head. "Anyway, Thibaan and I brought the goddesses back, and then we sort of met a whole bunch of people, there was a lot of stuff that happened, Vera became darkness and stuff, I got thrown into a wall, and…well, then I came here."

Sigrid sat there, waiting for things to sink in. They didn't. "What?"

"Oh! And don't drink winkie." Renarde nodded emphatically.

Her eyes closed as Sigrid silently counted to ten. She opened them once again and smiled thinly. "What goddesses? And what do you mean by their domains above the world."

"Well," Renarde scratched behind her left ear as the right one went flat, "I have to assume that the others have one. I mean, that's basically what everyone else implied at least. I know that Serenade has one. I was kinda raised there, so…yeah. It's different. Kind of like their castle, but not as…well, I'm not sure, actually. It's just different. More like a tiny island or something, really."

"And who is Serenade?" Sigrid asked.

Renarde's eyes grew into saucers. "You don't know who Serenade is? She's…Serenade! The Goddess of the Night. All that dark stuff out there is hers. She made it. Sort of."

"Wait…Ilta? Do you mean Ilta?" Sigrid's head pulled back. "Are you suggesting that you were raised by Ilta?"

"Uh, I dunno. Is that what you call Serenade?" Both of Renarde's ears went flat to the side.

"Are…are you her messenger?" Sigrid's voice fell low. "Do you know Koarr?"

"I have no idea," Renarde answered instantly.

"Koarr. The Goddess of Light and Life. She brings the dawn that gives life to the land," Sigrid explained.

"I think you're talking about Aubade, but it could be Etude," Renarde scratched under her muzzle. "Goddess of the Sun?"

"Yes," Sigrid said reverently.

"Oh, yeah, I know her. That's Aubade. Mostly really, really nice. Had a rough go of it there for a while, though," Renarde answered perkily.

"Don't joke about this." Sigrid's voice became cold and hard. "Don't you know where you are?"

"I'm not joking about this. I really do know Aubade and she really is mostly nice," she answered. "And no, I have no idea where I am, other than north of Harmonia."

"Harmonia? You're from Harmonia?" Sigrid asked. "Oh. Oh, I see. You went to see the castle they have there. You thought it had goddesses in it. I've heard of that place and what they claim."

"Well, no, not really. I mean, yes, I was there, but I didn't go there to see the castle. I saw the city because I was sent to the castle." She closed one eye. "So, kinda the reverse of what you're saying, actually."

Sigrid took another deep breath. "This is Dula Koarr. The whole of our nation is devoted to Koarr. It's her light that keeps us alive. Ilta is her sister, the one who punishes us. We pray to Koarr for aid and to Ilta for forgiveness."

"Okay," Renarde answered.

"Okay?" Her mouth fell open. "Are...are you mocking me?"

"What? No! Honest, I'm not," Renarde replied, reaching out to touch Sigrid on the arm. She pulled it back almost instantly. "I just...I don't know what to say."

Sigrid fell back against the tree. "I don't understand you."

Renarde shuffled over, pulling slightly closer to Sigrid. "Well, maybe it would help if I understood you. I'm new here." She shrugged. "Tell me about this place."

Sigrid stared up at the ceiling of their tiny enclosure. Renarde listened to her breathing, the steady rise and fall of her chest as she considered her words.

"Why not?" Sigrid clearly mumbled.

Crossing her arms over her chest, Sigrid pulled herself in tightly.

"Dula Koarr is taken from the ancient tongue of this country. It means 'The Light of Koarr.' I suppose to remind us to revere the goddess so we always have a sun there in the morning to bring us warmth. I imagine that's more important to the people in this Hundred and the ones around it than to the ones south of here."

"Hundred?" Renarde asked. "What's a hundred? And don't say the number after ninety-nine or I'll bite you."

Sigrid chuckled. "A Hundred is the area controlled by the Ranee of the region. It's an area of a hundred square miles. Each one set by the queen."

"Ooh, you have a queen?" Renarde's voice rose up.

"Yes. The current queen is Tatjana Berg, and she has ruled for almost twenty years. From everything that I hear, she is a hard, strict ruler—which is wasted here. We are so far from the throne that she doesn't understand what happens. She doesn't understand the rule of the Ranee."

"Okay, I'll bite—figuratively, this time—what's a Ranee?"

"The ruling priestess of the Hundred, set in line by tradition of the noble family of the region."

"Oh, so the rulers of each region are women, too?" Renarde bounced a little in place.

Sigrid laughed and looked over at Renarde. "You really don't know anything about where you are, do you? Everything in Dula Koarr is controlled by women. How did you come all this way and not know where you were going?"

"Well, Thibaan told me about this place," Renarde rolled her eyes, "but it got sooooo boring that I lost track of it right after she told me about some sort of something or other. I dunno. I just kept thinking about sex."

Sigrid blinked. "What?"

"Sex. It's way more interesting than listening to her talk about politics and stuff. Mostly 'cause Thibaan's reeeeally good at sex." Renarde's eyes seemed to glaze over for a moment.

"Okay. Changing subjects quickly," Sigrid continued, "and I'm sorry if this is rude, but…what are you exactly?"

"We talked about this. I'm Renarde," she answered with a giggle.

"That's your name. What are you, though. You…well, you look like a fox," Sigrid stated.

"Yeah. I am a fox. Sort of, anyway. The way it was explained to me—at least what I remember—is that I was given a little bit of a gift from each of the four goddesses, and then put here in Elan until I absorbed something here—which I'm guessing was a fox—

and then I was taken in by Serenade to be raised up until I could come back down here to help them out." She nodded. "Basically."

"I don't understand," Sigrid said closing her eyes.

"It's okay, you don't have to. I'm just me. Just like you're you. I just happen to be really soft and fuzzy and super cute," she pushed up against Sigrid. "See."

Sigrid went rigid and slowly pulled her shoulder back. She bit her lower lip, not hard enough to hurt, but hard enough to give her time to consider her words. Slowly, her body relaxed. "You aren't going to be happy unless you can sleep up against me—what did you call it?—cuddling?"

"Snuggling," Renarde corrected. "And it'll keep you warm." She grabbed Sigrid's hand and brushed it along her arm. "See? Fur. It's really warm. Trust me."

"Fine," she relented. "We need to sleep anyway. Dawn will be here sooner than I would like, and we'll need to be moving immediately."

"Because of those people chasing you?" Renarde laid her head down on Sigrid's shoulder.

"Something like that, yes," she stated.

There was a long pause of silence.

"Why are those people chasing you?" Renarde asked.

Another pause filled the small shelter. "Not tonight. We need to sleep," Sigrid answered. "I'll tell you about it in the morning."

Sigrid moved her arm around Renarde's shoulder, resting it on her back. This time Sigrid was sure she heard a purr.

"Okay," Renarde replied happily and wiggled in closer to Sigrid's body for the rest of the night.

. . . .

She woke the moment he stepped into her tent.

"What is it?" she asked trying to hide any hint of sleep still in her voice.

"You wanted us to come wake you when Hjalmar returned," the man stated.

She rose up, pulling the sheet up with her as she did. Underneath it was clear she was wearing a long-sleeved black shirt, possibly made of wool. Her hair was still braided, but was currently pulled up and tied on top of her head.

"Thank you. Tell him I will speak with him in the morning," she answered, and halfway lowered herself back towards her cot.

"Well…" his voice trailed off.

"What?" She was immediately up in her cot again. "Is something wrong?"

"He…he isn't back, ma'am," he explained.

"I beg your pardon?" There was no direct light in her tent, but the light from both the fire and the torches outside cast a gentle glow, tinting everything inside a gentle deep reddish-yellow. The angle of the fire kept the man's face hidden from her, but she could see the glimmer of sweat on his cheek.

"He, uh, he hasn't come back. Not exactly." His right hand wrung onto itself as he spoke.

She sat up completely, pulling her legs up under her slightly. "I suggest you start explaining yourself a little more clearly, soldier."

"He sent someone back, ma'am. He said that he needed to speak with you right away," he explained. "I thought it best to come and tell you."

"You mean to tell me—" She cut herself off instantly. A sound not unlike a growl rumbled out of her. "Yes, of course." She swung her legs out of the cot. A tight-fitting black set of leggings covered them completely. "Thank you. I'll be out in a moment."

The man saluted quickly and stepped out of the tent. The moment he was clear she shook her head and smiled. There was an almost palpable taste of fear in the air. It helped her to focus as she pulled on the more formal pants and boots. She stood and grabbed her coat, not bothering with the shirt of her uniform, and slid it on as she exited through the flap of her tent.

The grounds were mostly empty. Only a small smattering of soldiers were visible, most of them standing near the fire, facing out to watch for any movement in the darkness. Closer to her tent stood the man who had awoken her—at least she assumed it was from the expression on his face—and another man, one who had ventured out with Hjalmar earlier that evening.

"What is it?" She didn't bother with a formal greeting.

The man quickly saluted her and took a deep breath. "Hjalmar has instructed me to come here and tell you to continue on tomorrow morning without him and the others, ma'am."

"He what?" Her voice raked against her teeth on the way out. "He sent you here with orders for me?"

"He…I…." He swallowed visibly. "It was the message I was sent to give you, ma'am."

Her foot twisted into the ground and her upper lip twitched slightly. "Where is he?"

"He's gone after the woman and the demon, ma'am. He's tracking them through the night, and doesn't expect to be back soon. The last I saw him he was following a set of footsteps out of these woods and heading west."

"In the darkness?" she growled.

"Yes, ma'am."

Her eyes moved, straying from soldier to soldier awake in the camp. None of them met her gaze. It seemed obvious to her that all of them were purposely not looking at her. "Did any of my men come back with you? Or does he still have all of them?"

"Three of us came back, ma'am. He wanted to be sure that we made it safely through the woods. All of the others are still with him," he explained.

"So, him and four others have gone after her, then?" She nodded. "I see."

The two men watched her turn and pace a few steps back towards her tent slowly. She stopped, paused, and then suddenly turned to look at them directly.

"The two of you find two others. You're going to be staying behind waiting on him. If they don't return in two days, follow us back to the keep. If they do return, bring them along with you. And if you see that woman and her demon pet, kill them. I'm tired of this game." She turned and walked back into her tent without a glance back at them.

She removed her coat and held it tightly. Bypassing the hook meant for it, she threw it violently to the ground. Her boots came off her feet the moment that she sat on her cot. Without removing another article of clothing she lay back down and pulled the covers up to her neck.

"When I return back home, I will have a word with my sisters," she growled. "I am tired of their lapdog."

. . . .

Sigrid woke alone.

"Renarde?" She scratched her left shoulder with her right hand while letting her eyes slowly adjust to the morning. Tiny splinters of light wormed their way into the shelter through the cracks in the walls, creating a fractured panel of light in the small space.

Gently, she pushed the door closure out and open, feeling a sharp blast of morning chill race over her body. Reflexively her body shuddered, even as she wrapped herself more tightly with the heavy clothing she wore.

The unique smell of morning washed over her, with a sweet, fresh odor reminding her of a mix of pine and new snow. She stood and arched her back out, pressing her hands hard into her hips, followed by a short twist both left and right. A light mist hung loosely over the forest floor, obscuring the crushed needles, dirt, and leaves below it. Turning a full circle, she confirmed that she was alone.

"Renarde?" she asked again. There was no answer or indication of any life at all. "Huh."

She turned back to the previous night's shelter and reached inside to remove her sword, returning it to its normal home on her hip. Immediately, she began to deconstruct the simple shelter, starting with the roof and working her way down, pulling the leather straps she used to bind it tightly to the trunk of the tree and returning them to the bag she carried. Every piece that she used to create the enclosure was moved and carried to various distances, doing her best to make them blend back in with their surroundings.

Looking around, she was satisfied with her work. The forest absorbed her borrowed parts nicely. She pulled her hood back up over her head as she glanced around the area one more time.

"Renarde?" She didn't raise her voice much at all, simply hoping the words would find their goal. "Where has she gotten to?"

Sigrid leaned back against the same tree she had slept against the previous night and pulled her bag around to the front. Her hands rummaged through it without her eyes guiding them, knowing by touch where and what everything she felt was and why. In a few seconds they emerged from the bag holding a chunk of reddish-brown material in a long strip. At first, it almost appeared to be an odd colored leather—until she put it in her mouth and tore a chunk of it off.

Her mouth strained to chew the substance, causing her whole face to wince on almost every bite. She kept her eyes moving along an even line, searching for any movement at all. For an instant she was drawn to a small herd of caribou wandering between the trees, passing by with little regard to her at all. Her eyes slowly narrowed.

"I couldn't have imagined her, could I? That wasn't a dream," she thought aloud. She took another bite of her breakfast, once again chewing it defiantly. "No. No, too many details."

A faint sound drew her head around in a snap. Placing the strip of food back into her bag, her hand slid from the bag to the hilt of her sword. Cautiously she stood up and slid out away from the tree, her senses focused and alert, eyes fixed on the spot where the noise originated.

One careful footstep followed another as she made her way towards the sound—and what she quickly came to realize was the edge of the woods. Shifting back and forth, making sure to always keep at least one tree between her and a fully open view, she weaved through the tight forest, finally stopping still at the sight awaiting her.

In a large snowbank, she saw the ass-end of Renarde—her tail and butt down to mid-waist—sticking straight up in the air. The rest of her was buried in snow. For a second she considered turning back around and trying this again, but she couldn't actually pull herself away.

And before she could react further, Renarde popped back out of the snowbank, shaking her head and body, scattering snow everywhere. She turned around, saw Sigrid, and smiled.

"Hi!" She bounced up and through the snow, finally hitting the forest floor and trotting up to Sigrid. "Did you sleep okay? I did."

"What…where were you? You left early," Sigrid said.

"Oh, yeah. I don't actually sleep that much. I think it's Etude's fault. She said something about giving us energy and life and stuff, so she probably made it so I don't sleep much. That doesn't bother me, though. I like sleep, but you can't really do much while you're sleeping, so I tend to—"

Sigrid raised a hand up towards Renarde's muzzle, cutting off her words and causing the fox woman to pull her head back slightly.

"What were you doing?" Sigrid asked.

"Hmm? Oh, you mean here? Breakfast!" she smiled.

"Breakfast? You eat snow?"

"Huh? No. I mean, I have, but I wasn't then. Snow's a good way to get water, you know." She nodded knowingly.

"I did know that, actually." She took a different tactic. "Here. I've got food."

Sigrid reached into her bag and once again retrieved the stick of red-brown material. She held it out towards Renarde, who pulled away. Slowly she inched her way towards it, sniffing and curling up the right side of her mouth with every inhale.

"What is that?" Renarde asked.

"Kaisi," she answered. Renarde pulled away again. "It's okay, watch." She took a bite off of it and began to chew.

"Okay, but…what is it? It smells funny." Renarde stepped sideways, moving around to look at the kaisi from a new angle.

"Well, it's something we make in the fall for winter. It's basically a mixture of dried fruit, dried meat and animal fat that we cook slowly until it all melts together, and then we roll it up in cured leather until it solidifies." She took another bite. "It's pretty good."

Renarde stared at her with large, wide eyes. "Riiiiight."

Sigrid laughed. "Are you telling me that you're scared of food?"

"Oh no! No, not at all! I love food!" She pointed at the kaisi with her nose. "I'm just not sure if that qualifies."

"Suit yourself." Sigrid took another bite and put the bar back into her bag. She looked over at Renarde, who was staring at her intensely.

"So," Renarde smiled, "it's morning."

Staring at her, Sigrid stayed quiet for a moment before replying. "Yes, it is."

"So?" Renarde nodded.

For the first time this day, Sigrid took a deep breath and let out a slow sigh. She suddenly realized that it wasn't going to be the last time that happened. "Okay, what do you want?"

"Last night," Renarde said. "Right before we fell asleep snuggling." She paused, and then rolled her eyes. "You said you would tell me why those people are chasing you."

"Oh!" Sigrid chuckled. "That." She swallowed the last bit of kaisi in her mouth and wiped her hands against her pant legs. "They aren't."

There was a pause.

"Oh, well, thanks for that story!" Renarde threw her hands up in the air and rolled her head back.

Sigrid laughed. "Well, I'm not joking, they aren't chasing me. I'm chasing them. They just want me to stop, or find out why—or kill me, I suppose at this point."

"Okay, okay," Renarde's eyes glistened and her grin grew across her full muzzle, "now this is getting interesting. Why are you chasing them?"

Sigrid hesitated and she shook her head. "That's a long story, and this isn't the time or place for it."

"What? You can't start a story like that and not finish it!" Renarde pleaded.

Sigrid closed her eyes, and winced. When she opened them again she saw Renarde staring at her with a desperate, sad expression. A groan welled up as Sigrid rubbed her eyes.

"Okay, here's the very short version…" She took a deep breath and looked into Renarde's eyes. Her voice softened noticeably as she spoke, "They have my husband."

"What?" Renarde stood up straight, her smile fading away.

"They took my husband. Carried him off and away from me. I'm following them to find out where they took him." They stared at each other, neither showing any emotion at all.

"Why?" Renarde asked.

"That's a very good question. I'd like to know myself, actually," she answered.

"Who are they?"

"The personal soldiers of the Valpuri sisters. The twins who act as the Ranee for this Hundred," Sigrid explained.

"Okay, you're making funny noises again. I don't understand what that means," Renarde said.

Sigrid looked around, finally breaking eye contact with Renarde. Her hand came up and wiped over her eyes and she swallowed hard.

"That's all right. You don't need to understand that, actually." She squinted up towards the sun. "I should probably get going, anyway. They'll likely be on the move soon, and I need to try to keep tabs on them. Find out where they're going."

"Oh! Okay, hold on!" Renarde spun around and bounced up and over to the snow. She took a couple of steps in and paused. Moved a step and paused. Turned her head and paused.

"What are you—"

"Shhhh!" Renarde hissed back. She took another step into the snow and stopped. Her body slowly lowered itself down, her ears laid back, and her tail twitching constantly behind her.

In a sudden, graceful arc, Renarde leapt straight up and plunged down into the snowbank, burying herself up to her waist, leaving only ass, tail, and legs exposed.

Sigrid raised her eyebrows and blinked once.

Just as suddenly, Renarde pulled back up out of the snow, holding a large mouse in her hands.

"Got it!" she proclaimed with pride.

"A mouse?" Sigrid asked.

"Mouse. Breakfast. Whatever you want to call it. This thing has been taunting me for days!"

"A mouse has been taunting you," Sigrid said.

"For days," Renarde reassured with a nod. She held up the mouse. "Want some?"

Sigrid shook her head.

"Suit yourself." Renarde tossed the mouse into the air and with a single snap took it into her jaws. A few crunching sounds immediately followed.

"And you thought kaisi was bad," Sigrid muttered.

Renarde smiled broadly. "Okay, we can go now."

"We can go?"

"Yeah, you and I. We. And go is…leaving, basically," she explained.

"And where are 'we' going?" Sigrid asked.

Renarde's smile opened up, revealing a bright white set of fangs. Her tongue played against the canine hanging down on the right side of her mouth.

"We're gonna go get your husband."

end chapter one

CHAPTER TWO

THE CAPTIVE

The warmth surrounding his sex drove away any thoughts of the cold day. He felt her slowly bobbing her mouth up and down on him, pulling a groan from deep inside his body.

This is wrong.

Instinctively his hands fell down to her head, running his fingers through her hair, half of him wanting to hold and caress her gently, and the other wanting to push her head down further.

Don't do this.

He could feel her pull back until her mouth was free of him, only to have her tongue immediately begin to lick once more, while her hand came fondle him in her hand softly. With her hand still full she drove down onto him once more, taking all of him into her mouth until her chin lightly touched her wrist. His hand pulled back and gripped the sheet on the bed, filling his palms and pulling it tight beneath him.

Look at her. You have to look at her.

She brought her lips back up to just surround the tip once more, and then began to bob up and down in a much more shallow motion, her other hand moving to grasp the remainder of him and move in concert with her mouth.

"Sigrid," he moaned. *Open your eyes.*

Cool air washed over the him as she pulled completely free once more. Her hand remained around him, working up and down.

"I want you inside me," she whispered. He groaned in response.

He felt her body moving above him, positioning herself. He heard her take in a sharp breath through her teeth as she brought herself down on him, penetrating inside her.

It's not too late! Open your eyes!

His hands slipped up his own body until it found her hips and rested there, slowly gripping her more tightly by the second. In his mind, he was guiding her, suggesting the pace at which she rode him with his grip on her hips, but even he realized this wasn't actually true. All he was doing was sharing her ride in another way.

Look at her. Look!

His hands slid further back, coming to rest on the fullness behind her. The soft flesh gave way easily under his fingers, giving him a proper grip, and he curled his lip back in a feral position as he pulled the two cheeks apart. Seemingly in response, the speed of her thrusting increased, driving down onto his pelvis with renewed vigor as she leaned in towards him a little more.

What do you see? What do you see?

The image of his beloved filled his mind. Her creamy skin covered in a dusting of freckles, including the delightful row of them that journeyed from one cheek to the other across her nose. Her deep brown eyes becoming pools of lust and love as she carefully licked her deep pink lips before sucking the lower one between her teeth. Small, but—to his eye, at least—perfectly shaped breasts rose and fell in tempo with her hips.

"I want your seed inside me," she hissed.

No. No.

His hands moved up to her chest, filling his grasp. Her breasts felt heavy and full. His fingers massaged them, pulling outward until they found the peak of each globe. He took both nipples into his fingers and squeezed lightly, finding a pert, hard nub waiting. Her body gyrated on him, moving to pull his essence out.

It's not her.

His eyes blinked. For a moment he again saw his beloved Sigrid, her red hair waving wildly about her face as they shared this moment of intimacy. And with another blink her red hair turned pale. A blink and she was there, her body the perfect form that he remembered. Another and it was more delicate, with larger hips and breasts.

And she wore a mask over the right half of her face.

"No," he muttered, and then his voice became louder and more clear. "No. No! No!"

"Yes!" She grasped his neck, pulling him tightly to her as her hips ground against him at a desperate pace. As she pounded into him like a frightened rabbit, he could feel his body betraying him at the wrong moment.

He emptied into her. She moaned in pleasure, dropping her full weight onto his chest even as her hips continued to thrust against him, coaxing every drop from him and into her. Gradually, the spasms subsided and the two lay together in silence.

She rose up, arching her back and stretching her arms high above her head. A broad smile grew across her face as she pulled herself up and off of the man who lay still below her. After she swung her legs over the side of the bed and stood she faintly heard his voice behind her.

"You swore to me, Oikea. You promised," he breathed.

She turned and smiled down at him, her eyes running along the full length of his naked body. "Oh, Armas, I do apologize, but I walked in here and saw you and I was simply unable to control myself. You will forgive me, won't you?"

His eyes moved up to her, burning a hole through her silently.

"Well, I do hope you will." She reached down towards his arm. He jerked it away from her touch. She sighed, shrugged, and turned away. Walking across the room, her hips swayed out in an exaggerated motion with every step.

His eyes were firmly locked on the ceiling.

Her hand pulled the patterned red and black dress from the back of the chair in the room and held it as she turned the chair to face towards the bed. Sliding her legs across each other, she slinked down onto the chair and stared over at her recent conquest.

"I want to leave," Armas stated, still staring upwards.

"I know," she answered with a tone that attempted to soothe. "Unfortunately, you know that I can't allow that to happen. Not yet. When this is all finished, I will see to it personally that you are escorted back safely to your home."

He finally turned to look at her directly. "Of course you will. Just like you promised to never force yourself on me again."

"Well, I already explained that, darling," she stated as her lips pulled back into a thin smile. The leather mask over the right side of her face kept all of her mouth exposed, curving away just above her lips to angle back towards her jaw. This particular one was black with paintings of small red roses decorating it.

He pushed himself up from the bed, sitting upright. The room was lush and well afforded. High ceilings suspended multiple tapestries against the wood paneled walls. The floors were a complimentary wood to the walls, with long, wide planks polished to a near mirror reflection, only broken by the various area rugs at key points in the room. Two large windows sat opposite the four post bed where Armas lay, with the early rays of the morning breaking into the room past the heavy curtains which he never closed. The last remaining embers of a fire still struggled in the fireplace on the wall to the left of his bed, with the portrait of a woman whose resemblance marked her as relative of some sort to Oikea.

Oikea herself sat before a large desk in a high-backed chair covered in red velvet. She casually crossed her legs the other direction as she looked at Armas.

"I do apologize again, Armas," she began. "In truth, I was coming here to invite you to dinner with my sister and I. It has been several days since you last joined us, and we were hoping that you would want to spend some time with us today." She smiled. "Well, more time in my case, I suppose."

"I'm not hungry," he replied instantly.

"Well, this isn't about food so much as it is company. We feel like negligent hosts, we see you so infrequently anymore," she said with a sigh.

"I'm sorry, but I feel like staying in my room." His voice was cold and terse.

She stood from her chair, lounging up idly like a cat standing from a bowl of milk and turned her back to him. "I am afraid that I must insist. It's only a meal after all."

Bending over at the waist, she lowered her dress down to her feet, leaving her backside on full display for Armas to see. After slipping both feet inside, she slowly began to pull it up, shifting her weight to either side as is inched up her body. Once it was past her waist, she turned to face him once again.

"I'll tell you what, why don't you tell me what you would like the chefs to prepare for you this evening? I'll make it a point to see that they have it waiting for you." She slid first her right and then her left arm into the sleeves of the dress, leaving only the front of it open, displaying her breasts prominently.

"How about roast duck with a lovely berry compote for me, and poison for the two of you?" he answered.

"Why Armas, darling," she pulled the dress together, covering the majority of her breasts, but leaving a more than ample display of cleavage in the middle, "talking that way will do nothing to endear yourself to either of us. We have treated you more than fairly, or do you not like your accommodations?"

"Even the nicest prison is still a cage," he said.

Her hands closed a few buttons along the bottom half of her dress, still leaving her cleavage on display. The dress was black on the right side of her body, with the left half being a pattern of red vines growing over a field of white. "It is only a cage if you think of it that way, Armas. And only for a short while, no matter the case."

"And exactly how long is a short while?" Armas brow furrowed at her.

Oikea shook her head slightly, a warm smile that was frighteningly cold forming on her lips. "Alas, that entirely depends on you, and how cooperative you are with us. The more you assist us, the less time you will spend here." She grasped a pair of gloves and pulled a black one onto her right hand, and then followed with a white one on her left. Her feet slid one after another into a pair of short boots, one black and one white, matching the established pattern. With a stride that was more for attention than motion, she walked back over to the bed and stood over Armas. "I really don't know why you are fighting us on this. I can't imagine that it is torturous."

His expression remained flat. "I love my wife."

"Of course you do! As well you should. You are a fine man, Armas, but this has nothing to do with love. This is about duty." She raised her head up slightly, staring down her face at him. "We look forward to your company at dinner."

"I don't want—"

"It's no longer a request," she cut him off. "Wear something formal, won't you?" Her hand reached down towards his cheek, but he yanked his head away before she could touch him.

A sound somewhere between a laugh and a snort issued from her, and she turned and walked away at a much more direct pace. She stopped and knocked twice on one of the large double doors leading out of the room and then turned back towards him.

"Thank you for your time this morning, Armas." Her voice was light and chilling. "It was a pleasure on my end."

Loud sounds of locks and latches echoed from the far side of the door just prior to it opening wide, though the exit was blockaded by four armed men. Seeing the person who knocked, they quickly stepped aside.

"Until tonight," Oikea said with a smile and turned on her heel and spun around, her long, blond hair spreading out in a flourish. Once she had stepped beyond the guards, they wordlessly closed the door, followed by the sound of security sealing it instantly.

Armas squeezed his eyes closed. His right hand slowly moved up and ran through his hair, smoothing back the rather unkept growth. Reopening his eyes, he glanced around, quickly locating some light undergarments on the end of the bed. A quick lean forward allowed him to yank them back towards him, and he pulled them on as he rose from the bed in a single motion. Again his hand moved up and his fingers laced through his hair, doing their best to roughly organize it.

With a slight hesitance in his step, Armas walked up to one of the massive windows opposite his bed. He undid the latch and swung one of the three narrow parts of the window open. It was far too small for his whole body to fit through, but he could easily move his head outside. He couldn't recall how many times he had gone through this same procedure: open the window, stick his head out, and stare down at the suicidal drop. Like every time before, he pulled his head back inside and slowly closed the window tight once again.

Staring out the window, he filled his lungs completely and paused. The landscape of Dula Koarr stretched out before him, a glorious view from this high on the cliff. "I will find a way, Sigrid. I will find a way back to you."

He turned back and walked over to carefully stoke the dying embers of his fire.

•   •   •   •   •   •   •

Renarde stood there, cocking her head to one side, her ears twisting sideways and her tail flipping anxiously behind her.

"So, is that where we're going?" she asked.

"Would you get down!" Sigrid snapped. She yanked on Renarde's tail to emphasize her point. With a small yip, the fox woman dropped down beside her crouched companion.

"That hurt!" she growled.

"Good! Maybe you'll remember not to do that!" Sigrid glanced over at her for a moment before quickly returning her attention to the large group they had been following since that morning.

The soldiers had broken camp before dawn and started their march northeast, but a group that size was extremely easy to track, and by mid-day they caught up to them. They marched directly, with no attempt to hide or disguise their action.

Renarde brought her tail around and began to gingerly stroke it, her ears laying flat and her lips pouting out slightly as she did. "You obviously have never had a tail."

A full sidelong stare came from Sigrid this time. "No kidding?"

Renarde lessened her pout slightly. "You didn't answer my question. Is that where we're going?"

"I don't know. Maybe," Sigrid answered. "I think so, actually."

"What is it?" Renarde let go of her tail completely.

Sigrid rose up slightly, getting a better look over the rise they were hiding behind. A majestic, snow-covered mountain loomed on the horizon, dominating the landscape. On the southern facing of the mountain, seemingly growing from the rock itself, a massive keep protruded. Crafted from stone and wood, and with more than an occasional splash of red covering it, the keep was a brilliant spot of color against the snowy backdrop. Multiple towers grew skyward each starting on its own platform. The keep itself seemed to grow atop its own structure, with smaller tiers spanning into larger ones above.

"If I'm not mistaken, that is Valpuri Keep. Home to the Valpuri sisters, the Ranee of this Hundred," she said as she pulled back down with a heavy sigh.

"You don't know?" Renarde asked, twisting her ears forward.

"I know of it, but no, I'm not sure. I've never been here, and I can only guess from descriptions I've heard that that is Valpuri Keep." She peeked over the edge once more.

Renarde moved closer beside her, peeking up over the ridge as well. "Why are they going there?"

"The troops are from the Valpuri family. I am, sadly, very familiar with them," she stated. "It makes sense that they would be returning there."

"Well, if you knew they would be coming here, why didn't you just come here without them?" Renarde asked.

Sigrid pulled back down and looked over at Renarde. "Two reasons, actually. First, like I said, I've never been here. I didn't know the way. Secondly, I wasn't sure that was where they took Armas. I…I'm still not, actually."

"Well, let's go find out!" Renarde popped up, and once again found her tail in the clutches of her companion. And once more, she fell to the ground with a small yip. She looked over at Sigrid and growled. "Stop doing that!"

"Stop standing up!" she countered. "And besides, we can't just walk up to the keep and go inside."

"Why not?" Renarde asked, once again stroking her tail lovingly.

"Are you kidding? I don't know how to get up there, do you? And if we follow them," she gestured over her shoulder vaguely towards the troops they had followed here, "they will definitely recognize us, and that is just a quick way to our deaths. And even if they didn't, the ruling keep of a Ranee is not open to just anyone. They don't allow uninvited guests."

"Well, that's not very nice," Renarde let go of her tail and shifted around to peek over the ridge once again at the keep. She came back down and looked at Sigrid sideways. "How the heck did they build that thing, anyway?"

"I have no idea. From what I understand it has been in their family for centuries, so I doubt anyone actually knows how it was made," she answered. "And even if they did, they probably aren't sharing that information."

"Why not?" Renarde cocked her head slightly once more.

"To keep an air of mystery. Force the people to think that they are actually somehow superior to us in every way, even to the point where they can live in a magical castle growing from the side of a mountain." Her voice defied the doubt in her gut. "To remind us how small we are."

All of Sigrid's weight fell forward to rest against her legs, her head ducking slightly between her knees. She pulled her hood up and covered her head completely.

Dancing around on her haunches, Renarde moved to sit in front of her new friend. She sat down into the snow, crossing her legs and lowering her head down so that she could get a better look at Sigrid.

"Hey, what's wrong?" She kept dipping her head down, trying to find a clear view to Sigrid's eyes. "You okay?"

Without saying a word, Sigrid nodded.

Renarde slowly sat back upright. "Are you sure? You aren't acting like yourself. I don't think. Unless you haven't been acting like yourself since I first met you, which would be really odd because that would mean something was really causing you to act strange for a long time. And since I'm the only one that has been around you all that time, I would have to assume that it was me, and we both know that can't be—"

"I'm fine!" Sigrid interrupted. "I just…I just need a moment."

Renarde's tail flopped against the thin coat of snow covering the rocks where they sat, leaving a bare spot of stone as she lifted it back up. In an overly casual way Renarde looked around, seeing the same sparse trees and ever-present world of white that pervaded the area. Her lips smacked, and then smacked again. As she reached the full extent her head could turn to her left, she moved back to center and began to twist to the right seeing the same relative view that she saw to the left, only with a range of mountains looming in the background. A low, quiet whistle squeaked out of tune from her as her tail once again flopped against the snow behind her.

"Look, I'm fine!" Sigrid shouted quietly. "Stop bugging me!"

"Me?" she pointed at herself. "I didn't say anything."

"Exactly!" Sigrid sat up and yanked her hood back. "I don't need that!"

"Uh, okay," Renarde answered slowly. "Is there anything I can do? Or say, I guess?"

A short laugh burst out of Sigrid. She looked over at Renarde and smiled. "Believe it or not, you are already doing it."

"I am?" she asked with a smile. "Well, you're welcome, then!"

Sigrid responded with an open mouth and closed eyes, reversed those for a moment, and then spoke clearly and directly. "You asked if you could help. In fact, since I met you you've been doing nothing but trying to help me." She shook her head and narrowed her eyes. "Why?"

Her reply was a shrug of Renarde's shoulders. "Why not?"

"You don't know me. I could be a monster who is planning on doing something horrible. Why are you being so nice to me?" The second time the question appeared, she was more emphatic.

Leaning in, Renarde kept her eyes locked on Sigrid's. "You needed help. How could I have just left you? That isn't right."

Filling her lungs, Sigrid held her breath for a second. "You really believe that, don't you?"

"Well, yeah." Renarde nodded as her tail swept across the top of the snow, leaving a crescent shaped behind.

"Koarr's warmth preserve me, this is…. Wow." A quick breath of air and Sigrid turned around and snuck up on the ridge again, looking over to locate the troops as they marched ever closer to the mountain. "Okay, I think it's time we were on the move."

"Good!" Renarde popped up straight onto her feet. "We're going after them?"

"Nope." Sigrid stood and stepped back to stand beside the fox woman. She pointed off to her left, angling away from the mountain. "We're going there."

Lying perhaps a mile from the base of the mountain, buildings grew up from the frozen lands like the evergreens around them. A vast array of construction arranged in a regular pattern, with streets and courtyards peppering the design, providing a place for the citizens to move and gather. A city in the shadow of the mountain.

"Ooh! I like that idea even better." Renarde began to hop on the balls of her feet staring at the city. "I love meeting new people and doing new things. And we can go there and I'll be with you, and you can tell everyone that I'm not a demon," she looked over at Sigrid, "which I'm not as a reminder," and then looked back at the city, "and they won't scream or run or anything!"

Letting her eyes scroll up and down along Renarde's body, Sigrid took everything in at once. Her lithe female form. Her tail. Her ears and muzzle. Her paw-like feet. And all of that silver and black fur covering her from head to toe.

Noticing her, Renarde stopped bouncing and tilted her head. "What?"

Sigrid brought her left hand to her forehead and applied pressure.

"Crap."

•   •   •   •   •   •   •

The room was dominated by two separate things, depending on where your eye fell first. A half dozen massive windows lined one of the walls, running floor to ceiling and providing a flood of light into the space, especially at this time of day. Anyone stepping up to them was welcomed by an amazing view spilling over the valley below, including the city, which, at this height, appeared to be little more than a small maze meant to test the skills of rodents.

If a person's eyes were to land directly at the center of that same wall, however, they would equally be drawn to the massive stone fireplace warming the space. Easily twenty feet wide and six feet high, the flame in it had burned constantly for hundreds of years, fed regularly by a staff who only had that one duty—to keep the fire alive. To anyone inside the keep, it was known simply as The Burning Heart, as the heat from it helped to warm the entirety of the building. A mantle ran the full width of the fireplace, hewn from the trunk of a single tree and embedded into the mortar of the stone. Resting upon it, at its exact center, was a portrait of two women. The women in the portrait appeared identical, with the same lovely features and lush blond locks, though half of each of them was hidden in deep shadows—for one the left, and the other the right.

One of those women sat in one of two identically lush red high-back chairs in front of the fire, casually reading a book with a snifter of brandy on the small table beside her. She wore a dress that was black on the left side of her body, with the right half being a pattern of red vines growing over a field of white. Over the left half of her face was a leather mask, black with paintings of small red roses decorating it.

The massive doors to the room opened with the heavy sound of wood straining against the confines of hinges, filling all of the space for a moment. It caused the woman to glance up from her book and see another woman enter—dressed in black on the right side of her body, with the left half being a pattern of red vines growing over a field of white, and a black mask over the right half of her face with paintings of small red roses decorating it. A perfect mirror of her own appearance.

"Well?" the seated woman asked, lowering her book down.

The other woman sauntered across towards her, hips swaying wide with each step. "It's your turn."

The seated woman placed her book on the small table, rose, and stepped over towards the other woman, a smile growing upon her face. When they met, they grasped hands and leaned in, pressing each of their bare cheeks against one another, kissing lightly against the flesh as they did.

"I'm proud of you, Oikea," the woman with the left mask stated.

"Thank you, Vasen," she answered.

The two of them walked towards the fire, each of them turning and taking a seat in one of the twin chairs. When she sat down she grasped her snifter of brandy and lifted it slightly, nodding across to the other woman, and then took a small sip.

"Was he cooperative?" Vasen asked.

With a light sigh, Oikea answered, "Of course not. Fortunately it was easy enough to fan his breath with a little dream dust, letting him think whatever he liked for the majority of his experience." She shrugged. "As long as the goal was accomplished, I'm not upset."

"You rely too much on trickery, Sister," Vasen said, swirling her glass. "You must learn to take what you want and make it yours, and not simply borrow it through guile."

"It works for me, and that's the important part. Your methods are yours and mine are mine. Both work, so why complain?" Oikea glanced to her right, looking away from the fire and towards one of the servants by the door. She gestured with her hand as though it were an empty glass. Immediately, the man she looked at moved to find something to fill it.

"Oh, I'm not complaining. You know me better than that, dear, I just worry about you. I want you to be able to stand on your own," Vasen stated and took a small sip from her snifter.

Oikea's left eyebrow went up. "I am on my own, darling, remember?"

"Oh, I didn't mean it that way," Vasen lowered her glass and leaned forward in her chair, her empty hand extending out towards her sister. "And you are never truly alone, so long as I live. You are my other half, after all."

"And you mine," Oikea smiled. "I'm sorry, I suppose I am a bit jealous of you and Sebastian. I do love you both, though."

"I know, and we love you, too, dear." Vasen sat back in her chair. "I am lucky, though, I must admit. Sepi understands me so well."

"Well, we're both lucky about that part," Oikea laughed.

The servant walked up with a small silver tray. A single crystal glass, matching her sister's identically, sat upon it. With practiced grace, Oikea lifted the glass and dismissed the man with a glance. She cupped the snifter in her palm and swirled the brandy to warm it slightly.

When she felt the cool of the glass subside, she lifted her glass up towards her sister, and waited until she had copied her motion.

"To success," Oikea toasted calmly.

"To success," Vasen agreed.

Both brought the crystal to their lips gently and savored the aroma before imbibing the liquid directly.

"I figured I would find the two of you here."

The sound of the woman's voice turned both heads towards the open doors. Her boots clacked against the marbled floor as she strode towards the two of them. Still dressed in her black pants and coat, though it lay open, revealing the tighter fitting red shirt beneath. In her left hand she carried a pair of black leather gloves, while her right hand rested on the hilt of the sword still sheathed on her belt.

"Mathilda," Oikea said with a bright tone, "I didn't know you were back. I wasn't expecting you for another week or two."

"I'm sure," she answered, walking past the two of them to stand nearer the fire. "Circumstances dictated I come home a little earlier, however."

"Whatever the case," Vasen stood and walked over to Mathilda, kissing her lightly on the cheek, "it is good to see our little sister once again."

Mathilda made no move to return the kiss. "Your pet ran off again."

"Hmm? You mean Hjalmar?" Oikea asked.

A cold glance all but canceled the heat from the fire as Mathilda looked at her seated sibling. "Of course I mean Hjalmar. How many other lapdogs do you send off with me?"

"Oh, Tilly, don't think that way," Vasen brought her sister's attention back to her. "He is only there to protect you."

"He undermines me! He goes about as he wishes, ignoring my orders, and taking my men with him. How is that protecting me?" she snapped back. "Besides, I know why he is truly there."

Vasen's hand came to rest on Mathilda's arm. "Dear, you are our little sister. He is just there because we worry. We could never live with ourselves if something happened to you."

"Are you sure that it's not because you can't live with me?" Mathilda stared into Vasen's eyes.

The crackle of the fire drowned out the silence.

"Tilly, don't be that way. Sit. Have a drink. Tell us what happened," Oikea urged, gesturing over her shoulder vaguely. Within seconds one of the servants came rushing forward with a chair—not nearly the equal of the other sister's, though rich looking on its own—and sat it down between the other two.

It took a moment before she moved, but Mathilda did walk over and drop down onto the seat, spreading her feet wide to rest against the legs of the chair. Vasen moved back over to her own chair, smoothed out her dress, and lowered herself down, crossing her legs at the ankles.

"Now, tell us what happened," Oikea said softly.

Mathilda raised her hands up, letting the warmth of the fire play against her palms. The flames danced around in her vision as she recounted her story. "We were out testing, still, when we first discovered her. A woman who was following us. We aren't sure where we picked her up or how long she had been there, but she was definitely following us. She kept her distance, not wanting to come too close, so at first we ignored her. The longer she was there, though, the more difficult she became to ignore, so I started sending out patrols to find her and bring her to me. None of them could. So, I asked Hjalmar to do it." She finally looked over at Vasen once more. "He laughed at me." She turned to Oikea. "In front of my men, he laughed at me."

"That is not acceptable! I will see to it that he is properly reprimanded personally!" Oikea promised.

"You said he ran off, though," Vasen added.

The servant walked up to Mathilda with the same silver tray, presenting her with a very differently shaped crystal glass, this one half filled with a rich brown liquid. She took it, nodded to the servant with a smile, and then took a deep sip of whiskey.

"That's right." She took another small sip and her shoulders dropped visibly. "Yes, he did. He ran off chasing after a story that one of my men used as an excuse. He went off after a demon."

"A what?" Oikea blinked.

"Did you say demon?" Vasen asked.

Mathilda chuckled lightly. "Like I said, an excuse presented by one of my men. He couldn't accept that he wasn't able to overcome the woman who had been following us, so he made up a story about a demon coming to her rescue."

The silence returned.

"What type of demon?" Vasen asked.

"How should I know?" Mathilda took another drink. "He described it as looking like part fox, part woman. So, whatever demon that describes."

Vasen and Oikea looked at each other for a moment.

"Tilly, where is the orb?" Oikea asked.

Turning to her with a smile fully from ear to ear, Mathilda answered Oikea, "The orb? Oh, I think I left it with a couple of my men. They were supposed to return it to the Hall."

"Which men?" Vasen asked quickly.

"I'm not sure," she turned to look at the other sister, "they all blend together after a while."

"Mathilda! No games! Where is the orb?!" Oikea's voice turned colder.

She flipped back to look at Oikea quickly. "It's in the Hall! I put it there myself. I've been caring for that thing for months now. Why do you think I wouldn't know what to do with it?"

"I believe that Oikea was concerned that Hjalmar went off with it, Tilly. Nothing more," Vasen explained gently.

"I'm sure." Mathilda tipped her glass up, draining the contents down. She stood up and put the empty glass onto the seat of her chair. "I expect you to follow through on your discipline of Hjalmar, Oikea."

"And I will," she reassured.

"Good." Mathilda adjusted her pants and coat, making sure that her gloves were secure in her belt. "I'm going to go to my quarters, take a very long bath, and put on some reasonable clothes for a change. I assume dinner is still at 6:00?"

"As always," Vasen said.

"Then I'll see both of you later," she stated.

"It's good to have you home, Tilly, darling," Oikea said.

"Yes, dear, we are so happy to have you back," Vasen added.

Mathilda glanced at both of them briefly. "It's good to be home." She nodded once, turned on her heels, and walked from the room directly.

She wasn't even to the door before servants gathered up her chair and glass and carried them off. Once she was past the door, the two sister's looked at each other from their chairs.

"What do you think?" Vasen asked.

"I'm surprised that Hjalmar hasn't already killed her," Oikea groaned.

"Well, yes, that's true, but I was referring more to the woman and the demon in her story. The ones Hjalmar went off after."

"I know, I know," Oikea swirled her brandy, her eyes watching the thick liquid fleetingly cling to the glass for a moment with each pass. "Sadly, I outgrew stories meant to frighten children."

"But what about our sister's story?" Vasen reclined back into her seat and took a sip from her glass.

"Even more sadly," Oikea looked back at her sister, "I've learned to believe in the stories meant to frighten adults."

"Then we are in agreement?" Vasen asked.

Oikea laughed. "How could we not be?"

They once again raised their glasses to each other and took a small sip of their brandy.

•　•　•　•　•　•　•

More than a few eyes followed them as they walked into town. A few of them simply glanced and went on their way, but the majority stayed with them.

Sigrid smiled, trying to meet as many people directly eye-to-eye as possible, hoping to force them into looking away. She walked at a normal gait, despite her lack of cloak or overcoat to help warm her in this frigid weather. Most people would have been very curious about why—and possibly how—she was able to endure the cold air and biting wind if it were not for her companion.

To call her companion's walk awkward is a kind statement. It closer resembled the movement of a giant starfish, if it had been laced with rigid planks of wood—and then frozen. Her arms stuck out to her side, bent at the elbow to point downward, but showing no movement at all. Her legs were moving, but they were not taking the liberty of bending, causing her to waddle as much as walk, throwing her foot forward as she twisted her body.

The fact that her cloak hid her face completely thanks to the large cowl covering her head only added an extra level of mystery to this odd woman.

"Stop doing that," Sigrid whispered through her smiling teeth.

"I…can't." The words came forced from Renarde, fighting out with every awkward step.

"You were doing it a few minutes ago, why can't you walk normally now?" she asked as she nodded towards a man standing on the far side of the street.

"Yes, but…these horrible…things weren't…choking me," she gasped in response.

"Horrible things?" Sigrid shot her a quick sidelong glance. "What horrible things? Is there something in the clothes?"

"Yes!" Renarde barked. "Me! And these things itch and are making my fur feel strange. And my tail is strapped down to my body. It hurts."

Sigrid's eyes darted back and forth, watching the people begin to gather on the sides of the streets as the two of them walked. Some exited buildings to watch, while others simply stopped what they were already doing to stare.

She swallowed hard and grasped Renarde by the arm. "We are gathering attention. The whole point of this was to get you into town without anyone noticing."

"How can you live like this?" Renarde asked. "These things are so…so horrible!"

"Yes, you said that already." Holding on to her arm, Sigrid turned and began to pull Renarde along with her, forcing her towards a nearby building.

"Where are we going?" Feet scuttled along the ground, pulling at the cloth that was covering Renarde's feet in a makeshift shoe.

"Inside!" Sigrid kept her eyes forward, not wanting to draw any more attention.

"Inside where?" Renarde tilted her head back, hoping to see past the cowl, only to have Sigrid pull it back down with her free hand.

"Anywhere. Off of the street." They reached a door and pushed it open, a bell ringing as the wood jostled it above the sill. Renarde stumbled through, staying on her feet but staggering dramatically.

The room was filled with clothing. Coats, dresses, shirts, and pants in a variety of styles and colors adorned forms or were folded and placed on shelves. A young woman, still in her teens from the look of things, smiled at them both as they entered. Sigrid held onto Renarde's arm, who stood statue-like in the middle of the room.

"Tailor," Sigrid mumbled. "Of course it's a tailor."

"Oh dear," the young woman said, walking over to Sigrid, "you must be freezing. What are you doing out in this weather without a coat of some sort?"

"I was hoping you could help me with that," Sigrid's voice rose more confident with each word of her answer.

"We would be happy to help." The girl turned to look at Renarde, who remained in her awkward pose in the middle of the room. "And…can I help you?"

"I hate clothes," Renarde answered.

"Well, I don't blame you, those seem to be ill-fitting at best," the girl agreed, stepping up to Renarde. Her hand came up to grasp some of the clothing, but was stopped in Sigrid's grip.

"Don't do that," Sigrid said, holding the girl's arm tightly. "My friend is…sick. I don't want you catching anything."

"Oh, is that why she's bundled up like this?" she asked.

"Yes. Yes, it is. And she has a horrible rash, which makes her walk strangely." Sigrid began nodding along with her words. "She hates her clothing because it itches and feels strange to her."

"It sure does. I hate it," Renarde confirmed.

"Well, you shouldn't be out, then. You need to be in bed, resting," the girl said firmly.

"That's our exact plan!" Sigrid pointed at her. "In fact, we've just come here from out of town. We live in a small village a couple of days ride south of here called…Smallsby…and I feared for my sister's life, so I brought her here to see a doctor."

"You walked two days without a coat?" The girl's eyes went wide.

"No. No, I lost it this morning. Fighting off some wolves," Sigrid said.

"Ooh, tell me more about that!" Renarde said enthusiastically.

"What?" The girl looked over at her.

"Ignore her. She's delirious. We were just stopping here so I could get a new coat, hopefully. Do you have one?" Stepping forward, Sigrid forced the girl to take a step back from Renarde, and then positioned herself between the two of them.

"Why yes, we have many coats. Were you looking for something—"

"Cheap," Sigrid interrupted. "I need something…inexpensive." She nodded sideways at the still unmoving Renarde hidden in her clothing. "I have to have her cared for, after all."

"Oh, I understand. Let me think…." She tapped her chin a few times as her eyes looked at the ceiling. "I don't think that my mother would mind if I sold you one of the defectives we have. We aren't going to get much from them in any case. Wait right here."

The girl smiled again and walked through a door in the back of the room, leaving the two of them alone. Immediately, Sigrid turned to Renarde.

"You're sick," she explained.

"Yeah, I heard you say that," Renarde muttered under the hood. "I feel fine, though. Except for the clothing part."

"No, my point is that you need to act sick. It will keep people at a distance while we—"

"Here we go!" The girl announced her return right before she entered the room again. If she saw Sigrid jerk around from talking to Renarde, she made no motion about it. "I had to guess at your size, but then again, there aren't many options."

She held out a bundle of dark blue cloth which appeared to have white embroidery worked across it.

"I'm sure it will be fine." With a smile pasted on her face, Sigrid took the coat from the girl and slipped it over her shoulders. It fell down to mid-thigh and had a nice weight to it, but as she raised her arms up she noticed one particular issue. "One sleeve is much shorter than the other."

The girl nodded. "I know. And we can't replace it because of the stitching. That's why I'm willing to sell it at a low price."

"How low?" Sigrid looked at her arms. Her left arm had the sleeve covering all the way just past the wrist, while the right sleeve was easily two inches short. "Hopefully very low."

"How does twenty-five raha sound?" she asked with a slight wince.

"Twenty," Sigrid countered.

"Twenty-two," she replied, and then added quickly, "and my mother is going to be mad at that low price."

"Twenty-three!" Renarde jumped in.

They both looked over at her, one smiling the other...not.

"Ignore my sister," Sigrid growled. "She's ill." She looked back at the girl. "Twenty-two will be fine."

"But your sister said—"

"Is there a nearby place we can stay for a few nights?" Sigrid asked as she pulled some coin from her pocket. "As you said, my sister needs her rest."

"Oh, yes. About three blocks down and across the street there is a small lodge with rooms for rent. You shouldn't have any problem," she said.

Placing the coins firmly in the girl's hand, Sigrid looked her in the eye. "Thank you. You've been very helpful."

Grabbing hold of Renarde's sleeve, Sigrid pulled her along, causing Renarde to again stumble and dance awkwardly as she did her best to keep the clothes from rubbing up against her fur. Once outside Sigrid only increased her pace, causing Renarde to skip along behind her, occasionally making an odd whining noise. A few people still watched as they passed, but there was now a stronger look of amusement on their faces.

About three blocks later, on the opposite side of the street, Sigrid spied a timber structure with a small sign above the door that read simply, "Rooms." Without hesitation she burst through the door, dragging Renarde behind her. She saw a man standing at a desk and walked right up to him.

"We need a room for two, please. My sister is ill, and she needs rest. So, something away from others is probably best. Don't want to take any chances," she said quickly, giving the man no real chance for a reply.

"Sick? Is it something that—"

"No, you don't need to worry. She just needs rest. I just want her to be able to rest," Sigrid rattled off. "Everything is fine."

The clerk stared at her silently. Reaching into the desk he pulled forth a ledger, and laid it down on the desktop. He put a pen on top of it. "That will be fifteen raha a night, paid up front each night."

The pen felt surprisingly easy in Sigrid's hand as she scribbled down her name. As she set it down, her other hand went into her pocket and pulled out a fistful of coins. Using her thumb, she pushed out three onto the desk and looked up at the man.

He handed her the key as he scooped up the coins. "Up the stairs, all the way to the top, last room on the left."

"Thank you," Sigrid said quickly and once more grabbed Renarde's sleeve and pulled her along.

"Nice meeting you!" Renarde shouted as they hit the stairs.

Two flights up went quickly, and then the walk to the end of the hall was done. The door opened easily and Sigrid pulled Renarde inside. She fell against the door closing the room up behind her.

And at that moment, Sigrid's shoulders relaxed and she started breathing. Her eyelids slid closed and she exhaled all of the air from her lungs. "That was far more stressful than it should have been."

"I agree," Renarde stated.

Even before she got her eyes open, Sigrid sensed what had happened. Renarde was standing there naked. All of the clothing she had been wearing piled up in a mess beside her on the floor. As she tussled her hair with her hands, the fur on Renarde's tail seemed to puff out and groom itself.

"Thibaan and Porter make that look so easy," Renarde said mostly to herself and gave her whole body a shake, puffing her fur out for a moment before it once more fell flat against most of her body.

The next course of action was for Sigrid to lock the door.

"I know that you don't mean to be, but…." Sigrid looked at Renarde and hesitated. "Look, we just need to be careful, okay?"

"Yeah, okay," Renarde said. "I'm actually really good at sneaking around if we need to."

Sigrid took a moment to survey the room. Two beds, one chair at a small writing desk beneath a window. Sparse accommodations, but more than sufficient. The walls were washed white wood, with a dark stained wood on the ceiling. Walking over and pushing down on the nearest bed, she nodded and smiled. "I haven't slept in a bed in months."

"Really?" Renarde turned her head to the side, rolling one ear flat as she did. "I haven't either, but it surprises me that you haven't."

The window called Sigrid's attention. She spoke as she stepped over to it, "Why? Do I seem to be that pampered?"

"No. I mean, I guess not. I'm kind of used to pampered, though," Renarde sat down on the second bed, bouncing her rump up and down on it several times.

Satisfied that there was no clear view into the room through the window, Sigrid turned back. "You were pampered?"

"Yep! One of the perks of living with goddesses, actually." Her muzzle lit up in a huge smile.

Pulling out the chair, Sigrid spun it around and sat down, folding her arms and resting them across the back of it. "You still claim to be a harbinger of the goddesses?"

"Uh, no. I mean, yes I know Serenade and her sisters, but…" her words faded away. "Remind me again what a harbinger is?"

The short laugh barely preceded the smile that crept onto Sigrid's face. With all of the stress she had endured, it was nice to laugh.

The sudden knock on the door snapped that smile right off of her face.

The size of Sigrid's eyes quickly grew to resemble dinner plates, and she stared directly at Renarde. She pointed to the bed as she spoke softly, "Under the covers! Now!"

With wild abandon, Renarde spun around on the bed three times, before finally yanking the covers straight up and flopping down, pulling them over her completely.

"And don't forget, you're sick!" Sigrid whispered.

Seemingly in response, two quick coughs sounded from under the sheets. Satisfied, Sigrid stepped up to the door, took a deep breath, let it out, and opened it slowly.

A woman dressed entirely in black, with one red sleeve was waiting outside. Sigrid swallowed loudly.

"Welcome to Mirceby," the woman said with a smile.

Sigrid blinked several times. "I'm sorry?"

"I'm Sheriff Brynja Eydisdotter. I heard that you made quite an impression coming into town." The Sheriff was about the same height as Sigrid, with short black hair and strikingly blue eyes.

She leaned over to the side, looking into the room and at the bed where Renarde lay waiting.

"That's my sister," Sigrid explained. "She fell ill so I brought her to town to see if someone here could help."

Hearing what she thought was her cue, Renarde let out another pair of coughs.

"What's wrong with her?" The Sheriff leaned back, looking once more at Sigrid.

"We, uh, we don't know. That's why we came here. We heard that Mircleby had excellent doctors." A forced smile curled Sigrid's mouth.

"Mirceby. No 'L' in the name," she answered. "Where did you come from, anyway?"

"Uh…." She looked down at the Sheriff's waist. A sword hung there waiting. "A small village named…Smallsby."

"Smallsby," she repeated back.

"Yep. It's a very descriptive name, huh?" Sigrid laughed awkwardly.

"Sure is." She looked past Sigrid once more, seeing the lump of Renarde under the covers. "You didn't bring any sort of plague into my town, did you?"

"No. No, not at all!" Sigrid stated emphatically. "I wouldn't do that."

"Good." The Sheriff took a step backwards and pulled a pair of gloves from behind her. She slipped them on as she continued. "I'll send a doctor over here in a bit. In the meantime, you and your sister stay in this room. I don't want anything bad happening to you."

"Of course. Thank you, Sheriff…?"

"Eydisdotter. Brynja Eydisdotter." She smiled. "And what about you and your sister? What are your names?"

"I'm Sigrid Elsker." She nodded back towards the bed. "And my sister is Renarde."

"Well, as I said earlier, welcome to Mirceby, Miss Elsker," she said.

"Mrs, actually," she replied quickly.

"Oh, well then Mrs. Elsker, welcome." She nodded politely and turned to leave. "You can expect a visitor by the end of the day."

And with that the Sheriff walked down the hall. Sigrid closed the door, and by the time the latch clicked, Renarde pulled the covers down mostly off of her body.

"That was easy! I play a great sick person," Renarde said proudly.

"I don't know. I think she's suspicious," Sigrid answered, moving to sit on the other bed, looking over at Renarde.

"Of what? A sick sister?" Renarde's face lit up. "Oh, and thanks for making me your sister."

"Uh, you're welcome. We have a bigger problem, though. She's sending a doctor," Sigrid sighed.

"Yeah, I heard. That's okay, I can fake sick again," she said reassuringly.

"Sure. Right up to the point where the doctor takes a look at you and sees fur." She put her left hand over her face.

"Is my fur really such a problem?" Renarde's voice turned dusky and slow. Sigrid moved her hand and saw the fox woman sliding her hand up along her body, crossing down onto her chest and up between her breasts.

"What are you doing?" Sigrid asked.

"This bed would be kind of cozy to share, you know." Renarde's eyes fell half closed and her tail began to twitch slightly.

Shaking her head, Sigrid stood up and walked to the window. "Oh, that's all I need right now."

Renarde sat up, turning to follow Sigrid as she walked. "Hey! C'mon! I'm super cute!"

Sigrid stood at the window, waiting. Soon enough she saw the Sheriff walk out onto the street, directing two men in similar outfits towards the lodge before turning to walk away alone.

"Well, you better figure out a good use for that cute in the next couple of hours, or I think we're going to be in serious trouble." Sigrid's hand fell down to her sword, wrapping around the grip tightly.

• • • • • • •

The table was thirty feet long and over five feet wide, crafted from one single piece of wood. Artisans had carved it from a great pine that stood at the base of Valpuri keep for hundreds of years. It was the most grand tree in the land, dominating the landscape and serving as a point of reference for travelers for generations.

When the Valpuri sisters took over their family home, they saw only something that took eyes away from them. Two weeks after their parent's death, the had the tree cut down. Three months later the heart of that tree had been shaped and carved into a single massive slab. Other parts of the same tree were used to carve the five posts serving as the base for the table, and the wooden parts of the chairs sitting around it.

The wood was stained a rich, dark color, save for a section in the middle of the table where the Valpuri family crest—a raven with its wings folding over and in on itself—was inlaid in a lighter wood, creating a negative image of the crest on a dark field, rather than the traditional dark bird on white.

The room holding the table had always served as the dining hall for family and guests, though one window had to be removed to get the table into the space after it had been constructed. It was no easy task to pull that massive piece up the side of the mountain, either. Four men climbed alongside it, tethered by ropes to make sure that it did not fly about and damage itself against the cliff. The winds were not kind that day, either, and one of the men was badly injured by the furniture crushing him against the stone. The Valpuri sisters were grateful for his sacrifice, and allowed him to live his final days in the keep under the care of their servants. They sometimes even try to remember his name, though it remains a matter of debate between them.

Once in place, the sisters brought in decorators to make sure that every aspect of the room highlighted the table and the two seats at either end where they would sit. The lighting was specially arranged so the majority of it coming from the four chandeliers above the table, as well as the wall sconces, all seemed to highlight those two spots while still casting enough light for all to see.

As Armas was escorted into the room, he saw both of those spots filled by their normal occupants. On his right was Oikea, and to his left was Vasen. Directly across from the entrance, seated slightly closer to Vasen, was a smallish man with cragged features hidden under dark hair. All three of them turned to him as he entered.

It looked like he hadn't shaved for three days, and his hair was a jumbled mess, best described as being combed with his fingers moments before he entered the room. His clothes belied that rough look. A perfectly pressed white shirt, of which he left the top two buttons undone, sat beneath a heavy brown vest decorated with silver inlay that curled along the lapels. Simple black pants, with a crease looking like it could cut paper, and shining black boots completed his ensemble.

"Armas!" Vasen said happily. "I'm so happy that you joined us tonight."

The left side of Vasen's face was covered by a white leather mask with black filigree around the edge, matching almost perfectly the design on Armas' vest. Her dress was deep red, covering one shoulder and arm, leaving the other bare. A line of black roses began at her wrist and traced over one breast and down the rest of the dress.

"Well, I couldn't actually say no, could I?" He took a deep breath and walked forward. A servant rushed in front of him and pulled out his chair, one that was slightly closer to Vasen than Oikea. Taking the hint, he sat down with a nod to the servant.

"Despite what you might feel, we are grateful for you coming tonight," Oikea stated. She, too, wore a white mask, her's covering the right side of her face, as well as a red dress that near identical to Vasen's, only covering her right arm and shoulder. A perfect reflection of her sister.

"And why is that?" he asked, settling into his chair.

"Oh, darling, you do know that we want you to feel comfortable, and unless we get to know each other better by spending time together you might never have the ease you deserve in our home. Eating a meal together is the best way to bond. Food brings people together," Oikea stated.

"Mm-hmm," Armas droned.

"Armas," Vasen called his attention, "you do remember my husband, Sebastian, yes?"

"I'm sure he does," the man sitting across from Armas said. His voice was rough and cracked, and he wore a simple black jacket over a white shirt. "It's good to see you, Armas."

"Honestly, I'm surprised you feel that way," he answered. "Considering the situation."

"Well, I…I understand the circumstances." His smile appeared as though it might fracture his face.

"You're a very understanding man," he replied with a smirk.

"Sebastian is a wonderful husband," Vasen commented, and then looked over at the man. "Aren't you, Sepi?"

"If you say so, my dear," he answered with a glance her way. She smiled at him.

Sensing someone approaching, Armas glanced over his shoulder to see a servant approaching with a tray that contained three bottles upon it. He stepped up beside him, and placed the tray on the table.

"What's this?" he asked.

"The madams requested that you choose the wine for the evening," the servant answered. "I brought out what I thought to be three excellent choices."

"I don't know anything about wine," Armas admitted. "Anything I chose would just be a guess."

"Well, then let me help you, if I may. Do you like a dry or a sweet wine?" he asked.

"Uh, well, sweet I suppose," he answered.

"Do you prefer a light or a heavy flavor?"

"Light?" He shrugged.

The man picked up a bottle and presented it to Armas. "This is a forty year old vintage from the Valpuri label. It was produced at the end of the season, when an early frost struck the grapes and left them with a particularly sweet flavor. It isn't as heavy as a true ice wine, but it has a lovely bouquet and crisp finish. I think you will enjoy it." The man pulled what appeared to Armas to be a torture device from the tray and deftly removed the cork. With a slight flourish he handed the cork to Armas—who shrugged again and placed the cork in his vest pocket. The man poured a small quantity of the wine in a glass and presented it to Armas.

Taking the glass, Armas downed it in a single sip, and then presented it back to the servant. Suppressing a laugh, the servant poured the glass to the normal level, and then moved to pour the wine for the others at the table.

"A toast," Vasen raised her glass. "To a good night."

Two of the others raised their glass, but all four of them drank.

"Sorry I'm late." Everyone at the table looked to the door as Mathilda entered the room. Unlike her sisters, she was dressed in tight-fitting black pants and boots, with a very loose and flowing red shirt on top—one that was open down to her stomach, allowing an ample view of her cleavage. As she walked in she took a side trip to the servant's station and grabbed a bottle of whiskey, bringing it with her to the table. She sat down, popped the cork, and poured her glass completely full. "Did I miss much?"

"Hello, Mathilda. It's wonderful to have you join us. We so rarely get to spend a meal with you," Oikea said.

"Well, that's probably because I'm rarely here. The family has so many needs that I must fill." She took a deep drink from her glass.

"And we are very, very grateful for you sacrifice, Tilly," Vasen said. "You know how much we rely upon you."

Mathilda nodded slowly and glanced around the table. "So, how is everyone? Are you doing well, Sebastian?"

The man sat up straight, looking across the table with a crooked smile. "Yes, thank you. Quite well."

"That's good. I'm glad to hear that." She took another drink from her glass.

"Sebastian is a good man, Tilly. You know how much he means to me," Vasen replied.

"Of course! You two have been so close for so long now." The smile on Mathilda's face lingered as she turned to look at Armas sitting down from her at the table. "And what about you, Armas? How does it feel to be the house stud?"

"Mathilda!" There was a slight rattle of glass and metal near Oikea where she slammed her fist onto the table. "There is no call for that!"

Sitting back in her chair, Mathilda looked at first Oikea and then at Vasen. "You're right. You're right. I'm sorry." She turned back to Armas. "I should be more direct: do you like fucking my sisters? Are they any good?"

"Mathilda!" Vasen rose up out of her seat. "You are being rude to our guest!"

"Guest?" she laughed. "You must be joking. He's as much a guest here as the beasts in the stable. I don't see them being invited to the dinner table. The fact that you put on this pretense is the saddest part of the whole ordeal. I understand why he's here, but at least show some respect."

"How dare you!" Vasen spit. "You accuse us of showing no respect? We invited Armas to dinner and tried to make him feel welcome here, it's you who are sitting there mocking him. Do you really think that your words aren't making him feel worse? Oikea and I know what his role is here as well as anyone, but we are trying to show him some kindness along the way! Can you say the same?"

Silence reigned at the table. Turning up her glass, Mathilda emptied its contents down her throat. She put the glass back on the table and filled it once more. She glanced towards Armas under her brow. "I'm sorry," she said. "I didn't mean to belittle you."

With a growing smile, Vasen sat back down.

"It's all right, thank you," Armas answered. He leaned towards her and whispered just loud enough for her to hear. "And no, I don't like it, and no, they aren't very good."

The corner of Mathilda's mouth curled up.

"Well, now that we have that resolved," Oikea spoke with a heavy breath, "I believe that we should resume dinner."

"Of course," Vasen agreed. "We even have a special meal planned for the evening. Duck, by request."

Armas raised an eyebrow. "And am I also getting the other half of my dinner request?"

Oikea laughed. Vasen shook her head. "No, dear, we'll all be having the duck instead."

"There is an option besides duck?" Mathilda asked.

Oikea laughed again.

"I think that…. No, Tilly, dear," Vasen said slowly. "No, not even for you tonight."

The servants moved into the room carrying trays of food for everyone.

• • • • • • •

She turned, and walked back over the same stretch of floor she had tread for the past hour.

"You know, I'm pretty sure that I could jump from the window onto the roof and run away," Renarde said from the bed, legs crossed under her, tail swinging slowly back and forth.

"No," Sigrid answered. "If there is no one in bed when the doctor gets here, I'm going to be in just as much trouble. Besides, I'm reasonably sure they are watching for us to make a break for it. They'd probably see you anyway."

"Why?" Renarde asked, tilting her head, with no smile on her face at all. "I mean, what's so special about us that they want to watch us?"

Sigrid stopped in mid stride. She turned and looked Renarde directly in the eye. "I have no idea, but the fact they do scares me."

"So, if I can't leave, then what am I going to do? Hide under the covers again?" Renarde pointed at the pillow on the bed with her thumb.

"I don't know. I'm pretty sure that whoever this doctor is, they are going to want to take a close look at you." Sigrid said with a heavy sigh.

Renarde looked down at herself, turning her head from right to left. When she looked back up at Sigrid her familiar smile was back. "Well, I think he might notice something about me. I wouldn't call it wrong, but it's definitely noticeable."

"Yeah, I know." Sigrid said slowly.

An easy knock on the door caused both women to jump slightly, and turn their heads towards the sound. Almost immediately they turned to look back at each other.

"I'll hide under the covers," Renarde said. "If we need to run, I can carry you. I run pretty fast, maybe we can get away."

Without another word, Renarde dove under the covers, pulling them up over her head once more. Sigrid stared down at the lump in the bed with wide eyes. She swallowed once. "This isn't going to work."

Another knock came at the door, as casual as the first one, but still strong enough to give Sigrid pause. The pause passed, and she stepped towards the door, grasping the handle as she took a deep breath. She exhaled as she opened it.

The man on the other side of the door smiled weakly. His brown hair came down halfway to his shoulders, with a tousled, unwashed look to it. Deep lines ran through his face, but despite them he didn't appear old—just tired, which reflected in his voice when he spoke. "I'm Olav Karhu. I'm the doctor Sheriff Eydisdotter sent."

"Yes. Yes, of course," Sigrid nodded. She glanced down the hallway, but it seemed the man was alone. With another deep breath she stepped away from the door, giving the man passage inside.

"So, I hear you have a sick sister," he stated, walking inside. Seeing the lump in the bed, he gravitated that way. "What seems to be wrong with her."

"Oh, it's bad." Sigrid rushed around, getting between him and the bed. "Very bad. This is the first peaceful rest that she's managed to get in the past several days. I really don't want to wake her. Maybe I can just tell you what's wrong?"

"Well, we can certainly start there." He removed his coat, laying it down carefully, and sat down on the empty bed beside it, setting the small black leather bag he carried on top of the coat. He wore simple black pants and a heavy white shirt. "Describe what's wrong."

"Um, well," Sigrid licked her lower lip. "Well, you see, she started having trouble breathing a few weeks ago, and that led to coughing. It got really bad, and she became very, very weak. Then she, um, she started to…bleed." She winced as soon as she said the word.

"Bleed? From where?" the doctor asked.

"Her nose. She started to get bad nose bleeds," Sigrid nodded, and bit her lower lip.

"Nose bleeds? How frequently?" He leaned back, watching Sigrid.

"I…I'm not sure. A lot. More than she should." Sigrid looked away from him and at the lump in the bed.

"Had she had a problem with them before?" he asked.

"Uh, no. Not really. That's what made it so strange." She took a deep breath.

"Is there anything else you would like to tell me, miss?" The tone of the doctor's voice altered slightly.

"I hope not," she mumbled.

"What was that?" He leaned towards her.

"I was saying that I hope you know what's wrong." She turned back to him. "So, I suppose you'll need to go research this then?"

"Not yet." He stood up, bringing his bag with him. "I'm going to have to get a look at your sister."

"No!" Sigrid stepped in front of him. "I mean, uh, she needs her rest."

"Young lady, if I don't look at her, resting could be the least of her concerns." He moved to step past her, but Sigrid shifted with him.

"Please? Can you come back tomorrow?" she pleaded.

He looked her in the eye, and gently smiled. "What is the real problem?"

"I'm just worried about my sister," she answered.

"I can tell. I just want to know why? She's not really sick, is she?" His voice remained level and calm, which did nothing to help Sigrid stay that way.

"She…she's…."

"I'm actually okay," Renarde's voice came from under the covers. "I just don't think that people would react well to the way I look."

The doctor shifted over, looking past Sigrid at the lump in the bed. Sigrid's jaw fell open.

"Renarde!" Sigrid barked. "Stay quiet!"

"I'd like to hear what she has to say, actually," he stated. "So, Miss Renarde, is it? Why do you think that people would react badly? Are you deformed in some way?"

"Oh, heck no! I'm super cute!" She turned under the covers, bringing herself in line with his view, though still hidden under cloth.

"Renarde, don't do this," Sigrid begged.

"He was gonna look. What difference does it make when he sees me?" she asked.

"And when am I going to see you?" the doctor stepped to the side, looking down at Renarde under the covers.

Moving away, Sigrid stepped over to the door. Her hand slid down and touched the sword on her hip. She swallowed again.

The covers over Renarde started to move, sliding down from the top slowly at first. Her ears peeked out from the top, and moments later she yanked the whole thing down to her chest. A huge grin spread across the width of her muzzle.

"Hi! I'm Renarde." The way she introduced herself seemed as though it was as normal as a sunrise.

He stepped back, coming into contact with the other bed. His hands fumbled behind him as his legs gave out under him, causing him to sit awkwardly on his coat, the black bag he was carrying dropping to the floor with a dull sound.

Sitting up and letting the cover fall to her waist, Renarde tilted her head as her ears twisted out to the side. "I know, my cuteness can be overwhelming, can't it?"

Sigrid's grip on her sword hilt grew tighter.

"Did…did Oikea send you after me?" His voice was weak.

"Not that I know of," Renarde answered. "What's an Oikea?"

"You're not here for me?" His eyes narrowed as he pulled back a little more.

"Well, I like to think that I'm there for everyone, but at the same time, not for anyone in particular." Renarde's gaze slowly moved towards the ceiling, her eyes focusing on nothing.

"She's here to help me," Sigrid said. "Nothing more."

He turned to look at her, his eyes immediately falling to her hand on the sword. "You? And what are you here for?"

"I'm not here to hurt you, if that's what you mean. We don't want any trouble." Sigrid let her hand slip free of her sword. "You said 'Oikea.' I know that name."

"Everyone here knows that name. Oikea Valpuri, twin sister of Vasen Valpuri, the Ranee of this Hundred," he stated.

"Right. So, why would she send someone after you?" Sigrid adjusted her feet slightly, finding better balance.

"And more importantly," Renarde asked, "why did you think she sent me? That was your first thought, after all, and not 'ah! A demon!' I hear that a lot." She turned in the bed and crossed her legs, with her ears pointing towards him and her tail flapping against the covers.

"That's actually a good point." Sigrid stepped towards him, warily.

He took a deep breath and held it, sitting up straight. "If you aren't a demon, what exactly are you?"

Renarde rolled her eyes. "Okay, the short version. I was created by the goddesses and brought to Elan to help them return safely so that me and the others like me could then stop Aubade from destroying the world by being some big dark goddess thing, but she passed the power along to a human which let us actually stop her and lock her up, and now I'm looking for her children—sort of—and that led me up here." She smiled. "Whew! That was easy."

"I…I'm not sure that I followed all of that," he said calmly.

"You get used to it," Sigrid stated. "And now you get to answer our question: why weren't you more shocked by Renarde? You were afraid she was going to hurt you, not by her appearance."

He looked over at Sigrid, his eyes narrowing. "You were trying to hide her. What did you think I was going to do?"

"We were just wanting a warm place to sleep for a day or two, and then we would be on our way. That's all. That's all we still want," she grumbled.

"And you were going to go where? What was your plan?" he asked.

"Wow!" Renarde jumped up, startling both of them. She stepped over between them, flailing her arms the whole way. "You guys gotta just get past this whole intensity thing. I mean, seriously, what's the deal." She stopped and looked at Olav. "Sigrid is trying to find her husband. He was taken by the nasty people in the castle on the mountain. I'm helping her out. That's it! No big secret!"

"...not anymore," Sigrid growled.

"So, what's your deal?" Renarde asked Olav, putting one hand on her hip and crossing her legs.

He glanced over at Sigrid. Her hand was back on her sword's hilt. "You are planning to invade the keep? Are you insane?"

"Not invade, just find my husband," she said.

"How do you know he's there?" he asked.

Her hand was tightening and releasing on the sword. "I know. I followed them."

"Let him go," he said. "It's too late."

Her sword was out and at his throat in a flash. The blade pressed against his flesh, and would have penetrated had he not pulled back suddenly.

"What do you know?" she snarled.

"Whoa, whoa, whoa...." Slowly and gently, Renarde reached over and put two fingers on her sword and pulled it back away from Olav's neck. "Let's not give the nice man any reason to scream loudly and call extra attention to our room with all the nice people waiting outside."

Sigrid yanked the sword back away from Renarde, her eyes burning as she looked at the fox woman.

"She's right," he said. "There are many guards outside waiting for me to give them a signal if something is wrong." His hand came up to rub his throat. "I won't, don't worry."

"Good, good," Renarde said, her tail wagging behind her. "Now, let's get back to why you don't want her going into the castle thingie, and why?"

He was silent for a moment, staring at Renarde first, and then at Sigrid. He looked at her sword still turning in her hand slightly as she gripped it hard enough for her knuckles to turn white.

"I know the Valpuri sisters. I used to live in the keep." His eyes met Sigrid's.

Sigrid's eyes lit up. "Then you know the way in. You can get us inside!"

"No. No, I can't. I'm not welcome there any more. I live in fear that Oikea will decide that I'm better off dead and will send someone like her," he gestured towards Renarde, "to kill me. And if I try to leave, I know she'll hunt me down."

"Wow. She must not like you much," Renarde said.

"That's one way to put it," he replied.

"What do you mean, someone like her? Have you seen creatures—"

"People," Renarde corrected.

"—people like her before?" Sigrid asked.

"Not exactly, no, but I've seen things. The sisters have an obsession with finding the unusual. The exotic, shall we say. Hidden things from the past." He shook his head. "I wouldn't be at all surprised to see something—"

"Someone," Renarde corrected again.

"—someone like her in their service. They are capable of anything."

There was a pause. "You're joking," Sigrid said.

"I'm not. Not at all. You both need to leave while you still can," he said. "I'll tell them that you really are sick, and that I did everything I could. Leave town before it's too late for you."

"I'm not leaving without my husband," Sigrid said.

"Then you won't be leaving," he snapped back. "I'm sorry, but it's too late!"

"Why do you say that?" Renarde asked. Her ears were back and her tail was lying flat behind her.

"Because I know what happens to the men that are harvested from the towns each year," he answered with a sigh, shaking his head. "I know."

"It wasn't a Harvest," Sigrid answered softly.

They both turned to look at her.

"What do you mean?" he asked. "He wasn't—"

"No! It wasn't a Harvest. This was different," she turned away.

"Uh…." Renarde raised her hand. "Excuse me, but what are you two talking about? What do you mean by a Harvest? And…well, why don't you just tell me what happened?"

The sound of Sigrid's sigh filled the room. "All right." She turned to look at them. "All right, I'll tell you."

She sheathed her sword and wiped her hands together.

"It was several months ago…."

end chapter two

CHAPTER
THREE

THE COUPLE

Several months ago....

She was smiling and nodding, barely hearing a word the customer was saying. It was a skill she had mastered over a long period of time, where it seemed like she was deeply interested in every word of the ongoing conversation, but in truth none of it was remembered the moment she turned away.

Now, she didn't do this with every customer. Some of them were pleasant and actually had many interesting things to say, and those customers she knew by name and smiled when they came into her store. Regulars. The people that kept her going and provided the backbone of her business.

No, it was the other customers. The ones who came in and decided they needed to instruct her on how to do things, despite the fact that they had never done her job and she had been doing it for years. It always amazed her that there were so many people who thought that, by hearing something from a friend, or by once reading a book about something, that they knew all the nuances of a particular business. The audacity of it was almost matched by the humor of it all.

Nonetheless, she smiled. She nodded. She waited for the inevitable to come.

"…oh well, I suppose I need to be going. Roderick is waiting for me to return, and if I leave him on his own he's start to think he's capable of things. The poor thing. You have a nice day, and don't forget what I told you!"

Sigrid took the deep breath and smiled broadly, finally hearing her cue. "Oh, don't worry. I appreciate all of the advice. Very useful."

"Well, you do all of those things and I promise that your sales will triple! I promise!" She wagged her finger at Sigrid with all of the precision of her lecture. "You're such a sweet girl, Sigrid. I want to see you do well."

"You're too kind, ma'am." Ma'am was one of those catch-all words she used when she had no idea who was talking to her, even though they seemed to know her on a first name basis. Others included "dear," "darling," "sweetheart," "friend," and even the occasional "you." And that was just for her female customers. For the few men that actually did any shopping there was a much longer list.

The woman left, and as soon as the door shut, Sigrid picked up the newest order and turned to walk through the door behind her and towards the workshop where her husband labored. It was a good arrangement. She did all of the front-end part of the business: selling the wares, dealing with customers, handling the money—all of the actual business end of the operation. All her husband did was carve the furniture that they sold.

And she was in awe of his skill to this day.

To her, he could take a piece of wood and bring it to new life. It was as though there was a hidden structure inside every hunk of wood he touched, and it was asking him to bring it out—and he obliged.

"Armas?" Her voice rang out clean and clear, tinkling like a bell as she opened the door.

The heat of the room washed over her. Armas always kept the room hot, especially now, during the peak of winter. He said it had something to do with keeping the wood dry, which was apparently important in some way. She let him handle all of that.

At first, she didn't see him, but he slowly rose from below a table top, wiping sweat from his brow. She took a deep breath in at the sight of him, and thanked every lucky star she could think of for whatever brought him to her. He ran a hand through his thick brown hair, brushing it back slick with sweat. He had forgotten to shave today—again—but that never bothered her, it made his boyish face seem slightly more rugged and set his jawline.

"Sweetheart." He danced around the table and towards her, wiping his hands on his pants—and probably not getting them much cleaner. "What are you doing back here? Is there anyone watching the shop?"

"No, not right now, but I thought you would want this right away. One of the wealthier women in town came by with a fairly large order, and a bit of a rush on it." She pecked him on the cheek as he got close, and then patted his shoulder. "Are you almost caught up with the other orders?"

"Well," he turned around to look across his workroom. Every corner seemed to be stacked with lumber or furniture, in every level of completion, "not as much as I would like. I just want to make sure I get it right. I hate it when I send out something that isn't finished."

"You never think anything is finished," she laughed.

"Well, that's true." He scratched the back of his head, staring at the ground. "Well, what does this woman want?"

"A bed, a dresser, and two side tables for the bed," she answered.

"That's...that's a lot. When does she want it?"

"Three weeks." She smiled at him.

"What?! And you told her that I could do it?" His mouth continued to move well after he finished speaking, as though words were still trying to come out. "I'm not sure I can have the bed ready in that short a time, forget the other things!"

"You can do it," she put a hand on his shoulder.

"Dressers have drawers. Drawers need to be fit and made so that they can pull out easily. It's not just a matter of me—"

"Armas," she interrupted. "You can do this. You will do this. I told her you would, and you will. All right?"

"I…." He looked at her eyes. Deep brown, offsetting her pale skin nicely. "I'll try."

"You'll do it," she said. "If you have to bring in some help, we can afford it. I told her it was a rush job so I charged a little extra."

"Oh, well, that makes it much more possible." His face lit up. "Why didn't you tell me that to begin with?"

"Because I wanted to surprise you when you were panicked," she laughed. "It's my perverse nature."

He stepped up and towered a good four inches above her, without seeming to be anywhere but right at eye level. She wrapped her arms around him and pulled him tight.

"You're my man, right?" she asked. "You know I'll never hurt you."

"I know that. It's why I said yes when you asked me to marry you. I've never doubted how kind you are. You brought me here and took care of me. You made me a part of this town. Even this business was your idea." He brushed back a wild strand of her red hair. "You're amazing. I'm a lucky man."

Her lip curled up into a smirk. "Keep talking that way and you might just be getting lucky."

"Nope. Not right now." He slowly pulled her arms off of him and stepped back. "I've got two orders that I have to finish this week, and we're going to have to figure out a way to tell Brianna that her chair might be a little late, too."

"Let me handle her. We go back a long way. I'll be able to convince her that it's all your fault. She'll believe that," she laughed.

He nodded slowly. "Good to know that you've got my back."

"Always." She took a deep breath as their eyes locked. "You know how much I love you, right?"

He laughed. "Never a doubt."

"All right, get to work." She smacked him on his butt. "And start thinking of who you want to bring in to help. I'll get it arranged when you do."

"I will, Honey." He pecked her on her cheek. "I love you."

"Love you, too." She stepped back up the small flight of stairs and exited the workroom. A few steps later she entered back into the front of their furniture store—and stopped cold.

Through the windows, distorted by the ice and cold, she could see riders passing by the front of the building. Several of them. Dark horses and dark riders with a spot of red on one arm. She swallowed back a scream.

"No," she whispered, stepping back against the wall. "No, no, no, no, no."

A chill far colder than anything the weather could offer encased her spine. She stood there, motionless, watching as the obscure shapes made their way past the front of the shop. The abstraction of the ice made the figures appear as inhuman riders on beasts that were anything but horses. Elongated bodies stretching up past the range of the window on animals with broad chests and virtually non-existent waists.

And through all of that Sigrid saw the truth. She saw these shapes for what they were, and it was far more frightening than any monster her mind could conjure. Her hands tried to grip the wall. Her fingers desperate to find something to hold as they slid again and again against the smooth wood.

The shadows moved past the window, the light of day once again unobstructed into the front of her building. For a full five count she remained still, not even daring to breathe, trying desperately not to blink. On the sixth count her breath came out in fractured jolts, her chest jittering as it escaped. A single step forward really didn't change the angle of her view, but she twisted her head nonetheless, hoping to see something more than she could before. When nothing else appeared, she turned and hurried through the back door, rushing to see her husband once again.

"We have to go!" She blurted her words before the door had fully opened. His movement caught her eye a second later. "Hurry, we have to go!"

Setting down the length of wood that was in his hands, Armas stepped towards her slowly. "Go? Go where? What's wrong?"

She rushed to him, grasping his shoulders tightly. "The riders. The Valpuri. They've come back. We have to leave. We have to leave now!"

"The riders? That's not possible. They aren't due back for more than a year, still," he whispered. "What are they doing here?"

"I don't know." Frantically, Sigrid turned and moved through the room, pulling open drawers and opening cabinets, removing items almost at random. A small sack of nails. A hammer. Two pairs of gloves. Half a can of wax. "I don't care. It doesn't matter."

"It does matter!" She felt his hands firm on her shoulders as he spoke, urging her to turn to him. Obliging the request, Sigrid turned to him, dropping her armload to the floor in a heap. The look in her eyes was steel in a room filled with wood. "We don't know why they are here."

"Don't know…?" she gasped. "Of course we know! They're here for the Harvest! And I won't let it happen. Not again!"

"You don't know that! The Ranee have always been consistent and truthful about the Harvest. This may be something different," he stated, shifting his grip from her shoulders to holding her hands.

Thoughts raced through her mind, and with every one that passed, the grip she returned to her husband increased. By the time she spoke, he was wincing slightly.

"If we stay, we are risking your life. I can't…I won't do that. And trust me, the Valpuri are anything but honest and kind. You've never had to deal with the riders directly. There is nothing about them that is…. You don't want to meet them." She let her hands relax as she spoke. "We have to go."

His lungs filled slowly. "Where? We've discussed this. There is nowhere we can go. If we leave like this, I immediately become eligible for Harvest. We have to stay." He smiled reassuringly. "And we still don't know if that is why they are here."

Tears began to swell at the corners of her eyes as she brought her left hand up to his right cheek. She smiled softly. "You are so trusting. So kind. I won't let you be hurt."

"I won't be. Not with you here to protect me." He moved his hand up to take hers back from his cheek. "Now, when did they get here?"

"Just now. I saw them riding by the front of the building," she nodded towards the front of the shop as she spoke.

"Are you sure it was them?" he asked.

"Yes!" Her tone softened immediately. "I think. I suppose I should go and find out for certain."

"You might be getting worked up over nothing, Siggy," he said. "It could have just been some travelers."

"There were too many." Her eyes narrowed. "In fact, there seemed to be too many for a Harvest crew, too."

"See, you're probably worried about nothing," he answered with a smile.

"No. No, those were Valpuri riders. I know it. I've seen it too often. I still have nightmares." She turned and stepped away, massaging her shoulder gently.

"I know. I'm so sorry, Sweetheart." He stepped up behind her and placed his hand back on her shoulder.

She spun around to face him. "It's not right. I don't care if you came here from another town, you should be safe! I lost my brother, and I'm not supposed to lose anyone else in my family." Her voice became a growl. "I will fight it! I'll fight them all! I will!"

In response, he stared into her eyes. She felt her heart skip a beat and then simply wait until it found the pace best fitting with his, trying to get into sync across the distance. Her lungs filled up and slowly released. She closed her eyes for a three count and then looked at him again.

"Thank you," she said. "I was about to get a little carried away."

"I noticed. There is no reason to react to something that hasn't happened." His hand came to rest on her arm. "But if it does, I will support whatever choice you make."

"I know. I know that, and you know I will protect you every way that I can," Sigrid answered, taking hold of his hand.

"Of course I do. You've already done it just to get me here. I'm still amazed that people come into our shop at all," he laughed.

Her lip curled up. "They wouldn't dare not shop here. If they thought I was angry before, well, they haven't seen anything if I'm ignored."

"I don't think you can be ignored." He took a step back away from her. "I couldn't do it."

"Smart man." She nodded.

"I think so. I married you." He crossed his arms over his chest. "Now, what's the plan with these riders? I'm sure that others have noticed as well. Panic is probably setting in across town."

"Most likely, which means that Prisca is about to have—or already has—guests." Her right hand came up to rub her chin. "She's going to keep them as busy as she can, giving us a chance to get ourselves ready." She looked at her husband. "Prisca is a good woman." She took a step to the right, beginning a walk around the center bench of Armas's shop. "Which means that we'll have time to get an impromptu Thing together. Go into this with one mind and one voice."

She walked around the table a full turn, her hand still rubbing against her chin slowly.

"Which means you need to go. This will happen where? At the MuskOx? Or at the Great Hall?" he asked.

"MuskOx is the best place to start. The Hall would be too obvious. And they always set up there for the Harvest, so it's likely they'll be there for whatever this is," she surmised. Sigrid looked at her husband again. "And I pray that it isn't a Harvest."

"It's not," he said with a smile. "I can feel it. It's not."

"Well, I'm not sure, and until I am I don't want you leaving this room. Understood?" her voice was clear and firm.

"I'm not going anywhere." He pointed to the floor casually, gesturing to the small pile of debris scattered around their feet, and then ran that same hand through his hair, mussing it slightly. "I have several items to put back in place thanks to you."

A halfhearted laugh popped from her. "Well, I know how you feel." She stepped up and kissed him lightly. "I have some things to put in place, too."

Spinning on the ball of her foot, Sigrid found her bearing and strode across the room with a purpose. The door on the closet opened smoothly, and briefly Sigrid smiled to herself at her husband's craftsmanship and construction. She pulled out her heavy coat and slipped it on, pulling it tight and quickly tying the sash without taking the time to button it properly. As she turned to him once again, she put her hands on the sides of the hood, holding it for a moment.

"You promise to stay here." It was more of a statement than a question.

"Yes, love. I will be here. Don't worry." He smiled as warmly as he could manage.

"Too late. I'm far past worried already." She took a deep breath. "I love you."

She yanked the hood up and stepped to the outside door, opening it and stepping through in a single motion. It pulled shut quickly and tightly behind her.

"I love you, too," he said to the empty room.

• • • • • • •

The door opened up without a knock. It would have been a surprise to the people inside the building if they hadn't seen them coming long before they ever reached the entrance. Even so, the officials in the building had no real time to prepare, and by the time the doors were opened, they were still rushing about, trying to clean up the practically non-existent mess they were still seeing.

Two men held the door open as a single female walked in, pulling black gloves from her hands. A black fur hat covered the top of her head, with her blond hair still falling free behind it. A smile that was closer to a smirk was already on her face.

Several people scattered. Moving to the farthest reaches of the room or exiting it entirely. On the other side of a desk, a woman with brown hair, dressed in a slightly off white color suddenly stood nervously. "Madam Valpuri! What an unexpected honor."

"Hello Sheriff…Prisca, isn't it?" Mathilda Valpuri answered, walking up to the desk and tucking her gloves into her belt.

"Yes, Madam Valpuri. Excellent memory, as always." She gestured to the open chairs. "Please, will you sit?"

Without a word she sat down. The wood of the chair was dark, matching the color of the desk and the wooden walls all around the room. The room itself was spacious, with three doors to it: the northern one that Madam Valpuri entered through leading to the vestibule between this room and the outside, and two doors on the western wall separated by a series of cabinets leading to the rest of the building.

"Would you like anything? Some food? A drink perhaps?" the Sheriff asked sitting down in her own chair across from the Mathilda.

"A drink would be lovely, thank you," she replied while crossing her right leg over her left.

Instantly, the Sheriff waved her hand towards one of the few people left in the room, who rushed towards a small counter of glasses and bottles.

"So," the Sheriff turned back to her guest, "what brings you to Kyla? We weren't expecting you for almost another two years."

"We aren't here for Harvest. Remain calm." As Mathilda spoke, the Sheriff's body visibly relaxed. "It shouldn't take us more than two or three days to complete what we need to do, and then we'll be on our way."

"And what is it you need to do?" The Sheriff's voice wavered slightly.

"We simply need to speak to everyone in town." The man arrived with the drinks, presenting one to Mathilda, who took it with a pleasant smile. "Thank you."

"Oh, well, that seems simple enough, though I'm not sure we have a facility to hold everyone. If it's okay with you, Madam, I can arrange for you to speak on top of this building, with everyone—"

"No." Mathilda held the glass in her hand, swirling the brown liquid around for a moment. "You misunderstand, Sheriff. I don't want to speak with them all at once. I need to speak with them one at a time."

The Sheriff shifted the glass that was placed on her desk, bringing it closer to her. "I…I beg your pardon?"

"Everyone in town, Sheriff. No one can be missed." She locked eyes with the Sheriff, a glint in her own. She took a sip from the glass in her hand and smiled approvingly.

"I don't understand. You've never had to speak with everyone for a Harvest before," the Sheriff stated.

"This isn't a Harvest, Sheriff. I told you that." Her right leg began to bounce slightly.

"If I may ask, Madam Valpuri, what exactly is it that—"

"That's not your concern," she cut the Sheriff off abruptly. "It's a very simple matter and we will be gone before you even know that we are here."

"Of course. I'm sorry. I wasn't meaning to be rude," the Sheriff stated quickly.

"Oh, I know that, Prisca." Her leg was no longer swinging, but her foot was still bobbing slightly. "You would never be like that. The entirety of Kyla has always been very, very cooperative."

"Thank you," the Sheriff smiled. "And we will be happy to help you in every way you can while you are visiting our village."

Mathilda took another sip from her glass. "My village," she said before the glass was even clear of her lips. "While I'm here, this is my village. Everyone here will do exactly as I say." She swirled the liquid in her glass again, staring over it at the Sheriff. "Everyone. Is that clear?"

"Y-yes, Madam Valpuri," the Sheriff swallowed back.

"Excellent. Now, where is it that most of your people like to go for gossip?" Mathilda asked.

"Well, we aren't much of a gossiping village, Madam Valpuri. As you know, we are a simple group that always does what we can to support the Ranee and their officers." The Sheriff put her hand on her desk, letting it rest next to her still untouched glass of whiskey.

Mathilda stared at her silently for a moment. Slowly, she stood up and walked over to the bar where her drink had been poured. The servant who poured her drink took a step her direction, but was waved off without a word. At first she stood back, scanning over the bottles one by one, and then reached out and pulled the stopper from the top of a particular crystal flask. Bringing it to her nose, she inhaled in the aroma. Apparently content, she turned again and walked back over to the desk, this time stepping around to stand behind it. She looked down at the Sheriff and raised both eyebrows.

The Sheriff stood immediately and backed away from her chair. As Mathilda sat down in the chair behind the desk, the Sheriff moved around to the front. She stood watching as Mathilda set her glass down and filled it almost to the brim with the alcohol she brought over. With her left hand, she gestured to the empty seat she had just used. The Sheriff looked at it and then slowly sat down. Mathilda pushed the Sheriff's glass over towards her side of the desk.

"Ah, Prisca, we were getting along so well there for a while," Mathilda sighed. "And now you want to act like I'm stupid. I don't like being thought of as stupid."

Every little bit of color left the Sheriff's face.

Mathilda turned her gaze upwards, focusing on the ceiling. The Sheriff's eyes followed hers. "You live on the second floor of this building, don't you?"

The Sheriff's eyes snapped back to Mathilda, who slowly lowered her head to match her view.

"Y-yes, Madam Valpuri. My husband and I live there with our daughter." Her voice wavered with every syllable.

"Oh, really. Well, I'll need a place to stay for the next couple of nights, so you'll need to clear out your husband and daughter," she said.

Her throat swelled as the Sheriff swallowed hard. "O-of course, Madam Valpuri. We'll be glad to leave so that you can have a proper place to sleep."

Mathilda's eyebrows went up. "Your husband and your daughter, Prisca. Your husband and your daughter." She leaned in placing her elbows on the desk, letting her hands fall together. "Unless you have someplace else that I should be tonight?"

"I don't—"

"A place where I might meet other people in town. Someplace where your leaders might congregate in times like this," she interrupted, a growl hiding behind her words.

"The…The MuskOx. There is a bar in town called The MuskOx. It's usually busy at these times," Sheriff Prisca whispered. Her head fell down, staring at the desk.

Silence reigned for a moment, until Mathilda stood up and walked around the desk, stopping beside the Sheriff in her chair. She pulled the gloves from her belt and slipped them onto her hands.

"My soldiers and I will be setting up and sleeping in your Great Hall. I remember where it is."

The Sheriff looked up from the desk at Mathilda.

"I would hate to displace a daughter from her home on such short notice," Mathilda said. "When you see her tonight, tell her you love her, Prisca."

"I always do," she said back.

"Good." She turned and walked towards the door. "A daughter deserves a good mother. I will see you tomorrow at dawn. Make sure that you have at least prepared some of your citizens to begin meeting with us by mid-morning. It will take time to see them individually, and I want to be out of this village in three days."

She didn't wait for a response. With practiced ease she pulled her fur hat onto her head with one hand as she stepped out into the vestibule to exit the building. Sheriff Prisca watched until she was completely out of view before she stood up.

Tugging down, she straightened her clothes and walked back around behind the desk. Her eyes scanned over the bottle and glass that were left behind. She grabbed the glass and turned it up to her mouth, draining the contents. As quickly as it went up it fell down to the desk, the sharp sound of it echoing in the room. She looked over at the others in the room.

"Get together five groups. Go to the north side of town and tell the people there they need to be at the Great Hall early tomorrow morning. If you have time, go tell the western side they need to be there by noon. We'll tell the other half to be ready for the next day tomorrow." She stepped back around the desk. "And then go home to your family. Spend time with them tonight. I have a bad feeling about tomorrow."

She stepped to the back door on the side of the room, exited, and rushed towards her upstairs home.

· · · · · · ·

There are times when the free people of Dula Koarr come together to discuss issues and problems that have arisen. These meetings are called Things. Things begin at a local level and then progress to a regional level and upward until the Great Thing that contains a representative of every region as well as one from the Ranee of that particular Hundred. It has been this way since Queen Yngva Nowasdottir set them in place over five hundred years ago.

The last Great Thing in this region was held twelve years ago.

For the people it was not a forgotten tradition. They still gathered locally, and occasionally regionally, but never beyond that point. Ten years back a group of leaders from each region went to the Ranee to request a Great Thing, and were never heard from again. A statement was sent out to each region, explaining that the Renee Valpuri were too busy at this moment to organize and attend a Great Thing, and that they would let the citizens know when the situation allowed the tradition to return. It was the last statement made on the matter.

Even still, in times of great crisis, the leaders of a village—or even larger—would gather for an impromptu Thing. An emergency meeting to deal with the situation at hand, for better or worse.

In the village of Kyla those Things were held at one of several places, but most frequently they found themselves at the MuskOx. Owned by Krista Markkula and operated with the aid of her husband, Graham, it was in many ways the social hub of the town, with dozens of folks coming through it every day. It wasn't for the food, which was adequate but nothing special, or for the drinks that could be had at either of its competitors, it was entirely for something non-tangible.

There was no place like the MuskOx for laughing. Even in the most dire of personal times, Krista and Graham had a way to make anyone smile. Their personality was bouncy and joyous, and it seemed to be their personal mission to make everyone happy. They seemed to know everyone by name after they had visited only once—and on the rare occasion for their first visit. They told stories and tales about everything and anyone—so long as it wasn't rude or condemning—with flare and verve.

The only story that remained a mystery was why the place was called the MuskOx. Every time that anyone asked they got a completely different story. One time it was because of the family profession beforehand. Another might be because the couple met while hiding from a rampaging animal. Yet again it could be a special nickname that one of them had for the other due to their rather belligerent attitude. The only thing that the people of Kyla knew was that they would probably never really know the truth.

So it was that the MuskOx became a place where the citizens of Kyla visited when they were down and when they wanted to be happy.

It was also one of the places that had a large room where dozens of people could meet and speak on matters, and at this moment, that room was filled to the walls. And it was filled with the cacophony of many unrestrained voices.

"Calm down!" Her name was Gilda, with dark blond hair that had just a faint hint of grey trying to sneak into it casually, and her words were loud enough to echo off the timber walls of the chamber. "We have to speak in order! I know that everyone is concerned, but we cannot panic!"

"The Harvest is early! They are breaking their own rules!" An unidentified voice shouted.

"No!" Gilda took a breath. "Well, we don't know that. We don't know why they are here. Jumping to conclusions will do us no good. We have to keep calm and let this play out."

"Play out?" A dark-haired woman stepped forward. "You want us to wait until they are done? Until they have taken our loved ones and left? I won't stand for it!"

A roar built in the room again. Gilda took a deep breath and stood still. Her eyes stared out into the crowd, brow furrowed and lips a thin line on her face. She watched, and she waited.

"And then what?" She said calmly. The words fell onto only a few ears at the front of the room where she stood, but the impact rippled backwards, dulling the sound in the room once again. She looked at the dark haired woman who instigated it. "Let's say you take action, Rachel, and then what? Maybe you get killed, or maybe you get lucky and drive them off—or maybe we all band together and kill them all. Wonderful! We won." She looked over the room. "And then what?"

The room was silent.

"Do you think the Ranee are just going to hide from us? That they will ignore or forget what happened? Or not investigate if their soldiers disappear?" She pointed out over their heads. "There are three dozen trained soldiers out there. Do you think that no one knows they are here? We cannot afford to be foolish right now."

"She's right." Everyone turned to see the freckled woman with the frizzed red hair standing from her chair. Sigrid looked back at them and spoke again. "Most of you know me, but aside from Gilda, I don't see anyone here that shares our experience." She shook her head and looked around the room. "It's one thing to know about the Harvest. It's another thing to be a part of it. You talk from a place of fear, but Gilda and I speak from experience."

She stepped out, walking up to stand near Gilda, talking the whole time. "Let me make something clear, you should be afraid. You should be terrified. The Harvest is everything that you've heard it is. The moment they announce the name of the man you love—husband, father…brother—your heart falls. I was only eight years old, but my heart froze. My mother grabbed my brother and pulled him tight. I'm sure that more than a second passed, but it felt like far less until the soldiers came and took him from my mother's arms. To his credit, he never said a word, and my mother—the strongest woman I've ever known—cried. And that wasn't the difficult part."

Sigrid felt Gilda's hand grip her shoulder.

"It's that moment they come into your house and take everything that was his. Everything that mentions him, shows him, or has anything to do with him…it's gone. It's not called a Harvest because they take a person, it's called that because they take everything. Nothing is left behind. The men are taken and are gone forever," Sigrid finished.

"Is that supposed to tell us to stand down?" Rachel asked. "All that does is want to make me fight harder!"

"No, it's to make you think. I don't support the Harvest. I hate the Harvest! I imagine that there is no woman in this room who hates those riders more than Gilda and I! I'm telling you that we have been through that pain, and we are both telling you not to react. Don't do anything until we know what is happening." With every word, Sigrid's voice became softer.

"But by the time we know it's a Harvest it will be too late!" Rachel cried. "What do you expect us to do? Why should we wait?"

"It's not a Harvest."

Every eye turned to see the black-clad woman standing at the rear of the room, holding a bottle in her left hand. The top button of her jacket was undone, and she only had a glove on the hand holding the bottle. Her long, blond braid hung loosely behind her. Mathilda Valpuri smiled.

"It's not a Harvest. So stop all this nonsense," she stated coldly.

"Welcome, Madam Valpuri," Gilda replied. "We're not used to a representative of the Ranee joining us for a Thing."

She rolled her eyes. "Well, I'm not here as a representative of my sisters so that I can listen to what you have to say. I'm just here to make sure that no one does anything foolish."

"Why are you here?" Rachel asked.

After turning to look at her, Mathilda stared, eyes focused solely on her. "I just told you that. So you don't do anything foolish."

"Begging your pardon, Madam, but I believe she was asking why you and your troops were here. You can understand our confusion," Gilda explained.

"It's nothing to worry about. The Sheriff will be explaining everything soon enough," she answered.

Rachel spoke again, "Why can't you tell us? You're here now."

The smile on Mathilda's face grew larger and she raised the bottle up and took a solid slug of the whiskey. She brought it back down and stared at her again. "Because it's not why I came here. In fact, I don't need to be here at all. And from what I can tell, you're the biggest problem in this room, so maybe you don't need to be here, either."

"I'm not the one that needs to leave," she growled back. "This is my home."

Mathilda's eyebrow went up. "Really? I don't suppose it would help to point out that your home is inside of my home, would it?"

Rachel strode out, pushing her way through the crowd towards Mathilda. A twitch growing on her face.

"Rachel!" Gilda snapped. Mathilda raised a hand to quiet her in response.

By the time Rachel stood in front of Mathilda, a full snarl was on her lip. "I think that you are nothing but a coward who hopes that the people are too cowed to ever stand up and say anything to you." She raised up her head and looked down at the other woman. "I'm not afraid!"

"Oh," Mathilda answered calmly. "Does that mean that you intend to do something to me right now?"

Slowly, Rachel pulled her sword, leveling it at the other woman. "This is not your town. I have been awarded best swordswoman for four years in a row at the spring festival."

"Really? Congratulations! I'm sure that was no easy feat." Mathilda raised her bottle up to her, and then took another drink.

"You shouldn't be so flippant," Rachel snarled.

"Rachel!" Gilda shouted as she pushed towards the two. Again, she was answered by Mathilda's raised hand.

"So, despite the fact that I have told you we are not here for a Harvest, and that everything would be explained to you in time, you are still acting this way. Do you mean to harm me, Miss Rachel?" Mathilda's smile was thin and cold.

Rachel's lip curled up defiantly. "Only if you mean to stay."

A murmur had slowly built through the room, and space was clearing away from both women, leaving them with a wide berth. The only woman who moved inside that space was Gilda, with Sigrid stopping at the edge of the circle. The sword in Rachel's hand remained level with Mathilda's eyes.

"Your arm is going to get tired if you keep that up," Mathilda said.

"Then either you leave, or I find a place to put my sword down," Rachel stated, shifting her stance slightly.

She was answered by Mathilda raising an eyebrow and grinning. "I admire that you've had so much success in your tournaments. I've never had the opportunity to be in one."

It all happened in a heartbeat. Rachel lunged forward, her sword angling down towards the center of Mathilda's body. Screaming, Gilda reached out, desperate to prevent the assault, even though she knew it wasn't possible to stop her in time.

As Rachel's sword moved, so did Mathilda. Shifting to her left, her right arm flashed out, pushing against the blade as it and the woman holding it pressed past. Twisting around, Mathilda's left arm swung around in a wide arc, bringing the bottle she held against the back of Rachel's head.

Glass exploded with a sharp crack, covering both women as well as the floor beneath them in whiskey. The sword went clattering forward, haltingly coming to a stop on the wooden boards after striking a slightly raised plank. Rachel fell forward, her body slapping against the floor like a wet rag, and then lying motionless among the alcohol.

The room went silent. Gilda pulled back her hand, bringing it up near her shoulder as she stopped cold. After dropping the broken remains of her bottle, Mathilda pulled on the heavy leather of her right coat sleeve, prying apart the slice that remained from the sword. The barest hint of red on her flesh could be spied by anyone staring closely.

Mathilda looked down at Rachel, still motionless below her. A steadily growing patch of red was coloring the back of her head, and changing the color of the liquid beneath her. Mathilda knelt down, and grasped Rachel by the hair. When she pulled back a moan escaped Rachel, causing everyone in the room to let out the breath they were collectively holding.

"You owe me both a new coat and a new bottle. I'll talk to you about that tomorrow." Mathilda unceremoniously dropped the woman, her face again smacking against the floor with a dead slap. "And remember that fighting in a tournament isn't real fighting."

Mathilda started to stand, but noticed the blood on her left hand where she had grabbed the hair. With grimace she wiped her hand across Rachel's back, cleaning most of the blood, and apparently enough to satisfy her as she stood immediately after.

All eyes in the room were focused upon her. Gilda took a half step forward.

"I'm sorry about that. Rachel can be—"

"She was angry." Mathilda scanned the room. "I'm sure you are all angry. Anxious. Concerned." She nodded. "I would be too, in your position. What you need to know is that this is not a Harvest. And despite what some of you might think, my word is my bond. When I last left this village, I said there would be no Harvest for four years. I'll stand to that."

"Of course, Madam Valpuri," Gilda answered. "Thank you."

Mathilda nodded to Gilda and then looked around the room again. "Go home. All of you." She turned around and almost stepped onto Rachel's back. She looked back over her shoulder as she spoke. "And get this woman some medical help."

Stepping around Rachel, Mathilda walked to the doorway separating this gathering room from the main portion of the bar. Sigrid saw a handful of Valpuri guards at that doorway waiting on their commander.

And standing behind them was Armas.

The moment Mathilda walked out of the room the murmur returned, louder than ever. Several women rushed to Rachel, calling for help. Gilda did her best to calm the rest of the women in the room, mostly quelling a rising panic, but also quenching a patch of anger.

Sigrid walked out of the room and up to her husband.

"What are you doing here?" she asked.

He looked at her and sighed. "I was worried about you. Where else am I supposed to be?"

"At home, where you're safe," she answered immediately.

"Not possible." He shook his head. "Wherever you go, that's where I'll be."

She couldn't help but smile at his answer. He leaned to one side, looking at the women dealing with their wounded friend.

"Is she going to be okay?" he asked.

Sigrid turned at the waist and looked momentarily. Rachel had been pulled up into a sitting position while a bandage was being wrapped around her head. As soon as she turned back to her husband she started speaking again. "I think so. It was stupid of her to do that, though."

"Isn't she the woman who beat you at all those sword competitions?" he asked.

"Yeah," Sigrid nodded. "Every year for four years now."

"Wow," he said softly.

Sigrid grabbed him by the arm and started making her way towards the door. "That's a good way to put it," she looked up at Armas with a forced smile.

Amid the growing clamor, the couple exited the bar and headed home.

• • • • • • •

Before anyone entered into the Great Hall, the situation was explained to them quickly and briefly.

They would enter, wait for their turn, answer some questions, and then perform one simple task. They would bring no weapons and they would follow all instructions. After that, they would be done with the matter. They were told it should take less than a minute with every single person. Everyone was exiting the hall safely and quickly.

And even with that knowledge the tension in the line was palpable.

Watching her rock back and forth, Armas carefully stepped up and wrapped Sigrid into his arms. "You're cold."

She snuggled in tight against him. "Thank you. You've got to be freezing, too. I hate standing still in this weather."

The line stretched from the Great Hall back several hundred feet. A strong storm had developed overnight, covering the city in a new blanket of snow, which was still falling onto the waiting crowd. The wind whipped about, swirling and biting at their flesh, causing everyone to cringe and brace themselves against it. Armas and Sigrid were far from the only ones huddled together. They did have the advantage of being at the front of the line and just outside of the Great Hall, however.

"It's not going to be much longer," Armas said. "After that, we can just go home, curl up by the fire, and try to forget all of this."

She nodded curtly. "I'll forget it when these people are out of town and out of our lives."

"They will be. It will be over soon." His voice was warm and soothing.

The line stepped forward, and they moved along with it, putting them next to the door inside. Beyond it they could see very little, but they were able to ascertain that there were not many waiting inside.

"I don't understand why they couldn't just talk to us all at once," Sigrid stated.

"Because they want to see us personally. Maybe they want to catalog everyone in town for official reasons. It's probably just paperwork," Armas replied.

"No." She shook her head. "Why would they need such a large force just for paperwork? Something is happening."

"Well, whatever that something is, it's not too horrific." He pointed out to the side, watching people being ushered to their homes and away from the line after exiting on the side. Sigrid's eyes followed a pair moving quickly away.

"They aren't going to be able to keep them quiet. No matter how they try, word will get out to everyone in town what is going on. Every person going through this tomorrow will know what's happening," Sigrid scoffed.

"Probably. Who knows? I'm not going to worry about it," Armas said, pulling his wife closer and kissing the top of her forehead. He felt her arm squeeze tighter around his waist.

The door opened in front of them, and two guards motioned for them to step inside. Without hesitation they stepped through, feeling the warmth of the interior wash over them—a feeling that amplified as the door closed behind them.

The nondescript din of two dozen voices speaking at once filled the hall, echoing off of the distant walls. A curtain hung in front of them, with another guard standing at its opening. The cloth was parted just enough to allow glimpses of what lay beyond. From her vantage point, she could see several people gathered, including Mathilda Valpuri—at least it seemed to be her, it was hard to tell right now.

"Only four more people," Armas stated, looking at the tiny line in front of them. "In twenty minutes we'll be at home, with a fire and a warm mug of mulled wine to drown away these memories."

"Remind me of that again in twenty minutes," Sigrid stated.

She felt his fingers drag down her arm until they stopped to grasp her hand in his.

"You worry too much," Armas said with a squeeze of his grip.

A heavy breath sucked into her and was held. "I have my reasons."

He leaned in towards her and whispered, "I know. I know."

The next person stepped through the curtain.

"Well, I want to get back and get on with things," Armas said. "I have a lot of work to get done. You keep overselling what I can do."

"I don't oversell you. You've never failed to deliver, have you?" she countered.

He pulled back, his eyes growing wide. "I went a few days without sleep at times! You yelled at me about that, and it was your fault."

"No, no. You are better than that. There is no reason that you shouldn't have been able to get that done." A smirk grew on her lip.

"Oh, it's like that, is it?" he laughed.

"Completely," she agreed.

The next person stepped through the curtain. A moment later the door behind them opened, blasting them with frozen air as two more people stepped inside. Armas and Sigrid shuffled forward in line.

"We should take a trip," Sigrid said.

Armas blinked several times. "What? You…you never want to go anywhere. Ever."

"I can change my mind," she scowled at him.

"But you don't. You've always said that Kyla was the only place you ever needed to see." He turned his palms up, opening his hands to her.

"I'm not that stubborn." Sigrid put her hands on her hips.

"Compared to a mountain, no," he countered.

The next person stepped through the curtain.

"Are you calling me immovable?" Her eyes narrowed.

"Almost in those exact words," he said with a nod.

She opened her mouth and stared for a moment before closing it and turning away from him. A few seconds later she heard him giggle and turned back to stare into his eyes.

"Oh, you thought you had a tough work load before…." she threatened.

"You wouldn't!" he gasped.

The next person stepped through the curtain, putting them next. The door opened behind them, letting in two more people.

Sigrid shifted slightly, starting through the gap in the curtain. It was still difficult to see what was happening, but it was clear that the person was standing in front of a small group of people a decent walk beyond the curtain.

Turning with authority, Sigrid looked Armas in the eye again. "I'm going first."

"I don't want you to worry about me. I can—"

"I'm going first. This isn't a matter of debate," she repeated firmly.

He knew better than to argue. "Okay. You go, and then I'll meet you after."

"You will," she confirmed.

The curtain parted, and the guard pointed towards the gathering a distance away. Sigrid stepped through with confidence, taking a deep breath as she passed the opening.

Her eyes darted quickly, getting an assessment of her situation. There were several guards milling about, lost in their own world it seemed, but the majority of them were concentrated in one location—exactly where she was headed.

It almost appeared to be a funnel. Four guards on either side created a passage that led up to two other guards flanking to either side of Mathilda Valpuri. There were another half-dozen guards situated behind her in a loose cloud. None of that held her attention.

Resting on a wooden pedestal beside Mathilda Valpuri was an orb. At first glance, it was black, but after another look Sigrid's eyes began to play tricks on her. She would swear that it was shifting color, moving from black to blue to red and back to black once more. Behind the orb, standing perfectly still, was a towering man who paid her no heed, but simply stared straight out in front of him, arms crossed over his chest. Slowly, Sigrid walked to stand before Mathilda Valpuri.

"This will only take a moment," she stated.

Sigrid nodded compliance.

"First, I need to know if you have always lived in this village?" she asked.

"Uh, yes. All of my life," Sigrid answered, narrowing her eyes.

"Secondly, has your family always lived in this village?" Her tone was flat and level, and there was no discernible expression on her face.

"I believe so, yes. My mother always told me that we had lived here since—"

"Step over to the orb," Mathilda interrupted.

Immediately Sigrid's eyes fell upon the object once more. It seemed to be a deep purple color when she did, but shifted to black before she could blink. With a sharp exhale, her feet moved her over to stand in front of it. The orb was slightly less than a foot in diameter by her guess, and appeared to be perfectly smooth and even.

"Remove the glove from your right hand and place it upon the orb, gently," Mathilda instructed.

Her eyes darted back over to the commanding Valpuri. She was again met by a lack of emotional response. Tugging on each finger first, Sigrid quickly removed the glove from her hand, and then brought it up towards the orb—and stopped just shy of it. She felt herself swallow roughly, noticing for the first time that her mouth had gone dry.

She willed her hand down onto the surface of the orb. It felt warm and sticky to her touch.

"Thank you, you may leave," Mathilda stated.

Sigrid looked over to see the guard beside her pointing towards a different distant door. Sigrid removed her hand from the orb, feeling as though it pulled back against her flesh as she moved it away. With only a slight hesitation brought on by confusion, she turned and walked over to the door indicated by the guard, meeting two other guards. She passed them and stopped at the door, turning to see Armas walking to where she had just left. The guards did nothing, seemingly understanding she was waiting on him to go through the same procedure she had just finished.

The conversation began the same from what she could see. Mathilda asked Armas a question, and he answered, and then she asked a second one. Sigrid nodded to herself, waiting for the guard to direct him over to the orb. Instead, Mathilda asked him a third question. And a fourth. She began to shift uneasily, moving her weight from her left leg to her right and back again. When the fifth question came and she saw Mathilda Valpuri start to rub her left palm with her thumb she started to pace.

"What's going on?" Sigrid asked one of the guards. "He's getting a lot of questions."

"Stand beside the door, ma'am," he said strongly, pointing to the exact location intended.

She turned and paced back to that spot. After she stopped she began bouncing slightly in place and twitching two fingers on her right hand. Finally she saw the guard point to the orb, and she let out a heavy sigh.

The orb shimmered blue for a flash as he approached. He had removed his gloves before walking over to speak with the Valpuri, so there was only a slight pause before he placed his hand on the orb in the same manner she had.

Immediately she felt a deep throb pulse through her body, and from the reaction of everyone else in the room, they felt it too. Within a breath, far before she had time to say anything, a brilliant glow emanated from the orb, reflecting a rainbow of color across its surface.

Everyone was frozen, staring at what was happening dumbfounded. The huge man behind the orb moved before anyone else. He grabbed Armas by the shoulder, holding him firm in place as Mathilda began to shout orders and other soldiers moved and circled him.

"Armas?" Sigrid whispered to herself.

The entire facility was suddenly active. Three men corralled Armas, ushering him quickly beyond the point where Mathilda Valpuri had been standing. The two guards in front of Sigrid turned and were coming up to her quickly.

"You have to leave right now," one of them instructed.

"Armas!" she shouted, extending her hand out. That hand was immediately grabbed and turned, forcing Sigrid to turn with it. She lashed out, spinning her other hand back towards the guard holding her, but it was intercepted by the other guard who helped to bullrush her towards the door. She slammed into the door, forcing it open and falling out beyond it in a heap.

"Go home, ma'am. Now!" The guard slammed the door shut.

Instinctively, her hand fell to her waist, looking for her sword. The empty air reminded her, and she pictured it sitting beside the door leading to their bedroom back at their home. With a snarl she leapt up and rushed to the door she had been thrown through, and found it locked tight. Her body slammed against it twice, but it was firmly in place.

She turned and ran towards the front of the building, heading back to the entrance they originally used. As she rounded the corner she saw the people outside stepping away from the door as it closed.

"No!" Sigrid pushed herself to run faster, hoping to somehow reach the door even as she saw it shut only a few steps into her sprint. That didn't even bring her pause. In a handful of seconds she was at the door, pulling on it firmly and finding it locked tight. Her fist slammed into the door. "Let me in! Open this blasted door! Damn you!"

"Sigrid!"

She felt a hand grab her shoulder. She shrugged it off and slammed that same shoulder into the door.

"Sigrid, stop!"

She ignored the voice and continued to pound against the door. She felt her shoulder shift after one thrust, but ignored the pain, driving into it again. Hands were grasping at her, trying to pull her away, but they couldn't hold her or contain her. Again and again she battered the door, propelling herself against it with all her might.

A sharp pain shot through the back of her head and she felt her knees buckle under her. Before she was on the ground the world went black.

• • • • • • • •

The thought kept running through her mind: why was someone hammering so early?

"Stop it, Armas," she mumbled through the haze. "I'm trying to sleep."

He was always working in the morning. She kept telling him that she hated him doing that, but she was secretly jealous. It always took her longer to get going in the morning than it did him. There was no way she was going to tell him that, though. The continuous pounding, however, that was still annoying.

"Armas…." she raised her voice slightly, trying to get his attention. Which was going to be difficult with him locked in the Great Hall with all of those Valpuri soldiers. Her mind wrapped around that one more time. He was locked behind the doors of the Great Hall with the Valpuri soldiers.

She sat up like a bolt. "Armas!"

"Relax." The voice was soft and soothing, and she recognized it instantly. Sigrid turned to see her just as she sat down on the bed beside her.

"Gilda? Where am I? What happened? Where's Armas?" Her head darted around the room to assess her surroundings. Sunlight fell into the room, but that was all she took in before her body objected. A sharp pain hit the back of her head and she reached around to put her hand on it, feeling a huge knot back there. Her eyes fell to her body, and she noticed that she was wearing only her light underclothing. Nonetheless, she felt her midsection to confirm the fact.

"Take it easy," she cooed. "You took a nasty shot back there. You need to rest."

Sigrid squeezed her eyes shut and winced. When she opened them again she spoke, "Where's Armas?"

"Let's worry about you first," she said.

"No. No, where's Armas?" Her arms pressed up against the bed raising her up—and she almost made it halfway before they gave out and she dropped back down to the mattress.

Gilda's hands braced Sigrid's back, keeping her in an upright, sitting position. "Yeah. I think it's best if you rest a little more."

Looking around the room, Sigrid took in her surroundings once more. It was a smallish room. Very clean. The red drapes flanking the sole window went well with the warm tone of the wooden walls. The bed she was on was only large enough for a single person, but was comfortable and soft, with linen sheets and a heavy blanket. A small brown rug rested on the floor in front of wooden chair near the bed. A table sat between the bed and chair. The door leading out of the room was open, revealing a hallway beyond.

"Where am I?" Sigrid asked. "What happened?"

"This is my house. We thought it was best to bring you here." Gilda stood and stepped over to the table. She poured a small glass of water and handed it to Sigrid.

Sigrid took a sip from the glass, and then immediately went back for a larger drink. She rested the glass on her leg and looked at Gilda. "We? Who's we? What happened?"

"That's...that's a little more complicated." Gilda stood up and scratched the back of her head before she walked over to the window. She took a deep breath and turned back to look at Sigrid. "What do you remember?"

Narrowing her eyes, Sigrid's gaze fell to the floor. She spoke slowly as she answered, "I...I remember going to the Great Hall. The Valpuri they...." Her head snapped up and her eyes grew huge. "They took Armas! They pushed me out of the hall and kept him!"

Gilda nodded slowly. "That's right. And you were beating on the door, trying to get into the Hall."

"Yes!" She put the glass on the table. "I was working on the door and...and...." Her eyes turned dark. "And I heard your voice telling me to stop—just before I was hit on the back of the head."

"Yeah," Gilda sighed.

"You hit me!" Sigrid growled. "You hit me and dragged me away from there!"

"I didn't! I was only trying to talk you down. Get you to stop," Gilda pleaded.

"Then why did you hit me?!" she shouted.

"She didn't." They both turned to the voice, seeing the figure standing in the doorway. "I did."

"Prisca?" Sigrid pulled her head away slightly. "What? You did?"

"I did. And I would do it again." She stepped into the room, nodding briefly to Gilda. "I'm sorry, but I had to do something, for both you and the village."

"What is that supposed to mean?" Groggily, Sigrid forced herself to her feet. "I was trying to get to my husband! I still have to go to them and find out what—"

"You can't," Prisca interrupted her.

"If you try and stop me again, Prisca, so help me I will—"

"He's gone," she interrupted again. "They took him."

"What do you mean, they took him? They told us many times that this wasn't a Harvest. They weren't going to take anyone," Sigrid growled.

"I know. They told me that, too, but, nonetheless, he's gone. They took him." She stepped towards Sigrid, holding out her hand gently. "I'm sorry, Sigrid."

"Gone? They've already left?" She looked around the room for her things. "I can't believe you didn't wake me. I've got to catch up to them."

"You can't," Gilda said.

"Don't tell me what I can and can't do. Even if they left last night, they can't have gotten far away." She continued to look for her clothes.

"Sigrid," Gilda called to her softly. She raised her voice slightly the second time. "Sigrid."

"What?" Sigrid looked over at her friend.

"They left five days ago," she swallowed. "I'm sorry."

Sigrid blinked. "What? What do you mean five days? I was just…. I can't have been…."

"I gave you kaverian root. I wanted you to sleep," Prisca stated. "I couldn't afford to let you go after them."

"You did what?!" Sigrid took a step towards the Sheriff, who stepped away cautiously. "You helped them steal my husband?! Why?!"

"Calm down," Prisca ordered. "I understand why you are upset—"

"Upset?! You haven't seen upset, yet! If I don't get some quick answers, you will," Sigrid rumbled.

"What was I supposed to do!" the Sheriff shouted back. "If you were to start something then everything could come crumbling down. I had to keep you either sedated or locked up. I chose the former."

"It's what we talked about at the Thing, Sigrid," Gilda stated. "If you went after them, what would happen to the rest of the town?"

"It's not the same!" Sigrid staggered backwards. Her legs hit the side of the bed and bent naturally, depositing her on its surface. Her next words were weak and soft, "It's not the same."

Both of the other women held themselves, each wanting to step over and comfort her, but waiting for the proper moment.

"I…I only have Armas. They took my brother. My mother is gone. There is nobody for me. Nobody." Tears fell down her cheek.

Not able to hold back any longer, Gilda quickly went to her side, sitting next to her on the bed. "You don't have to be alone, Sigrid. You…you can live here with me. I'm alone, too. We can comfort each other."

Tears welled up in Gilda's eyes, hidden somewhat by her smile. Sigrid looked at her and opened her mouth, wanting to say things to comfort the woman beside her, but only speaking what her heart allowed. "No. I have to go after him, Gilda. He's everything to me. I will find him, and I will bring him home."

"You can't!" Sheriff Prisca said with a huff. "They've been gone five days, and for three of those days we had near blizzard conditions. There is no way to track them. We don't know where they've gone. It would just be suicide to leave."

"Then I'll look everywhere." Sigrid stood up again, gathering herself slowly. "And if I die, then you don't have to worry about them figuring out it was me and coming back to Kyla, do you?"

"I don't want you to die, Sigrid," Prisca stated.

"Then we do share one opinion," Sigrid answered. She turned to look at Gilda, who remained seated beside her, tears still threatening in the corners of her eyes. "Gilda, come with me. Please?"

A single tear finally broke free as she smiled and shook her head. "I can't. It's too late for me. I'm sorry."

Sigrid smiled weakly in return and nodded.

"Don't do this, Sigrid," Prisca urged.

She turned to look at the Sheriff. "Are you going to stop me?"

"No. You're free to do what you want," she answered. "But do understand that I feel you are making a huge mistake."

"It's not a mistake. I'm doing this because I love him. That's not a mistake." She looked back at Gilda. "Where are my things?"

With hesitation, the other woman stood and went to gather Sigrid's items.

• • • • • • •

She knocked on the door firmly. After only a couple of seconds she did it again. As her hand pulled back from the second knock, the door opened.

"Sigrid?" Rachel turned her head slightly. "What are you doing here?"

"I'm going after them," she stated bluntly.

"Going after who?" Rachel looked past her at the street. The mid-day sun was shining down, but the cold kept the roads mostly empty.

"The Valpuri." Sigrid's face burned hot.

"What? Are you serious?" Rachel stood up straight.

"Very. I want you to come with me. You hate them and you're the only one in town better with a sword than I am. I could use you," Sigrid explained.

"What? You were trying to talk me out of it last week!" Her face twisted to a scowl.

"Things have changed." Sigrid reached out her open hand to the other woman. "Please, Rachel, come with me."

Turning her head away, Rachel shrunk down again. "I…no. No, I won't." She looked back up to Sigrid, showing something new on her face. "Things have changed for me, too. I…I can't."

"Why not?!" Sigrid demanded.

Rachel's mouth opened and remained silent for a moment before the words began. "She…she didn't have a sword, Sigrid. She was just standing there and…." She trembled in the cold air. "I can't. I'm sorry."

She hesitated. Sigrid looked Rachel in the eyes, searching for the fire that was there the week prior. Hoping to see at least an ember that she could fan into flames. A few seconds later, she looked away.

"Good-bye, Rachel." Sigrid turned and walked away.

"Wait! Hold on!" Rachel turned and rushed inside. Sigrid turned back and waited. Less than a minute later she reappeared, carrying a small bundle with her. "Here, take this."

"What is it?" Sigrid took the package from her, realizing the weight at once. "Is this your sword?"

"My best one," she answered with a nod. "Take it, please."

"But what about—"

"Take it," Rachel's eyes said more. "Please."

Sigrid bowed her head slightly. "Thank you."

"Good luck," Rachel said.

Without another word, Sigrid turned and began to walk out of Kyla, with a crystal clear goal, but no certain direction. By the time she reached the edge of the village the wind had risen, whipping up the snow around her, and she disappeared from view.

end chapter three

CHAPTER
FOUR

THE COURSE

Renarde sat on the edge of the bed, her hands balled into fists and resting underneath her chin beside each other while her elbows rested on the knees of her crossed legs. Her ears pointed up, high and strong, and turned straight towards Sigrid, and were only outshone by the wide, bright eyes focusing on her as she finished her tale. A soft slapping sound echoed from where her tail beat against the bed.

"And?" Renarde asked anxiously.

For the duration of her story Sigrid stared down, focused on the ground between herself and the two listeners. With Renarde's words she slowly looked up, blinking several times as she came back to the present.

"I…I spent months wandering around, going from city to city, looking for the Valpuri soldiers who took Armas. Eventually someone described them perfectly, telling me they had left the day before." Sigrid nodded slowly as she spoke. "I finally had found them. Of course, Armas wasn't with them, so I just started to follow them. I spent my spare time training, getting better with the sword. I knew that they would lead me to him eventually and I had to be ready for whatever might happen. And then you found me, and you know the rest."

Sitting up straight, Renarde's hands fell away from her chin, opening up slightly as they did. "That's it? No more story?"

"There's plenty more story," Olav stated and then took a deep breath, "it just has yet to be told."

Sigrid stretched her back out and leveled her eyes at Olav. "You believe me?"

"Sadly, I believe every word." He looked over at Renarde. "Though I didn't get to hear the story of how you became involved in all of this."

Pointing over at Sigrid, Renarde answered, "I kept following her."

"That's…not too far off, actually," Sigrid nodded.

"So you were following Mathilda and her soldiers," he pointed at Sigrid to start and then moved over to Renarde, "and you started following her?"

"Oh, well, there was a fight and a chase and stuff like that, too. Oh, and we slept together," Renarde replied.

Olav's eyebrows raised high on his forehead.

"Slept!" Sigrid added quickly. "Literally sleeping side-by-side in the forest to keep warm. That's all."

"Oh come on," Renarde purred. "Would it really be that bad? I'm super cute."

"You are a fascinating creature," Olav said to Renarde. "You claim to be a child of the goddesses, yet you act with none of the grandeur and demeanor I would expect from a deity."

"Thanks!" Renarde smiled with her tail wagged excitedly behind her.

"I'm not sure he meant that as a—"

"We're going to have to do something," Olav interrupted. "Quickly."

"We? What do you mean by that?" Sigrid asked.

"We," he reinforced. "There are many people both in and around this building, and if I don't return to them soon, they will suspect something—and might already—and if they think that I'm conspiring with you, then I'll pay the price as well."

"So, if they think you're helping us, then you'll get in trouble. And to make sure that doesn't happen you're going to help us?" Sigrid narrowed her eyes at him.

"Would you rather I betray you?" he asked.

"I wouldn't!" Renarde raised her hand.

"Of course not, it's just…. You understand, I'm sure," Sigrid said.

"I do, but we can't argue about it. Time is a concern." He stood and walked over towards the window, glancing out at the dark street in passing. One of the guards below looked up and saw him, causing them both to nod in accordance. "They look to be impatient."

"How long were you supposed to be in here?" Sigrid asked.

"Long enough to diagnose the problem and correct it if needed. Not as long as I've been here," he answered.

"But you didn't know what was wrong or how complicated it might be. How could they be so impatient?" Sigrid asked.

"Yeah! I'm really complicated. I could have lots wrong with me," Renarde added.

"As I said before, I'll give them a diagnosis explaining that you have a rare malady that will take some time to cure. That it would be best to stay clear of you and this room," he said.

"Thank you," Sigrid said.

"Don't thank me just yet. You are both still in a tremendous amount of danger. Confirming that one of you is ill won't stop them watching you. I'll do what I can to move them away. Follow my advise and leave town. Otherwise…. They won't be coming directly after you, but they'll want to make sure they know where you are. You'll be trapped," he explained.

"Better trapped than in a prison—or worse." Sigrid stood and put her hand on his shoulder. "Again, thank you. Time gives us a chance."

"A chance?" Renarde stood on the bed, glancing down at both of them. "A chance is more than we need. These guys can't keep us in here if we want to get out." She hopped down off the bed and walked between the two, causing Sigrid to pull her arm back quickly.

"We have a goal and a purpose," Renarde continued. "We're here to rescue her kidnapped husband, and she thinks that he's in that big castle thingie on the mountain, so we're going to do it!" Her ears went down flat on the sides of her head and her tail fell down low. "So these guys better think twice about trying to lock us in this room, because they don't know who they're dealing with!"

"I'd say that's true," Olav replied slowly.

"Renarde," Sigrid drew her attention, taking a step towards her, "I appreciate your support and enthusiasm, but you might be oversimplifying things a little. We're two people and they are a whole guard, not to mention the Valpuri militia in the castle. We are the ones who need to watch out, not them."

"Nah!" Renarde bounced over to the door, putting her back against it. She pointed over her right shoulder with her thumb as she spoke. "You keep forgetting your secret weapon: me! I'll be able to get inside and get your husband and run out of there before they know what's happening. Then I'll find you two and we can celebrate and stuff." She beamed a smile at both of them.

"Two?" Olav asked. "I'm not a part of this."

"Yeah, you are. You don't really have a choice with all the stuff that's going to happen," she said. "Besides, someone has to take care of Sigrid while I go get her husband."

"Uh, it's not that easy. How do you expect to be able to do that?" Sigrid asked.

"Oh, that's easy. I'll get inside—I'm good at that, trust me—and once I'm in there, the rest is just finding and running away!" Renarde nodded.

"That's…that's really not an answer," Sigrid stated. "And that's really not going to work."

"Sure it will! What could go wrong?" Renarde's impossible smile grew larger—for a second.

A section of the door behind her shattered, sending splinters of wood across the room as a pair of hands reached through and grabbed Renarde by the throat, holding her tight against the wood of the door. Both of the other occupants of the room jumped back reflexively, with Sigrid going for her sword as she landed.

As Renarde's hands went up to her throat to grasp the powerful grasp holding her, her feet went up on the door, bracing herself against it to help provide pressure. The wood creaked and groaned under the strain as she pushed against it. Her hands tried to pry away the grip on her throat, but found almost no give.

Another crack of wood opened up enough of a space to see through from both sides. A large man with dark hair and dark eyes, wearing a bearskin over his shoulders stared through at them.

"That was a merry chase, little demon," Hjalmar growled at Renarde, "but your little tricks back in the trees were just a delay. I never lose my prey, and all it did was make me hunger for you so much more. And now I have you in my grasp. What do you have to say to that?"

Renarde winced, closing her right eye most of the way and twisting her ears around until they were laying flat on the back of her head. Her hands still tried to pull the fingers off of her throat, deep indentions appearing in the flesh under her fur.

"Ouch?" Renarde answered.

• • • • • • •

The bed was amazingly comfortable. It was large, soft, and luxurious, with finely woven sheets that felt softer than silk and as warm as wool. A mound of pillows rested on it, each one overfilled with amazingly plush down that sank when anyone touched them with hand or head. It was the ideal place to sleep and what so many people dreamt of when they slept in their own bed.

Armas lay on it, shifting and squirming in constant discomfort.

He punched the pillows behind him, pushing up into them again and again. He wiggled his whole body down, hoping to find a cocoon to ease into, only to shift out of it moments later. He sat up in frustration and ran his hand through his hair.

When the door to the room opened, he only slightly turned to look. He already knew who it was.

"Good evening, Armas," Vasen said smoothly. "I hope you are well."

The door closed and locked behind her, leaving the two of them alone. Vasen was wearing a simple two-tone gown of black and red. The hem of it played along the floor, defying the grip of the wooden surface with every step, as though repelled by the idea of getting dirty. Light shifted against the dress with every step, cascading over the feminine form beneath it, revealing each of Vasen's curves.

"If you must know, I'm actually having a very bad night and would rather spend the evening alone, thank you." He punched the pillows again and pushed his back up against them, his legs tenting the covers as they bent.

"Heh." Vasen laughed once as she slinked over to the bed and stood beside it. "Are you sure that a little company wouldn't be easier on you?"

"What would be easier is having clothes!" he shouted. "They took all of them when I came back from dinner."

"A temporary setback, I'm sure," Vasen answered.

"And I can guess who arranged that little setback," he snapped.

"You're angry, Armas. I thought dinner went well, despite the attempts my sister made at ruining it," Vasen stated.

He snorted a laugh. "Really? I thought she was the best part of it."

"Well, she certainly added flavor, didn't she." Vasen slinked up to the bed, rubbing her leg against it gently.

Armas lowered his head, staring at the sheets covering his body. He took a deep breath and ran the fingers of his left hand through his hair. He raised his head back up and softened his face. "Vasen, please, I honestly am not in the mood tonight. Can we please—please—not do this? Just for tonight?"

With a sigh, Vasen sat down on the bed next to him. She smiled warmly. "Oh, Armas, dear…no. Everything has already been put into motion, and I need to follow through with it. This is going to happen."

"Dammit!" He punched the pillows again. "You can't even give me one night. One night!"

"Don't be so dramatic. You have had a great many nights to yourself. It's not as though she and I are in here constantly," Vasen answered calmly.

"It feels like it!" he shouted at her. "You don't let me have any sort of life. I can be in this room or where you direct me, no place else. I'm nothing but a trumped up pet you keep locked away for your entertainment. The two of you disgust me."

Vasen's expression never faltered, half hidden behind the mask of white covering the left side of her face. She waited a few seconds before she spoke. "Are you finished?" When he didn't say anything she continued. "I'm glad that you are passionate about your situation. Hopefully it will motivate you a little. So far, you have been nothing but resistant to what my sister and I have asked and offered, and it has gotten you nothing. You are still here and under our control." She smiled, all the warmth from before gone. "Perhaps you should try another tact. Work with us and not against us, and you will find that we can be very accommodating."

Armas laughed. Vasen sneered in response.

"Well, it doesn't matter, really." Quicker than Armas could respond, Vasen's hand darted under the covers, immediately finding and grasping her erect target. "This is what matters."

In slow, smooth strokes her hand began to work up and down.

"Let go of me," he growled.

"Why? You might be arguing, but part of you is already interested," she answered in a slow snarl, her hand continuing its ministrations. "Even before I touched you."

In one fluid motion Armas stuck his own hand beneath his sheets and grasped Vasen by the wrist. "I said, take your hand off of me!"

The snarl on Vasen's face transformed into a smirk. "Make me."

Tightening his grip, Armas twisted his hand, trying to turn her's away, but at the same time her grip on him tightened, turning his sex with her arm. The resulting pain caused Armas to ease his grip slightly. As soon as he loosened up, her hand began to slide more quickly up and down.

"One try? Is that all?" she mocked. "I thought you might be made of sterner stuff than that. "

He pulled himself up as tall as possible in the bed. "If you are trying to goad me into striking you, you are going to be very disappointed."

"Oh, I don't want you to hit me. Not at all." She continued to slide her hand along his sex. "But why not take this opportunity to do something about me? To me? Why not punish me?"

"Punish you? What?" He recoiled slightly.

"Take me however you want. Show me how we make you feel." She pulled in closer to him.

Her hand continued to massage him, and he could feel his pulse pounding inside his chest in response. Heat flowed through him, collecting in his shoulders and head. A single bead of sweat rolled down his cheek as his lip quivered. And then, suddenly, everything he saw turned red.

"Is that what you want?!" The covers flew through the air and gathered beside the bed as he threw them off. "You want me to do this?!"

His hand grabbed hers, and this time she released her grip. Still holding her tightly, he bounded to his feet beside the bed, burning a glare into her. Yanking her arm, he pulled her up with him, her body only a heartbeat away from his.

Dropping her wrist, both of his hands found the center of her gown, filling both fists with fabric. In one motion he shredded the material, revealing her alabaster skin and flawless body. Another swift motion pulled the fabric from her arms, leaving her completely naked beside him. He dropped the cloth to the ground, and his right hand reached up towards her face—and was stopped by a vise-like grip when she caught it.

"The mask stays." Her voice was absolute.

He jerked his hand back with a snorting laugh. "Who cares? Keep it." The same hand immediately went to her left breast, gripping it tightly. He squeezed, feeling the flesh pressing up between his fingers. The expression on her face didn't flinch and he grimaced in response. He let go of the whole breast and moved out to grasp only the tip. Immediately he pinched and pulled on it, tenting out the breast away from her body.

She sucked in air through her teeth, bringing a wide grin to his face.

Switching his grip to both of her shoulders, he spun her around, and with one push between her shoulder blades, he bent her over the bed. A moment later she shifted her weight slightly, flattening her body against the mattress and pushing her lower half higher into the air.

"Go on," she purred over her shoulder.

His hand met the fleshy part of her backside with a loud slap that resonated through the room. It wiggled from the impact, and continued to twitch slightly as she moved in response. His hand fell again, leaving a bright red mark for a moment on the surface of her right rear cheek, fading almost instantly. A third impact elicited a moan from the core of her, causing him to grab a handful of her buttocks and squeeze tightly.

With only a slight shift of his body, he was positioned directly behind her, the head of his manhood pressingly against her slick opening. The length of his shaft slipped along the span of her sex as she pushed herself back against him, and then again as she moved back forward, once again positioning him behind her.

Both of his hands gripped either side of her hips and he angled himself forward until he felt her lower lips open and accept him inside—and that was all he needed. With all the force he could muster he thrust forward, impaling himself into her until his hips slapped against the flesh of her ass.

Another deep moan swelled up and she writhed on the bed, shifting the position of his length inside her. He pulled back until he was almost free of her, and then slammed into her again, feeling the impact of his pelvis against her body. His lips curled back, revealing clenched teeth as he repeated the action again and again. The slick sound of slapping flesh filled the room, accompanied by the moans and growls of the two participants.

"Harder," she moaned.

A fistful of her hair yanked her head back as he grabbed it and pulled, causing her to gasp excitedly. Her head bobbed slightly with every thrust as he used her hair as leverage to drive himself into her as hard and fast as he could manage. A guttural growl grew from Armas, louder and louder with each impact of flesh, until it reached a crescendo and erupted into a deep roar from him.

"Yes!" Vasen moved her hips, driving back against him as far as she could as he pulled on her hair and pressed his pelvis forward.

For several seconds they remained that way, broken up by a trio of twitching jolts of action that attempted to further push the two of them together. And then, it was over.

Armas stepped back, staggering, his breath rapid and shallow. He looked down at her, still bent over the bed, twisting her body in the moment. Slowly, she pulled herself back, sliding upright until she stood on her own. With a practiced grace she turned around to face him again.

"Thank you," she purred.

"Wh-what just happened?" He shook his head, bringing his right hand to his temple. "I don't…. I've never…." He looked back at her. "I'm not like that."

"Oh, you poor dear." She stepped to him, her hand reaching up to caress his cheek. He recoiled at her touch. "Every man is like that inside. Every. One. You just needed to have yours released."

"Released? What are you—" he stopped himself in mid sentence. His face fell as his eyes grew to fill the space. "You did something to me. You did something to me!"

"I told you that I had put things into motion. I couldn't take the chance that you would be difficult again tonight. These things do take planning, you know," she said with a laugh. With a swing in her step she paced over to the armoire in the room and opening the door. She glanced back at him. "And all I did was release the passion you keep bottled up. Men are easy, dear. Timing is hard."

"Damn you," he muttered. "Damn you both."

"I assume you are including my sister in that curse, despite the fact that she isn't here. You should really appreciate what's in front of you, Armas. Well, that aside, you did perform wonderfully."

She turned back to the armoire and pulled out a long silk robe.

"What?" Armas quickly walked over to stand beside her. "This thing was empty. I know it was. I checked."

"Mostly empty," she answered, slipping her arms into the robe. Slinky black fabric washed over her, covering her in a perfect coating of luxury. She walked away from the armoire, leaving Armas behind.

"Well, I hate to run off so soon, but I feel you don't really want my company." She turned back to face him. "Though I think you should consider that option. Consider spending all of your time with me. I could give you a life beyond your wildest dreams."

"Your dreams, not mine. Don't get those things confused," he answered.

She shrugged casually. "Just think about it, dear." She turned and walked towards the exit, stopping just short of it and turning back to him again. Her eyes played over his naked form, and he quickly stepped over to grab the sheet from the bed and cover himself, causing her to chuckle. "I'll see to it that your clothes are brought back to you. Oh, and I'll also send up something to drink and a snack. I want you to keep your strength up."

Over her shoulder, Vasen knocked casually on the door twice. Armas stood still, quietly, as the door latch was thrown and then opened slowly, revealing the armed guards beyond.

"Consider what I said, Armas. Although we haven't yet achieved our goal, I find that I am enjoying you. It would be a shame to see you go," she said with a thin grin. "Goodnight."

With a turn she walked from the room, and moments later the door closed, and once again he heard the heavy latch lock behind her.

Immediately he walked back to the armoire and examined the inside. His hands roamed across the surface, searching for a seam or break in the wood. His fingers knew the texture of wood and anything that might alter it. To his surprise, he found nothing unusual.

"I looked in here," he muttered. "I know I did." He took a step back, fixated on the empty cabinet. The fingers of his left hand slipped through his hair. "So, where did she get that robe?"

•　•　•　•　•　•　•　•

"Renarde!" Sigrid's sword was out and ready in a single motion as she rushed towards the door.

In response, Renarde raised one hand out, stopping her, while the other still attempted to pry Hjalmar's hands from her throat. "Hold...on."

Her feet pushed off from the door, launching the lower half of Renarde's body upward, twisting in his grip and flipping her around completely—loosening his grip. She pushed off with her free hand while still pulling at his fingers and twisted free completely, spinning in the air and landing directly on her feet.

Renarde glanced over at Sigrid and smiled. "Thanks, though."

The door creaked more, and splintered completely as Hjalmar pulled the remaining portions out into the hall with him, clearing the passage completely.

"Impressive, demon. Very impressive," Hjalmar stated, his body filling the doorway.

"Ha! You haven't seen anything yet!" Renarde retorted, and then turned to Sigrid. "So, what's next?"

"Me? I don't know!" Sigrid's eyes flashed from Renarde to Hjalmar and then beyond him, to see several other members of the Valpuri military waiting in the hallway. "We're in trouble."

"Not too bad," Renarde whispered. "Do you think you could get past two or three of those guards?"

Taking a half step backwards, Sigrid nodded slowly and whispered, "Yes. Maybe."

"You are trapped. Surrender." Hjalmar looked at all three occupants of the room. "All of you."

"Dammit," Olav mumbled.

"But they aren't demons!" Renarde shouted. "Well, actually neither am—"

"It doesn't matter. You will all be coming with me." He stepped into the room, closing on Renarde quickly—causing her to smile broadly.

A powerful leap propelled Renarde up and above Hjalmar, arcing over him towards the door. She felt his fingers brush against her fur as he attempted to grab her. Landing on the far side of him, she immediately fell down to all fours, lowering herself almost fully to the ground, ears plastered down on the back of her head. The four soldiers in front of her stepped back reflexively as she smiled up at them, showing a full row of fangs and teeth. She quickly looked back over her shoulder.

"Close, but you haven't caught me yet, which means I can't go with you. Sorry," she giggled, and then leapt against the far wall, bounding sideways and running down the hallway.

Without a second thought Hjalmar ran after her, shouting commands as he sped past the other soldiers. "You two with me! You other two keep them in that room!"

Sigrid stepped forward at the same moment the other soldiers closed into the space, blocking her exit.

"Dammit!" Olav repeated as he backed up against the far wall.

No words came from Sigrid. Her blade flashed up and was met by one of the soldiers, and then quickly moved over to drive against the other man's blade. The sound of metal clashing filled the room as blade met blade and neither party gave way.

Sigrid jumped back suddenly, providing separation between her opponents and herself. "I'm surprised. The two of you are actually capable with those swords."

"Put your's down, witch! If you don't we will not hesitate to down you," one of them growled.

"That doesn't sound like a good idea, actually," she replied and stepped back into the fray.

Feigning to her left, Sigrid shifted at the last moment and drove the heel of her boot into the stomach of the soldier on her right. He doubled over and she drove the pommel of her sword into the back of his head. Twice, just to be certain.

As he crumpled to the ground the other man moved, shifting to his right in an attempt to move into one of her blind spots. The man she struck slid against Sigrid's body, making it difficult for her to turn.

She felt the movement behind her, the hairs on her neck prickling up, but could see nothing. In desperation she threw her sword over her head. In the breath after she moved her sword his struck, driving hers back down, twisting it behind her head.

Slipping down to one knee, Sigrid put the sword back up above her, only to have it battered down again. Her mind raced, considering options and possibilities, but found that the only time allotted to her was enough to raise the sword back up again. Two…three more times it was driven back down, and her arm was growing weary with each blow. She knew that her strength would not be enough to hold him off any longer.

And that was when she heard a crash and his body slumped down beside her.

She looked at him, lying beside her, unmoving, and then behind her to see Olav standing there with the remnants of a broken chair in his hands.

Popping up to her feet, she spun to look at him. "Thank you," she said through labored breath, and then noticed his breathing was easily as forced as hers, if not worse.

"Dammit," he repeated for the third time.

"I have to go help Renarde," Sigrid said. She turned, but was stopped before she could take a single step.

"No. She gave us this chance. We have to take advantage of it," he told her.

"We can't just let her die!" she screamed, shaking free of his grasp.

"I don't think she will! Hjalmar could have killed her on sight, but he didn't!"

"Hjalmar? Who the hell is Hjalmar? That big guy?" she asked.

"Yes. Yes, and he is in the service of Oikea and her sister. We can't go after her. We won't be able to win." He placed his hand gently back on her shoulder. "We have to go."

"How do you know that? And what do you mean, 'we?' You aren't a part of this," she said.

"I am now. They saw me up here, and I did nothing to show there was any problem. Oikea won't take that. Hell, Sheriff Eydisdotter wouldn't take it. She's nothing but a mealy mouthpiece for them, anyway." Olav stepped over and grabbed his bag and then looked back at Sigrid.

She paused, letting various factors run through her mind. "Fine. You come along, but we've got to go downstairs anyway, so we'll be helping out Renarde in any case."

"No, we won't." He stepped past her and glance both ways down the hallway. "There's another way out. Those soldiers won't know about it, and with Renarde down there causing mayhem, the locals won't have time to look there."

"I can't just—"

"Do you want to save your husband?" He glared at her. "If you do, then you come with me. I'm the only chance you have left."

He took a few steps down the hall, drawing Sigrid out of the room to follow her. She stopped, looking towards Olav and then the other direction of the hallway. Sounds of fighting echoed up the hallway. She stared down the hall and took a deep breath.

"Be safe, Renarde." She turned to Olav. "Let's go!"

The two of them rushed down the hallway, away from Renarde and the others.

• • • • • • •

Renarde crouched down immediately to all fours, lowering herself almost fully to the ground, ears plastered flat against the back of her head. The four soldiers in front of her recoiled reflexively as she smiled up at them, showing a full row of fangs and teeth. She quickly looked back over her shoulder at Hjalmar.

"You haven't caught me yet, which means I can't go with you. Sorry," she giggled, and then leapt against the far wall, bounding sideways and running down the hallway.

Without a second thought Hjalmar ran after her, shouting commands as he sped past the other soldiers. "You two with me! You other two keep them in that room!"

Renarde sped down the hallway, pausing only to make sure that the large man and his soldiers were in pursuit. Confident they were going to stay with her, she grinned and scampered forward, keeping the same distance between her and the others.

The stairs greeted Renarde and she responded by hurdling the rails and forgoing the majority of them, touching only twice before her feet contacted the ground floor, where she was met by a whole new group. A half-dozen people, a mix of town guard and Valpuri soldiers, turned as one and drew their weapons.

"Uh, hi," Renarde said, waving and smiling at the gathering.

"Get her!" One of the town guard shouted it, and an even blend of local and Valpuri moved towards her.

"Really? What did I do?" Renarde dropped to all fours and ran at them, reaching them well before they were prepared. Two of them ended up flat on their back as their feet gave way from attempting an emergency backpedal. The others were equally surprised—though they managed to keep their footing—when she sprung into the air, passing over their heads in the open lobby.

Behind her, Renarde heard Hjalmar's feet hit the floor, causing a rattle to the building—or at least it seemed that way to her. She couldn't be sure, since she was far more focused on what was ahead of her, including the two men who were now blocking the exit out of the building.

"Do not let her out!" His voice echoed off the walls, loud enough to make Renarde wince. "Block the exits!"

She turned her head to him. "Would you keep it down! That was really loud!" Her eyebrow shot up in surprise. He was only a few steps behind her. "And slow down!"

The guards in front of her moved closer together and stepped into the doorway itself, filling it to the best of their ability, blocking the closed door.

The grin on her face ran from ear to ear.

Without slowing down, Renarde continued straight towards the exit—and sprang into the air less than a body's length in front of the men. Her feet hit the wall above them, and she used that to reverse her momentum and direction.

Hjalmar's hands once again passed against her fur as he skidded to a stop. His feet gave slightly, causing him to slip far enough so that one hand was on the floor. With the aid of her tail, Renarde twisted around, landing again on all fours and not missing a single beat as she continued to run.

But her directions were running out.

"Would someone mind opening a window?" she asked. "It's a little stuffy in here." Her eyes scanned over each window. A guard stood in front of each one, cutting off that avenue from her. Another look over her shoulder showed Hjalmar once again in quick pursuit. A new idea came into her mind.

She skidded to a stop, turning around and standing at the same time, staring directly at the onrushing man. Her eyes narrowed, ears fell flat, and her tail began to twitch anxiously behind her. When he got close enough, she made her move.

Her hand came out, open and inviting. "Hi! I'm Renarde!" She smiled bright and broad, ears popping up and eyes going wide.

Unfortunately, Hjalmar didn't slow, aiming directly for the center of her body as he attempted a tackle. The attempt failed.

Too fast for his eyes to follow, she popped up, her feet pulling up just high enough for him to pass under her. In mid air, she turned and landed back on her feet, just in time to watch him tumble to a stop several feet away.

"What's your name?" she asked in her friendliest tone.

His only response was a growl, as he once more came at her— though much slower than before. He stalked up to her, and she met him, bouncing on the balls of her feet.

"I don't want to be a pain, but can you tell them to clear the front door? I really have someplace that I need to go," she asked.

"The only place that you'll be going is with me, demon," he answered.

"Okay, we'll get into the demon thing later," she began, "and even though I appreciate the invite, I really do have someplace to be. I kinda made a promise."

"You'll have to break it," his hand shot out, grabbing for her, only to find air as she took a small jump backwards. "Stand still!"

"Uh, no." She shook her head. "That would be kinda stupid."

"You have no choice in the matter, you will be taken," he growled.

"I'd really rather not," she replied. "Nothing personal, but…well, yeah, it's kinda personal, I guess. I don't trust you."

She skittered back, staying just out of his reach while her eyes surveyed the room for another way out.

"Maybe we can make an arrangement to meet again later on? Say in fifty or sixty years?" she suggested.

His hands swept in front of her, grasping side to side, not managing to touch her at all. To everyone in the room it appeared he was taking part in a futile task, but he saw it differently.

Once more his hand swept to the side, and once more she skipped back—and that's when he acted. While she was still in mid air his other hand moved, balling into a fist and slamming hard into the floor, shattering the wood and sending the boards up.

Renarde's feet hit the board sooner than she expected, and she stumbled. It wasn't much, but it was enough of an opening for him. His hand grabbed her wrist, locking down on it. Her eyes became saucers and her mouth hung open as he pulled her tight against him, wrapping both of his arms around her in a tight, secure hug, trapping both of her arms. A short blast of air escaped Renarde as he squeezed sharply.

"That's…friendlier than…I wanted…right now," she gasped. "Could you…loosen up a little?"

"You are quick, but not quick enough, demon," he answered. "You're mine now."

"Wow, you're…the possessive type…aren't you?" She squirmed, wriggling against his grip. "And strong, too. Really strong."

He squeezed harder, pushing another blast of air from her lungs. "You will be down soon enough, demon."

"Okay, see…that's the thing…I'm not…. Oh, never mind." Her mouth snapped out, clamping down on Hjalmar's nose. He snarled and squeezed tighter.

Renarde pulled back, her tongue repeatedly pushing out of her mouth in rapid succession. "Bleh! You…taste like…." She looked at his face. The point where she had punctured his flesh on his nose was an open wound. The faint gleam of metal sparked through the skin—which was rapidly mending itself again.

"What…are you?" Renarde's voice faded away as her eyes rolled back, taking her head with them. The world around her turned into a blur that shifted to a dull gray, and then eventually black.

Her body went limp in his arms, head draping to the side, tongue lolling out of her head. He continued to squeeze her tight for another full minute before finally releasing her.

She slumped to the floor in a heap as he rubbed the tip of his nose carefully.

• • • • • • •

The door opened so suddenly that Armas actually jumped. He felt his heart race in his chest as a single figure walked in, then followed by another. The second figure was carrying a tray laden with fruits, bread, and cheese. The first person held only a bottle and two glasses. With a nod of her head, she directed the second person towards a small table.

"Go ahead and set that there and leave," Mathilda instructed. "We'll be fine."

"What are you doing here?" Armas asked. He stepped away from the window where he stood, wearing a simple loose fitting shirt and comfortable pants. He moved towards her and the other woman, who set the tray down and then walked directly back towards the door.

Mathilda put both glasses down on the table and poured a healthy amount of liquor into each one. Picking them both up, she held out one for Armas. "I figured you could use some company."

The door to the room closed, the sound of the locks once again falling in place, leaving the two of them alone inside.

"Not you, too," he sighed. "Vasen has already worn me out tonight. I'm sorry."

"Please," she laughed, "you aren't my type." She shook the glass slightly, the liquid threatening to slosh over the edge of the rim each time. "Besides, my sisters would probably kill me if I did."

He hesitated. Slowly he reached out and took the glass from her hand. With a short breath, she turned and walked over to a chair and sat down. Both of her legs extended out straight, crossing her feet at the ankles.

"So, your life sucks, doesn't it?" she said and took a healthy drink from the glass.

"You don't know anything about my life," he replied and walked over to his bed and flopped down onto the mattress.

"That's where you're wrong, remember? I'm the one that brought you here," she stated. "I know you better than anyone else in this place."

"But you still don't know me." He took a drink from his glass and winced.

She chuckled at his reaction.

"That's probably true." She nodded. "So, why don't you tell me about yourself, then?"

He shook his head. "Why should I?"

"I figure you're pretty lonely at this point. My sisters have probably been paying a lot of attention to you, but not in the way that you need." She took another drink from her glass. "Trust me, I know about that."

"What does that mean?" He took another sip from his glass.

"Oh no, we're not getting into that just yet," she laughed. "You tell me yours and I'll tell you mine."

He sighed. "All right. The basics are that I'm a woodworker. I build furniture, like my father did. When I was a little kid I hated it. He used to make me come in and help him out—holding wood while he planed, fetching a plank right next to him, that sort of thing—instead of letting me go out and play with my friends. Not every day, but…often enough." A smile crept onto his face slowly. "It wasn't until much later that I realized he was teaching me. Making me watch what he did."

"Sounds like a smart man." Mathilda poured her glass back to full and then downed half of it in single shot.

"He was." Armas' voice trailed off wistfully.

"Was? What happened?" she asked.

"Nature. The only thing necessary for woodworking is wood. It was spring and he went out with three other men to gather some birch for a custom job." His eyes fell to his glass and his finger circled the rim. "Only one of them came back. They came across a mother bear and her cubs." He shook his head.

"I'm sorry," she replied softly.

"I was fifteen when it happened. And…and the only thing that still haunts me is that I never really got the chance to tell him… thank you. I was young and stupid, and he did so much for me that I can never repay." Armas took another drink from his glass and sighed gently.

"What about your mother?" Mathilda asked.

Armas sat up straight, completely unaware that he had been slumping. "Mother took another husband two years later. After my father's death she turned the business from crafting to repair, only trusting my skills so far at that point. She ended up taking in my father's main competitor when his wife died under mysterious circumstances."

"Really?" Mathilda's eyebrow went up and she sat back in her chair.

"Yes, and it didn't sit well with the family. The daughter of the dead wife challenged my mother, and ended up taking her life. She assumed the role of head of the household and—"

"And you were excommunicated. Banished," Mathilda finished for him. He nodded agreement. "Did you lose everything?"

"I only had my own clothes," he answered. "It was summer, so it wasn't too dangerous to travel, and I made my way from town to town, hoping to find someplace that would take me."

"How did you end up in that small village I got you from? What was it called? Kyla?" she asked.

"Yeah, Kyla. I was lucky enough to arrive there for the fall festival. Right in the middle of a big party, and I got food and drink and good times—and I met Sigrid. She was beautiful. Took my breath away instantly." His smile grew wide. "And then I heard her talk. She was amazingly drunk, and that worked to my advantage, actually, as she saw me and decided that I was a welcome conquest." He shrugged. "I must have done something right because she didn't throw me out of her house the next morning. She put me to work a week later, and then asked me to marry her only three months after that."

Mathilda laughed under her breath.

"What?" he asked.

"Your voice. It changes when you talk about her." She drained her glass dry and poured another. "It gets a bit of a…a singing quality to it. It's cute." She smirked. "I'm jealous."

The idea of pursuing that comment briefly ran through Armas' mind, but he decided it might be best not to know what—or who—she was jealous of right now. He decided to redirect the conversation.

"Okay, it's your turn. Tell me about yourself," he sipped from his glass, "and about your sisters."

The room turned very quiet, broken only by the popping of the wood in the fireplace. The expression on Mathilda's face changed, losing some of the light it held only moments before. Her tongue clicked against the roof of her mouth and then suddenly stopped. In a single motion she put her glass down beside the half-empty bottle and stood up. Then she walked with a deliberate pace over to the fire and stood. The light from the flames licked up her body, which also warmed her considerably. She turned and looked at Armas with a forced smile.

"Have you seen under their masks yet?" she asked.

He answered with a slow shake of his head. "No."

"Not surprising. They're a little private about that, but I thought there might be a chance," she replied. Her right hand went to the mantle of the fireplace, where her fingers began to strum rhythmically.

"When they were younger they were perfectly identical. No one could tell them apart. No one. Not even our mother." Mathilda nodded slowly, her fingers sit rapping gently on the wood above the fire. "They were beautiful. Truthfully, I suppose they still are beautiful, at least for the most part.

"They also had another quality as children: they loved to play games. With each other, with me, and with our parents. Father enjoyed it. Every time they came to him he became a child along with them. I was very young, so I only just remember it, but it's a good memory." Mathilda's voice softened, easing out of her gently.

"He sounds like a good man," Armas said.

"I like to think so," she nodded. "I really don't remember anything about him other than his smile and laugh."

"What happened to him?"

Her lungs filled slowly and then she spoke, "Mother didn't share our father's enthusiasm. She found my sister's games to be a waste, and even called them childish," she laughed, shaking her head. "Childish. She said that about children."

She pulled her hand back down and rubbed it on her leg. "One of my sister's favorite games was switching places. One of them pretending to be the other one, or even both of them pretending to be the same one and showing up together at the same time. Mother hated that."

Armas slid forward, his eye's widening slowly.

"On their ninth birthday Mother said that she was giving them a special gift. Something that they would remember forever. She gave it to them at their party, held at The Burning Heart. I was there." Her words became dark and shallow. Armas slowly stood beside the bed. "The guards held each of them still while she pulled the iron from the fire. She took her time and dragged it slowly across the left cheek of one and the right cheek of the other." Her voice faltered.

Armas took a step towards her.

"They screamed. Who wouldn't? I screamed, begging mother to stop, not really understanding what was happening. I was only six." She closed her lips, pulling them tight. "I'm sure you don't know this, but their real names aren't actually Oikea and Vasen. Those are ancient words for both right and left—I'm sure you can guess which is which."

"What…what are their real names?" Armas stepped towards her again, meeting her at the fireplace.

"I don't remember. Not accurately, anyway." She walked past Armas, heading back to the table and picking up her glass. She turned back to him and downed the contents. "I've used their current names since that day. Was punished if I didn't."

"Your mother changed their names? I don't understand." Armas stayed by the fire.

"No, she didn't. Three days after their birthday they finally showed themselves again, only they were now both wearing a mask—and they changed their own names. Everything about them changed that day. I don't remember them playing a single game after that. It took them years to smile, actually." She turned and poured herself another drink. "They were the ones who punished me if I used their old names."

"What?" Armas gasped.

"The next time I saw them smile was on their thirteenth birthday. That…that was a special day." She raised the glass to her lips and emptied the contents down her throat. After setting the glass down she pulled the back of her right hand across her lips.

"I can't say how they did it, most likely they hired someone to do it for them, but that morning both my mother and father were killed, and my sisters declared themselves the new Ranee. Not a single person argued with them. Our parents entire bedroom was a bloodbath. It was like both mother and father were torn apart completely." She forced another smile. "I don't know how it happened, and I don't want to. I just know that as of that day I became afraid of them."

She picked up the bottle, forgoing the glass completely, and took another drink. "They sent me to the military academy the next day. I didn't see them again until I was sixteen, and by then they had found Hjalmar. To this day I have no idea where he came from, but I know that he does whatever they tell him to do."

The bottle swayed at her side as she walked over near him, sliding over to lean up against the wall beside the fireplace. "They faked being happy to see me—like they always do—and graciously gave me the rank of Commander of the Valpuri." She raised the bottle up. "I have my own army, thank you!"

She took a deep swig from the bottle.

"You might want to slow down on that." Armas pointed to the bottle.

A huffing laugh was her only reply. "The only problem is that it isn't my army. It's their army. I'm just in charge of it to keep me away from here. I get to do the dirty work. Go out and harvest men from cities and be the frightful face of the Valpuri." Her eyes met his squarely. "Trust me, I know what everyone thinks of me."

"Then why do you do it?" he asked.

"Because I want to stay alive. Isn't that obvious?" she laughed.

She raised her bottle up again, and looked at the level of the liquid inside. Waving it back and forth, she measured the liquor visually. Her head shook back and forth slowly.

"Well, it looks like our conversation is about done," she said. "I've got to go find something more to drink."

"You're going to kill yourself if you keep drinking that way," he said.

A short walk over brought them face to face. Her hand came up and brushed his cheek with the back of it. Without a word she turned and walked over to the table holding her glass, and set the bottle down.

"I'll leave that for you." She pointed to the nearby food. "Oh, and you might want to eat some of that, too, actually."

With a grace that belied the amount of liquor she had consumed, she walked towards the door to leave.

"Mathilda," his words stopped her and she looked over her shoulder. "Why did you come tell me all this?"

She shrugged. "To commiserate. Share a burden. Besides, I know that it will never leave this keep."

Stepping towards her his voice went low. "What do you mean?"

A light chuckled preceded her words. "You know exactly what I mean." She nodded once. "Try to get some sleep, Armas."

Walking up to the door, she knocked twice. The door opened and she exited quietly, leaving him behind.

• • • • • • • •

Her lips smacked against each other several times. Arms and legs extended out, her ears curled around the sides of her head and her tail went rigid behind her as a loud yawn caused her to stretch her whole body, first straight and then arcing out to the side.

And then everything came to a drastic halt when the chains reached their limit.

Renarde's eyes shot open and she looked at first her right wrist and then her left, both of them anchored down by a hefty manacle attached to a thick chain leading down below the surface of the bed. Raising her body up as much as possible, she looked down the length of her body and saw another pair of cuffs around her ankles, both attached to an equally imposing set of chains.

"Not good," she mumbled. Both of her arms pulled tight against the chains and strained, testing them. Her muscles pulled, the chains didn't. "Yeah, not good."

"Oh, you've awoken. Lovely." The voice was thick silk laced with iron. A short turn of her head allowed Renarde to see the speaker. It was an evocative blonde woman dressed in a white dress with intricate black lace running down the right side of her body. "My name is Oikea. Welcome to my home."

Renarde looked at the chains on her wrists and ankles. "Uh, thanks?"

"I apologize for any discomfort, but I'm sure you understand."
She walked to stand beside the bed.

"Um, not really." She shook the shackles and chains.

"Mmm." Oikea walked around the bed and made her way to the
nearest window. She pulled open the drapes suddenly, causing
sunlight to blaze into the room, washing over Renarde and her
bed. Slowly, Oikea turned back to look directly upon her captive.
"Well, that confirms that."

The colors of the room came into focus for Renarde. The deep
blue walls were mostly barren, with only a sole painting of a regal
looking woman with an expression that chilled the whole of the
room. The room was permeated with a smell that was half musty
and half perfume, with neither winning the duel—and something
deeper lying beneath. A few pieces of furniture were scattered
about, covered in a thick layer of dust, while others were covered
by a heavy cloth—with the exceptions of a single chair and the
bed.

"Great. What did we confirm?" Renarde asked.

Oikea smiled. "You're not a demon." She moved to the next
window and pulled open those drapes.

"Well, yeah, I knew that," Renarde answered while rolling her
eyes. She twisted her head slightly as she continued, "Wait, how
did you know that? Nobody else seems to."

"You didn't scream," she said as she continued to open drapes,
flooding the room in light. "Demons of your ilk—or rather what
I thought you might be—don't like direct sunlight. But that does
leave a question," she opened the last drape and turned back to
Renarde, "what exactly are you?"

"Oh! I'm Renarde!" She stuck her hand out as far as it could go,
rattling the chains.

In response, Oikea walked up beside the bed, just out of reach of Renarde's hand. She stared down, peering out from behind the white silk and black lace mask covering the right side of her face.

"What's that on your face?" Renarde asked. "Is that a mask? Why do you wear a mask?"

"I'm going to assume that Renarde is your name, am I wrong?" Oikea asked.

"Uh, no, you're not wrong. I just told you that," she answered and pulled her hand back.

"Then perhaps you will answer my question: what are you?" Oikea worked on a smile, baring her teeth.

"Wow. Everyone always has the same questions," Renarde sighed. She closed her eyes and her ears drooped for a moment before the eyes opened up again. "Can you let me up? I talk better when I don't have chains on my arms and legs."

"I don't understand why. There is nothing covering your mouth— yet," Oikea stated.

Renarde pulled herself up off the mattress. "Haven't you ever known someone that couldn't talk without using their hands?"

"You want me to free you. Have I already given the impression that I'm foolish?" she asked.

"No!" She looked over her completely. "Though you do kinda dress funny."

Chuckling, Oikea sat down on the bed beside Renarde. Her hand fell onto her captive's thigh, rubbing gently. "You aren't doing anything to win me over, you realize. Why don't we start with the basic question I asked, and then progress from there?"

"The what am I thing? Well, okay...." Renarde took a deep breath. "I'm some sort of mix of the four goddesses and some kind of essence of Elan that was mixed up and then taken into Serenade's domain where she raised me to eventually come back to Elan to help them get back here and hopefully stop Aubade from destroying Elan because she was possessed by a big, bad spirit of something nasty, which we didn't have to do because Aubade gave the nasty to a human who turned into a different nasty and then we fought her and got beat up but ended up saving Harmonia and then I came here." A huge exhalation followed her words before she quickly added, "Oh, and I'm a super cute fox, too."

With the exception of a broken smile crossing her lips, Oikea appeared unfazed. "Did you say that you are a creation of the goddesses?"

A vigorous nod confirmed Renarde's acknowledgement.

"And that you were raised by Ilta? The goddess you call Serenade?" she asked calmly.

"Yep! That's the basic version." Renarde's mouth smiled wide, with her eyes matching it completely.

Their eyes met. Renarde's glinting in the morning light, while Oikea's stayed placid. "Prove it," Oikea stated.

Renarde blinked. "Uh…what?"

"If you are the child of a goddess, then you should have something that shows that. I want to see it," Oikea explained.

"Well, let's see…. I'm very athletic and active. My upbringing made me exceptionally curious, though I always try to do the right thing. Oh, and I LOOK LIKE THIS!" She nodded down her body. "What the heck do you want? I told you I wasn't a demon and you agree, so…?"

"It's not quite that simple. There is always the possibility that—" Oikea's words were suddenly cut off by the sound of a door swinging wide. She stood smoothly, turning towards the sound. Renarde lifted her head to see what was happening.

She saw a woman who looked remarkably like Oikea walking in, though she wore a black dress with white lace on it, with a matching black mask—both decorated on her left side.

"Sister!" Oikea's voice turned soft and joyous as she walked across the room. "I see that you are awake."

"Yes, I am. I would have been here earlier, but I didn't determine that you were up here until a few minutes ago. I was surprised to discover that you brought someone to our mother's old room. Naturally, I rushed up here to see about our guest," Vasen answered.

They met in the middle of the room and kissed each other on their exposed cheek.

"I've been trying to find out more about her. When they brought her in last night you had already retired, and I didn't see the point in disturbing you until I knew more," Oikea explained.

Nodding reassuringly, Vasen answered, "Of course. I understand completely. Fortunately, I'm here to help you now." She looked past her sister at Renarde—who smiled warmly back at her. "What have you learned?"

"She claims to be the offspring of Ilta. I was looking to confirm that fact." Turning and walking back to the bed, Oikea stood at its foot, staring down at Renarde.

"Her name is really Serenade," Renarde stated. "Though she'd probably be okay with that Ilta name, too."

"And what is your name, dear?" Vasen asked as she came up beside the bed.

"I'm Renarde! What's your name?" she answered.

"I am Vasen. It is a pleasure to meet you." She glanced beside her. "If you haven't surmised it, I am Oikea's sister."

"Hi, Vasen!" Renarde looked between the two sisters. "And it's nice to know your name, Oik-a."

"Oikea," she corrected.

"Well, let's get you up and out of that bed, shall we?" Vasen turned to Oikea. "Where is the key, Sister?"

"I'm sorry? Shouldn't we discuss this first?" Oikea asked, a slight tinge behind her voice.

Smiling softly, Vasen stepped over to her sister and took her hand in her own. "What good is it to keep her chained here? If we are going to find out anything about this creature—"

"Woman," Renarde interjected in a happy tone.

"My apologies," she said to Renarde and then returned to Oikea. "If we are going to discover the truth about this woman, then we have to spend time with her. Perhaps show her the orb?"

"The orb?" Oikea raised an eyebrow.

"If she is the child of Ilta, then perhaps she might have something to show us," Vasen closed her eyes slightly as she looked at her sister.

A light washed over Oikea as a smile grew across her face. "Why, that is a wonderful idea, Sister."

"Thank you. We could have already been there if you had shared her being here with me earlier," Vasen stated.

"Let's not bicker, Vasen. We have a guest to attend to," Oikea said.

"I agree," Renarde said. "Attend to me. I'm the guest." She lifted her wrists and rattled the chains. "Please?"

"Of course!" Oikea's tone brightened suddenly. She reached her left hand into her right sleeve and pulled out a key, moving first to Renarde's feet and freeing them from her shackles. Immediately Renarde stretched her legs up high, flexing her canine toes out wide—causing Vasen to stare despite her best effort.

"That feels good!" Renarde purred. Oikea reached across her body and unlocked Renarde's right hand first, and then her left.

Oikea stepped back beside her sister as Renarde sat up in the bed, twisting her body and reaching her arms up high above her head.

"Oh that feels so good! I was worried I wouldn't be able to move them anymore." Her eyes closed and her ears twisted around slowly, her tail flipping from side to side slowly.

"You only knew you had them on for less than ten minutes," Oikea growled.

"Nonetheless," Vasen stepped forward, offering her hand to Renarde, "please, allow us this time to show you our home."

"That sounds great. I'd like to meet everyone in the place, please," Renarde popped up to her feet, ignoring the woman's hand, with head swiveling to get a good look at the place, while at least one ear remained pointed towards the sisters.

"That…will take some time. Why don't we begin with the more simple task of just giving you a tour of the building first?" Vasen suggested, pulling her hand back gracefully.

"Okay. Do I get to see all the rooms?" Renarde turned back to her.

"Maybe," she answered. "Why don't we start with some of our favorite rooms."

"Can I choose?" Renarde turned and twisted her head slightly, a grin growing across her muzzle.

"You should be grateful," Oikea stated. "We could always put the shackles back on you."

Renarde turned to her, eyes closing slightly and chin lowering. "Ooh. I hope that you are saying that in a fun way."

"Hmm." Vasen's response brought Renarde's attention back to her. "What did you say your name was, again?"

"Renarde." She extended her hand. "And you are Vasen Valpuri and your sister is Oikea Valpuri, and the two of you are the Hundred of this Ranee."

Vasen took her hand gently, and then squeezed it warmly as she spoke, "Close. The Ranee of this Hundred, actually. Now, how do you know that?"

Oikea walked across the room, opening the door and waiting. Taking the hint, Vasen began to walk towards her sister and the exit, drawing Renarde in her wake.

"Well, it's right, isn't it?" Renarde stepped in alongside Vasen easily. "I picked things up from the locals, listening and figuring things out."

"Locals? Is that what you are calling the woman you were here with?" Oikea asked, watching them approach.

"Sure. I'm from Harmonia—sort of—and that's not local. So anyone here in your country would be local for me," she answered.

Stepping through the door first, Vasen spoke over her shoulder. "What was the name of this local?"

"Does it matter?" Renarde waited for Oikea to go, but she gestured for the fox woman to go first.

The upper hallway was well lit from a series of long, narrow windows, creating a hatch work of sun slicing the shadows off the floor. As Vasen walked, Renarde saw her fade into and out of the light in quick turn.

"It could," Vasen said.

"Sorry, I don't remember," Renarde answered. "I think it started with a 'C' or something. Maybe."

"Of course not," Oikea said from behind her. "Where did you meet the poor woman?"

"In the woods," Renarde answered immediately. "She was coming this way and I came with her."

"And she let you come along with her, darling?" Oikea asked.

"Uh-huh," Renarde nodded over her shoulder. They moved to a grand stair, walking down its large spiral slowly. Two maids walking up spied them and froze. One of them dropped the linen in her arms and cowered against the wall.

"You?" Oikea continued. "She just let you go with her?"

"Yep! I'm really charming and super cute!" Renarde beamed as they passed the women. The cowering one began to weep in terror and dropped to the floor, hiding her eyes.

"Obviously," Oikea stated.

"Why was she coming this way?" Vasen asked as she led the trio along through the corridors of the keep.

"I'm not sure. It had something to do with coming to see someone she knew," Renarde answered.

"Olav," Oikea sneered.

Renarde turned to look at her. "Wasn't that the name of the doctor who came to look at me?"

"I believe it was," she answered. "And I'm told that he and the woman in the room disabled two of our guards and escaped.

"Who told you that?" Renarde asked, still looking back at Oikea. Ahead, beyond Vasen, she could hear the sound of scurrying feet rushing from the hallway.

"That would have been Hjalmar, dear," Vasen answered. "From what I understand, he's the one who brought you here."

"Oh! The big guy with the metal nose," Renarde said calmly.

Vasen stopped completely, causing Renarde to catch herself and freeze, with Oikea walking immediately up behind her.

"What did you say?" Vasen asked.

"Big guy. Metal nose," Renarde repeated.

"And why would you say such a thing?" Vasen's eyes and tone turned to ice.

"Um…I bit his nose. It looked and tasted like metal," she answered.

"Did you?" Vasen's eyes shot from Renarde to Oikea, and then back. "I didn't hear about that."

"We haven't had time to properly discuss anything, darling," Oikea replied. "We will have that discussion after we've dealt with our new guest."

A deep breath filled Vasen's lungs, and she let a smile grow back onto her face. "Of course. After." She turned back around and walked ahead. Oikea gently prodded Renarde forward.

They walked in silence, no questions being asked at all. Renarde began to hum a song to herself, her head on a constant swivel as she took in everything they passed, her tail a perpetual flutter behind her. Vasen remained in front of her, and Oikea behind her as they moved. Finally, Vasen stopped in front of a large door with iron braces across it. She knocked on the door three times.

"You should feel honored," Oikea whispered from behind Renarde. Her left ear pivoted around to pay strict attention to what was being said. "There are only a handful of people who have ever seen this room."

"Why?" Renarde asked.

"Because," Vasen answered, "there are only a handful of people worthy of seeing it."

The sound of metal unlatching from metal reverberated through the hall, and the doorway in front of them slowly swung inward. A shortish man with a cragged face surrounding dark eyes peered out at them. A smile slowly cracked across his lips.

"Vasen, my dear," his voice was gravel drawn over a fire. "What an unexpected…."

His voice trailed off as he looked beyond Vasen and fixed onto Renarde. He opened the door further and stood, his mouth hanging open.

"Sepi, dear," Vasen turned and presented her companion, "this is Renarde. She claims to be a child of Ilta."

"Amazing," he mumbled.

"We were wanting to show her the orb," Vasen stated. Those words pulled his attention back to her. He blinked and glanced back over at Renarde. He nodded slowly.

"Yes. Yes, I understand." Stepping backwards, he pulled the door with him, providing the space needed for the others to pass inside. Vasen stepped in through the door quickly.

Renarde hesitated. Her head shifted back and forth, trying to get a view beyond the door. There was plenty of space, but she couldn't see what lay ahead.

"Go on," Oikea urged, gesturing towards the door.

"What's in there?" Renarde whispered. "I can't see anything. It feels weird."

"My sister is in there, among other things," Oikea answered.

A single step brought her close enough to extend her arm and reach beyond the door. Instantly, she snapped it back, quickly looking it over and sniffing it. Her tongue ran over her lips, which led to the lower one being sucked up between her teeth. She closed her eyes and took three steps forward.

When she finally reopened them, she discovered herself in a long, narrow room, perhaps fifty feet deep and maybe fifteen feet wide. The ceiling towered above her, allowing at least twenty feet from floor to ceiling. And all of the surfaces—walls, floor, and ceiling—were gold. She wasn't sure if it was just gold in appearance or gold in reality, but they had the exact look and sheen of polished gold. There were no windows, and light came from an unseen source, bouncing around the room and creating an odd tint to everything inside it.

Dozens of curious relics—to call them anything else would seem inappropriate—were in the room, spaced out along both walls, either resting on tables or standing independently, depending on the item in question. Two of the relics rested near each other, with one of them being flanked on either side by Vasen and the short man. Renarde turned when she heard footsteps beside her.

"We call it The Hall of Wonders," Oikea said.

"Uh-huh." Renarde let her eyes wander down its length and back. "Wonder why?"

"Please," Oikea gestured over to the others and the item between them. Straightening herself, Renarde walked over to them.

"Renarde, allow me to introduce you to Sebastian, my husband," Vasen looked at the short man.

He stood a couple of inches below Renarde, with an unruly mop of black hair that was slicked down to the top of his head, providing an overhang for his face. Wrinkled lines sank into his skin, deepest around his eyes and the corners of his mouth. He stared at Renarde with a fire in his eyes—a hunger. Renarde looked at him, then over at Vasen, and then back at him, and then settling back on Vasen.

"You're kidding, right?" she asked with a blink.

"My Sepi is a brilliant man, dear," Vasen explained. "He has enlightened and aided me—and my sister—in many, many ways."

Renarde nodded slowly. "Ew."

"He's not important," Oikea stated. "What's resting between him and my sister is."

Between them rested an orb. Even with the yellow light filling the space, it appeared black—at least, at first. Several colors began to play across it. Blues and purples. Reds and oranges. She stared at it, lost in the myriads of colors and forms dancing over its surface.

"Intoxicating, isn't it?" Sebastian asked.

The words snapped her back, and she shook her head briefly to clear it. She looked at the small man and nodded. "What is it?" she asked.

"Something wonderful that my Sepi discovered," Vasen purred. "Could you do us a tremendous favor and just…touch it?"

"Why?" Renarde took a half step backwards.

"It's a test," Sebastian explained. "We are testing your bloodline."

"I don't think I have one of those," Renarde stated.

"You said you were the child of the goddesses." Oikea remained behind her.

"Well, yeah," Renarde said, "but see I wasn't born with any… any…. Uh, is it going to hurt?"

"Not at all," Sebastian said. "It won't do a thing to you."

"Renarde," Vasen's voice became firm, "touch the orb. Please."

Her left ear began to twitch as Renarde stepped back towards the orb. The sides of her cheeks pulled back from sniffing the air repeatedly, and her throat bulged out from a nervous swallow.

Then, with a shrug of her shoulders, she reached out and placed her right hand on the orb.

Nothing happened. Renarde looked over at Sebastian.

"What was supposed to—"

Her words cut short as a sound not unlike thunder reverberated through the room. The yellow tinge to the Hall shifted and all color was lost, transforming everything visible into shades of grey.

Everyone in the room leapt in shock. Their muscles involuntarily spasmed from surprise, causing a short, sudden movement— which included Renarde. Her hand yanked off of the orb and she immediately dropped down to all fours, recoiling backwards.

"What the hell was that?!" Renarde shouted.

"I…don't know," Sebastian whispered. His eyes shot to Renarde. "Do it again!"

Her eyes went wide as she scrambled backwards. "No!"

"No, don't! I mean, don't worry, darling," Oikea stated. "You don't have to do anything at all."

"Wrong," Renarde said quickly. "I have to get away from that thing." She stood up and pointed at the orb.

"Of course!" Vasen offered. "Sister, why don't you take our guest out of here and show her the rest of the keep. We can meet up shortly for lunch, perhaps?"

"Yes, that sounds lovely." She moved to Renarde and gestured to the door. "Why don't we move along to a more secure location."

"Yeah. Yeah, let's do that." Following Oikea's suggestion, Renarde scuttled towards the door, keeping one eye on the orb the entire time.

Vasen moved to stand beside Sebastian, watching as Oikea opened the door and ushered Renarde out of the room. She waited a full heartbeat after the door closed before she turned and spoke.

"What was that? What happened?" Vasen's voice was low and intense.

"I…I really have no idea. That isn't what is supposed to happen when someone touches it," he answered with a slight stammer. "It shouldn't do that with her kind."

"With her kind? What do you mean?" Vasen asked.

"Hmm? Oh, um, simply that it shouldn't do that with anyone. Especially not someone who isn't from Dula Koarr," he explained.

"Well, you need to find out why. You need to find out what that means." She stepped in front of him and smiled. The fingers on her right hand traced lightly up and down his chest. "I need to know, Sepi. You figured out the orb once, you can do it again."

His eyes traveled down to her hand, and the corners of his mouth slowly turned upward. "You know I will do my best, love. I can make no promises, but I will do my best."

"I need you to. She acted without me again." Vasen turned away and walked a few steps from him. "I can't let her gain an upper hand. I know her."

"I'll do everything I can, love. I will keep it safe from…everyone. That's all I can offer," he assured her.

Her back remained to him. Slowly, she crossed her arms, staring at the large object. At first glance, it appeared to be a slightly oversized cabinet, not unlike an armoire, painted a rich, deep black. Two doors remained closed on its front, but without any handles or locks. And then the color began to dance across its surface, and shapes began to move inside the wood.

"You have to, Sepi," Vasen growled. "I won't let her have this. It will belong to me."

·   ·   ·   ·   ·   ·   ·

He looked out the window again before closing the shutters tight. A simple latch secured them, and he turned back to the other person in the room.

"They don't seem to be out there," Olav stated, "and that bothers me."

"Why does it bother you that they aren't looking for us? I'm actually rather glad they aren't," Sigrid replied.

She was sitting on a chair, holding her sword in her lap and rubbing it with a cloth. It already had a sheen on it crisp enough to show a reflection.

"It bothers me because it means they are waiting on us," he said. "They aren't desperate, and therefore aren't likely to make any stupid mistakes."

Her eyes remained focused on the sword in the dim light of the room. During the night, Olav led her to this room. A small, simple chamber at the base of a residence. It was meant to hold goods needing to be kept cold, which meant there was little barrier from the weather, but adequate protection to keep out creatures wanting to steal the food. Except for hungry humans, it seemed.

They spent the night there, huddled against the cold, waiting for the dawn. When it came, they waited some more. Watching the movement of the people, and more importantly, any of the Valpuri forces.

"I like that they aren't out there. It will give us a chance to move tonight," she said.

"Move? Where do you think you are going to move?" He pointed outside. "Didn't you hear me? They are waiting. They want us to come to them."

"Well, maybe I should!" She rose up, griping the sword in her hand and turning its blade. "It's better than waiting. It's better than knowing that he's up there and I'm down here. It's—"

The moment ended as she turned her back to him. Her arms pulled in tight to her body as she took in a deep, careful breath.

"I'm sorry," she whispered. "It's the cold. My mind is feeling it."

"I don't believe that any more than you do," Olav said. He sat down on a box near the window, keeping his eyes on her. "You told me yourself that you've been looking for your husband for many months now." He pointed back over his shoulder. "And now that you think you know where he is, all that patience is coming to an end. Your emotion is bubbling out of you." Shifting on the box, he leaned in towards her. "And that is perfectly fine."

The entirety of her body stiffened. With a slow, steady motion she sheathed her sword and turned to face him. He looked up and saw puffy, red eyes staring down at him.

"I can't. I just can't." She took a sharp breath in. "You said it yourself. My husband might be in there. If I break now everything I've worked to do is for nothing. I fail in one place and I fail everything." The breath eased out of her completely. "It's not fine."

The wind punched into the room, and she pulled herself in tight once again.

"I suppose not," he answered.

Her lips stiffened and her eyes narrowed, but it had nothing to do with the wind or the cold. "I am going in there. As soon as possible." She paused. "I don't expect you to help. That's not your concern, but any advice that you can give me would be welcome."

There was no answer. Not for several seconds as he sat there staring first at her, and then past her to the back of the tiny room. "It's suicide."

"It doesn't matter. I'm going to go," she replied immediately.

"I know," he grumbled. "That's the problem."

"It's not your problem." Almost imperceptibly she shook her head.

A deep laugh slowly welled up from him. "You're wrong." He looked straight at her. "For two years I've been sitting in this city, waiting for her to act. Hoping that she wouldn't." A deep sigh came from him. "You've been a wake up for me. I'm alive right now, but I'm not living."

"Then come with me," she said. "Help me rescue my husband. You can come with us back to our village. You would be welcome."

"It's not about that," he said as he stood and smiled at her. "Thank you, but this is about me having the freedom to leave. Being out from under the fear of Oikea Valpuri."

"Good. Then you will go with me into the keep?" she asked.

"No." He shook his head.

"But I thought you said—"

"Not into the keep," he interrupted. "That won't work, but I might have an answer. There are ways into that place that aren't so heavily guarded. At least not on the way in. And that, I will do."

A small smile crept onto her face. "That's more than I can ask. How are we going to get inside?"

"That you aren't going to like," he answered with a sigh.

"I don't care what we have to do to get inside. Where we have to go. Just so long as it gets us to my husband," she stated firmly.

"You will care," he answered.

"Why? Are we going to crawl up through the sewers and in through the waste tunnels? I'll live through some filth," she answered.

He shook his head slowly. "No. Not that kind of filth, anyway. We'll be going up through the mines."

"The mines? What mines?" Her head recoiled slightly in surprise.

"The ones under the keep. The ones that the majority of the people in this city either don't know about or refuse to acknowledge," he explained.

"Why?" she asked. "What are they mining?"

"It's not what they are mining, it's how. It's better to show you. I don't want to say." He turned and stepped towards the window, looking outside again.

"That sounds ominous," she commented.

"It is," he answered as he turned back to her. "Okay, we need to go."

"What? Now? It's hours before it will be dark," she stated.

"Exactly, and they aren't out there looking for us right now, but I'm willing to bet they expect us to move at night. There are plenty of people on the street right now, so we'll blend in." Pulling on his gloves first, Olav made sure he was safely wrapped up and protected against the weather.

"I thought you said you were concerned because they weren't looking for us." Mimicking his motions slightly, Sigrid pulled her gloves tight and secured her jacket around her body.

"Oh, I am, but that doesn't mean that we are going to wait. We have to act. They have the upper hand in this and are hoping we'll do something stupid," he said with a smile.

"Isn't that what we're doing?" she asked.

"Yes," he smiled wider, the crow's feet around his eyes sinking slightly deeper, "but not the stupid they are expecting."

"Then let's get out there and disappoint them," she slapped his shoulder.

Gently grasping the handle, he opened the door. "After you."

She stepped outside, with him following right behind.

· · · · · · ·

"I don't believe it," Mathilda mumbled, barely audible to her, let alone anyone else in the room.

Leading her in like an honored guest, Oikea escorted Renarde through the doors into the dining hall. Mathilda was standing over near the windows, glass in hand, and currently somewhat slack-jawed. Vasen sat comfortably at the head of the table, near where Mathilda stood, calm and collected, smiling at the fox woman. Shifting uncomfortably in his seat nearby, Sebastian pulled himself towards the table, getting a better look at their new lunch guest.

"Hi!" Renarde waved to everyone. "This is a big place."

"Yes, it is," Vasen agreed. "I'm glad that you were impressed. I hope you enjoyed it."

"Well, except for all the people running, screaming, crying, and that kind of thing, it was pretty good," Renarde stated. Her eyes fell onto Mathilda. "Oh! Hi! I'm Renarde." She bounced lightly around the table, coming to rest right beside the other woman, her tail flailing joyously behind her.

"Mathilda Valpuri," she answered blankly. "I don't believe it."

"Don't believe what? Is that not really your name?" Renarde twisted her head while her ears turned to stay directly towards Mathilda.

"Mathilda is our sister," Oikea explained, walking around to Renarde. "And she is also the Captain of our guard."

"What manner of creature are you?" Mathilda asked. Her hand reached out and gently touched Renarde's arm, brushing along the fur. "Are you a demon?"

Renarde's eyes rolled back in her head. "Ugh! No."

"We discussed that, Tilly," Vasen said softly. "Renarde is a child of Ilta."

"I wanted to hear it from her," she answered, her hand still running over Renarde's fur. It traveled up to her shoulder, her eyes staring blankly at what she did, and then back down the length of her arm.

Looking down at the hand stroking her fur, Renarde spoke softly, "Um, did you want to sit next to me for lunch?" She smiled broadly at Mathilda.

Quickly she pulled her hand back. "My apologies," she mumbled.

"Why don't we all sit, actually," Oikea suggested. "Lunch sounds lovely to me."

"Yes!" Renarde nodded sharply. "I'm really hungry."

"Well then, why don't you come here," Oikea gently placed her hand on Renarde's arm and gestured towards the other side of the table. Willingly, Renarde went with her and sat in the seat to which she was directed.

Moving on past her, Oikea took her place at the opposite head of the table from Vasen. Keeping her eyes on Renarde the whole time, Mathilda moved to sit directly across from her. Renarde watching and smiling the whole time.

"So," Renarde kept her eyes on Mathilda across the table, "what does everyone want to eat?"

"I believe that the chefs have prepared roasted chicken over a melange of vegetables," Vasen stated. "Is that something that you can eat? I hadn't thought to ask about any dietary needs."

Five servants came into the room at that moment, each carrying a plate with a silver cloche. Four of them quickly stepped into place, with the fifth approaching a bit more cautiously, but eventually he came into place as well. As one they lifted the cover, revealing the food beneath: half a chicken resting on top of several vegetables beneath.

"No, this looks good." Renarde licked her lips and smacked them together softly. "Very good."

"Oh, excellent," Vasen said happily.

"Would you care for some wine?" Oikea asked.

"What?" In a jerky motion as she fought to take her eyes off of the food, Renarde turned to Oikea. "What would I want?"

Oikea held up a bottle. "Some wine?"

"No!" Renarde shouted. "Uh, no, thanks. Just water. Water's good."

A short laugh came out under Mathilda's breath.

"Of course," Oikea said. "Well, please," she lifted a fork, "enjoy your meal."

"Thanks!" Renarde grabbed her fork in her right hand and stabbed the half bird on her plate. With a twist of the fork she ripped a chunk of flesh from the bird and lifted it up. With her left hand she then took the meat and put it into her mouth and began to chew. Her eyes closed and a purr-like sound welled up from her.

It wasn't until she opened her eyes once again that she realized the rest of the table was sitting there watching her eat.

"Uh, are you going to eat, too?" she asked, looking around the table in general.

"Of course we are," Vasen stated and immediately cut a small piece of chicken from her plate. Oikea mirrored her actions almost perfectly.

With a grin coming back to her face, Renarde went back to her meal.

"Excuse me, miss," Sebastian directed towards Renarde, "may I ask you some questions?"

"Sure," Renarde looked up and pulled more meat from her fork and ate it.

"That noise that you just made, what does it mean?" His focus remained on her, and his food untouched.

"What noise?" she answered through a full mouth of food.

"Well, I'm not sure. It sounded, well, not exactly like a cat, but similar." His hands waved around slightly as he explained his query.

"Oh, that." Renarde shrugged casually and stabbed her chicken again. "It's just a sound I make. I dunno."

"What does it mean, though? Is it a happy sound, or a nervous one, or what exactly?" Sebastian's fingers drummed in syncopated rhythm on the table lightly.

"Happy mostly. It just happens. I don't really turn it on or off or anything." She gingerly pulled the chicken apart on the fork, putting smaller bits into her mouth as she spoke. "Why?"

"Forgive me, but you are a curiosity. I just want to learn about you. I am actually hoping to get a chance to examine you closely when everything is finished," he said.

"When everything of what is finished?" she tilted her head to the side and squinted one eye.

"Nothing you need to worry about just now, dear," Vasen stated.

"When should I worry about it, then?" Renarde asked.

Her answer came in the form of a small, soft laugh.

"If I may continue," Sebastian came back, "I was still curious about you, Miss Renarde."

"Oh, no miss, just Renarde." She smiled across the table at him.

"Well then, Renarde, we can see that you eat the same food as us, but is everything else about you the same?" Sebastian asked.

"Uh, define everything else," she answered.

"Yes, I'm curious about that, too," Mathilda said to Sebastian. "Why do you want to know everything?"

"It's what he does, darling," Oikea answered. "Let him ask."

Bypassing the sister's conversation, Sebastian addressed Renarde. "I mean everything in the sense of your body. I can see that you have hands, but your feet don't look human, and there are other more visible differences. What about everything else? Do you need to breathe? Does the cold affect you? What about heat?"

"Um, yes, not badly, and I don't know," Renarde answered. She put the fork beside her plate and began to pick the flesh off the chicken carcass with her fingers. "As far as I know I work basically the same way everyone else does, except for the fur and stuff. I have normal people parts, too."

"But you aren't human. You aren't normal. And if the cold doesn't affect you badly, then you are more durable than a person, too," Sebastian stated. "Have you ever been tested? To see how you compare to a human standard?"

"Nope." Renarde began shuffling the bones around on her plate, trying to find more meat hidden amongst her uneaten vegetables.

"Would you be willing to be put to such a test?" he asked.

"Nope." She pushed the plate away from her, content that she had gotten all the meat from it, and smiled across at Sebastian. "That sounds like it would take a lot of time and be really, really boring. I have other things to do. Sorry."

Taking a deep breath, Renarde yawned and stretched her hands high above her head.

"You have more time than you think," Vasen stated. "You'll be staying with us for a while."

"Uh, sorry, but no." Renarde smacked her lips and her eyelids closed slightly. "I...I think I need to...."

Moving from person to person, Renarde looked all around the table slowly, and then turned to look blankly straight ahead. A warm smile crossed her face.

"That was some funky chicken." She fell flat, face hitting the place where her food had recently rested.

"Renarde!" Mathilda jumped up from her seat, palms flat against the table.

"Calm down," Vasen said easily, holding her hand up. "She's fine. We just don't know what she is capable of, so it's best to keep her controlled."

"There are other ways to do that," Mathilda glared at her sister.

Both Vasen and Oikea stood and paced around to meet behind Renarde's slumbering body. As the arrived, Vasen nodded to one of the guards standing in the doorway.

"She is an interesting creature," Vasen stated.

"Somewhat annoying, actually," Oikea replied. "You haven't spent as much time with her."

"Well, that might change." Vasen turned to Oikea calmly. "I tested myself this morning. Negative."

Oikea snorted a sigh in disgust. "He's proving to be useless," she growled.

"Perhaps it isn't him," Vasen replied, causing Oikea to bristle and straighten her body.

"You are not implying that—"

"I'm saying that this might be a matter of finding two beings that both have a similar bond. Say invoking a response from the same artifact?" Vasen smiled on one side of her face.

One of Oikea's eyebrows went up. "Interesting theory."

"The two of you are not suggesting what I think you are," Mathilda said as she stormed around the table. "We don't even know what this woman is, or if she would be interested in that."

"I wasn't planning on asking her," Vasen's look stopped Mathilda cold.

"I can't believe that you are even suggesting that Armas—"

"You seemed interested enough," Vasen interrupted. "So obviously, she isn't without some degree of charm or attraction. At least for some people."

"What? I...I was just—"

"We know what you were doing, Tilly," Vasen sneered. She turned to the open door and saw Hjalmar enter. He was cleaner, but still wore the same bear cloak over his shoulders. The guards gave him plenty of room.

Looking back over the table, Vasen smiled at Sebastian. "Sepi, may I have the collar?"

He stood and produced a metal circlet the color of tarnished gold, about the width of a closed fist. Deep inscriptions laced the whole of it in a pattern that no one at the table understood or recognized. Reaching across the table, Sebastian handed it to Vasen.

"What is that?" Mathilda asked.

"Control," Vasen snarled. The circlet opened in her hands, and Vasen placed it around Renarde's neck, closing with a clink that echoed through the room. She turned to Hjalmar and calmly gestured to the unconscious fox woman. "Hjalmar, if you would please carry our guest upstairs, we will join you in a moment."

Responding immediately, Hjalmar grasped Renarde by the arm and pulled her up and out of her chair and hoisted her across his shoulder. Without a word he exited the room with her.

"I don't approve of this," Mathilda said forcefully.

The twins walked together following Hjalmar's path, with Vasen pausing just as they reached the door. "That's the beauty of this, dear," her smile was sharp and cold, "your approval isn't required."

Only a moment later Vasen left the room, just behind Oikea. Mathilda stood and watched them until they were completely out of view. And at that moment she spun around and slammed her fist onto the table. The plate and glass from Renarde's meal jumped in response. Sebastian remained perfectly calm.

"Try not to be angry. It's just the way they are," he said to her.

Raising her head up, her gaze burned the space between them. "Yes, it is, isn't it?" Storming over to the side of the room, Mathilda grabbed a full bottle of liquor and slammed through the servants door from the room.

All alone in the dining hall Sebastian slowly turned back to look around the table at all of the empty chairs. He picked up his knife and fork and cut into the chicken on his plate with practiced precision.

· · · · · · ·

She glanced behind her again, looking at the horizon and everything between it and her. Trees kept the city from view, hiding them from anyone looking out from town—and hiding anyone who might be carefully following them.

"We're alone," Olav stated. "You can stop looking over your shoulder now."

Sigrid chuckled. "Let me know when you stop looking over your shoulder and we'll talk."

"I'm meaning it literally," he grumbled.

"What I'm doing is cautious. I'm too close to become complacent." She turned back to him. "Which reminds me, how close are we to our goal?"

He pointed to a ridge just ahead of them. "That's it. At least it's the start of that part of our trip."

Looking to her right, Sigrid leaned back, attempting to get as wide a view as possible to the other side of the mountain in front of them. "And you're telling me that we are going to get into Valpuri Keep from here? I can't even see it from here."

"I know. That's intentional. What's up there isn't meant to be immediately associated with the keep," he answered. "In fact, this is a good time to prepare."

"Prepare? Prepare for what?" Sigrid asked.

"For what you are about to see." He pulled his bag out and rummaged through it, pushing things aside until he had a clean line to the side of the bag's lining. Tugging firmly, the lining gave way. Olav reached into the gap between the lining and the leather and pulled out a small metal vial.

"What's that?" Sigrid asked.

"The thing that will let us get inside." He shook the vial in front of his face, judging the contents by feel as he stared at the dull metal. "But we'll have to hurry. There isn't much."

"Okay, you're going to have to explain yourself," Sigrid said. "None of this is making any sense."

"It's easier to show you. Let's get a little closer first." Sealing his bag, Olav once more began the trek up the slope with Sigrid behind. A few minutes later they were almost at the crest. He stopped and turned around.

"This isn't pleasant, but it's better than the alternative." Olav opened the vial and poured a tiny amount of a thick liquid into the palm of his hand. Immediately he smeared the oily material across his face, spreading it out in a thin coating. He handed the vial to Sigrid. "Go ahead."

Contorting her face, she pulled her head back slightly as she took the vial from him. "What is that smell?"

"The oil. Put it on," he instructed.

"Why?" she asked. "It smells horrible."

"Yes, I know. You'll have to trust me. Please," he motioned with his hand towards her face.

Taking a deep breath, Sigrid held it inside as she considered her options. She removed her gloves and opened the vial with a sharp exhale, and then poured the oil onto her hand. The container emptied with only a small dab. Following Olav's example, she smeared it across her face, rubbing it in slightly. Her eyes closed as she tried her very best to close off her nose from the noxious smell assaulting her.

"Oh, that's worse," she mumbled.

"It's better than what you are about to see, but it will keep us safe long enough to get past," he explained, and then walked on up to the ridge and paused.

As Sigrid joined him she felt her heart and stomach come together. Her heart might have stopped, but she wasn't sure. It was possible that her stomach tried to lurch up and out of her at that instant. She wasn't aware of much of anything in that moment, except for the fact that she was sickened.

Below them was a pit, easily two hundred feet across with a depth she truly didn't want to know, because the deeper it was, the worse the moment became. From edge to edge, the pit was filled with bodies. Hundreds, if not thousands of bodies lay unmoving in a heaping pile.

"Sigrid?" She heard the voice and looked over, suddenly becoming aware that Olav was holding her shoulder to keep her steady. Her shock turned to disgust, which quickly fueled anger.

"What is this?" she growled.

"The end of the Harvest. What happens to all of those men that are taken from the villages," he said softly. "I'm sorry."

"Wh-what?" She glared down at the bodies, seemingly thrown haphazardly into the pit. She shrugged free of his grip. "Tell me you weren't involved in this. That this is the reason that you left."

"It is," he answered. "I couldn't bear this."

She stepped back, turning to face him directly. "How is this happening? Why is this happening?"

"The how and why are the same answer. The mines. These men are used and broken, and once they die they are tossed here for... disposal." He spoke as though the words were bile in his mouth.

"How do the people not know about this? It's little more than an hour's walk from the outskirts of the city. They have to come here all the time!" The volume of her voice raised dramatically.

"Shh!" He raised his hand in a halting manner and looked into the pit. "Don't raise your voice."

"Why not?" While still lower, the volume of her voice was high as she turned to follow his view to the pit.

And she saw the bodies move. Not in a natural way, but shifting and sliding like a blanket might move if someone was beneath it.

Her eyes went wide. "What is that?"

"That's the reason no one knows of this place. No one who sees it lives," he glanced over at her, "unless they have an oil that masks their presence. We have to go."

"Right," she replied in a dull tone. "Let's go. Where?"

"There." He pointed to an opening that would be easily overlooked. A cave growing up into the mountain which was quickly lost to shadow and darkness. "We go in there."

She nodded, and without another word he began working his way around the rim of the pit, with Sigrid close behind. The first part of the journey was short and easy, taking them around to the face of the small cliff holding the cave opening. The rest of the trip looked much more difficult.

"How good are you at climbing?" he asked.

"As good as I have to be," she told him and then looked down at the pit. The movement had stopped. "At least that thing has calmed down."

"It's the colder months. It isn't as active. It will go through all of those bodies in the spring," he said reluctantly. "It works out. The cold hides the smell of the bodies and then when it gets warmer, the creature devours them."

"Have you seen it?" she asked.

"Once. That was enough." He began working his hands along the cliff face. A narrow ridge ran from where they stood to the cave. If they could hold onto the rock, they should be able to make it across.

"Why were you here?" Her eyes traveled the distance between where they stood and where the cave waited. It was thirty feet at the most.

"I was the doctor of the keep. Someone had to confirm those men were dead," he mumbled.

"Yeah, it looks like great care was taken on their behalf," she grumbled.

He turned and faced her. "I did what I could. When I realized that I couldn't do any more I left. I'm lucky I'm not in that pit with them."

Their eyes met, locked in a brief understanding. She nodded slowly.

"Let's go," Sigrid said and pointed to the cliff.

Olav turned back and worked his hand high onto the wall once more until he felt happy with his grip. His foot slid out to the side, half of it hanging off of the small ledge. As he found a solid grip his other foot moved beside the first one, and the process began to repeat. Ten minutes later he was almost halfway across, and Sigrid stepped forward to begin her climb.

Repeating his actions, she moved hands and feet slowly, sliding and gripping in a long, careful scaling of the wall. She felt her breath grow narrow and short, doing her best to keep herself thin, subconsciously thinking it might help her stay on the ridge.

She lost track of time. All she could do was remember to find a grip and then move her feet. It was working out exactly as it should—until it didn't. She felt something snag. It caught on the rock face. It was on her right, and the position of her arm over her head blocked her view. Taking a calm, deep breath she tried to move backwards, hoping to dislodge whatever was holding her to the wall. She felt the same tug as she attempted to move the other direction. Whatever was caught, it was firm.

"Sigrid?" She heard Olav's voice off to the side. Glancing over her left shoulder she was able to see him inside the mouth of the cave, looking out at her. He was only ten feet away.

"I'm stuck," she replied as loudly as she dared. "Something has caught on the rock."

He nodded to her. "We can work through this. You need to try to pull straight back. Just push your hips away from the wall until you feel it start to give and then ease back until it's free."

"All right." She swallowed. Her hands re-gripped the wall and her feet shifted in place to secure her footing. She took a quick breath and tried to relax.

With great care she began to push away from the wall with her hips, and once more felt the snag. She increased the pressure, hoping to feel something start to give, with no success.

The sides of her jaws expanded as her teeth clenched against each other. The possibilities ran through her head, and the solution options followed. The clearest option presented itself, and she followed it.

She pulled her right hand off the wall and slipped it down to where she felt the snag. Somehow, a jagged piece of stone had pierced her coat and was holding her tight to the wall.

"Be careful," Olav encouraged from a distance.

She didn't take the time to acknowledge him, concentrating instead on her own issue. Her vision was extremely limited, so she was forced to work mostly from feel. Tugging on the coat, she tried to pull it off of the stone, but couldn't move it above the point needed.

Her hand shifted, moving under her coat again and feeling for one of her knives. Slipping it free from its sheath, she pulled it out and held it with half of her hand as she felt for the opening to the snag. Pulling back slightly, she kept her eye on the relative spot as she moved the knife in her hand, bringing the tip to the point of the rock. Slowly, she began to slide the knife down the rock, feeling the rough texture of the stone sliding against the edge of the blade. Her tongue played along the back of her teeth while she slowly worked to cut herself free.

The sharp sound of cloth tearing welled up, and she felt her balance shift. Instinctively, her right hand came up the wall, trying to grab onto her handhold, only to be rebuffed by her blade against stone.

She tumbled down, falling freely from the wall. There was only about twenty feet from the edge of the shelf to the bodies below, but the fall seemed to take minutes to her. Arms and feet flailed about, hoping desperately to find something to slow her descent.

All of the air was forced out of her when she impacted the bodies. Everything above her turned blurry for the moment, with a loud thrumming echoing in her ears. She blinked and the world came back into focus. Then she heard a voice above her, calling her name repeatedly. Her head rolled slightly, finding the source of the voice falling down with hushed urgency. Olav looked frantic above her. Taking a deep breath, she nodded and raised her arm up to show him that she was still alive. She breathed out as she came to realize that same fact.

And then she felt movement beneath her.

. . . .

His hands ran over the inside of the cabinet once more. Carefully trained fingers traced the grains of the wood, looking for anything that felt out of place. Occasionally he would pull back from the surface and let two fingers thump against it, listening for anything unusual.

"Something has to be here," Armas muttered to himself. "Clothes do not just appear from nothing."

The sound of his door clicking open caused him to lurch upright. His arm hit against the door slamming it into outer section of the armoire. He grabbed it immediately and then closed the door as quickly as possible.

He turned to the door, doing his best to compose himself. "I'm sorry, you startled me. I was just…."

There was no one there. His eyes narrowed and he shifted over to the side, staring over at the door. "Hello?"

A sound came from near the door. Low and primal, just barely above a growl. Slowly, she came into view. Crouched near the ground, moving on all fours. The look in her eyes was feral and raw, with something burning deeper beneath. She bared her teeth and a line of drool ran from her to the ground.

Armas leapt backwards, fumbling to find something to grasp. "Koarr preserve me!"

She was covered in silver and black fur, with pointed ears and a thrashing tail behind her. Armas swore that he was staring at a fox woman. A very angry fox woman.

end chapter four

CHAPTER
FIVE

THE CHATTEL

"Hello, how are you," Sebastian mumbled with a nod as he walked through the hallway. The staff was in full motion, working and striving to complete their daily tasks away and hidden from the owners of the keep.

Everything the staff did they kept hidden from the mistresses of the house. Both Oikea and Vasen insisted upon a house bordering on perfection, with nothing out of place and everything immaculate at every second. If there was something out of place or missing, it was noticed. Anything causing them a moment of consternation was taken out on not just the person the sisters thought responsible, but on everyone who might have overlooked it. So, to that end, the entire staff worked constantly and diligently to make a home that was beyond reproach.

To make that matter even more difficult, the mistresses of the house did not like to see any work being done. Seeing the staff moving about in small numbers was allowed, but to actually see them working was not permissible. That meant they had to work wherever they weren't, and do it as quickly and efficiently as possible so as to never be at a point where they couldn't move and be done at a moment's notice.

None of the staff's rules and fears applied to Sebastian. The staff never saw him as the husband of Vasen, but as one of them.

As a part of what kept the house running smoothly and calmly through any and everything. After all, the story was well known that he had been one of them not that long ago.

An expert on antiquities brought in to help and assist the sister's with their collection, Sebastian soon found himself more than slightly useful. Useful enough that Vasen claimed him as her own, and eventually married him. His current status elevated him above the others in the house, but he carried himself with his more humble beginnings.

So, every time he passed one of them they smiled warmly and said hello. Each and every member of the staff greeted him by name or waved if they couldn't speak. In response, he nodded and mumbled to them as he ambled to and fro, going about his own business.

His current business was taking him down to the lower levels of the keep. The lower he went, the fewer staff he encountered and the more his smile grew. His surroundings went from lush to sparse, to the point of no furniture or decoration at all. The walls slowly shifted from wood to stone, constructed to carved, as he worked his way down.

Eventually, he found himself at the door. Thick wood with heavy bands of iron, latched three times and guarded by two soldiers, fully dressed and alert. Immediately upon seeing him they saluted. He nodded and waved his right hand casually.

"Any activity?" he asked them, raising his voice above a mumble.

"None, sir," the first responded. "Another quiet day."

"Ah, I suppose that is to be expected," his voice went back down to a low murmur. He waved at the door, moving his fingers up and down. The same guard who spoke to him stepped over and unlatched each lock, starting from the bottom and working upwards, until the door pulled away from the sill slightly. The guard grasped the door and pulled, swinging it wide into the rough hewn stone hallway.

"Leave it open," Sebastian instructed. "I will only be a short while."

"Yes, sir," the guard answered.

Sebastian stepped through the door and onto the massive stone platform beyond. The two guards waiting on that side saluted as he passed, with him waving them off casually. Even before he reached the rail at the edge of the terrace the smell struck his nose. His head pulled up as his nostrils flared open to take it in.

A fusion of almost every conceivable odor mixed into a noxious fume that attacked him. Images of waste, worry, and fear filled his mind, causing him to close his eyes as he reached the railing awaiting him. His hands stretched out before him, finding the cold metal and guiding his body up to the precipice where he opened them and looked down below. Figures moved about, moving like huge ants obeying a hidden queen.

He took a deep breath, breathing in the smell once more and smiling wide as it overwhelmed him.

"Marvelous," he muttered to himself.

· · · · · · · ·

He backpedaled while reaching out around him to find something, anything that he might be able to use as a weapon. The figure on the other side of the room moved quickly, shifting along the ground, sliding effortlessly towards him, and he kept his eyes on her constantly, doing his best to keep her directly in view.

There was an overwhelming sense of inevitability as she moved. Despite her indirect journey towards him, he had a sense that she was going to be on him sooner than he realized. Time slowed to a crawl. He saw her move, all of her fur shifting over her body, lean muscle rippling as she slipped from light to shadow and back again. His hands touched everything within reach, desperately grasping for hope.

A shadow loomed above him at the same moment his hand closed around a something solid. With all of his might he swung the item, smashing it into the side of the beast, seeing a chair shatter against her body as she let out a sharp yelp. Briefly the fox woman skittered back and Armas used that second to regain himself, taking the broken leg from the chair firmly in hand.

By the time he put eyes on her again, she was already leaping for him. Again he swung the chair leg, only to have it snatched from his hand and thrown across the room in an instant. The momentum of the woman slammed him to the ground, with her pinning his arms above his head.

He pressed back, squirming and shifting below her weight. Looking up at her face, he saw her lips pulled back into a tight snarl, a small line of drool falling towards him. His lips closed tightly as the spittle fell against his lower lip and trailed down the side of his cheek. She lowered her face more, inching closer to him, and he closed one eye and turned his head to the side to avoid her.

"Don't…fight…" she growled. "Please."

His eyes fluttered as he turned back to look at her directly. "Did…did you speak?" he whispered.

For a moment he thought it was imagined. That his mind was tricking him the moment before his death. She dropped her head down next to his, and he heard her inhale deeply.

"So…sweet…." Her voice seemed rough, as though ripped over jagged rocks as it came out of her. Suddenly her head pulled up again, and she stared down. Her lip quivered and her tongue came out and licked across her teeth. "Don't fight. Please…don't."

"Are…are you going to kill me?" he asked softly.

She shook her head no and released his arms, pulling herself up until she was sitting on his stomach. He felt her tail swiping back and forth across his legs. Her hands fell onto his chest, and he felt claws dig into the cloth of his shirt. In a single swift motion, she tore it open. The look in her eyes terrified Armas, but he lost sight of them quickly as she moved her face to his chest and he felt a long, wet tongue drag across his skin.

He recoiled reflexively, and felt the claws that tore away his shirt dig slightly into his flesh. She looked up at him and growled, deep and primal, causing his blood to freeze and his body to lock up. She ripped the remaining bits of his shirt away and began to drag her tongue further down his body, shifting her position from his stomach to his legs.

"Wha-what are you doing?" he stammered.

No verbal answer came, but he felt the claws move to his pants and grip them tightly. A moment later they shredded away from his waist. Immediately, she pushed her nose into his groin and took a deep sniff.

"No. Oh, no. You've got to be—"

His words were replaced by a sudden gasp as teeth clamped down on the cloth covering his privates. A second later she pulled her muzzle back and took his underwear with her, leaving him completely exposed.

"Please don't." His voice was soft, but his words were urgent and desperate.

She hesitated. Their eyes met and he saw the conflict in her. Her chest rose and fell more and more rapidly as her breath came in shorter and shorter spaces. He watched her lip quiver more frequently and realized what was happened before it occurred.

It overwhelmed her and she fell down, pushing her muzzle against his flaccid sex. No time passed before he felt her tongue lunge out of her mouth and drag itself across the length of him. The second time her tongue went down further, beginning on his scrotum and sliding up and over him.

A mix of fear and confusion filled him. He swallowed, his arms spreading wide and fingers grasping at the floor in an attempt to keep himself from attempting to pull away again—especially with the large, pointed teeth well in view near his manhood.

The tongue lashing continued, lapping anxiously and covering him in a thick layer of saliva. He noticed that he was no longer breathing, holding his chest still in an effort to remain perfectly motionless. Slowly, he let his breath return while keeping an eye on the woman and her tongue playing over him. Fear gripped him with the thought of what might happen next.

There were two possibilities. Either he would become aroused and she would take things to the next level, with unknown potential for violence and pain—or he wouldn't. If he didn't become aroused, how angry would she become? What extreme would she take it to if she became frustrated or rejected? And he knew there was no arousal in him at this moment.

Which is why he was surprised when he saw his manhood twitch. A low growl worked up from her as she felt it move under her tongue, and that only increased his fear—and his confusion. There was no arousal in him. Nothing. The reality of what was happening created many emotions inside him, but none of them excited him sexually.

Despite his innermost feelings, he watched as his erection grew under her tongue. A small sound not unlike a purr came from her as she took her mouth and surrounded his shaft all the way down. He felt her tongue continue to swirl around him, drawing up and down in unison with her mouth.

A warmth welled up and spread from his groin to the rest of him, bringing a tingling sensation along with it. The arousal that wasn't there washed over him, bringing more confusion along with it.

His mind raced, trying to fight down a growing sensation of lust inside him. A feeling he had felt once before.

"Vasen," he muttered, feeling it grow stronger by the second. "Damn you. You did this—again."

He stared down at her and felt his passion grow. His hand slipped down, brushing against the fur on her head, causing her ears to twitch and her eyes to open and look back up at him. Out of the corner of his eye he saw her tail rise up and begin to slap down side to side against the floor beside him. His hand moved to the longer hair growing from her head and he wrapped his fingers in tightly, losing all sense of reason and succumbing to raw, carnal desires.

His fingers grew tighter, his muscles pressing down, urging her to not only continue, but to take more of him into her mouth—even though she already had taken him completely. Pushing down, he held her in place, grinding his pelvis upwards.

When she suddenly pulled up and away from him, he gasped in surprise. Shallow, rapid breaths matched her body as it lurched back and forth. His eyes fell onto her fur-covered breasts, spying a point pushing out on their apex. A thin line of spittle trailed down from her mouth, falling onto his thigh, as her lips pulled back into a snarl, exposing all of her fangs.

Rolling off of him, she fell flat onto her stomach. A second later she brought her knees up under her, raising her hips off of the ground. Her tail flicked to the side, exposing her sex to him, and he could see a glistening moisture in the light of the room. Turning back, she looked at him with expression that bordered somewhere between pleading and insistence.

The tension sparked between them, waiting for the inevitable. It only took a moment for him to shift around to his knees and move in behind her. Shifting her hips, she maneuvered herself, wanting to force him inside her, but he held himself away. Waiting. Building. Her tail flipped back and forth in front of his face, causing him to twist out of its way with every motion. The next flip back brought the tail into his waiting hand, and his fingers circled around it tightly.

A sharp yelp came from her as he pulled the tail up and out of the way, pulling her up off the floor for a brief second. Still gripping her tail, he positioned himself and thrust his hips forward, burying himself completely inside her.

It wasn't quite a hiss, nor was it a bark, but the sound that came from her filled the room. Their bodies slammed together, again and again, the pace increasing each time. With one hand still holding her tail, his other reached up and grabbed a fistful of hair, and then pulled both simultaneously.

Her mouth fell open, tongue lolling out to the side, as she was relentlessly pounded from behind. His face was a tightly contorted scream, like a flame caught in the midst of igniting.

And then it exploded. Both voices crested upon each other, and the two of them pressed together tightly, their energy merging and expelling out together. Spasms of pleasure wracked through them for several seconds, until their energy was gone and they collapsed motionless to the ground.

The room rested in silence, only broken by the periodic deep breath from the two inhabitants as they collected themselves.

"Wow," she said. "That was...intense."

Armas rose up looking over at the fox woman lying on her back, smiling up at the ceiling. A quick push of his arms backed him away from her. "You can talk. What are you?"

She let her head turn to the side. "I'm not a demon. Let's not even start that."

"What are you doing in here? Vasen sent you, didn't she? Why?" He backed away a slight bit further.

"That's a little more complicated." She sat up and shook her head, tossing her hair loose around her shoulders again. "I'm just hoping that Sigrid isn't pissed because of what just happened."

"Sigrid?!" He lunged towards her. "You know Sigrid?"

"Yeah, I do. She's really nice. We kinda—"

"Pet," the voice cut her words short, "heel."

A bright glow surrounded the woman's neck, revealing a circlet Armas had previously overlooked. All human expression dropped away from her, replaced by primal obedience as she jumped and ran over towards Vasen and Oikea, who stood just inside the door to the room. She ran between them and sat down. The moment she sat, her expression returned as she glanced up towards the two sisters.

She looked angry.

"Allow me to introduce you to Renarde," Vasen said to Armas, who slowly stood up covering himself with the remains of his clothes. "She's my new pet."

"What was that about?" Armas shouted. "Who is she?"

"Now, now, Armas darling," Oikea soothed. "There is no need to raise your voice."

"Depends on your point of view," Renarde growled.

"Who is she?" he repeated.

"I told you, she's my new pet. She's wonderfully obedient, don't you think?" Vasen explained.

"She's not a pet. She's…she's intelligent," he replied.

"If you say so," Oikea stated. "I just think she looks good here beside us. Don't you?"

Armas' eyes dropped down to Renarde, who looked back at him. He could see the fire burning inside her as she barely shook her head to him.

"Get out," he said. "Get out of this room, and leave me alone." He dropped down and picked up the chair leg and strode towards them. "I'm done with this. I'm not a toy, and I'm willing to bet that she's not a pet. If you come near me again, I will make you pay."

As he got closer, several guards stepped into the room, moving towards him, only to be stopped by a wave of Oikea's hand. She and her sister stood still as he walked towards them with a purpose.

"Don't do something you will regret, Armas," Vasen growled.

"Or make us do something we will regret," Oikea added.

"What would that be? Kill me? I don't think that you will. I still haven't fucked the two of you enough, it seems! Or fucked other people, or whatever the hell she is either, have I?" He gestured towards Renarde as he neared them. "So, what can you do? What are you going to do?"

The two sisters looked at each other and nodded. Oikea waved her hand forward once more, and the guards responded. Five of them rushed towards Armas. He swung wildly, trying to buffet them away from him. It worked for almost three seconds.

They closed on him and took away the chair leg, and then forced him to the ground, onto his stomach, pinning his arms and legs to the ground. All he could see were the feet of the two sisters as they walked up to his face.

"Take him to a cell," Vasen said. "Something very sparse. Don't hurt him permanently, but do make sure that he understands his situation."

"You are being very foolish, Armas. After some time in less accommodating quarters perhaps you will learn to appreciate what we can provide," Oikea explained. "We'll let you know if we need your services anytime soon."

The toe of Vasen's shoe worked its way under his chin and then pushed up, bringing his gaze in line with both sisters. "You belong to me. Never forget that. We would prefer your stay to be pleasant, but never, ever threaten us. This is a lesson. Learn it."

She pulled away her foot suddenly, and his head fell to the floor, chin first. He saw Renarde still sitting on the ground where they had called her, the corner of her lip pulled back into a snarl as she looked at the guards on top of him.

With the first blow that landed in the small of his back he shut his eyes tight, and saw nothing more of what happened. Through the sudden, continuous rain of fists that fell upon him he listened to the few words the sisters spoke as they walked away.

"Come along, Pet," Vasen said. "I'm going to place her in her cage and then meet up with you again."

"I'll see you in the Hall, darling," Oikea replied.

He could still hear them. Despite the beating he was receiving he could still hear them. He refused to let any sound come from his lips. He wanted to stay perfectly quiet and hear them.

And he hoped they heard his silence.

• • • • • • •

Everything beneath Sigrid shuddered. She felt the bed of bodies beneath her undulate as something below them moved, creating a ripple in the dead. Above her she saw the figure of Olav waving wildly, a dull echo trying desperately to sync up with his mouth to create words.

"What?" she asked weakly.

The ground moved again, jostling Sigrid's memory, clearing away a corner of cobweb. She turned her head to the side and saw a bulge forming amidst the dome of bodies.

"Don't move," a voice said from above.

The voice drew her head back, causing her to look up at Olav once more. He was pointing beyond her towards the bulge she had already seen.

"What?" she asked louder.

"It tracks by scent and motion. Don't move! Just stay still," he urged.

"Tracks by scent and motion?" She shook her head, and squinted as she rose up on her elbows. "What are you…?"

The memory of what just happened began to reappear in her mind. A fall and impact, and before that a message and vision of death.

The sound of cracking bones turned Sigrid back to the mound where a massive talon broke through the surface. Bodies fell away as the beast rose up from below. Everything in Sigrid's view shifted as the world seemed to fall away and bring the creature clearly into view. A massive form crawled up and out, coming clearly into the picture. The head was squarish, covered in a thick, rough, reddish-purple skin. A deep, wide slit indicated an overly large mouth at the bottom third of the face, shards of torn flesh hanging loosely from its lips. Centered over the mouth, practically at the top of the face lay two small, black dots for eyes. Beside them, leading down to nearly touch the mouth were a pair of long, narrow nostrils that flared wide with every breath. A huge foreleg lumbered forward, revealing a three toed foot, with gnarled five-inch claws digging into the flesh as it placed its foot down and dragged itself forward. The two small legs further back seemed vestigial and appeared incapable of supporting the monster's weight. The rear legs sat at around the mid-point of the creature's overall length, which narrowed to a pointed tail far behind. In a short transition behind the head, the hide shifted from the rough skin to a more brownish-black series of plates, almost armor-like, covering the rest of its near twenty foot length.

And it was heading towards her.

"Don't. Move." Olav's words fell down on her with weight. She swallowed hard, feeling her breath catch in her throat as she did.

The beast rose up, its nostrils opening completely as it drew in a deep breath. It twitched, its head bobbing slightly as it measured the air. With first its left, and then the right foreleg, the beast dragged itself across the floor of bodies with surprising speed, pulling closer to Sigrid.

"It's trying to scent you," he told her from above. "The oil you put on earlier should mask you, but it won't hide you completely. Stay still."

She shot a glance up at him, and then quickly back to the creature. A harsh smell hit her as it neared, burning her nostrils and making her wince in pain and shut her eyes tightly. Bile built in the back of Sigrid's throat, trying to force its way up and out of her. Clenching her jaw she fought the rising sickness back down, unwilling to let it betray her in any way. The burning sensation fell back down, and she swallowed to usher it on its way. Finally, she opened her eyes again.

The face of the creature was only inches away, filling her entire field of view. Nostril's flared open and hot breath hit her face, once more bringing the bile to action in her stomach. Every muscle in her body clenched tight, trying to keep her perfectly still—and making her tremble as a result.

The beast pushed forward, its blunt face impacting Sigrid and causing her to shift backwards. Bodies shifted below her, causing her grip to slip away from her and she fell flat, loosing a gasp of surprise as she hit. The creature followed, once again bringing its face close. Short, jagged breaths ripped from her lungs as panic started to bubble up in the core of her being.

"Relax! You have to stay calm!" Olav shouted from above. "Just for a second. Please!"

Its mouth opened, revealing dual rows of short, dagger-like teeth. A long, thick tongue slithered out, slipping downward. Faintly green slickness looking somewhere between slime and saliva hung loosely above Sigrid, threatening to fall on her face.

Something crashed behind the creature, causing it to spin around suddenly. The bulk of the beast crashed into her, sending her sprawling. All of her breath rushed out as she impacted the floor of bodies, and with it came an accompanying sound. Glancing over her shoulder, she saw the creature shuffling in the middle area of the pit. The weight of the situation measured in her head, and in less than a second she made a decision. She stood up and ran towards the wall.

"Hurry!" Olav shouted. "It's turning back!"

Even before he said anything she knew it. The ground beneath her trembled as the massive monster moved towards her. Without slowing, she unsheathed her sword. The fall and impact had left her roughly fifteen feet from the edge of the cliff, and the impact from the beast drove her another five or so feet away, leaving a short sprint to the cliff wall—and then a climb.

"It's gaining! Run faster!" he yelled down at her from above.

Speed wasn't the answer. If she was lucky, she might reach the wall ahead of it, but she wouldn't be able to get up the wall beyond its reach. She knew that something else was going to have to happen if she wanted to get out of there alive.

Her right foot hit the wall at full speed, and she used that force to help her turn and propel her back towards the pit—and the creature. Twisting around in air, she brought the sword up in front of her, leveling it beside her shoulder.

The sword impacted the creature's face, slightly piercing the thick, rough skin. It roared, unleashing a sound unlike anything Sigrid had ever heard, rattling her very bones. Her feet landed, digging into the frozen flesh filling the pit, and sliding backwards as the continuing momentum of the monster drove it forward. Her hands fell back to her shoulder as she leaned in harder, trying to drive the sword in deeper, but the hardened flesh was too tough.

She screamed back at it, feeling the wall hit the heel of her boot. Its tongue lashed out again, knocking the sword free from its face. The beast reared up, opening its mouth and preparing to strike. Its claws hung in the air and its nostrils flared wide, casting a chill into the frozen air. In return, Sigrid lunged forward and drove the point of her sword deep into the creature's right nostril.

The beast howled, throwing its head to the side and ripping the sword from both Sigrid's hand and its nostril, sending her weapon flying and her toppling down. It lurched backwards, its clawed front leg rubbing at the wound leaking a black ichor of blood. A sound between a cry and a squeal followed it as it jumped up and away, giving space to Sigrid.

"Now! Get out now!" Olav shouted.

Her head turned on a swivel, finding her target quickly. The ground shifted below her feet slightly, partially from her movement, and partially from the beast's tremendous bulk as it moved.

"What are you doing? Get out of there!" She ignored his words and snatched her sword from the ground as she ran past it and then quickly sheathed it. Turning at that point and racing to the wall, she used her momentum to leap up the wall, springing along it as high as she could until she found a slight handhold.

Her hands scrambled as quickly as her feet, pushing and pulling her way up the stone face. Above her, Olav extended his hand, reaching down towards her, the inches separating them feeling like hundreds of feet at that moment.

He wasn't shouting words at her. She knew what needed to happen and so did he. The stone beneath her fingers was scalable, but time was the key here, not possibility. Olav extended further, pushing himself to close the gap.

The squealing sounds behind her subsided, and her heart rose up in her throat. Throwing her left hand up she brushed against fingers. Her feet began to scuttle, trying to push her up just enough. She let her left arm swing down and then back up, shifting her weight and pushing off completely.

Palm wrapped around wrist and she brought her feet back to the stone, running up the wall as Olav leaned back, using both strength and mass to pull her upwards. The impact of the monster against the wall below resonated through both of them as they collapsed beside each other in the passage above the pit.

The sound of it scraping the walls was barely audible over their own heavy breathing.

"Wh-what is that thing?" she gasped out.

He sat up and looked down beyond the edge of the passage. It was already burrowing back down into the depths of the bodies. "That was an ahemait." He turned back to look at her as she propped up on her elbows. "That was a demon."

Shifting up to a full sitting position, her eyes narrowed. "What? You mean like a demon but not—"

"I mean demon," he stopped her. "An ahemait. A devourer of the dead. An eater of souls. An actual demon."

Sigrid shook her head. "That's not possible. How is that possible?"

"Because Oikea and Vasen brought it here." He looked her in the eye. "They're witches."

• • • • • • •

The door closed with a barely audible noise, not unlike the sound of a pillow falling to the floor. Jerking back, Oikea turned to the door, seeing her sister walk in alone.

"Sister, darling, welcome," she said, walking up to greet her. Vasen met her, grasping each other by the hands, and kissed each other on their exposed cheek. Oikea pulled back smiling. "No problems, I assume?"

"Of course not. As long as she wears the Collar of the Beast, she is under our control. We have nothing to fear," Vasen answered as she stepped forward past her sister.

"I do hope you are right, darling, because it would be ever-so-much a bother to have to reign her in again." Oikea moved to walk alongside her sister.

The golden glow of The Hall of Wonders tinted their outfits, giving the cloth a glow that seemed to radiate around both of them. "She's a beast, dear. The collar allows us total control over any beast."

"Total control?" Oikea glanced a smirk at her sister. "Then why didn't you bring her down here so we could test her on the cabinet?"

Vasen laughed. "As always, dear, you make an excellent point. Precaution always gets the better of me, doesn't it?"

"I wouldn't go that far," Oikea answered. "You are gifted with an abundance of boldness, darling."

They stopped before the cabinet. The deep, shimmer blackness slipping on the surface, drinking in light and reflecting nothing. Both of them stared at it for a moment. Oikea's lower lip was pulled between her teeth while she watched. Vasen licked along her upper lip. A noise, low and distant, seemed to resonate between the pair and the cabinet as they stared in silence.

"You were testing yourself again," Vasen said, breaking the quiet. They turned to look at each other. "I saw you pull away as I entered."

"Yes." Oikea nodded. "Yes, I was. I was hoping for a delayed response."

"Pregnancy is not a delayed response, dear. If Armas were ever successful in his attempts the results would appear almost instantly," Vasen said. "Neither of us is pregnant, Sister."

"Assuming that damn thing would register it," Oikea spat out. "And assuming that carrying Armas' child would be enough."

One of Vasen's eyebrows raised. "Are you questioning whether or not Sepi is correct about that?"

"Why shouldn't I? For all we know he isn't right about it testing for compatibility at all. He claims that those stones stated it was a test, but how can we be sure? All of that text is ancient and no one truly speaks it anymore," Oikea responded. "And where is he anyway? I thought he was supposed to be here working on these things."

"Oikea, dear, the reason we brought him here was because he could read Antediluvian writings. The stone was found with the cabinet and orb, and it was fairly clear in what it said," Vasen said calmly.

"Yes, yes, I know. That the orb would reveal who could open the cabinet, and that those people must be kept around because of evil inside it," Oikea said with a sigh. "We both know that, darling."

"You paraphrase, though. It said it would, and I quote, 'find those who control the cabinet and the evil that is kept within.' I believe in accuracy," Vasen said.

"Do you?" Oikea asked.

"Is something bothering you, Sister?" Vasen asked.

A wide, thin smile grew upon Oikea's face. She took a deep breath and spoke clearly and slowly, "We."

"I beg your pardon?" Vasen blinked.

"Earlier. Up in Armas' room. You were speaking to him, and you forgot to say 'we,'" Oikea said.

"You'll have to be a little more clear, dear. I said many—"

"Armas does not belong to you, darling. And Renarde is not your pet. They are both things that WE possess. You seemed to have forgotten that." Oikea's smile grew steadily wider as she spoke.

"I don't think that anyone in the keep would think anything different, dear. If I misspoke and said such a thing, it was just a slip of the tongue. Nothing else." Vasen let an equally wide smile develop on her face.

Facing each other, with the masked side of their faces towards the cabinet, the golden glow from the room faded halfway across their bodies, leaving their faces drenched in shadow.

"Well, I'm not worried about the rest of the keep, Sister. They know their place," Oikea said.

"Of course they do. Everyone in the keep understands that sort of thing. So we have nothing to worry about, do we?" Vasen's voice was even and soft.

"Naturally. It was just something I noticed and wanted to point out to you. Especially since you are so keen on being…accurate." A polite nod accompanied Oikea's words.

"Well, then let me thank you for noticing and bringing it to my attention, dear. I won't make that mistake again," Vasen said.

"I'm sure you won't." Oikea took a deep breath and let it out slowly. "I suppose we'll have to wait a while to see if she is imbrued with Armas' child."

"Yes, but if she is, then we will have a child of more than noble lineage to add to the family—if we still agree that Renarde is a child of the goddesses, that is," Vasen said, stepping away from the cabinet and towards the orb.

"Even if she isn't, we both have seen that she possesses an amazing inherent power. If we can breed that out successfully, and train those offspring from birth, then we will still become greater." Oikea's right hand balled into a fist as she spoke.

"And use that greatness to cast out the impostor queen and return true nobility to the throne of Dula Koarr. To put us on the throne, where we belong." Vasen's chest swelled out, filling with equal parts breath and pride.

The two sisters turned to look at each other once more, a warm smile spreading over their lips. A pair of steps later they embraced, holding each other tightly.

"Oh, Vasen, we are so close. We can accomplish such wonderful things," Oikea said.

Vasen pulled back to see her sister face-to-face, with only a half-foot separating them. "We will accomplish them, dear. We will accomplish them."

Breaking away with a spin, Vasen quickly stepped up to the orb and placed her right hand upon it. A hush hung over the room for a half-second, and then fell flat as nothing happened. She turned back to Oikea. "Like you said, it was worth checking."

A hearty laugh echoed from Oikea as she glanced around the room. "Sister, you still haven't answered my question: where is Sebastian?"

"I don't know," Vasen said. "I was just as surprised as you to be let in by a guard and not him. I imagine that he is off doing some research or some such. He does manage to keep himself busy."

"Yes, he does. Sometimes I wonder doing what, actually," Oikea replied.

"Don't worry about Sepi, dear. He's harmless. And we have Hjalmar watching over him right now, remember?" Vasen said, and then rested a finger on her chin. "Though, about Hjalmar…."

"Yes?" Oikea stepped towards her sister, tilting her head to one side. "What about him?"

"Our new pet might have damaged him," Vasen said. "We should check to make sure."

"A nip on the nose? Are you serious?" Oikea laughed. "He was built to withstand an army. One small bite from a fox—god-child or otherwise—is not going to hurt him."

"Probably not, but we don't know, and I'd rather be sure," Vasen said as she took her sister's hand in her own. "Renarde is a wild card in this equation."

With a gentle sigh and smile, Oikea gripped her sister's hand back. "Very well, I will check on him. Test him to see that he is fit. As you said, it's better to be certain. Why don't you go and find Sebastian? I would like to know what he is doing."

"Yes, I was planning on doing just that," Vasen said.

Vasen leaned in, and Oikea met her half way, bringing their cheeks up and beside one another. Each of them felt a light kiss brush against their skin for a moment before they pulled back away. Their eyes met bringing a smile to both of them simultaneously.

"Meet for dinner?" Vasen asked.

"Of course! I will see you in the dressing chamber." Oikea released her sister's hand and stepped back. "But now we have work to do. You go. I will have Hjalmar summoned to me here. It's best to look him over in private."

A shallow nod was Vasen's answer. With a graceful turn she made her way back towards the only door to the chamber, where she paused. A slight turn of her head brought her cheek fully into Oikea's view. "You do know how much I love you, Oikea, don't you?"

"I do," Oikea answered, "and I love you just as much."

A smile crept back onto Vasen's face. She turned back and opened the door. Two seconds later she was closing it behind her, leaving Oikea alone.

"Don't worry, darling, my love for you will never change." Oikea raised her hand up and spread her fingers wide, as though a flower coming into bloom. "It just seems that you have to learn a lesson regarding proper etiquette towards your betters."

A spark jumped from her fingers, arcing across her open palm.

•　•　•　•　•　•　•　•

"Vasen?" she spoke as she stepped inside, making sure her presence was announced.

"Not here." The voice was familiar, but not the one she was expecting.

Mathilda followed the sound of the voice further into the room. As she moved past the entry hall and into the middle of Vasen's private chambers she spied a large cage. Dull black metal bars crossed each other in a square pattern, lacing across the entirety of the five-foot cube. A large black lock kept the hinged door shut tight, sealing inside its sole occupant: a silver and black fox woman.

"Hi," Renarde said flatly.

With no reply, Mathilda continued her stroll, walking up to stand beside the cage. Renarde sat in the exact middle of the cage, legs crossed and resting her head on her right hand, elbow resting on right knee. Staring inside, Mathilda began to pace slowly around the cage. Renarde sat up and turned her head as she walked, following her around one way, and then snapping her head around the other way to catch her on the other side. Eventually, Mathilda arrived back where she started her circuitous path and stopped once more.

"What are you?" she asked levelly.

"I'm Renarde!" she answered cheerfully, and then twisted her head to the side, folding her ears back. "I thought we covered that back at lunch? You know, where you were rubbing your hand all over my arm?"

"Don't be snide with me, beast. There is no one here to protect you now." Her voice chilled slightly.

"Ooo-kaay. That turned snippy quickly." Renarde sat up straight, ears swiveling forward, and tail beginning to twitch behind her. "Well, then I won't be snipe—whatever those are."

"I admit that you fascinate me. There is an aura about you. Something…unusual. I will not let that cloud my mind, however. In fact, I should kill you right now," Mathilda said. "My sisters are too blind to themselves to see you for what you are."

She turned her head to the other side. "And what is it you think I am?"

"Trouble." Mathilda's hand open and closed repeatedly while she continued to focus her attention on Renarde.

"Well, I have been accused of that, too. At least I understand that one more than the whole demon thing. Do you know how annoying it is to be called a demon again and again and again?" Renarde asked.

The words appeared to impact Mathilda, causing her to step backwards. Her jaw fell open and her mouth went slack. "You. It was you."

"What was me?" Renarde leaned forward slightly.

"The demon. The one who scared my men. Who drew Hjalmar away and sent me back here. It was you," Mathilda said softly. "It was you!"

"Umm, maybe?" Renarde shrugged. "I'll have to know more about…wait, Jall-Mark? That's the guy with the metal nose, right?" Renarde asked.

"Metal nose? No. He's my sisters' bodyguard. They send him along sometimes to make sure that I'm keeping in line," Mathilda explained. Once more she started to pace around the cage, her eyes wandering over Renarde more fully. And again, Renarde sat there following with her head. "Why did you say that?"

"Because his nose is metal. I bit it. Trust me." As if to demonstrate her knowledge, her tongue pushed out of her mouth as her face scrunched up.

"You bit his nose," Mathilda stated from behind her.

"Yeah. When he caught me and brought me here," she answered, trying to get a good look at Mathilda.

"I see." Mathilda stopped cold directly behind her and paused, waiting for a reaction. Renarde simply continued to twist her head from one side to the other quickly.

"Why are you doing that? Just sitting there trying to watch me?" Mathilda asked.

A sudden huff of air preceded Renarde's words, which sounded closer to a growl. "Because your sister told me to sit here and stay."

"And you can't move?" Mathilda asked.

"I can move my head and my arms." She raised her arms up to demonstrate. "And my tail. Other than that…. Yeah, I'm very happy about this."

"They said the collar would control you, but…but I wasn't expecting anything this complete," Mathilda said, remaining behind Renarde.

"Yeah, me either," Renarde snarled. "And let me repeat that I am so very, very happy about it."

"You claim to be the child of Ilta, don't you?" Mathilda asked.

Renarde twisted her head around as far as possible to her right. "Didn't you just ask me what I was?"

"And I just asked again for clarification, but you have yet to answer," Mathilda snapped back.

"Well, I…." She spun her head around the other way, "I just was…." She spun back to the other spot. "I was just going to…. Dammit, would you come around in front of me so I can see you!"

Both of Mathilda's eyebrows went up "That's the most direct thing you've said since I got in here." She slowly walked around to the front of the cage. "Why don't we keep things that way."

"Fine. Just stay there so I can see who I'm talking to." She took a deep breath. "Okay, so yeah, I don't exactly call myself the child of Serenade, but…basically, I am. Sorta."

"You're back to being vague," Mathilda stated.

"Not really. You're no better, using the name Ilta when you mean Serenade, but I understand you," Renarde said, wagging her head slightly.

Mathilda laughed. "Ilta is her name. After all, why would she name herself after a song?"

"Oh! Okay, I see why you are confused," Renarde smiled. "You have that backwards. The song is named after Serenade. It's how her power works."

"By her singing?" Mathilda replied.

"Uh huh! It's how all of their power works. Serenade sings the night into being. It's really pretty, actually. Same with Aubade, Etude, and Threnody. Though I guess no one remembers hearing

Threnody sing." She glanced upwards in thought as she finished speaking.

Mathilda stood there in silence. Her lips smacked twice, and then she continued, "Back to the matter. You were the one in the woods. The one who scared my men when they found the woman who had been following us."

"Um, maybe. I can't really say for certain," Renarde answered.

"You can, and you will," Mathilda said. "The consequences for you are far more severe if you don't."

Renarde glanced around the cage, looking at the bars that surrounded her and then at the door with the large lock upon it, and then finally back up at Mathilda. "Um, how? I'm pretty bad off already."

"Do you really want to find out?" Mathilda let the words hang in the air.

"Hmm, good point." Renarde looked calmly at her. "Yes, that was me. Well, it was probably me, anyway. I can't be sure, but the description sounds right."

"And what were you doing there? Why did you even bother attacking my men?" she asked.

"Well, I didn't attack them. I more stopped them attacking. I never really fought them. They just kind of got scared and ran after that," Renarde explained.

"You stopped them from attacking, but not attacking you? So they were attacking someone else. Which means that you saved whoever that was. And it was probably that woman. Did you stay with her?" Mathilda asked.

"Define stayed," Renarde replied.

Mathilda turned to the side, peering out one of the large windows of Vasen's room that looked out over the city. "You did. And you ended up here, eventually, after coming into town with the woman. She was following me for some reason, and you joined her," she glanced over at Renarde, "but you didn't know who I was. So, I wasn't the reason you were following, was I?"

"Umm…." Renarde twisted her muzzle slightly.

"And if my men and I weren't the target, that means something else was. Something severe enough to cause her to be very driven." She walked towards the window slowly, the fingers of her right hand strumming against her thigh. Her head turned slowly, looking at the finery of the room. The high walls covered in thick tapestries. A fireplace with a burning hearth keeping the room warm. A bed three times the size needed for her sister to sleep luxuriously. And a large portrait of Vasen she kept hanging over her own bed. The room was a temple her sister kept to herself.

"This place," she mumbled. "That's why she stayed so far back. She was following us. Waiting for us to come back here." Mathilda spun on her heel and strode back to the cage. "Who brought you here and why? What is her plan?"

Recoiling slightly, Renarde laid her ears flat against her head. "I don't think there was an exact plan. In fact, I know there wasn't. It's okay though," her ears perked up and she smiled broadly, "I got inside."

"And that's what you wanted," Mathilda said slowly. "You meant to get caught. And if it wasn't for the collar, you'd have already done what you meant to do." Her eyes grew larger. "Armas. This is about Armas. I heard how he spoke about his wife, and she has that same passion. She's come to free him."

"I didn't say that," Renarde said.

"You didn't have to." She turned and began walking briskly towards the door.

"Where are you going?" Renarde shouted.

"To speak with Armas!" she answered.

"Wait! What about me? What am I supposed to do?" Renarde asked quickly.

"I don't care what you do!" The door shut just behind Mathilda's words, leaving Renarde alone in the room again as a bright glow surrounded the collar on her neck.

A twitch started in her tail, and quickly turned into a thrashing wave. The smile returned to Renarde's face, curling up the edge of her lips until they almost touched her ears. "I'm really glad to hear you say that."

She got up from her sitting position, reached out of the cage, and began fiddling with the lock.

• • • • • • •

"I'm still having problems with this," Sigrid said.

The passage was narrow, but more than high enough to accommodate even the tallest person. Parts of the walls appeared to be natural, but the majority of it was clearly carved, with a set of stairs winding upwards into the mountain.

"Think back," Olav said. "Surely your mother told you tales of the Ranee when you were a child. Of the original Ranee and the founding of Dula Koarr."

"Of course she did. Every little girl hears that story, but that's all that it is, a story to amuse children," Sigrid said.

"Well, amuse me, then. What do you remember of the story?" Olav glanced back at her as they continued up the stairs. "No details, just the basics."

Shaking her head and sighing, Sigrid thought for a moment.

A few seconds later she began her story. "Back before there was a Dula Koarr as we know it, just after the time of the Antediluvians, there was a lot of war. Men and women fighting each other over the best land in all of Elan. Then Koarr appeared to a group of women who would become the first Ranee, and told them that they needed to form their own country, where they would rule. The problem being that the only place they could do that was the far north, a land so harsh that no one wanted it. So, in order for them to be able to survive, Koarr promised to protect them and give them the ability to survive in the coldest winter. They went north and spread out over a large area, each of the original Ranee taking a piece of the country to populate, which became the Hundreds that we know today." She took another deep breath. "There, happy?"

"And?" Olav asked.

"And what? That's the story. Koarr sent the original Ranee north, they formed Dula Koarr, and now we have all the Ranee ruling over their own Hundred. It's just a story to tell girls how the country was created," Sigrid said.

Their voices echoed very briefly against the cold stone walls as they continued to walk, the only light to guide them coming from a small torch in Olav's hand.

"How did the Ranee survive? What did they do?" His tone was sharp and prodding.

"I don't know! I told you the story. What does it have to do with the Valpuri's being witches?" she barked back.

"Because the original Ranee were all witches! That's why some people still revere them so highly, so unnaturally. In some places the story of the Ranee being witches is still very strong and very real," he explained.

"Wait. Are you telling me that the people of Mirceby believe that the sisters are witches because of an old story, and that's how they are able to rule so firmly?" Sigrid hurried slightly, getting closer to Olav and his light.

"No, not at all. What I'm telling you is that they KNOW they are witches." He turned to look at her again. "And it's not just a story. Koarr gifted the original Ranee with the power and ability to survive in this harsh place, and it was because of them that the war never reached us. We are safe because the Ranee had power, and they used it to make Dula Koarr safe."

Sigrid walked in silence, letting her thoughts catch up with her. "So all of the Ranee are witches?"

"No. Not all of them. Some, but it's rare. Neither Vasen and Oikea's mother nor grandmother had the gift." He took a deep breath. "But they do. Both of them. I've seen it."

"Seen…seen what exactly? What are we talking about here?" she stammered.

The flickering light began to play tricks on Sigrid's eyes. Suddenly every shadow revealed images of faces, staring out at her, watching her as she walked up the stone stairs.

"I'm…not sure. They can do amazing things—dangerous things—but they can't do everything. They can't directly control others or read minds, for example." He sighed. "Not that they haven't tried."

"But that thing back there," Sigrid pointed behind her, "you said they summoned up that monster?"

"Yes, they did. I didn't see it happen, but Oikea told me they did and I believe her," he answered.

Thoughts raced through Sigrid's mind. "What have you seen them do?"

There was a prolonged silence. "Change items. Transform them from one thing to another. Nothing alive—not successfully, anyway. Everything I've ever seen them do to anything alive resulted in death. Very painful death."

"How many times did you see that?" she whispered.

"Too many."

"Is...is that why you left?" she asked.

He laughed. "No. Oh no. I didn't leave. I was told to leave. I was far too frightened to leave on my own. Oikea got mad at me and.... Well, I suppose she still had something in her that cared enough for me to just send me away."

"Why?"

"That is a totally different matter. She brought me to her because I was a doctor and I was supposed to cure her. Things just didn't work out," he said.

"What was wrong with her?" Sigrid's voice returned to her normal tone.

"The same thing that is still wrong with her: she's infertile. She and her sister both." He glanced back at her again. "I was supposed to make them whole. They are convinced that the problem doesn't sit with them, but with something around them. They blamed everyone in the world but themselves. When I couldn't cure her, Oikea became angry and eventually sent me to the city, and I believe you know the rest."

"Earlier you said you left because of what happened with the Harvest," Sigrid stated. "Which is it?"

"Both. I wanted to leave because of the Harvest. She sent me away because of her own issues. I'm guessing me confronting her about the Harvest had something to do with her anger towards me," he answered.

Sigrid looked at the dancing light on the wall, trying not to see the faces in the shadows staring back at her. Turning her head down took them out of view for the time being.

"What have I gotten myself—what have I gotten Armas—into?" she muttered.

"So, you believe me?" he asked.

Her chest swelled and emptied with a heavy sigh. "If you had told me all of this not that long ago, I would have laughed at you and called you crazy. A lot has changed in my life recently, though. I met a fox woman who is supposedly a child of the goddesses and fought against a monster that I'm told is a demon." She looked back up, finding him looking back at her. "So, sadly yes, I do believe you."

"Good," his voice was deep and troubled, "because it's about to get worse."

A heartbeat passed. "You're joking, right?"

"I'm afraid not." He stopped on the stairs, stepping to the side to reveal a light at the end of their path.

"The end of the stairs? That's worse?" Sigrid asked.

"At the top of these stairs there is likely to be a guard, perhaps two," Olav continued. "Our sole advantage is that they will not be expecting anyone approaching from this side. They can't be allowed to raise any alarm."

"How likely is that?" she asked.

He took a deep breath and pulled his lips tight against his teeth. "If they aren't taken out quickly, it's very likely. I brought a vial filled with chloroform, intending to break it and knock them out, but I had to use it on the demon back there."

"Wait, that breaking sound was you?" Sigrid's eyes lit up.

"Yes, and I think it slowed the beast down when you fought it. I'm just glad it worked," he said. "In any case, we're going to have to figure out a way to stop them quickly."

"How will they raise an alarm?" Her voice dropped down an octave.

"There's a flag tethered little more than an arm's reach away from them. If they throw the holding lever, a weight sends it up high enough to alert the watch above. That's all it takes," he explained.

"Where's the flag?"

"To the right. The guard will likely be standing beside it, and probably looking out towards the rest of the chamber," he said.

"Chamber? What chamber?" Sigrid asked as she wrapped her fingers around the grip of her sword once more.

"That's where we're going. What I want to show you. I don't know the status of it, but there is a chamber beyond this stairwell. Not a single open one, but a…a honeycomb chamber. It's difficult to explain." He shook his head.

"Okay. Fine. I'll deal with that when I have to. First, we have to eliminate the guard before he can signal anyone," she stated.

"Yes, and hopefully he's alone," he said, glancing up the stairs.

"How often would he not be?" Sigrid asked as she moved past him.

"There's no regularity. At least none that I know of, but there is a chance. If there is a second guard, he'll either be right beside him or a few feet away towards the wall on the left." Olav gestured with his hands, indicating vague directions as he spoke.

"Well, the one nearest the flag has to be taken care of first." She swallowed hard. "So, I'll do that. I can do that."

"What's wrong?" he asked. "You sound uncertain."

"I'm not. I'm just…." She took a deep breath and looked back at him. "I've never killed anyone before, and I think that's about to change."

"Are you all right?" With delicate ease he placed his hand on her back.

She snorted a sharp laugh. "No. No, I haven't been all right for months now. My entire world has been ripped apart and I'm fighting to bring it back together, and all I have for help is you and a…whatever the hell Renarde is, assuming she's still somewhere and able to help."

One step further up on the stairs allowed him to move his hand up to her shoulder. "We don't know what's going to happen. You might not have to kill him."

"I hope not, but honestly that's not the thing that's bothering me." She took another step forward, pulling his hand off her shoulder, and spoke to him without looking back. "It's the fact that I'm so easily willing to do it."

Olav watched her walk up the stairs. Eventually, his mouth turned down slightly and he started after her. The rest of the ascent was spent in silence. When they were only a few steps shy of the top, Sigrid turned to him and placed a single finger in front of her lips, signaling for him to stay quiet.

Silently slipping her sword from its sheath, Sigrid slinked steadily upwards. With her eyes darting rapidly from side to side she made her way up one step at a time, looking for anyone or anything unusual. Her head crested above the level of the final stair, revealing what lay beyond.

Odd shapes towering up in a vast cavern were overrun by innumerable strands of black rock forming an intricate latticework, appearing almost like the workings of a spider who spun its web in stone. For a second she was lost in the oddity of it, until she heard a faint sound off to the right of the opening.

Her hand loosened and re-gripped around her sword. With great care she stepped up, keeping to the far right of the stairs to stay hidden from whomever awaited beyond the stairs. The pounding of her heart grew louder and louder in her ears as she reached the last step, and then in a single bound she jumped into the area beyond the staircase.

The guard waiting there spun around at once. His hands fumbled for his sword, slipping over the sheathe and handle once and then pulling back to get a solid grip on it. Sigrid didn't wait for him to pull it.

A full sprint run to him ended with her knee rising up and impacting his midsection. As he doubled over she brought the pommel of her sword down on the back of his neck, driving him to the ground. He landed and remained motionless.

She stared down at him, waiting for him to move at all. To do anything. The only thing that snapped her back to the moment was hearing how hard she was breathing. Turning her head around quickly, she moved back to the top of the stairs and motioned Olav up.

"Hurry. I knocked him out," she said in rushed words. "Where do we go now?"

Olav reached the top of the stairs and glanced over at the man and then back to Sigrid. "Are you all right?"

"I think so." She nodded. "Yeah, I'm okay."

"Good," he answered as he stepped up beside her. "I suppose that—"

"Adar, what's all the noise…." The guard's voice trailed off as he saw his unconscious friend. Sigrid and Olav stood and stared blankly.

In a flash his sword was in his hand, and he was lunging towards Sigrid. The two weapons met creating a sharp metallic sound that echoed from the nearby walls. Slipping away, Sigrid shifted around, trying to maneuver behind him. In turn, he pressed back, turning his sword up and grasping the blade, driving it towards her.

Sigrid stumbled backwards, unbalanced by his attack, and toppled to the ground. Pressing his advantage, the guard swung down at her, narrowly missing as she rolled to one side. His foot moved, kicking her in the side as she came to a stop, but not hard enough to drive the air from her.

Swinging her arm in a wide arc Sigrid drove the edge of her blade into the side of his knee. Screaming in pain he fell, dropping his sword as he grabbed for the wound. Without hesitation, Sigrid rose up and twisted her body, driving the sword point down and into his body. With a second lunge she moved it to the side, shifting the point inside him.

He twitched once and then became motionless.

Once more she heard the laboring of her own breath. The expression on her face went blank as she slowly rose up, pushing herself into a standing position using the sword still inside him. She stared down, watching the blood slowly begin to slide free from his wound.

"Sigrid," Olav's voice startled her, causing her to flinch briefly. "Let me in. I need to stop the bleeding."

"Why? He's dead," she droned.

"I know, but we're going to have to hide the body, and we'll need to remove as much blood as we can," he explained.

She nodded and pulled up on her sword. It took three tugs before it came free. Gently, Olav moved her aside and pulled a vial from his bag. A degree of fascination gripped her as he sprinkled a fine silvery powder over the wounds, and then pulled back slightly. After that he pulled another bottle, a clear liquid, uncorked it and poured a small amount onto the powder.

In a brilliant flash of light the powder ignited, causing Sigrid to shield her eyes with her hand. When she pulled it away, all the wounds were closed and a deep black. A moment later the smell hit her nose.

"Oh goddess! What did you do?" she gasped.

"Burned the wounds closed. Those chemicals—" He turned to look towards her, and his eyes became saucers. He pointed behind her. "Sigrid!"

Following his finger, she spun around just in time to see the first guard—the one she had knocked unconscious—grabbing the latch to the signal flag and setting it free. Her eyes traced the path up as time slowed down for her. To her, it almost felt as though she stepped outside her body to witness the events. Her body twisted, her arm extended, and the tip of her sword drove itself through the man's neck. Before he had the chance to slump down to the ground she pulled the sword free and slashed through the rope trailing up after the flag.

"No!" Olav screamed and leaped forward, though far too late to grab the rapidly retreating flag.

"Are they going to see it? Did I stop it?" Sigrid asked.

"No. Cutting the rope just means that we won't be able to reset it," he explained. "We've got to get out of here. Hide the bodies and try to move up there before the investigating troop arrives. They'll put the platform on lockdown."

"I…I don't know what that means," she said.

"It means that we have to buy time. They're going to come down here. They're going to find out someone got inside. We're just hoping to delay it," he said. "Grab his body. I'll grab that one. Follow me."

She sheathed her sword and turned to look at the guard she had just killed. A line of blood trailed down his body. "Are you going to stop his bleeding?"

"Dammit!" He ran over to the body, poured out both chemicals and in another flash seared tight the flesh. His neck was charred and the smell once again assaulted her nose. Olav moved past her and began to drag off one body, and she quickly followed.

"Over here." He moved to a small alcove, only a few dozen feet away. "We'll drag them in here."

It was barely three feet high, causing Olav to crouch down and drag the body more awkwardly than before, but he was able to work it inside. She glanced into the tiny passage, trying to see anything. The light that pervaded the chamber—she still wasn't sure from where—quickly disappeared inside that small space. Nonetheless, she crouched down and began to shift her weight back and forth, dragging the body behind her.

Light erupted from the end of the passage, and she turned to see Olav huddled down, the body he was dragging now behind him as he held up a burning match.

"What are you doing?" she asked.

"We're not the first ones here," he muttered.

"What?" She let go of the body and worked her way down the passage to get closer to him. "What is it?"

He stepped aside, revealing another body. Smaller than the two guards, this one seemed much older and more frail. His flesh was pulled tight and the early signs of decay had set in around the corners of his mouth and eyes.

"Oh," she mumbled.

"He's been here for a couple of months it looks like. I know him," Olav said. "I just don't know what he did to get down here. Why they would put him here."

"Who put him here? Who is he?"

He turned to look at her.

"That's Vasen's husband. His name is Sebastian."

• • • • • • •

The door opened on its own and he stepped through quietly.

"My pardon, Sebastian," Oikea said, "but as you can see, I'm rather busy at the moment."

Blue light tinged the golden walls and ceiling, tinting everything near her that same color and casting a green light in the more distant reaches. Hjalmar sat still in a large, sturdy chair, with Oikea standing directly behind him. Both of her hands were beside Hjalmar's head, palms towards him, as arcs of blue light passed from her and into him. The light flashed back and forth behind Hjalmar's eyes.

"No worries, Oikea." He walked slowly towards them with his head swaying back and forth slightly with each step. "Has something happened to Hjalmar?"

"Simply a precaution. Vasen was concerned there might be something wrong with him," she explained.

"Is there?" He stepped in front of them, staring into Hjalmar's eyes.

"Of course not. His construction is amazing. He's been flawless since the day we found him," she said. "And he will remain so forever, I believe."

"He was the first wonder you discovered, was he not?" he asked.

"Yes. He was standing guard over the old keep—or at least he had been. He was inactive when we found him. Our magic reanimated him and bound him to us." She looked over Hjalmar's head at Sebastian. "But you know all of this already, so why ask?"

He laughed. "I'm an old man, Oikea. Sometimes I question my memory. It's always good to have some things reinforced."

The arcing energy coming from Oikea's hands stopped and she took a large step backwards. She stood there, staring forward, more or less looking at Hjalmar, though her focus was unclear. Gradually she moved around him, coming towards the front to stand beside Sebastian.

"He's a wonder, still," Oikea said. "An artificial being, animated from metal and meant to follow instructions perfectly." She looked over at Sebastian. "It's important to have servants who follow instructions, don't you think?"

Sebastian smiled at her. "I went to oversee the progress at the old keep, Oikea. I do that every day. You know that. Vasen said you were upset that I wasn't here earlier."

Oikea kept her eyes on Hjalmar. Her voice was cool and even. "I still am, actually. Performing your job is exactly what you should be doing, and that includes making sure things are progressing at the old keep." She finally turned to look at him. "What I don't like is how you always seem to be just away or just arriving all the time. Don't think I haven't noticed. It's a recent thing, only a couple of months old now, but I've noticed."

"Really? I'm…I'm sorry. I would never do anything to upset you or Vasen." His voice broke slightly. "I…I don't know what to tell you. I'm sorry."

"I'm not Vasen. She has a blind spot for you and will overlook a great deal," Oikea continued. "I won't. So let me suggest that you stop whatever it is that you are up to. It's not a good idea to challenge me to become your enemy."

"I'm aware of that," Sebastian swallowed. "Again, I'm sorry."

With a slight flourish she turned and began to walk towards the door. "He should be back active in a couple of minutes. Make sure he's all right and then send him back out to his quarters. I want him available if needed."

He nodded at her, despite seeing only her back as she walked. "Of course, Oikea. I'll get it taken care of."

Reaching the door, Oikea stopped and turned back to look at him. A chilling smile grew on her lips. "Oh, and Sebastian, if you think I would be a problem, let me assure you if Vasen found out you were betraying her in any way, you would dream of having me as an enemy."

All he could do in response was nod.

"I'll see you at dinner in a bit, then." Oikea's tone shifted to light and pleasant as quickly as a candle flame is snuffed. She turned and exited the room without waiting for a response.

The moment the door sealed shut his back straightened and his eyes narrowed. Quickly turning, he looked directly at Hjalmar. His fingers snapped sharply just before he spoke. "Wake!"

Hjalmar's eyes blinked once, and then looked around with the sentience they normally possessed.

"What happened? Did she do anything to you? Has she altered your status at all?" he asked.

"No, Master. Nothing has changed," Hjalmar answered.

Sebastian's shoulders visibly relaxed. "Good. What happened to cause her to work on you?"

"That fox creature bit me and exposed the shell beneath my skin. It seemed there was concern that my strength was fading," he explained.

"Of course. The damned spawn of Serenade," he growled. "Between her and Oikea's suspicions I'm running out of time."

He motioned with his hand for Hjalmar to stand, and he obeyed. Together they walked across the room to the massive cabinet, darkness dancing over its surface. Pausing in front of it, Sebastian brought his hand up to his jaw, stroking along to the point of his chin.

The flesh on Sebastian's arm darkened. Thin lines of black appeared on his skin, twisting and moving towards his fingertips. All of his hand began to fill with a darkness that moved and shifted just under the surface.

As he stretched it out towards the cabinet, the shadows of the wood reciprocated. They moved and gathered, almost swarming in a rush around a single point. As his hand touched the surface, a shadow of a glow appeared, surrounding the point where the two met, obscuring them slightly.

"Soon, my brothers. Very soon."

He pulled his hand back and looked at Hjalmar.

"The waiting game is over." He smiled. "Let's go pay Armas a visit, shall we?"

end chapter five

CHAPTER
SIX

THE CABINET

There are no mirrors in Valpuri Keep. At one time there were many—some on walls, some free-standing, and several hand-held mirrors owned by individuals—but in the current day none were allowed on the premises. Everyone was told about it the moment they set foot there, and there was no forgiveness for breaking that rule. To bring a mirror into the keep was to beg to be banished from there forever, assuming you were allowed to leave at all.

With that lack of self-awareness, other means of grooming became a necessity.

The room had been re-designated and redesigned years ago. After entering into an antechamber through either one of the small doors to the side or the larger one that emptied into the hall, the only way to continue led anyone into the main part of the chamber. On either side of the large room was a massive wall of clothing. Forty feet of cloth, all of it carefully arranged in a precise order. At first glance, it appeared that the two walls were identical, until the subtle difference became obvious. Either side was a mirror view of the other.

In the middle of the room, carefully centered, stood a beautifully crafted dressing table—or perhaps it could be called a pair of tables. Two identical sides that met in the middle, with exactly the same items positioned directly across from each other on top. It appeared as if a large mirror rested in the precise middle of the desk creating two identical images, but there was none.

At this moment, on either side of the desk, sat one of the Valpuri twins. Neither of them wearing a mask.

Each of them held a small cup filled with lip blush in one hand and a brush in the other—the hands they used created a perfect mirror of the one across from them. As one they dipped the brush into the red color and pulled it out. Slowly, they dragged the brush over their lips, tinting them one shade closer to blood. They pursed their lips in perfect unison, followed by a nigh-identical smile.

A smile that quickly faded as their eyes traveled to focus on one particular side of their face. With delicate care they both reached up and brushed their fingers across the rough texture of their scarred flesh. The crags and projections creating the scars felt cold to their fingers—and the cheeks felt nothing of the touch. Gradually their expression turned as cold as the feeling on their flesh.

Both of them slowly let their hands move to the top of their desk. The leather mask was waiting for them, and they retrieved it by rote and brought it up to their face, slowly positioning it in place. With practiced precision they tied the mask in place and brought their hands back around in from of them, resting on the desk. The smile returned to their faces as they stood up.

"As always, thank you," Vasen said.

"And you as well," Oikea replied.

The two of them walked around the desk and came together. After a quick hug they pulled back and kissed each other on their exposed cheek. They stared at each other for a long moment.

"You should gather our pet from your room," Oikea said. "I want her to be with us at dinner."

"Of course. She's still in training. The more time with her, the better. It will help her learn her place," Vasen stated.

"Yes, and that can be a difficult lesson to learn sometimes." Oikea smiled broadly.

"What about Armas?" Vasen asked cooly. "Should we bring him up to dine as well? Or does he deserve at least one meal in his current living quarters?"

"Oh, one meal at least. To teach a lesson, there must be consequences," Oikea said. "A reward cannot be given too soon."

"True. And we wouldn't want him to become overconfident, either. It would be wrong to allow him to have the illusion of control over the situation," Vasen said with a nod.

Oikea took a short, sharp breath. "Well, why don't you go fetch our pet. I'll wait here for you and we can parade her down together."

"You don't want me to just meet you?" Vasen asked. "I'll be happy to bring her in on my own."

"Oh no. I think we need to do this together, darling," Oikea's voice dripped from her.

"Well, then we should probably fetch her together as well. That way we can just leave from my private chamber," Vasen said.

"Fair enough." Oikea turned and walked towards the exit from the dressing room. Vasen followed immediately and moved beside her. "Though I was thinking that we should move Renarde out of your room. I don't want her causing you any undo trouble."

"Really?" They turned together in the antechamber to head towards Vasen's chamber to the left of the room. "Where did you have in mind? Your room wouldn't do, of course, as that would just move the problem instead of solving it." She turned and smiled at her sister. "I wouldn't want her to bother you, either."

"Why not put her where I first had her? Up in our parents old room? We can turn it into a…a kennel of sorts," Oikea laughed.

"I suppose that is a good compromise." Vasen looked forward once more. "Though you still should have informed me she had been captured, instead of me simply discovering her there with you."

Oikea raised an eyebrow. "Are you still going on about that? You shouldn't concern yourself over such things, darling."

"Well, I promise you that I—" Her words stopped cold as they entered her private chamber.

Across from the door sat a large cage with latticework bars. Dull black metal measuring about five feet on each side. The door on it was open, and the cage was empty.

Vasen turned suddenly to her sister. "What did you do?"

Recoiling, Oikea's expression soured. "Me? What are you talking about? You were the one who put her in the cage. Though apparently not very well."

The left side of Vasen's lip curled up. "I'm very, very good at what I do, dear Sister. She was locked and secure in the middle of that cage, with no way to move," she leaned in, "unless someone released her. And since you are the only other person who could have done that…."

"Interesting speculation," Oikea hissed. "Why don't I give you one of my own? You put her here, and in your normal level of proficiency you forgot to order her in place, and she found a way to escape her rather pathetic cell."

"How dare you!" Vasen's left hand raised up, forming into a claw-like grip. Sparks arced between her fingers. "If I hadn't stepped in you would have either killed her outright or wasted whatever potential she might have. And if you think my cell is so sad, then you won't mind spending some time in it!"

Oikea took a step backwards. The knuckles on her right hand tinged white as she formed a fist. "Did you just threaten me, darling? I don't believe that would be a wise course of action."

"Dear, dear Sister, I did not threaten you at all," Vasen growled. "I was simply saying that if you ordered Renarde free, then you must have been opening up the cage for yourself."

"I did nothing of the sort! This is so typical! Blaming others for your own incompetence," Oikea shouted.

"Don't lie to me, Oikea! I ordered her to stay in that cage, so she had no option to do otherwise! You know as well as I do that the collar is bound to our blood, so you are the only other person who could have given her a command!" Vasen's arms pulled back as her chest thrust forward.

"I do know that! And I also know that I didn't do anything! So, if it wasn't me, it had to be you!" Oikea's fist moved up in front of her, glowing an odd shade of blue.

"Well, that's very interesting, dear, because I know it wasn't me. And if it wasn't me, and it wasn't you that means—"

Both of them stopped. They turned together to look at the cage, and then slowly back to each other.

"Mathilda," they said as one.

"Why would she free her?" Oikea asked.

"I don't know. We should ask her," Vasen stated.

They stared at each other blankly as their hands relaxed back down to their sides. Slowly, they stood upright, relaxing their shoulders. A cold smile fell onto both of their lips.

"We need to alert the guards that Renarde is free," Oikea said. "I'll go and inform Hjalmar. Set him on her trail. Sebastian should have returned him to his chambers by now."

"Excellent. I'll try to find Mathilda. Perhaps she is unaware of what happened. She is rather oblivious, after all," Vasen said.

Oikea took a step towards her sister, which Vasen replicated, until they stood directly in front of each other. They leaned in and kissed each other on their bare cheek.

"We should go," Oikea said as they pulled back. "The longer we wait the more dangerous this could become."

"Agreed." Vasen walked into her room and turned towards the main exit. Oikea followed, and soon they were in the main hallway. Without a word, Oikea moved down the hall towards Hjalmar's room.

"Oikea," Vasen called out, causing her sister to turn. "We should discuss things later. Clear the air."

"Of course, darling. I would never want to leave anything unresolved." She smiled. "I love you far too much."

"And I you, dear. Good luck."

Turning away from each other, they both headed towards their separate destinations.

• • • • • • •

It was never the look of the cells that bothered her. She knew what they looked like. More than a few times she had put people into them herself, and had been responsible for attending to even more prisoners than she directly caged. The size and shape of the cells was consistent—a six by eight cage with no windows, just the view of the one next to it through the bars. Not pleasant by any terms, but these were not supposed to be pleasant accommodations.

The smell of the place, however, still almost made her gag. Despite the fact that there was currently only one occupied cell, and it that guest had been there for less than a full day, the horrid reek was still as strong as ever.

Mathilda shook her head as she marched forward, amazed that her sisters never even bothered to try and clean it completely. The fact that they had placed Armas in a cell so far back in the room also confounded her. What was the point?

When she turned the corner and saw him, she almost stopped. He was lying on the floor, naked, his body bruised and battered, with only a single blanket lying beside him and a small pail of water. Hearing her footsteps, he looked up at her. One of his eyes was swollen shut, but he was still able to scowl at her.

"Come to finish me?" he muttered roughly.

"No." Mathilda walked up to his cell and stopped. She tugged on her gloves, pulling them tighter to her hands. "I want to ask you about Sigrid."

His face changed, filling with a new light. "Why?"

"How determined a woman is she? To what lengths is she willing to go?" she asked.

He turned himself, sitting up on the cold stone floor. Grabbing blindly, he finally found the blanket and pulled it over himself, wrapping it around him. "You sound…concerned."

"Answer the question," she stated coldly, shifting in place.

"I already told you about how we met. How she took me in.
Do you really think she would do that if she was even slightly
worried about her own self?" He smiled, and winced in pain
through it.

"Enough to come after you, then. Come after you here," Mathilda
stated.

He sat up straighter. "What do you know? What's happened?"

"Do you know that fox creature? Renarde? Had you met her
before?" she asked.

"No. Never," he said with a shake of his head.

"She knows your wife." Mathilda shifted to her left, trying to get a
better look through the bars.

He stared up at her, waiting patiently.

"You already know that, don't you?" she asked. "She told you.
What else did she say?"

He shook his head. "I don't know what you're talking about."

Grabbing onto the bars, Mathilda used them to help lower herself
down to a crouched position, putting her on the same level with
Armas.

"Tell me what you know, Armas," she ordered.

He laughed. "What I know? I know that your sisters are monsters.
I know that they have some strange desire for me that they refuse
to explain. And that I only want to see Sigrid one more time
before they finally decide to just get rid of me for good."

She nodded. "What will she do, Armas? How will she try to get in
here?"

"How the hell should I know? I don't know how to get in here.

Everyplace that I've been in this keep I've been guided and
secured. The only part of it I really know is my—heh, my—
bedroom."

"Dammit, Armas, answer me!" She slammed her hand down on
the bar, jolting a sharp sound through the room. "I need to know
what she's going to do!"

He glared at her. "I do, too. I want to talk to Renarde. If I do,
maybe we can both find something out."

"I don't think so," she answered.

They stared at each other, neither moving for the longest
moment. Finally, Armas lowered his head. When it came back up
his expression was drastically altered.

"Mathilda," he said softly, "please let me go. I just want to go
home to my wife. Surely you understand."

"I do." She shook her head. "I'm sorry, but no. I may not approve
of what my sisters do, but as much as Sigrid is yours, they are my
family. I am bound by honor to protect them."

"You mean by fear," he said.

"I prefer to think of it as a misunderstanding between us that
we'll someday resolve," she said.

Rising to her feet, Mathilda looked down upon Armas and pulled
her gloves tight to her hands once more. She snapped her shirt
down, stiffening the collar and shoulders.

"I believe that I'll soon be attending to your wife, Armas. I will
send your regards, and hopefully send her away peacefully," she
said.

"Don't hurt her, please," he pleaded.

"That entirely depends upon her," she stated.

Footsteps approached from behind, causing Mathilda to look over her shoulder. A pair of guards walked briskly towards them.

"Captain!" one of them shouted as he saluted.

She turned and returned the salute. "What is it?"

"An alarm has been raised. We were told to put the keep on high alert," he stated, a slight nervous tremor in his voice.

"Why?"

"I'm sorry, ma'am, but I don't know. We were told to be on alert, and I was instructed to locate you and inform you," he said.

Mathilda quickly glanced over her shoulder at Armas, and then back at the guards. "Stay here, both of you. Don't let anyone near this cell without the express orders of myself or my sisters, is that clear?"

"Yes, ma'am!" they said in unison, snapping to attention.

Armas pulled himself up on the bars, rising to his feet as she began to walk away. "Mathilda!"

She stopped without turning back.

"What are you going to do?" he asked.

A second later she answered. "My duty."

The echoes of her footsteps filled the hall as she left.

• • • • • • •

With every person who passed, her head twisted left to right, following their footsteps. Timing was everything, and there was no second chance—at least not yet. For a brief moment she considered leaping out and waving her arms around, just to see if any of them would be able to catch her, but she kept reminding herself that it wasn't about her this time. After all, this was so she could help out someone else.

But damn it was tough not to have fun.

Renarde's tail was twitching, despite her desperate attempt to keep it still. For some reason her lips were feeling constantly dry, making it almost possible for her to measure each minute by the number of times she wet them.

Sneaking around this place was much easier a little earlier, too. With everyone running around so actively now, it made it tough just to cross a hallway, let alone try to find Armas. She remembered Vasen saying that he wasn't going to be in his room anymore, but she still checked just to be sure. It was sure. He wasn't.

Which meant that he had to be in a cell, because that was where Vasen told those guards to take him. So, all she had to do was find out where they were keeping the cells, get in there, get him free, and then get out with him. A curt nod to herself confirmed all of this and put a smile on her face for having a plan.

Now if she could just figure out how to execute it.

She figured some of these people rushing around—especially all the ones who seemed dressed up in the black and red outfits and carrying swords—must be going to where Armas was being kept. Unless they were all just looking for her. That idea made her tail twitch again.

Inhaling as deeply as she dared, Renarde waited a moment before letting it out in single slow exhale. No matter how exciting it sounded, nor how much it made her heart race, nor even how much absolute fun it felt to her, she couldn't be chased. Not right now. After she got Armas, sure, but first she had to get Armas.

Which meant she had to be the follower for a change. Stay in the shadows. Remain out of sight. Figure out where they were going and what they were doing. Which would be a lot easier if she could just hear what they were saying.

That cloth she stuck in her ears and then wrapped around her head to keep it in was making it impossible to hear anything. And that thought made her smile even wider.

She waited for the next group to pass, and then trotted down the hallway behind them.

•   •   •   •   •   •   •   •

"Stop, sir."

He did as requested, holding up his hand to stop Hjalmar behind him. Bent over slightly, Sebastian smiled, his eyes almost disappearing due to his cheeks pushing up into his squint.

"I'm here to see the prisoner. To see Armas," Sebastian stated with a slight crack in his voice.

With a gentle raise of his hand and a smile, the guard replied, "I understand, sir, but we are under very explicit orders not to let anyone see him. I'm sure you noticed the activity."

"Well, yes, but that's why I'm here. I was told to come and speak with Armas about all of this mess," Sebastian stated. "So, if you would just stand aside."

"I'm sorry, sir, but no. I'm under orders that only one of the Valpuri sisters themselves may speak with him," the guard said.

"And I represent Vasen Valpuri. You know that, boy. Now, move aside." His voice took on a sharper edge.

The guard shifted his weight and put his hand on his sword hilt. "No, sir. Captain Valpuri gave me my orders directly. You cannot pass, nor may you speak to the captive."

"What do you want, Sebastian?" Armas asked loudly. He stood up in his cell, looking past the guards to the old man in the hall. The scowl on his face said as much as his words.

"Keep quiet!" The other guard struck the door of the cell firmly, causing a loud echo in the corridor.

"Or what? You'll beat me up and lock me away?" Armas answered snidely, and then shouted past him. "Tell Vasen I'm not interested, whatever it is."

"Don't answer him, sir," the guard instructed to Sebastian. "In fact, I'm going to have to ask you to leave, since he won't cooperate."

"I think you would like this idea, Armas." Sebastian ignored the guard. "Or would you rather not be allowed to leave?"

Armas laughed. "Leaving this cell for a nicer one isn't that much of a change, you know."

"Stop it, both of you!" the guard ordered, holding up his hands between them.

"Oh, I'm not talking about leaving the cell." Sebastian shifted over, moving to once again get a clear view of Armas. He smiled when he saw a change in expression. "I want you to leave the keep. Return home to your family."

"You want that? What do you mean?" Armas replied.

"Enough!" The guard drew his weapon and held it out. "I am ordering you to leave, sir! I will not repeat myself again."

The reaction was immediate.

From Armas' perspective it appeared as though the guard dropped his sword for no reason beyond clumsiness. It took a moment longer for him to notice Hjalmar now standing beside the guard, having somehow moved past Sebastian in the hallway.

A second later the guard screamed, his good hand reaching over to grasp the shattered portion of his forearm from where Hjalmar's fist had crushed it in a single blow. The arm tilted at an impossible angle, bending around his grip and sagging down.

"Do not threaten him," Hjalmar said directly. He then turned to look at the other guard. "Are you afraid, boy?"

The guard's sword was already in hand and held before him. It trembled in his grip.

"You'd be a fool if you weren't." Hjalmar took a step forward. "This is the time when you get to make an important decision. You get to choose whether or not to listen to what he says," he motioned his head back towards Sebastian, "or to be forced to listen to him by what I do."

The first guard fell to his knees, his scream completely transformed to sobbing. The second guard looked at him and then quickly back to Hjalmar. He swallowed hard.

"Why don't you gather that poor man up and get him some attention," Sebastian said calmly. "I would hate to see both of you hurt over something so trivial."

The second guard's upper body lurched back and forth in rapid order, despite his best effort to control his breathing. His jaw trembled. Slowly, he shifted to his left, moving towards the side wall and up towards his blubbering partner. Hjalmar's eyes never faltered from watching every step.

He reached down and grabbed his fellow guard by the collar, pulling up while not taking his eyes off of Hjalmar. The first guard got his feet under him and stood beside him. Sebastian stepped aside, giving a wide berth for the two of them to leave— which they did in short order.

"Don't be foolish enough to come back here," Hjalmar said as they retreated. "I may not be as kind the next time."

Both Sebastian and Hjalmar turned to see Armas standing slack-jawed. "Wh-what did you do to him?"

"I hit him," Hjalmar answered.

"That's not important." Sebastian moved past Hjalmar, standing between the huge man and the cell. Armas retreated several steps to the back of his cell. "What is important is you listening to me and understanding the situation."

Armas' eyes were wide. "What situation?"

"I'm so glad you asked," Sebastian said with a voice of silk over cream. "You do know that Vasen and Oikea have been trying to get pregnant by you, yes?"

"I…I didn't really want to admit that, but I suppose so, yes," he answered.

"That's because you are special, and as an extension your child will be equally special. They both want to be the mother of that child," he said, and then continued before Armas responded. "And the entire reason? To open a box. That's all."

"A box?" Armas asked.

"Yes. A box. Sounds silly, doesn't it?" Sebastian laughed.

"What type of box?" His tone bordered between curious and uncertain.

"Oh, a large one to be sure. Rather intimidating by appearances, too. The thing is, they don't know what's inside. No one does. That's why they don't want you opening it. If it's something precious, they fear that you could claim it for yourself. As much as I love my wife, she can be a little self-centered." Sebastian raised his right hand up as he spoke, his thumb pressed close to his index finger to show the smallest of gaps, the hand shaking the entire time.

Nodding slowly, Armas let his eyes travel from Sebastian to Hjalmar and back again. "And why are you here telling me all of this?"

"To rectify the situation of course. This mess has gone on long enough, to the point where they now have a beast-woman rutting you in the hopes that she might spur you to greater...shall we say success? I find myself increasingly disturbed by it," he replied with a crooked smile.

"And how are you going to fix it?" He was now shaking his head.

"By doing what they want! I want to take you to that box and have you open it." He paused and then chuckled. "As long as you promise not to steal whatever's inside."

"Wait." He closed his eyes tight, help up his hands, and shook his head vigorously. "This isn't making any sense. Why do I have to open a box? I mean, why does it have to be me? Can't they open it?"

"Ah, you see, that is the issue. It is a magical box—a cabinet, actually—sealed by ancient magic, and awaiting the touch of the...right person," he answered. "You are that person."

"Me?" He stood there silently, and then suddenly burst into hard laughter. "Me? Oh, you so have the wrong person. There is nothing magical about me. I'm a carpenter from a small town. That's it. You've got the wrong man."

Taking a deep breath, Sebastian straightened up somewhat, though the smile on his face remained bent. "Then it won't do any harm for you to try. If you fail, then we were wrong and you go home. If we're right, then you open the cabinet and you still get to go home."

"That...seems too easy." Armas shuffled in place, still keeping a safe distance away from the door to his cell.

"Of course it does. With all the machinations Vasen and Oikea have put you through, how could you feel anything but mistrust?" Sebastian leaned in towards the bars of the cell, his hands wrapping around the cold metal. "But I am not them. I am far too often a victim of Vasen's ambition as well. Or do you think I enjoy being a cuckold?"

Eyes narrow and straight at Sebastian, Armas continued, "I'm worried that my wife is in danger. That she might be the reason for the commotion in the keep right now. Promise to help her and I'll go."

"I see," Sebastian's eyes softened. "Is she here? I hadn't heard." He nodded as he spoke. "Yes, yes of course I will help her as best I can." He pulled back. "But we have to go now. If we don't, then I do not know if I will have the time to help."

"All…all right." Armas nodded sharply once. His eyes fell to the cell door. "Go ahead and unlock the door."

Sebastian's smile fell into shadow as he stepped away from the door. "Hjalmar, if you will, please?"

The large man stepped to the bars, staring through them at Armas, who moved back until the cold of the stone wall pushed back against him. Armas still didn't feel like he was far enough away.

Hjalmar turned his attention to the door. His left hand moved out and slid along one of the bars, moving up and then slightly back down before he circled his fingers into a grip around it. His right hand followed, moving onto the opposite side of the door, sliding until it was in position and gripping tight. All of Hjalmar's muscles tensed, rippling beneath his flesh until they appeared ready to burst through.

"What is he—"

Armas words were cut short when the door creaked. It was a clear sound of metal straining. Fighting against an outside force determined to win. He swallowed and his mouth fell open, no words or sounds threatening to come out.

Hjalmar's jaw clenched tightly and his shoulders moved behind his chest as he fought against the cell door. The battle was already decided, it was just a matter of one of them admitting defeat. The sharp sound of metal snapping echoed off the wall behind Armas and he instinctively closed his eyes.

Shards of iron exploded through the room, breaking away at the hinges and lock of the door. Armas felt a small piece bounce off of his chest, causing him to open his eyes, even as he turned his head away.

At the opening of his cell, Hjalmar held the iron door in his hands. Moving it to the right, he placed the door against the other bars and stepped back. Sebastian immediately stepped into his place. He raised his arm up and held his hand open towards Armas.

"Th-that's not possible," Armas stammered. "How did he do that?"

"Hjalmar is an amazing specimen. Much like yourself," Sebastian said with a grin. "Now, it's best if we hurry. There are things we must do before time gets the better of any of us."

There was a long hesitation before Armas took Sebastian's hand and stepped out of his cell.

• • • • • • •

"What the hell is that?"

She stood there staring, looking at a massive structure buried on top of itself. Brilliant white walls without seam or line stretched the length and the height of the structure, shaping it inside the cavern. Light emanated from it, filling the entire chamber in an odd glow. The bright color gave the structure a weightless quality. At a glance it appeared as though it would float away were it not tied down.

Like a spider web spun by the ground itself, strings of black rock criss-crossed through the pocket inside the mountain, tethering the building and holding it in place. Some strands ran above the walls, others through them, piercing into unseen parts of this odd structure.

"That is the true keep of the mountain," Olav answered, "and the true reason why the Valpuri built their home here."

"But what is it?" Sigrid's eyes remained fixed on the white structure. Her head shifted to and fro slowly, trying to change her perspective enough to comprehend what she was seeing.

"I don't know. No one does. As far as I know, it predates everything else in Dula Koarr, and perhaps all of Elan."

It appeared to be neither stone, wood, nor metal. Walls rose up at odd angles, twisting at times to become almost perpendicular to their original direction, with no obvious signs of how that was possible.

"What…what are they doing with it? I mean, what—" She turned to look at Olav. "I don't understand."

"I told you I couldn't really explain what was in here, didn't I? Well, this is part of that reason. The other is a little less savory," Olav answered.

She shook her head. "Please stop with the vague statements. I just need to hear something honest and direct right now. No demons. No odd buildings in the middle of a mountain. No fox women. Just something normal."

"This is why the Harvest exists," he said bluntly.

The light coming from the building moved over Sigrid's face as she twisted her head, maintaining a solid gaze on Olav. Her lips moved over and over again, but no words came out.

"This building—or whatever it is—is the reason the sisters have been taking men out of villages," Olav continued without prodding. "They are using them to…to mine that structure."

"Mine? A building? How do you mine a building?" The words came back.

"I know that it's confusing. I'm not sure it's so much a building as it is a…well, a chest. Something that has been locked tight to safely contain as much material as possible." He pointed at the black tendrils. "Those things aren't part of it. A long time ago something happened and the mountain ate it. Sort of. I don't know. Like I said, we may never know, but Oikea and Vasen want to know. So they keep sending men inside to find what they can and bring it out."

"Bring out what, though?" She looked over at the structure. "And where are they? I don't see anyone at all."

"They're inside. They only come out to eat and then go right back in." Olav sighed heavily. "They work constantly. The sisters have put something into their food to control their minds. All they want to do is eat and work. They never sleep. They never speak. And they will work until they collapse and die."

"I…you're joking. Exaggerating at least." Sigrid's voice was weak and frail.

He shook his head. "No. I promise you that every nightmare I have reminds me how real this place is, and how much a coward I actually am."

"Coward?"

He dropped his head down, avoiding both Sigrid and the building. "I could have done more. I should have done something. Instead I did what Oikea asked for the longest time, and when I finally couldn't take it anymore, well, we've covered that—and still did nothing. I told no one. I'm just as guilty as they are."

He said nothing more and she simply stood there until the need to act overwhelmed her. Stepping to him, she put her hand under his chin and brought him eye to eye with her. Then, with her other hand, she slapped him as hard as she could manage across his face. Stumbling to the side, he grabbed his cheek and turned back to stare at her.

"Stop feeling sorry for yourself. Doubt I understand. Fear I understand. This isn't either of those. Pity will do you nothing. You want to change things, you do something. Yes, I think I would hate myself if I were in your position, too, but right now you have a chance to do something about it. That's why you came here, isn't it? To try to make amends with yourself?" She pointed at the white structure. "Well, here's your chance. Let's get those men out of there."

"We can't!" He spat back. "I tried that. They won't leave. Their minds are too muddled to understand." He shook his head sharply. "The only way they get out is if no one is keeping them here."

"Which means the Valpuri." Her hand fell to the grip of her sword. The ridges and grooves played across her fingertips, seeking a compatible match to hold. "How are we supposed to do that? They have an army. And from what you've told me, they're also witches."

"Exactly," he answered.

She glared at him. "I didn't say we couldn't. I was just trying to figure out how to do it."

"Well, the first thing that needs to happen is we need to get past that thing." He pointed at the white structure. "On the far side of it are stairs leading up to the tunnels that go into Valpuri Keep. If we can get that far, then we'll worry about the next step."

Sigrid's tongue ran over her upper teeth. "A sensible plan. Take things one step at a time." With no flourish her arm swept to the side, indicating direction. "You know the way."

He didn't argue. The way down was awkward and ill-formed. A good distance from them were the carved stairs that made the trek easier, but that was also the way the guards would inevitably be coming. This section was originally planned as a second stair, as he understood things, but Oikea and Vasen decided it was a waste of time and energy, so there was only one easy way in or out.

They trekked on in silence, cautiously moving through the shadows cast from the huge edifice. Prudence was only one side of the coin, however, and they understood that speed was also of the essence. Soon enough, they were standing beside the structure.

Speaking in a raised whisper, Olav gave his instructions. "Now we work our way around. When we see the stairs we move quickly. Surprise is our only hope. If we can get to them fast enough, we might—just might—be able to get to the top, and then inside the keep."

Sigrid gave a curt nod and then motioned him forward. He responded and began walking. After only a few steps, Sigrid's attention was stolen away when her hand brushed up against the building.

It wasn't that the building was warm. She almost expected it to be warm from the odd light. Nor was it the fact that it was smooth.

Even from a distance she could tell it was a smooth surface, though it was smoother than she expected. The alarming part was the odd vibration she felt. A rhythmic drone just under the surface, strumming against her skin. A part of her wanted to jerk back, but the greater part of her kept her hand there, trying to measure it somehow.

"Eerie, isn't it?" Olav's voice brought her back to him. "I try not to touch it. For a long time I did exactly what you're doing right now. Feeling it. Trying to understand it. I finally decided I didn't want to."

"Why not?" Her hand slowly pulled away from the wall.

"Because I thought I figured it out, and it scared me. And before you ask, yes I'll tell you," he swallowed, "it's a pulse."

"A what?" she whispered.

"A pulse. I don't know how or why, but that's the only thing I could match it to," he said.

"That's not possible. This is a building." She looked at it to confirm her words.

"I know. Why do you think I stopped touching it?" He walked on. Sigrid followed, moving a step away from the wall.

"In a minute or so we'll be passing by an opening," he turned back to stare at her, his eyes adamant as his voice, "do not look inside."

"You realize that only makes me want to do it," she answered.

"Don't. You don't want to. Trust me. We have to keep moving." His shoulders slumped slightly. "Please."

"What's in there?" Sigrid turned her head slightly towards the building.

"Men, mostly. And all of the things that they are trying to find. The…the maze of items that are laced together. There are hundreds—thousands, likely—of things inside this building, but they aren't just waiting. They've, well, they've almost grown together, and they aren't easy to get free. And half of the time if someone does, things happen. A chain reaction." He pointed to the black stone resting just overhead. "Sometimes one of those will come free."

She shook her head. "I'm starting to feel like an idiot, asking questions every time you speak. What do you mean, come free?"

"They can move. Shift if the pressure inside changes. I've seen men impaled straight through by it. I've also seen men lose limbs as the piles shift and trap part of them with the interior of the place." He turned back away. "Just trust me. Don't look."

"How many are in there?" she asked, her eyes once more turning to the walls of the building.

"Two, maybe three dozen. They don't want too many or they are hard to control, and they have to keep a fresh supply coming in. A half dozen or so are probably already in the keep, being fed mind-controlling food until they are completely obedient. As soon as they are ready, or as soon as they are needed, they'll be brought in to replace the others."

"And the dead go out to the pile and that monster," she muttered.

"Exactly." He paused and pointed at the opening in the wall. "Now remember, don't look. You can't. Please."

"I…I'll try," she nodded.

With a nod of his own he walked on, moving quickly past the opening. Sigrid waited before she followed—and waited longer than she intended. Closing her eyes, she stepped forward, her face screwed in determination. When she felt a rush of heat and an odd metallic smell wash over her, she hesitated. Somewhere inside she heard the sound of a man humming, most likely to himself, and then suddenly stopping. A wet sound followed it, with a short echo, like a droplet hitting a pool. Her mind wanted to know why. Wanted to see what was inside.

With all of her strength, she strode forward, keeping her eyes squeezed tightly shut. When the heat passed by her back she opened her eyes and remembered to start breathing again.

"Good," Olav said. "You did good. We just have to go there." He pointed to the corner ahead. "The stairs are just past that. We can get up them quickly and get to the keep."

"Guards will be at the top?" she asked.

"Yes. Probably two," he answered.

Her chest swelled up with a deep breath and then slowly exhaled. "Okay. Thank you."

"For what?" His face drew tight.

"Getting me this far. I couldn't have done this without you." Her breath was returning to a more normal rate.

He smiled. "You're welcome, but we aren't done."

Her hand fell down to her sword once more and she nodded once, and then stepped past him heading towards the corner of the building. With every step her posture rose and her stride grew stronger. She felt Olav quickly pacing her from behind.

They reached the corner together and turned. The staircase rose in front of them, going up a hundred feet or more, with a width of around five feet. And halfway up it stood at least a dozen guards, each of them holding a sword—and all of them now looking their way.

"Oh crap," she muttered, drawing her sword.

A loud bell rang throughout the entire chamber as she rushed towards the stairway, with Olav shouting her name from behind.

. . . .

"RENARRRRRDE!" Vasen's scream could be heard throughout nearly a third of the keep, and vibrated off the huge windows of the room. "COME HERE! NOW!"

The scowl on her face was amplified by the way she stalked through the room. A handful of guards stood at the entrance, watching her pace before The Burning Heart and mumble to herself between screams. She glanced through the windows, seeing a snowstorm raging, whitewashing the world outside.

"I know you can hear me, beast!" Her voice was lower, but no less forceful. "And I know you must obey." She took three more steps. "So why aren't you?"

"Did you find Mathilda?" Vasen turned at the sound of her sister's voice. The scowl transformed into a fragile smile.

"Hello, Sister. Mathilda wasn't in her quarters. I've sent guards to find her and summon her here. I'm not sure where she is at the moment. I assume that you have sent Hjalmar off hunting for Renarde," Vasen replied as she walked towards Oikea. When the met they leaned in and kissed each other on their bare cheek.

"So you have not seen Hjalmar either, then?" Oikea asked. "I was hoping that you and he had found each other."

A single eyebrow raised on Vasen's face. "So, both Hjalmar and Mathilda are missing. How coincidental." She narrowed her eyes at Oikea. "You did send Hjalmar to his quarters when you finished, didn't you?"

Oikea screwed a smile onto her face. "I instructed your husband to send him when he was active once more. You have trained him to follow our orders, I assume."

"He always does what I ask of him without question. Out of respect," Vasen said.

"Of course he does." Oikea walked past her and towards the hearth.

Vasen stood in place and turned to watch her walk all the way to the fire. "I'm sorry if you cannot command the respect of any man, dear. Perhaps one day you will find one that values you."

Standing with her back to her sister, Oikea held her hands towards the flame, spreading her fingers wide and closing them several times. "I heard you screaming for the lost pet, darling. You sounded quite upset. I wouldn't let it bother you so much. You can't blame yourself for things like that."

"Blame myself for what?" Vasen took a small step forwards.

Oikea turned back with a smile. "Oh, nothing. Nothing at all. I'm sure that things will right themselves soon enough. I've sent reliable people out."

Returning the smile, Vasen took a deep breath and smiled. She glanced over her shoulder at the guards gathered by the door. "Would you all be so kind as to step outside and close the door? My sister and I need to speak privately for a moment."

The two men standing just inside the doorway all but stumbled over themselves as they rushed out the exit, pushing others back as they went. Two other guards quickly stepped in and grabbed the doors, pulling them until the latch closed with an audible click. By the time the door had fully closed, Oikea and Vasen were staring at each other. Each sister's hand glowed for a moment, and the wood on the doors grew over and across, binding and sealing them together.

"Sister, dear, we have too many outside elements causing us stress at the moment. There is no reason that we should be taking this out on each other." Vasen's voice was level and soothing. "We are not enemies, after all."

"Of course not! I have never thought of you that way, darling. You are right, there is just an inordinate amount of stress on you right now, causing tempers to flare," Oikea sighed.

There was a long moment of silence.

"Don't worry, dear, I realize that you have some feelings of inferiority, but there is no need to be quite so dramatic about it." Vasen placed her hands slowly behind her back, drawing her shoulders up.

Oikea laughed loudly. "Inferiority? Whatever do you mean?"

"Transposing the stress of the situation from you to me. Your passive manner of handling things. Unlike you, I'm willing to confront the issue directly," Vasen replied. "Namely, your constant insubordination."

"I believe you use the wrong word, Sister. You can only be insubordinate to a superior." Oikea stiffened and slipped her hands behind her back.

Both sisters began walking, one to the their left and the other to their right, until they stood directly across from each other in the middle of the room. A chill wind howled outside, barely audible over the sound of the fire.

"Apologize," Vasen growled.

"Me?" Oikea laughed again. "Whatever for, darling. If anything you should be apologizing to me."

"Why would I ever do that?" Vasen asked.

The flame in the fireplace rose higher, increasing the heat between the two sisters.

"Well, for being so rude for one thing. It would be a nice start, and something that I could use as a basis for forgiveness." Light danced over Oikea's eye.

"Forgiveness? Hmm." Vasen nodded slowly, narrowing her eyes to piercing intensity. "What an interesting idea, considering how I've already done everything I could manage to forgive you for all of these years."

"Ah yes, all of these years." Oikea took several steps backwards. The movement was reciprocated by her sister. "Dating back how far, darling? Five years? Ten? Or maybe a few more. Maybe enough to get us back to being children."

"Oh, so you do remember. Good. Then I shouldn't have to explain it, should I?" Vasen stopped walking and pulled her hands to her side, a blue glow resting in her palms.

"How could I forget, darling? There is nothing I can do to make me forget. Every damned day I wake up and remember!" The volume of her voice gradually increased with every word. Oikea's hands moved in front of her midsection, a faint spark charging across her fingers.

"Then you should be begging me for forgiveness!" Vasen spat back. "It was your actions that made mother angry! If you hadn't been so damnably annoying she would never have taken it out on me! I should be beautiful!"

The smell of ozone filled the room.

"You were never beautiful! Even then you were a foul-hearted, cruel monster masquerading in my reflection. It was you that mother hated. She only burned me because she couldn't stand the thought of seeing someone who looked like you in the house." The furniture near Oikea rumbled and shifted on the floor.

"Oh, don't be so pathetic! You wanted to be me, you just never could. Instead you tried to whine and manipulate your way into things. You twisted everything mother ever said to be what you wanted. Just like you're doing right now! The saddest part is that you don't understand how much you need me." The air around Vasen began to swirl, kicking up dust and debris into a miniature whirling cyclone.

"You are at least right about one thing: I do need you. We need each other. You know as well as I do that our powers would dim considerably without the other one," Oikea stated, "but that doesn't mean I can't make it clear which of us is in charge, darling."

Vasen glared over the distance, her teeth clenched and hands glowing. "I was questioning for a moment whether or not this was the proper time to instruct you on that course, dear Sister," her eyes glowed blue, "but not anymore."

The huge row of windows exploded. A shower of glass and snow mingled, sweeping through the room, swirling around the perimeter of the space before focusing its attention on Oikea. Four solid streaks of white and blue raced towards her, and in response she raised up her right hand and the flames from the fireplace obeyed. A torrent of flame circled her, blocking her from view. The room quickly filled with steam as the snow smashed itself against the fire, both of them dying to create a new atmosphere.

"Oh, Vasen, darling, don't you realize that you cannot hope to overwhelm me with your ability?" Oikea chuckled. The furniture around her shattered, falling to pieces on the ground. They didn't remain settled however, as they shuddered and shifted, pulling together to form a trio of figures—upholstered men with ornate arms and legs.

"How quaint. It's a shame you are so limited, or you might be dangerous." Vasen's hair raised up into a halo around her head just as every shard of glass from the windows rose into the air, hovering for a moment before rapidly flying together, shaping and forming themselves into six human-like figures of glass.

The three wooden soldiers marched out, standing between the sisters. All six of the glass men shifted and slid into position across from them. The heat of the steam fell upon them, condensing into water once more to cover them all in a glistening sheen of moisture.

Both sisters stood behind their warriors, perfectly dry. It was as though the heated water was afraid to touch them at all. Their dresses waved in the bustling air, and their hair moved to the side, a steady wind blowing in a single direction away from the windows and towards the doors. The two of them remained a reflection of each other in almost every way.

A loud banging began on the doors as their loyal guards attempted to break into the room. If they could hear it, they showed no visible sign.

"Out of love I will give you this one chance to surrender," Vasen said. "All you need do is apologize and admit that I am better than you, and we can get back to the matter at hand."

"Oh, darling, that is so cute. Your bravado has always been a point of entertainment for me," Oikea replied. "It's ridiculous at the moment, of course."

"I do believe I will have to correct you on that as well, dear," Vasen stated.

They smiled at each other. The snow flew through the windows as the temperature dropped noticeably inside. With a rush, the crafted soldiers suddenly moved towards each other.

• • • • • • •

"You are relieved." Sebastian's voice was soft and easy.

"Sir, he's not authorized to be in this—"

"I said, you are relieved." His voice turned harder and more direct. The young man blinked at him, looked at Hjalmar standing behind Armas, resting one hand firmly on his shoulder, and then looked back at Sebastian.

"Sir, no disrespect, but the keep has been put on alert and—"

"DO NOT…." He hesitated. "Do not worry about that. You know me. It's all right. We will handle things here. It was decided that bringing him here was the safest choice. You know that this is the safest room in the keep, after all."

"I…. Yes, sir. I understand, sir." The young man stood up straight, looking again at Armas and Hjalmar.

"You're dismissed. Go to your station. I will handle things here," Sebastian said with a smile. His voice was once again soft and soothing, and his body slightly bent over.

The young man looked back at him. "Yes, sir. Thank you."

A strong grip redirected Armas, turning him towards the center of the room. Hjalmar moved forward, pushing Armas along in front of him, with Sebastian walking close behind.

The wonders of the room washed over Armas as he struggled to take everything in. It had taken him a moment to get used to the gold walls when they first entered the hall, but as they moved further into it, his attention moved from the walls to the items it held. Then his eyes fell upon a very familiar orb resting near a large cabinet. Both items had the same black sheen, with a reflection sinking far below the surface. He licked his lips and swallowed, his mouth and throat suddenly dry.

When the door clicked shut loudly, Armas jumped. He turned back to see Sebastian laugh and straighten himself, rising to a much taller height.

"Finally, we're alone. I thought he would never leave," Sebastian said. "Relax, Armas. This is why we're here, and as I'm sure you can surmise...."

He walked past Hjalmar and Armas, finally coming to stand beside the cabinet. His chest rose as he filled his lungs and let out a slow, breathy sigh. Both of his hands moved out at waist height and gently caressed the cabinet, fingertips running along its surface lightly.

"This...is the cabinet," Sebastian purred.

Armas stood there in silence. Instinctively he stepped backwards, running into the immovable object known as Hjalmar. "I'm...I'm having second thoughts."

"Whatever for?" Sebastian spun towards him, smiling. "This is what you want. It's what we all want. It will get you your freedom and my emancipation."

His eyes narrowed. "What's in there?" Armas asked. "The way you touched it. It's...."

"Think of your wife, Armas," Sebastian stepped towards him. "If she's here, she's in danger. You saw the activity in the halls. The keep is on alert. Something has happened, and they are reacting. You know how Vasen and Oikea can be. Harsh. Cruel. Torturous. Is that what you want your wife to endure?"

"Of course not! I just—"

"You are that close to having her back, Armas." He turned sideways, holding out both of his arms as though to bring the cabinet and Armas together. "Those doors hold your freedom. You simply have to open them and everything you want will be yours. Everything."

"I don't want everything. I just want Sigrid," he replied warily. He glanced quickly behind him, confirming Hjalmar's position behind him.

"Then that is what you will have! The two of you back home. Sitting by the fire, this entire nightmare quickly fading into memory best forgotten!" The position of Sebastian's hand turned, opening up, pleading to Armas.

"You know more than you are saying. You know what's in that box, don't you?" Armas asked.

"What does it matter?! If you open it all of this ends!" he answered, urging forward.

"It matters if opening it only makes things worse! That's…." He pointed vaguely towards the cabinet, waving his hand up and down. "It's not natural! Look at it!"

"I do look at it. I look at it every day. I spend hours here desperately trying to find a way to open it myself, but I cannot. You can open it, Armas. Only you. I promise you that nothing in there will harm you or your wife, ever. You have my word on it." Sebastian took a step towards Armas, his breath growing shorter with every passing second.

"How can I trust you?" Armas asked.

Sebastian stepped back, opening the passage to the cabinet. "It is your decision, but it is one you must make now. Time is up. I urge you to do the right thing. For yourself. For your wife. Listen to your heart."

The black cabinet stood before him, and Armas stared into its surface looking for answers. The colors shifted across it, and for a brief moment he thought he saw something—some shape— move. Two steps later he realized he was moving towards it, drawn to its call.

And then he was there, standing in front of it. His eyes danced back and forth, skittering from one point to the next, trying to find something to focus upon and finding nothing. He licked his lips and swallowed. He heard something, a voice perhaps, and he hoped that it was coming from Sebastian, or even Hjalmar, but since he had no idea what the voice was saying, he couldn't be sure.

Armas' hand reached up towards the cabinet's surface.

• • • • • • •

Most of the blood on her belonged to someone else. Most, but not all.

There were already eight bodies behind her, and she genuinely hoped they were going to stay that way. She didn't have a chance to make sure they were dead, and her mind ventured back to the cold woods where she met Renarde and her fight with the guards there. Much to her own shock, she wished that Renarde was with her right now.

Olav was with her. Behind her, doing his best to keep up. The entire time she was running to the stairs he screamed behind her, trying to call her back and away from the guards on the stairs. She knew better. If they ran those men would chase them, and eventually catch them. Where they caught them was only a matter of chance, and that could be disastrous. At this moment, in this place, she knew what awaited her. A set of stairs wide enough for two of them at best to fight her. Not ideal, but the best she could hope for, given the circumstances.

For months she had trained. She watched the soldiers from afar, knowing that one day she would have to fight, and likely fight more than one. Time and again she came in second place at the tournament back home. That wasn't good enough. Every day she trained. In her head or in the field, practicing against unseen enemies. These enemies were very real, and putting every second of her training to the test.

Initially, there were twelve men to fight. At the moment, she had no idea. Eight behind her, but more than four in front. The bell was still ringing, too, which meant there were more men who could potentially arrive. An endless fight, but one that was steadily moving upwards.

It moved because she kept on the offensive. They fell back as she pushed forward, and she had no intention of slowing down. Darting and dashing with her blade, the guards did little more than parry and riposte. If she was lucky enough to get one of the ones on the outside off balance, she used that momentum to drive them off of the stair. So far, none of them had come back up behind them.

For his part, Olav was making sure that none of them came back or stood up. The sword in his hand felt awkward, and looked far worse. Knowing better than to run up beside Sigrid, he stood back, prepared to do his best to anyone who made it past her or came from below. His head was on a swivel, spinning back and forth from above and below.

In his mind he was shouting words of encouragement. Urging her forward with a show of verbal support. In reality he was dead silent, not daring to say anything that might distract her from the overwhelming odds in front of them.

If either of them had taken a moment to think about their situation they would be terrified. Luckily, they weren't allowed the luxury of time. Olav stepped aside as another man fell past him and watched another fall of the side. Ten down.

Sigrid twisted and turned, lunging and driving forward, each motion another step up. They were over halfway to the top, and from what she could see, there were only six more men ahead of her.

Two minutes later there were only three. Sweat poured down her face, matting her hair to her head and touching the corners of her eyes. The grip on her sword was damp and threatening to slip from her hand, causing her to change tactics. Bellowing a scream she leapt forward, slashing into them and immediately sending another one off the side. The two remaining men came at her suddenly, one of them finding themselves impaled upon her sword. She wasn't as lucky with the other. As she pulled her sword free, he tackled her, knocking the blade from her hand.

Toppling down to the stair, she tumbled over, the guard on top of her. All manner of orientation was gone, and she struggled to push him off of her. They came to a stop as suddenly as they fell, the weight of the guard pinning her down. Her hands drove into him, punching at his kidneys with all of her might, but he didn't budge.

And then he rolled off of her. She scrambled towards the wall, pushing herself up to a standing position. Olav stood there, bloodied sword in hand, staring at the dead guard at his feet. Eyes wide he remained motionless, aside from the obvious rise and fall of his chest as he gasped for air. She moved to him instantly.

"Olav," she said sternly. "Olav! We have to go. We have to."

He looked at her and nodded. She nodded back and then turned to scan the stairs. Her sword was there and she bent to grab it. A sharp pain ran through her side, causing her to drop one hand to it and wince. When she rose back up with her sword in hand, her head swam. The world spun for a second and she stepped sideways, regaining her footing.

"Are you okay?" Olav asked.

"Yes. Yes, let's go." The way to the top of the stairs was finally cleared, and she wanted to wait no longer. One foot after another she forced her way up the stairs, momentum increasing with every step until she reached the top.

Tall and blond, her hair pulled back into a long braid, a familiar figure awaited her on the platform at the stair's end. She held a sword before her and stood directly in front of the only door leading out of the space.

"You must be Sigrid," Mathilda said. "Armas speaks highly of you."

Rising up, Sigrid wiped her hand across her face, pulling away sweat and leaving a slight stain of blood. "Get out of my way."

"That's not going to happen." Mathilda looked past her at the man coming near the top of the stairs. "Hello, Olav." He froze in place.

"You saw what I did to your men," Sigrid growled. "I won't hesitate to do it to you, either."

"I did see, actually. Not the whole fight, mind you, but enough of it. I got here about halfway, I estimate. Very impressive," she answered.

Sigrid raised her sword up, pointing it across towards Mathilda. "Move. Aside."

"No. I'm actually guessing that you are rather spent. Fighting that much will exhaust anyone. Right now you have virtually no chance of winning a contest against me, so I offer you this instead: surrender. I will take custody of you and, while I cannot promise any sort of leniency or guarantee of survival, I can promise to take you to Armas so the two of you can say goodbye." Mathilda kept her voice level as she spoke.

Her lungs were burning with each breath, but Sigrid found enough air to shout, "Fuck you!"

Mathilda snorted a sharp laugh. "You have no idea. Your husband did ask me to go easy on you, so I had to try."

They stared at each other. Sigrid's chest rose and fell rapidly as she fought to catch her breath, while Mathilda stood calmly across from her. The youngest Valpuri turned her blade in her hand. Long and thin, it gleamed a mirrored reflection, even in the distant light where they stood. She brought it up slightly, smiling across at her opponent. Sigrid raised her sword up, dark and covered in blood, a gift from a now distant friend, and snarled.

Her scream echoed through the chamber as Sigrid rushed towards Mathilda.

• • • • • • • •

Light streamed from the point where Armas' fingers touched the wood. It raced and circled the cabinet, finding every unseen seam and seeping into it like water over a broken stone. A rush of air swept past everyone, centered on the cabinet, disappearing into the box in a violent vacuum.

A sound began to fill the room, or rather the distinct rushing of sound disappearing. Items fell from their perches, smashing into the ground, but making no audible noise as it was absorbed into the cabinet. Armas tried to pull away, but his fingers betrayed him, refusing to leave where they touched the dark wood.

He looked behind him, the fear in his eyes countered by the exuberance shown in the man behind him. Sebastian's mouth moved, forming words no one could hear. He pointed to the cabinet, causing Armas to turn to it once more. The seams broke apart, barely noticeable at first, but gradually growing wider.

All at once it seemed to burst. The wood shifted, sliding open without hinges or runners, parting until the doors rested open at the sides of the cabinet. The rush of air inward stopped, and for a heartbeat the room was still. After that heartbeat all of the sound and air that had been sucked into the cabinet burst forth, staggering back all three who stood nearby, and toppling Armas to the ground. Crawling back up to his feet, Armas looked to the cabinet, his mind reeling from what just occurred, unsure of what was to come.

The cabinet stood there, doors open, and completely empty. He stepped closer, closed his eyes and reopened them. It was a plain wooden armoire, with nothing inside.

"What...?" He turned to look at Sebastian, whose smile was larger than ever. "After all that I expected there to be something. It's empty."

Sebastian laughed. "It's empty now, but only just now."

"What are you talking ab—"

Once more Armas was sent sprawling, tumbling to the ground as he fell forward, landing near Sebastian's feet. His hands flew over his head, protecting himself instinctually. A deafening sound raced above him, a mix of a scream and a roar that he felt as much as heard. It continued and continued, lingering and swirling through the room.

Braving a look, Armas turned his head, looking up towards Sebastian. He stood above him, arms spread wide and head back, reveling in the chaos around him. Hundreds of long, black streaks spun through the room, circling and twisting around each other. Several of them flew to Sebastian and wrapped around him for a second before continuing their flight. And when Armas looked more closely he saw something else in each of those streaks of black: a pair of eyes.

"Finally!" Sebastian called. "After all those centuries, finally free again!"

"Wh-what?" Armas muttered.

At the sound of his voice, Sebastian stared down and Armas' blood turned cold. Sebastian's eyes were now solid pools of black. "Armas! Armas, my dear, dear friend. You have no reason to fear. I promised that neither you nor your bride would have any reason to fear us, and I keep my word. But still…."

Sebastian looked at Hjalmar, who remained still through the cacophony of chaos, and motioned him over. The massive man reached down and grasped Armas, yanking him up by his arm until he stood awkwardly, his arm still higher than normal.

"What's going on?" Armas said in a panic. "What are those things? What's happening?"

"That is a lot of questions. Let me just answer it by thanking you for freeing my brothers. And now we can once again continue what we started so very long ago," Sebastian said with glee. "You and your wife will join the Valpuri sisters and that damned celestial spawn in getting to watch it all occur. I do hope you don't become too overwhelmed with grief and end yourself."

He tried to pull his arm free, but Hjalmar held onto Armas firmly. "Your brothers? This…I…."

"Take him someplace away from here. I don't care where," Sebastian said to Hjalmar, "as long as he isn't here."

Hjalmar nodded as Sebastian walked past. Armas head was in constant motion, watching the numerous black shapes move through the room, abjectly moving with Sebastian as he approached the door. Hjalmar joined them, following behind Sebastian and dragging Armas along with him.

"Wait! What are you doing?" Armas voice cracked.

Sebastian turned back, raising an eyebrow. "Why, I'm releasing my brothers. Between the guards, staff, and eventually all of those hapless fools in the retention shell—once we drag them out of it—there is enough life for each to form themselves a new body. After that, we'll move to the city and then…. Well, we'll see, won't we." He turned back to the door. "Again, I cannot thank you enough, Armas. Your name will always be revered among my brethren, though I imagine you will be cursed and reviled among humanity for a great time yet to come."

Grasping the door, Sebastian swung it wide, pushing back on it until the wide gate was completely open. Immediately, the chorus of black entities streamed out of the room, turning either way, moving down the halls, filling them with their own unnatural wailing and the screams of the people they immediately met. In seconds, the room was empty of the black creatures.

Sebastian stepped into the hallway and paused. He glanced behind him with a wide smile. "Goodbye, Armas." He turned right and walked down the hallway, quickly disappearing from view.

Wordlessly, Hjalmar pulled Armas into the hall, turned left, and strode away.

About a half minute later, something stirred in the back of the room. Stepping out from behind one of the relics on display came a silver and black fox woman with her head wrapped up in cloth. She raised up to her full height, wavering back and forth, her tail sliding to either side to help keep her balance as she visually surveyed the space.

Dropping down to all fours, she sprang forward, arriving at the cabinet in three leaps. Sticking her nose out, she sniffed carefully while her eyes darted around the view of the interior. The tip of her tail twitched rapidly as she eased forward. With delicate care she stepped up and into the cabinet. Her hands ran along the interior surface, feeling the warm smooth wood. By the time she turned back to face the opening, her face was twisted up and one eyebrow was raised.

A brilliant flash of white light filled the room, and when it faded the cabinet was empty.

end chapter six

CHAPTER
SEVEN
THE COVETOUS

They faintly heard the pounding on the doors and the shouts from beyond them, but neither of them gave it a second thought. All of their focus was on each other.

Shards of glass and splinters of wood littered the floor, but still the animated warriors battled. Behind either line stood their creator and commander, two women who only had eyes for each other. Giant arcs of blue light were met by sparking streams of green electrical might, igniting a massive display of color and pyrotechnics.

The room was beginning to suffer extreme casualties. More than one fire burned, charring heavily the ancient wood that mixed with stone to become the backbone of the structure. And if these flames were not enough, both sisters still drew the flame from the hearth, daring to pit it against the other, or summoned in the cold, hoping to freeze the fight out of her twin. The only true casualty of the battle thus far was the keep itself.

"You're tiring, Oikea. Why don't you simply surrender?" Vasen shouted. "You've proven yourself worthy, as I always knew," she smiled, "simply not quite to my level."

"I would hate to be at your level, darling. That would mean that I've had to step down a notch or two," Oikea answered. "But it's cute that you think I'm tired. I have scarcely begun."

Vasen's glass soldiers ripped across the wooden warriors, shredding shards over the floor, but leaving fragments of glass behind. Only two of Oikea's wooden constructs remained, one of them in a very fragile state. Three of the glass creatures continued to fight, but two of them were showing severe cracks in their structure.

"You are nothing but a filthy excuse of a whore, Oikea. No faithfulness. No honor. Nothing of any merit," Vasen spit.

"What an interesting comment from a common slut such as yourself. Or did you forget that it was your plan to copulate with the villager in the hopes of seeding your womb? It was your only chance to do something to make yourself feel like a true woman of Dula Koarr," Oikea said.

"I am more than just a woman of Dula Koarr! I am the true Ranee of this country! Your ambition is to do little more than lie with as many men as you can fit between your legs. I will carry us to our rightful throne, even if I have to drag you to it on a leash!" Vasen spat.

"At least men want to be between my legs! The only appeal you have is when they mistake you for me. Your best quality has always been looking like me. A pale reflection of ambition, attitude, and power. You cannot help what you are, but you can— and will—realize what I truly am!"

A sharp crack of thunder shook the building, causing the constructs to fall to the ground. The painting over the fireplace slipped askew and fell to the floor, cracking the frame holding it. Each sister glared across the barren room.

"How quaint. You've decided to fall onto parlor tricks now," Vasen said.

"Parlor tricks? I assure you everything I do is far more dangerous than a trick. I am hoping, though, that you haven't become desperate enough to actually damage the core of the keep, and that little sound was just for effect," Oikea said with a chuckle.

Vasen took a step backwards. "I didn't do that."

"Of course you didn't. I'm not so easily lulled into complacency, Sister." Oikea raised her hands, sending tendrils of eldritch energy flying across the room. Vasen raised her hands up, bringing a bright blue barrier between them both. The tendrils shattered against it.

"Don't be an idiot, Oikea! I'm telling you I didn't do that! And if you didn't, then something else did!" Vasen shouted.

"Naturally, and that something else is a dangerous threat. Which means as soon as I lower my guard then your magic will course through me. The threat is you, darling," Oikea insisted.

"For once will you stop! Listen!" Vasen pointed to the door.

Oikea turned to the door, one eye still on her sister, listening cautiously. The banging serving as a constant background rhythm during their battle was gone. It had been replaced by screaming.

The sisters looked at each other warily, and then as one turned and walked towards the door. A wave of both of their hands broke the wood sealing the door shut. A second gesture flung them open wide as they grew closer.

They were greeted by streaming strands of blackness with eyes, flying into the room and towards them. From Vasen's hand a perfectly blue bolt of energy erupted, striking and shredding one of the flying creatures. In unison, Oikea let fly a jagged lash of green that ripped along the outside of one of them, grasping it and tearing it into several pieces.

"What the hell are those?" Vasen shouted.

"I have no idea, but look." Pointing past the doors, Oikea gestured to a handful of guards who lay on the ground, their bodies shriveled and lifeless. Above them, still holding on to the front of the fallen guard's clothing, were their identical match, save for the halo of darkness currently surrounding them.

One of the new guards turned and smiled, revealing a row of sharp, pointed teeth. Even as he smiled at them, his teeth changed, turning into those of a normal human.

Together, both Oikea and Vasen let loose a volley of magic, striking the creature and rending its flesh apart. As the hull of a man fell to the ground, a figure of black energy rose up from it and flew off.

The sisters looked at each other.

"Do you know what this is?" Vasen asked.

"Not a clue," Oikea answered.

"Truce?" Vasen suggested.

"Of course! Blood is so much thicker than…." Oikea looked at the flying shapes coursing through the hallways and the shadowy men rising above the fallen corpses of their guards. "Darkness."

They strode out together towards the screaming and the death.

• • • • • • •

Ultimately, where she stood there was nothing. A sea of white extending in every direction. Below her there was nothing, nor above, nor any other direction she looked. Yet she walked as though her feet were on solid ground, and she breathed as normally as ever.

"Hello?" Renarde shouted. "Helllllooooo?"

She walked on a bit, her tail slowly swaying from side to side, and her head still wrapped in a large, white cloth. With every step she looked around, hoping to see something, and she sniffed deeply, trying to smell anything, but the only thing she discovered so far was herself.

"Wow. This could get really, really boring," she muttered.

"Not really."

When she heard the voice she leapt straight up, spinning around in anticipation of discovering who it was who had snuck up behind her. Like everything else here so far though, there was nothing.

"Who said that?" She spun in a circle, head and eyes darting every which way. "Where did that get said from?"

"…get said from?"

Dropping down to all fours, she ran in a small circle, keeping on the move. Her eyes still scanning constantly. "There you go again. Talking without being here, which isn't a thing you should be doing."

"Why are you wearing that odd thing on your head?" The voice asked. "It looks uncomfortable."

"So I can't hear anything!" she shouted back, checking below her just to make sure she hadn't missed anyplace the voice might be hiding.

"And how well is that working?"

Renarde stopped. All of her mouth shifted, moving slightly to the right as she thought for a second. As she stood up, she unwrapped the cloth, and a moment later dropped it to her side. Her ears sprang up and twisted on the top of her head, rejoicing in their rediscovered freedom.

"Good point." Renarde slowly looked around, her ears moving with her head as she listened pointedly. "You're still hiding, though. Where are you? And while we're talking, who are you?"

There was a pause.

"I'm not sure, exactly," the voice answered. It was neither exactly male or female, but could easily have been either depending on the moment in each word. "I think the appropriate question might actually be, what am I?"

"Okay," Renarde answered, "what am I?"

"No. That's not what…. You didn't understand…." The voice went silent.

"I think you misunderstood." The voice's return made Renarde spin around, locating the source directly behind her. A shadow of pure white stood in this world of white, only visible because of its shape in a shapeless void. "You are a child of the celestials, are you not? One of the original four?"

"Uh, maybe?" she answered. "I'm Renarde. Hi." She waved, casually.

"Yes! Renarde. I knew I remembered you. Tell me, are there still four celestials? And just the four of you as well, correct? Or has the war already happened?" the figure asked.

Renarde nodded slowly. "I have no idea." She twisted her head. "What are you talking about?"

"My apologies. It's difficult to remember which time we are in. They all seem the same. Pay me no heed." The figure bowed slightly. "I am at your service."

"You are?" Renarde bobbed a quick bow herself as she spoke.

"Of course. I cannot obey you, but I am indebted to help you for all that you will do for me," it said.

"Riiiiighhht…." Renarde replied slowly. "Well, if you are gonna help me, maybe you can tell me where I am?"

"You are inside me." The voice stated.

"Well, before this goes to a kinky place," she took a deep breath, "what the heck does that mean?!"

"You passed through the portal and into the central portion of my containment vessel," it explained.

Renarde's right ear began to twitch spastically.

"Perhaps you need to return to your original question." She could swear she saw a smile in the area where the shape should have a face.

"Or you could just assume that I asked that question and go ahead and tell me!" A lock of Renarde's hair fell up and over her face. With a puff she blew it back away from her. "But fine, what are you?"

"I am a class one containment vessel, designed for the accumulation and confinement of negative life entities," it said.

Renarde blinked. She then shook her head violently before looking at the shape once again. "I have no idea what you just said."

"I am a box designed to hold the shadows." The tone was the same genderless, soft voice.

"Okay! That I understand!" Renarde bounced on her feet slightly. "Right. Now…what?"

There was a prolonged pause. "I'm sorry, but I don't understand that question."

"What are you doing? Why do you hold shadows? How do you hold shadows? And I have lots of other questions if you can get through those!" Renarde grinned, still bouncing.

"I believe you are asking for an explanation of my being. Very well. A long time before the present one, in the way that you measure it, at least, there was—"

"Simple version? Please?" Renarde put her hands together lightly.

"Have you heard of Antediluvians?" it asked.

"Yes! I have heard that word used!" she answered with a bounce in her voice.

"When the Antediluvians ruled this world, they dealt with the same threats the celestials must contend with today. Namely, the encroachment of the negative life entities, or shadows as you call them. I was one of the containment vessels they crafted to hold the shadows safely," it explained.

"Until today," Renarde said.

"I was crafted to respond to Antediluvians," it replied.

"Uh, yeah. You kinda opened up when Armas touched you," Renarde answered. "I think. I was kinda hiding in the back of the room when it happened. I saw Metal Nose and Old Guy dragging Armas into what turned out to be a fancy gold room, so I snuck in behind them when they weren't looking. I'm good at that."

"Yes, you are."

"Thank you!" Renarde beamed. "So, anyway, about that whole shadow and you thing: I don't get it."

"I am a construct of light, given form and sentience to maintain my duties more manageably. As such, the shadows are powerless against me," it said.

"Right! Aubade kinda did that with herself!" Renarde said, raising a finger in triumph.

"Yes. Her undoing." The voice turned solemn.

"Okay, I don't get it. You said that you were made by the Andyoldeans—"

"Antediluvians."

"Whatever. You got made by those people, but you know me and my friends, and...the future?" Her head tilted to one side as her eyes squinted half shut.

"There is no future, just possibilities and remembrance," it answered.

Renarde nodded slowly. "All right. I now understand why people get frustrated with me. Kinda." Placing her hands on either side of her nose, Renarde pulled all the way back along her muzzle, over her ears, and down the length of her hair.

"To continue," the voice spoke, "the shadows themselves are powerless inside me, but that does not mean that I am invulnerable. I was placed inside the hollow mountain, hidden away from them as I radiated against the shadows in all directions. In time, they still discovered me, and pitted war against me, attacking from the rock itself. I was wounded severely, and I fear that my guardian was damaged. When the Antediluvians gave their existence to destroy the shadows and bring forth the celestials, the assault against me was halted. And for the millennia I waited, content in doing my duty.

"When the witch-children arrived, they captured my guardian and restored him, altering his purpose and design. Afterwards, they attempted to delve into my being, pulling forth the contents and shards I held within. Most notably, they found the Cabinet of Shadows, holding the majority of the shadow spawn I had captured. Now, thanks to the Antediluvian, those spawn are once more free."

Starting at the far left side of her mouth and slowly tracking along the full length until it reached the right side, Renarde slid her tongue along her lips. "Okay. Except there's one problem. Armas opened you up. I have no idea how, but I saw him do it. So, it wasn't one of the Angryfallopians—"

"Antediluvians."

"—at all. It was Armas, wife of Sigrid, seemingly nice guy, and surprisingly good lay."

"Well, then this Armas, as you call him, is an Antediluvian," the voice replied.

The words lingered in the white nothingness for a second.

"How…but…?" Renarde raised her hand up and held it there. "What? I thought they were all dead?"

"Apparently, so did they," it answered. "I assure you, though, the only being able to release the shadows is an Antediluvian."

"Okay. Well, that's not good. So, we have a whole bunch of ancient shadow thingies flying about, ready to do all kinds of nasty stuff, I'm sure, which is not good." Her mouth wrinkled up and her ears fell flat as her tail drummed against…nothing, it seemed. "Now all I have to do is find a way out of here, figure out a way to deal with all the old—and likely really, really mad—shadows, two really nasty witch women, and then get Armas and Sigrid back together while keeping everyone, including myself, alive. Right. Got it."

"You sound troubled," the voice said.

"It is kind of a big job, actually. And I am just one small—but really super cute—woman." She looked over at the shape. "Got any suggestions?"

This time she was sure she saw a smile.

"I'm so glad you asked me that."

• • • • • • •

Olav was chewing his lip. Repeatedly. The two women in front of him maneuvered carefully around each other, measuring each other. For the past several minutes they had been engaged in a fight. Swords clashing combined with the sporadic attempt—or success—with a punch or kick. From a casual perspective, they were both giving as well as the other.

Unfortunately, Olav did not have a casual perspective. He watched Sigrid's chest heaving, fighting to gather her breath. Across from her, Mathilda showed only the slightest indication of labored breathing.

"You drop your left shoulder before you attack," Mathilda said, pointing at the shoulder. "Keep them square. Let your body move fluidly."

"Shut up," Sigrid snarled. "Just shut up."

"I'm only trying to help. No need to be snippy," Mathilda chuckled.

"What the hell is wrong with you?" Sigrid spat. "Either end this or let me pass!"

Mathilda clucked her tongue. "Ah. Do you value yourself so poorly? I've actually been quite impressed with you so far."

"Bitch!" Sigrid lunged forward again, driving the point of her sword directly at her enemy's midsection. For what seemed the hundredth time to Sigrid, Mathilda slid to one side, parrying the attack away from her body. This time at least, Sigrid caught a piece of fabric and tore it away.

Leaping away, Mathilda brought her free hand to the cloth, inspecting the rip with her fingers. The corners of her lips pulled tight.

"Almost," Sigrid said with a smile.

Raising her head slightly, Mathilda nodded. Her next movement brought her to Sigrid, who fumbled backwards, avoiding the angled, shallow slice. Swinging upwards, Sigrid pushed the blade away from her, and thrust out again, but this time missing wildly. Arcing overhand, Mathilda swung down at Sigrid, who fell to the floor and rolled off to the side.

"Not…gonna make it easy…on you," Sigrid gasped.

"Obviously," Mathilda grumbled in response. "You do understand that if I wanted to kill you I already would have."

"Seems like you've been trying to me," Sigrid said as she regained her feet.

Mathilda took a step back, circling slowly to her left. Shuffling her feet, Sigrid stayed across from her, only to have her foot catch momentarily and stagger. Wasting no time, Mathilda moved in with a slight backhand swing. A wave of Sigrid's sword knocked it to the side. Three more times, from three different angles, Mathilda swung on her, each time only to have the blade rebuffed.

Mounting what she could, Sigrid swung low, finding only air as Mathilda leapt backwards. It gave Sigrid the time she needed to regroup, pulling herself up and letting her re-grip her sword.

"She's only here for her husband!" Olav shouted, unable to stay silent.

She glanced his way, maintaining her focus on her opponent. "I know that. What would you have me do, Olav? Let her take him?"

"Yes! Please!" he pleaded.

"It doesn't matter," Sigrid said with a growl. "I'm taking him whether you let me or not."

They continued to circle each other, looking for an opportunity.

"And what makes you think that?" Mathilda asked.

A piercing scream preceded her attack. Sigrid threw herself into it with a powerful overhead strike. Mathilda was able to get her sword up in time, but the force of the blow drove her arm down. Immediately, Sigrid followed with a second swing driving Mathilda's arm lower. The third swing took her down to one knee. Before she could swing a fourth time, Mathilda grabbed Sigrid's ankle with her free hand and pulled, toppling her over onto her back. Sigrid's arm flung out as she went to cushion her impact, and as she did her sword skittered away.

Leaping forward, Mathilda landed atop Sigrid, driving her forearm into the woman's midsection, forcing the air out of her. Sputtering and coughing, and pinned down by Mathilda's weight, Sigrid felt something cold against her throat.

"You fight well, woman, but this is not your day to win." Mathilda was close enough to whisper the words. "I will say your goodbyes to your husband."

Something suddenly pushed against Mathilda's ribs.

"Put your sword down." Olav's voice cracked. "Now. Do it now."

There was no response. She remained motionless, her sword still in hand.

"I mean it! Put it down!" Olav pushed forward, driving the point deep enough to draw blood.

With a flick of her wrist, Mathilda threw her sword behind her, away from Olav. The moment she felt him pull back, she rolled away and came up on her feet. Her eyes moving along to locate her sword. It was well within reach.

Finding her sword took her eyes away from the fight, however. With all of her strength, Sigrid kicked her foot up, driving it directly into Mathilda's groin. A sharp yelp accompanied her buckling knees, though she didn't fall to the ground.

"Give me my sword!" Sigrid scrambled backwards, pushing herself up to her feet beside Olav. Her breath was labored and blood trickled from the corner of her mouth. All of his attention was focused on helping her—healing her—but before he could even speak she yanked the sword away from him.

The sound of scraping metal drew their attention back. Rising back to her feet, sword in hand, stood Mathilda. Teeth clenched, she raised her arm, leveling her sword at Sigrid. Olav took a full step back.

Before any words could be uttered, the door on the platform flung open. Two guards rushed through, streaming trails of black mist behind them, swords raised. Without hesitation, Mathilda attacked, cleaving the head from the first one to her in a single stroke. The second one was close behind, his sword cleaving through the air towards her neck.

It was met and stopped by another steel blade.

Sigrid pulled back from her block, pushing the attacker away and giving Mathilda the opportunity she needed to dispatch him as quickly as the first.

From the two bodies on the ground, long tendrils of shadowy black rose up, curling and coalescing into elongated shapes not unlike human bodies with faint glowing eyes. They moved together, spiraling over each other as they flew the short distance between them and their new target—Olav.

Spinning around, Sigrid turned her blade up through the air, cutting through one of the inky shadow's, rending it in half. In concert, Mathilda swung down, cutting the other one in two equal parts. For a moment.

The segments of shadow slid through the air, finding their other halves and rejoining them. With a shriek they flew towards Olav once again, who stumbled backwards until he was against the stone wall at the edge of the balcony.

Sigrid and Mathilda ran towards him, slashing through the air at the shadows outracing them. They flew past the balcony, circling around to come back again, and giving time for the women to reach Olav. Each of them grabbed one shoulder and pulled him back, standing between him and the shadows. They flew in again, and both women brought their swords up. Sigrid swung across, cutting one in half again. Mathilda shifted her blade, meeting the shadow directly and dividing in down the middle, either part falling aside.

The two halves of Sigrid's shuddered and then rejoined. What was left from Mathilda's attack fell and faded into nothingness.

"Their eyes!" Mathilda shouted. "Aim for the eyes!"

A flash of steel brought Sigrid's blade into the face of the reformed shadow, splitting the front portion and cleaving the eyes apart. With an unholy wail it disintegrated into nothing.

"What in the holy hell are those?!" Sigrid shouted.

"I have no idea." Mathilda turned to look down the open hallway, seeing nothing but hearing the sound of more shrill, inhuman screams. The two women turned to look at each other.

The mutual expression on their face was concern. The underlying tone was resolve. Narrowing their eyes they measured each other once more.

"This isn't done," Mathilda said.

"It is for now. We can resume later if you want," Sigrid answered.

They nodded once to each other, and then turned to Olav.

"Stay close," Sigrid said.

"Grab a sword. Use it. Aim for their eyes," Mathilda instructed.

The moment Olav picked up a weapon, the three of them ran into the tunnel, Mathilda leading the way.

• • • • • • • •

Walking together, side by side, through the halls of their own keep, Oikea and Vasen came upon the occasional shadowed figure hunkered over a fallen guard or servant. Once identified, they didn't last long. They paid little heed to the withered husk of a shell the shadow had stolen life from. It was little more than debris needing removal. Though they did pause at times to consider the best method to hire or acquire additional people to fill the roles being vacated.

It wasn't until they found themselves in the main hallway of the keep, staring at a hundred whirling shadows, that they began to consider the threat. A simple glance towards each other was enough to tell them what needed to be done, and a second later they unleashed a torrent of magic, arcing through the hallway like lightning striking the peak of a tree, with similar results. The shadows shattered, scattering to the walls and floor—and parts the ceiling—and even leaving scorch marks along some of the surfaces of the hallway itself.

What surprised them was seeing some of the shadows pull together and reform. Not all, but some.

"These creatures are unknown to me," Oikea said. "You've studied more on the creatures of the nether realms. Do you recognize them?"

"No, dear, I do not. With the number we are seeing here that surprises me a good deal, actually," Vasen replied.

"Do you think that some idiot in the mines stumbled and released this plague of…shadows, I suppose?" Oikea moved slightly away from her sister, looking at the outline of a figure that was burned into the wood on the walls.

Vasen waited while her sister examined the spot. "I suppose it's possible, but that just doesn't seem right, somehow."

"It's not." The voice preceded the figure, and it caught the attention of both sisters. Oikea moved to stand beside Vasen in the hallway, facing towards the approaching outline. "Well, not directly, anyway."

"Sepi?" Vasen turned her head. "Sebastian, is that you?"

"Interesting question." Stepping clearly into view, Sebastian walked down the middle of the hallway. Behind him a dozen shadow forms twisted and turned in the hallway, following his lead. "In one way, yes. In another, no."

"This isn't the time to be cryptic, darling," Oikea stated. "We are feeling just a teensy bit antsy right now."

"Oh, I assure you that I do not want to provoke you. Either of you." He walked towards them, standing tall. "I do value my current existence, after all."

Vasen's eyes traveled up and down the length of Sebastian's body, narrowing more and more with every second. "Who are you? You are not Sebastian. Do you represent these…creatures?"

He laughed. "Well, that's a more difficult question than you realize. I actually am Sebastian. At least I'm the Sebastian that you have known for over two months now." He smiled. "And yes, I do represent my brothers."

"Perhaps you are the right one to discipline over this affront, darling." A crackle of energy surrounded Oikea's hands, but Vasen gently lowered them with her own.

"One moment, dear," she said to her sister softly, and then turned to Sebastian. "Are you saying that you replaced my husband two months ago? And you call these things brothers. Are you one of them?"

"Close. I'm a distant brother, but still one of them. I heard their call a few miles from here and simply had to come visit. I bumped into your Sebastian downstairs, and borrowed him for a bit." He smiled. "I do hope you don't mind."

An eyebrow went up on Vasen's face. "Well, you did just admit to killing my husband."

"A loveless marriage. You were using him for your own means, which is all that I've done. We have far more in common than you think," he replied, and then looked to Oikea. "All three of us."

"Darling, don't compare me to you or these…things." Oikea waved her hand casually at the shadows twisting in the air behind him.

"My sister brings up a very good point. What are those things, and what are they doing here?" Vasen asked.

"That is precisely what I came to speak with you about!" He stepped forward a step, stopping as soon as he saw the magical energy arc across both sister's hands. "Ah, well, let me explain. You see, I have recognized your power—the one the two of you share—and I have no desire to confront it. I would much rather help it. Help you."

"Explain yourself, dear," Vasen answered.

"The two of you have great dreams of power, yes? Dreams of ruling the whole of Dula Koarr. I think that is quite a reasonable goal. We," he gestured to the floating shadows, "can help you to become the Queens of Dula Koarr. We are more than willing to share this world with you."

"Interesting," Oikea strummed her fingers on her thigh, "but you didn't answer the question, darling. What are those and where did they come from?"

"Ah, you see, that's the thing. The two of you were on the right path, but you didn't know how to complete it. You have potential. You simply did not know—"

"Stop skirting the answer and tell us," Vasen interrupted.

"The cabinet. They came from the cabinet," he stated softly.

"And just how did they free themselves?" Vasen's chin lifted up as she stared down at him.

"They didn't. I freed them." He moved back to the center of the hallway.

"You? If you could open the cabinet, why didn't you do it long ago? I don't believe you," Vasen said.

"Well, true, I did have help. Armas technically opened it, but he did so at my behest." He bowed his head slightly.

"He did? You forced him to open it?" Oikea asked.

"No, no! That wouldn't work. He had to open it on his own accord. Now that he has, however, I—"

"And where is Armas now?" Vasen asked.

"Safe. I have Hjalmar watching him," he answered. "He needed to be moved."

"Hjalmar should have been in his room. Why is he is listening to you? Shouldn't he be only following our commands?" Oikea shifted her weight from her right to her left, bringing her closer to her sister.

Sebastian nodded. "Ah, well, I understand a bit on his inner workings, and was able to—"

"You altered our orders. You made him obey you," Vasen said, sliding to her right. "Is that basically it?"

"I needed his help to bring Armas to the cabinet," he explained.

"Why didn't you do that much sooner? Why the wait?" Oikea asked.

"I had to see who you were. What you offered and how we could benefit each other," he answered. "But all of that is not important! What is important is that we are now working together towards the same goal. You want this country, and we can help you get it." He brought his hands up and the shadows moved around, swirling past him and then back behind him again, circling him in the hallway.

Slowly, with growing smiles, the two sisters turned to each other. They nodded as one, and turned back to Sebastian.

"Dear Sebastian," as Vasen spoke, her right hand moved out to grasp Oikea's left, "you have made a compelling argument. One that strikes us near our heart." She took a deep breath and shared a smile with Sebastian. "So…no."

He blinked and shook his head. "What?"

"Do you really think us so shallow, darling? I must say, for some…thing that has been studying us for two months, you are sadly lacking in information," Oikea said. A glow surrounded their joined hands.

"You may have Sebastian's form, but you certainly do not have his wisdom." The glow intensified. "If you had approached us earlier, before you made such a move, you may have been able to convince us, but now...." Vasen shook her head.

"Now you are acting out of fear, darling. If you weren't afraid, you wouldn't have done anything of the sort. You know that we can hurt you, and for some reason your 'brothers' avoid us." Oikea looked at her sister. "We believe there is something you aren't telling us."

"And we believe that something starts with the cabinet," Vasen added.

Darkness fell over Sebastian's face. "You idiotic whores! I offer you a place in the world and you cast it aside? Fine. Die with the rest of your kind!"

The laugh from the sisters was easily lost amid the sudden shriek of the shadows. Scattering through the hallway, the shadows flew out, invading the walls themselves. Moments later, the wood creaked as the hallway began to constrict upon itself.

"Oh, darling, that's not a good idea." Oikea raised her right hand.

"Not at all." Vasen raised her left hand.

A blinding light filled the hallway, erupting from the sisters and flooding down the hallway, invading every nook and cranny, penetrating to the core of the wood and beyond. The shrieks of the shadows took on a very different tone, changing to high-pitched screams as they shredded amid the brilliant assault.

When the light died, the hallway was empty.

"Hmm. Sebastian scurried away," Vasen said, pulling her hand free of her sister.

"You expected something else, darling? Bugs like him hate the light." Oikea rubbed her hands together gently, wincing slightly. "I do so wish that wasn't so painful."

"We both do, dear." She turned to her sister and stepped closer, kissing her lightly on her exposed cheek. "It's so wonderful that we can share something like that, though."

"Oh yes! So intimate, in its own way." Oikea pulled back. "Where do you suppose he ran?"

"Where else? To the cabinet. I'm wagering he wants to protect it from us, somehow." Vasen took a step away and rubbed her right hand lightly.

Oikea's face lit up. "Do you suppose there is a way for us to control these shadows ourselves? Directly, I mean, using the cabinet?"

"A wonderful suggestion!" Vasen nodded. "Why don't we go and find out?"

"After you," Oikea gestured.

"No, no. After you," Vasen countered.

They both hesitated, and then spoke simultaneously, "Together."

With a slight nod to each other, they turned and walked down the hall.

· · · · · · ·

The wind whipped around them, slinging snow and blinding them to anything more than a few feet away. Armas felt it as well. He was chilled to the bone, shivering and desperately trying to find any comfort. He tugged on the rope around his waist, testing the strength of the knot once again. Tracking the rope to the other end, he had no doubt that the knot around Hjalmar's waist was just as strong.

In one sense, he was dejected. There was no way to free himself without a blade, but that wasn't necessarily a bad thing. A glance behind him brought his stomach into his throat, seeing the ground falling away behind him. Though he could only see a short distance, the feeling of the huge distance was no less powerful. He swallowed back the lump in his throat and closed his eyes, ultimately grateful to be tethered to the powerful man ahead of him.

"Don't do that."

Armas turned back, seeing Hjalmar glancing over his shoulder with a stern expression. He nodded quickly, digging in his heels and re-gripping the rock face. Off to his left was Valpuri Keep, now a hundred feet away, and he had no idea how far down. Since Hjalmar dragged him out onto the mountainside and began the climb up, he struggled to keep up. With the increasing cold, the drop off below him seemed more and more ominous.

"Wh-where are we going?" Armas asked. "Shouldn't we be inside?"

"To a keeping room." Hjalmar's voice was deep and rumbling, carrying through the wind clearly.

"What's that?"

"A room where you keep things. I thought that was obvious," he answered. "Stay close. You need to follow me precisely. I do not want to carry you."

"If it's a room, then why," he climbed up, trying to get closer, "why are we outside? Shouldn't it be inside?"

"The keeping rooms were carved into the side of the cliff and meant to be difficult to reach. They are safe and secure." Hjalmar continued his climb, threatening once more to outpace Armas.

"I'm…I'm going to freeze to death," Armas stated, his teeth chattering through the words.

Hjalmar looked back again. "Then climb faster."

A sudden burst of wind cut through Armas. "You're supposed to keep me safe. That's what…that's what Sebastian said. You're killing me."

"No, I'm not. You may become very cold, perhaps even frostbitten, but you won't die. The keeping rooms are protected as well. You'll recover. And we are almost to a trail, which will speed things along."

As if on cue, a gap in the snow appeared, giving them a clear view ahead. An obvious break in the face of the cliff revealed itself, giving a brief moment of hope to Armas—very brief. The next blast of cold air hit him like a hammer on an anvil. He felt his body reshape and twitch, pulling up and causing his muscles to contract sharply. His hand slipped from the rock, followed immediately by his other hand. Instinctively he grabbed blindly, hoping for a handhold, and raking his left hand across a jagged stone, gashing him deeply. He screamed, both from pain and terror. A second later his fall ended with a sudden yank on his waist, as the rope linking him to Hjalmar pulled taut.

The big man on the mountain didn't move, other than to reach above him and begin climbing faster. Armas made an attempt to grab the cliff again, finding firm grip with his right hand, but discovering the left to be worthless. His feet slipped off the stone multiple times, never truly aiding him up the mountain, but his excited nerves kept them in constant motion.

The rope around his waist pulled suddenly tighter, and he accelerated up at an alarming rate. Once more he screamed, flying up above Hjalmar. With one arm, his captor and protector had tossed him up in an arc, and he landed on the ledge quite unceremoniously.

Armas lay there, his chest heaving as he tried to regain his breath. The pain in his left hand suddenly became a sharp throb as he pulled it close to his body. He barely noticed Hjalmar climb up onto the ledge with him.

Grabbing his wrist, Hjalmar pulled his left hand up and studied it. Shaking his head, he tore a piece of cloth from his sleeve and wrapped it tightly around Armas' hand. He examined it once, and then let it go, standing slowly above the wounded man.

"That was a really good throw."

They both turned to look up. Like a splinter of stone that hadn't quite fallen away, the rock loomed almost ten feet above them, a small pillar of granite with rough edges towered along the cliff face. Atop it, crouched down on all fours, rested a silver and black figure, her fur spotted with small bits of snow.

"Renarde?" Armas sat up, once more clutching his hand to his chest.

"How did you get here?" Hjalmar asked.

With a quick glance that way, she pointed the direction of the keep with her right thumb. "I ran."

"That isn't what I meant." Hjalmar reached to his side and pulled a small axe free. "I meant how did you find us? You were imprisoned."

"Was. That's the important word there. I was imprisoned." She nodded. "Oh, and I just listened after I got out of the building. I already had Armas' scent, and while I'm no Porter, I can do that a little."

"You prattle like a child," Hjalmar said.

"Well, one of us has to." She leaned down slightly. "So, are you gonna give me Armas, or do I have to take him?"

A single huff of a laugh preceded his words. "You cannot take him little non-demon. He is in my custody and will remain there."

Renarde shook her head. "Y'know, even when you don't call me a demon you call me a demon. You are one obsessed…thing." She stood up on the pillar, her tail waving behind her to keep her balance as the wind blew her hair and fur in swirls. "Which reminds me, I had a very illuminating," she laughed briefly at herself, "conversation in a box recently. Found out a few things. Want to guess one?"

"No," he answered flatly.

"Well, okay. Fine." Her hair flew back away from her head, and her ears flattened down. "I have this thing about hurting people. It makes me feel really bad. So, I really don't do much actual fighting. Then the box told me something very, very important." She bared her teeth. "You aren't a people."

Leaping from the pillar, she sprung against the wall and struck Hjalmar in the side with her foot. The impact moved him slightly, but did little else. The axe swing that followed missed her by inches and she flipped in mid-air to land on all fours beyond Armas, looking at Hjalmar and snarling.

"The beast reveals herself," Hjalmar said, pulling another axe from his waist.

"Never tried to hide that part," she answered with a grin. "Besides, I already hid a little today. I'm not just a one-trick fox."

As she moved, so did he. Armas fell to the ground, flat beneath them as they fought above him. With one eye closed, he barely made out any details, but could see flashes of metal and fur. For him time moved slowly. The direct conflict that took only a second or two unfolding in an unreadable long blur. When they separated, he felt a drop of blood land on his face.

"You do know that you aren't a person, right?" Renarde growled from past Armas' head. "The white box said that you probably couldn't be fixed at this point, either. That you had been infected or something, and that your brain was broke."

"I follow my orders, beast. That's all I need to do." He nodded towards her. "And it is your body that is breaking, not mine."

A thin line of red ran from Renarde's back, down her side, and dripped onto the ground.

"I've had worse, trust me," she said.

"And you will again." Hjalmar stalked forward, raising the axes.

Renarde leapt backwards, flipping once completely before landing on two feet, far back of the onrushing Hjalmar. She smiled and waited.

Only a few feet short of her, he jerked suddenly, tugging Armas forward with him and snapping the cord between them rigid. That slight hesitation was Renarde's signal to move. She ran past him, moving high along the wall, only to drop down immediately. Her teeth fell on the rope, and with a sharp snap she sliced the cord in two.

Hjalmar whirled, both axes spinning with him, and narrowly missing Renarde as she ducked low.

"Well, I'm glad that's done. It makes things easier," she said.

"Not really." A flurry of blows fell from Hjalmar, each one striking stone as Renarde ducked, dodged, and dove around them. "My body restores itself instantly. Nothing can damage me."

"First point," she snarled, "I'm quicker than you. Second point," she jumped at him, landing on his chest, and rearing her head back, "I'm magic, so, actually, I can hurt you."

Her jaw clamped around his neck, but only for a brief second. She heard the axes rushing through the air, and fell back to the ground in time—almost. One of them missed her completely, but the other caught her in the side, leaving a bit of an open gash.

Hjalmar's neck was exposed. Lines of metal strung up under the torn flesh, like cables on a clock, pulling and straining as he moved his head. One of them snapped, jerking his head to one side and causing his lip to curl up sharply. He staggered.

In a short sprint, Renarde flew into him, leaving her feet and kicking him with all her might in the mid-section. He bent over, dropping one axe as his hand fell to the ground in support. Tumbling over his back, Renarde dropped to the ground and rolled up until she was directly under him.

"Bye-bye!" She waved at him as her feet pushed up, driving him into the air and back away from her—and over the edge of the cliff.

Bouncing to her feet, Renarde looked over the side. A few feet below the ledge, Hjalmar was grasping a large stone and slowly pulling himself up.

"Dang, you are stubborn." Her eyes scanned the ground until she found his discarded weapon. She pulled it up next to her head as she looked down at him again. "Hey! Hey Metal-Nose!" He looked up at her with black eyes. "You forgot this."

The axe left her hand with a flick of the wrist, striking the stone in his grip. The blade embedded into the frozen rock with a sharp cracking sound. Before a heartbeat passed, a fracture appeared in the rock. He didn't look away from her eyes as the stone crumbled, and then he fell away. She watched him tumble over the rocks silently, passing down beyond her range of sight and into the swirling snowstorm below them.

"And don't come back," she said down to no one visible, and then plopped down onto her butt. "Ouch." She reached up and felt the wound on her side.

"Are…are you okay?" Armas crawled over to her, his expression still fairly blank.

Her lips curved up into a wide grin as she looked at him. "Me? Oh yeah, I'm good. I'm actually kinda hard to kill. Gift of Threnody." She moved her hand away from the wound. "This hurts, but it won't keep me down." Her eyes fell to his hand. "Are you okay?"

"My hand is cut badly, and I'm...very cold," he muttered.

"C'mere!" She grabbed him and pulled him close. "I'm a warm person. I can help." He moved in and braced against her fur. "Besides, we gotta get you back inside."

"Yes, please," he mumbled.

"I really need your help," she said. "Oh! That's right, you don't know. You're an Angledeludean."

"A what?" He blinked.

"One of those really old dead people that don't exist. You're one of those," she said quickly. "So we need to get you inside."

"Do you mean Antediluvian?" He shook his head. "No, I'm not. Those don't exist."

"Yeah, they do and you are. Don't worry, you'll see." She jumped up quickly and held her hand down. "C'mon, I'll get you down to the crazy ladies' house. I know a short cut." She tilted her head to the side. "Okay, it's really more of a very fast drop, but it'll get us there, honest."

She smiled down at him, beaming from ear to ear. With a hard swallow he reached up and took her hand.

・　・　・　・　・　・　・

"What happened here?" Sigrid turned around, checking behind her quickly, before looking back at the scene in front of her.

"I'm not sure." Mathilda gently ran her hand over the metal's edge, feeling the inconsistency of the surface. "The door was pulled off of the hinges. You can see where it bent."

"How's that even possible?" Olav asked.

"What difference does it make? Where's Armas?" Sigrid's voice teetered on the brink.

Turning back to her, Mathilda gripped her sword tightly and smiled. "Not here, obviously. Beyond that, I don't know."

"You said he was here!" Sigrid stepped towards her, arms wide.

"And he was when I left. Someone or something has moved him since," she answered, stepping towards Sigrid.

"Ladies," Olav stepped between them, "this isn't between you." He turned to Sigrid. "There isn't a body, so he wasn't taken by shadows. We know that much. We just have to find him." Then he addressed Mathilda. "Who—or what—could have done that? Pulled that door off?"

"Nothing." She shook her head. "That's impossible."

"Obviously not," Sigrid retorted.

"Well, then let me say that I know of nothing that could make it possible, is that more to your liking?" Mathilda stepped just to the right to get a clear view of Sigrid when she answered.

"Stop it! Both of you!" Olav shouted. "I don't know about the two of you, but I'm terrified, and the two of you bickering is not making it easier!" Neither woman flinched as he took a deep breath. "Mathilda, you know what's going on better than we do—and I know you are just as confused—so do you have any idea where he might have been taken?"

Mathilda turned back to the cell and took a single step inside. Turning slowly, she surveyed the whole space. "I left two guards here." She turned back. "They aren't here now. They weren't taken by the shadows, either."

A shadow screech echoed through the hall, passing by the outer door quickly, and causing all three of them to tense up. Even after it was gone the tension remained.

"Why aren't they coming after us?" Sigrid asked. "They've come after you, Olav, but left Mathilda and I alone. Why?"

"It must have something to do with why they are here. Something about the two of us. I would say it was that we are both female, but we've seen other women being attacked. So…." Mathilda nodded. "It's because of who we are. They have orders not to attack us."

"Orders?" Olav asked.

"Yes. When I instruct my soldiers to do something, they do it. They follow orders, and that includes who they can and cannot attack. These shadows are under orders," she stated.

"Then who is giving them orders?" Sigrid asked.

Mathilda looked at her. "My first thought is my sisters, but they wouldn't do this to the rest of the keep." She shook her head. "I don't know, but I'm willing to bet I know the location where the order came from. That damned hall. Something in that hall did this."

"What hall?" Sigrid asked.

"The place where Oikea and Vasen keep their…relics," Olav stated.

Mathilda was already walking before any more words were said. The others fell in quickly behind her, moving out into the larger section of the keep. Immediately they were confronted by shadows flying past, screeching down the hallways. Any that dared come close were met by steel from Mathilda or Sigrid.

They raced through the halls, Mathilda guiding them directly to their destination. From the corner of her eye, Sigrid saw several figures with shadows over them in adjacent rooms and hallways. With no time to wait, she didn't know if they were alive or dead, and didn't dare stop or she would be lost behind Mathilda and Olav. Eyes forward, head straight, she pushed through, ignoring any screams she heard from without or within.

One final turn brought them to a sudden stop. A massive door was wide open, revealing a hall-like chamber lined with gold. Sigrid's eyes jumped from item to item, looking at the various marvels in the room. Mathilda was immediately focused on one in particular.

"It's open," she whispered. "Those things were inside it." Her face contorted, wrenching into a twisted, painful countenance. "Those idiots! They didn't know what the hell they were doing!"

"Mathilda?" The voice was soft and fragile. All three of them turned to find a small, frail looking man walking towards them quickly.

"Sebastian?" Mathilda stepped towards him. "What's going on? Do you know what happened?"

"Oh, yes. Yes, I do." His breath was labored, and he all but staggered towards them. "Your sisters went mad. They…they forced Armas to open the box. You see what happened. They couldn't control it. And now they have gone insane, killing everything they see."

"What about Armas?" Sigrid stepped forward. "Where is he?"

"Oh, I don't know. They sent him away with Hjalmar. He took him someplace. I couldn't stop them." He looked at Sigrid. "Who are you?"

"I'm his wife," she growled. "Where did he take him? Which direction?"

"It doesn't matter," Mathilda said. "We need to deal with my sisters first. This must be stopped." She looked at Sigrid. "I need your help."

"But I have to—"

"If we don't stop them, then you, me, Armas, and everyone else here will all die! We save them, and we save him. Understood?" She moved to stand in front of Sigrid, rising up to her full height.

"It makes sense, Sigrid," Olav said.

"Yes. Yes, listen to him. You have to stop them," Sebastian shuffled past the three of them, moving into the golden hall.

"Fine, but as soon as this is done…." Sigrid took a deep breath and let it out slowly.

"Agreed," Mathilda said with a nod.

"Oh, thank you! Thank you!" Sebastian took a few steps deeper into the hall. "They already tried to kill me once."

"Get inside," Mathilda ordered, directing Olav to go with Sebastian. "The two of you lock yourselves in. We'll find my sisters and deal with this, one way or another. Don't open these doors until everything is safe, do you understand?"

"Yes," Sebastian nodded. "Don't worry. I'll make sure no one gets inside."

"Good. We'll be back soon," Mathilda answered.

"Stay safe," Sigrid said to Olav.

"Don't worry. I'll take care of him." The two women turned and headed down the hall. Behind them the door slowly closed, causing a shadow to fall over Sebastian's face.

end chapter seven

CHAPTER
EIGHT

THE COLLOCATION

Every few steps another shadow creature would appear. Most of them immediately retreated, disappearing into the actual shadows or racing down the hall with a shrill scream. A few of them, however, came closer. And those that did quickly learned the error of their ways. Bursts of magic shredded them apart, destroying them utterly, and doing nothing to slow the advance of the Valpuri sisters.

They weren't walking with haste or excitement, but a steady pace towards their destination. It lay one floor below them, where Sebastian was undoubtedly waiting. They stopped briefly at the top of the stairs, looking down them to make sure it was safe.

"I suppose you'll want to apologize," Oikea stated as they began their descent.

"Apologize? Whatever for?" Vasen stepped with her, remaining at her side.

"For Sebastian, of course. If it's truly been two months as he claims, you should have noticed that he was replaced long ago, darling." Oikea glanced at her sister on the last word.

"Well, I suppose I should be getting one from you likewise, then," Vasen retorted. "You've seen him every day for those two months as well."

Oikea tutted with her tongue. "True, but he isn't my husband."

"Ah yes, that would make you more oblivious, wouldn't it." Vasen sighed heavily. "Let's not tread these trails again, dear. At least not right now. We have more important matters at hand."

"Oh, I agree, darling!" Oikea turned to her sister as they neared the bottom of the stairs. "I just thought you might want to say something before we dispatched your false husband."

"Why no, dear," Vasen looked her in the eye, "my conscience is perfectly clear. Thank you for your consideration, though. I do appreciate it."

"Don't think of it! I'm always here for you," Oikea said as they stepped off the staircase. A few steps brought them into the main hallway.

Shadows scurried away, finding corners and cracks to squeeze into. Disappearing into the walls and floors themselves it seemed. Neither sister thought anything of it as they strode towards the great hall holding their variety of their treasures.

"Locked," Oikea said.

"And we can both guess who is waiting on the other side," Vasen replied. She glanced at her sister and then gestured casually to the door. "Would you like the honor?"

"No, no. He's your husband. You go first." Oikea smiled and took a small step backwards.

She nodded back to her sister. "Thank you." Stepping up, she gently rapped her knuckles against the door. The sound echoed through the hallway like a battering ram pounding against a fortress. "Sepi, dear, would you please open this door? We don't want to get violent."

The answer was a moment in coming. A distant statement barely crossing the barrier between them. "I'm sorry, but no. You know I won't do that."

"Ah, Sebastian, I think you were confusing what I said as a request. It was more of a statement of what you should do, lest you suffer something rather harsh," Vasen explained. "Now, open the door."

There was a long silence.

"Sebastian!" Oikea stepped beside her sister. "What do you think will happen to you if you don't open this door? Whatever it is, I assure you that you aren't thinking about it enough. You do not want to press this matter."

"How will it be better if I open it? You're both mad with power," he replied.

They glanced at each other. A brief smile accompanied the chuckle they shared.

"Please don't make us out as insane. We are both in full control of our faculties, darling," Oikea explained.

"It is true that we are mad in another sense, however," Vasen continued. "And you do not want to see that pushed to the level of furious."

A brief delay before he responded. "I'm not opening the door. You've lost, Vasen. Take your sister and leave. I know you can't get through this door."

Her eyes narrowed to slits. Rolling her shoulders back, Vasen lowered her chin and stared at the door. "You have brought this upon yourself. Do not blame us for what happens next."

"Darling," Oikea spoke to him through the door, "just so you know, when we get inside, I plan on slipping off little bits of your skin and feeding them to you. I assume you still have skin and the desire to eat, yes?"

Vasen smiled. "Oh, that does sound lovely." She reached over and pecked her sister on the cheek. "You are clever at times." She turned back to the door. "Oh, and Sepi, dear, you are right about one thing: I cannot get through this door. We crafted it so that it would even withstand our own assault."

A giggle filled the hallway, coming from both sisters. Oikea spoke, "But that was against one of us, darling. To stop us individually." She extended her right hand.

Reaching over with her left hand, Vasen took her sister's in her own. "We never tested it against our combined strength." A spark ran across their arms, over their chest, and to their free hands. "We'll see you soon."

The hallway filled with light. The smell of ozone pervaded as energy crackled and washed over the door in a display of magical might. In response, the hallway itself seemed to groan, resting weary under the onslaught waged against a single door.

Oblivious from the roar their own magics created, neither Vasen nor Oikea heard the sharp sound of wood cracking echoing through the rest of the keep.

• • • • • • •

"What the hell was that?" Sigrid shouted.

Pacing ahead of her, Mathilda strode into the room, staring at the destruction littered across the floor. The Burning Heart held its flame, but the heat it gave off couldn't fight off the bitter cold rushing in through the shattered windows. Mathilda recognized the tell-tale signs of battle.

"That was the keep," Mathilda answered. "The whole keep shook."

"That isn't normal, is it? You don't get earthquakes here, right?" Sigrid asked.

She shook her head and walked further into the room. Only a step behind her, Sigrid followed, her eyes scanning the room for trouble as Mathilda crouched down to look at some debris.

"This glass shouldn't be all the way over here." She looked up at the windows, snow building up inside the room, covering the floor just beneath the openings. Determination mixed with curiosity propelled her to walk to the window. Dragging her foot in the gathered snow, she cleared a spot on the floor. There was nothing beneath. No debris at all.

"This isn't possible," Mathilda stated. "There is no way that all of that glass could get over there, but not be here."

"Is this really important right now? We're supposed to be finding your sisters, not figuring out why the windows broke," Sigrid growled. "And if we don't get back on that soon, I'm going to go find Armas, with or without you."

Even with Mathilda's back turned to her, Sigrid could see her take a deep breath and close her eyes. When she finally turned around to face her, she wore a placid expression. "No. You won't. We are staying together, and you are going to do what I tell you. Understood?"

In a slow, even move, Sigrid brought her sword up level, pointing it at Mathilda. "You do not tell me what to do."

"Are we going to do this again?" Mathilda took a step backwards, bringing her sword around and spinning her grip around once before firmly grabbing hold. "Let's at least make it quick so that I can get on with the important task of finding my sisters and your husband!"

"Leave your hands off of him!" Sigrid shifted her feet, adjusting her stance, and dropping her sword to a lower position.

"I haven't touched him. My sisters, on the other hand, have been having their way with him practically every night." Mathilda snarled. "If you want to keep him safe, then you need to listen to me and stop this foolish anger! It accomplishes nothing!"

"It's gotten me this far!" Sigrid snapped.

They stood only a few feet apart, their swords separated by less than the span of one hand. A snarl curled on each of their lips, the flame of the nearby hearth reflected in their eyes. A single line of sweat ran down one of their faces, anticipating the short fall to the floor. Waiting for a signal to drop.

"Wow, this room is freezing and you guys still need to cool off."

The voice snapped them back and turned their heads in the same direction. On the far side of the room, leaning casually against the sill of one of the destroyed windows, stood a lithe silver fox woman with a massive smile on her muzzle.

"Renarde?" Mathilda pulled back slightly.

"Renarde!" Sigrid said with elation.

"Hi." She smiled, her tail flipping behind her. "Okay, so now that I've interrupted the two of you about to try to cut each other up, can I ask what's been happening? I've been outside."

"Why were you outside?" Mathilda asked.

Without hesitation Sigrid stepped in front of the Valpuri Captain, and spoke directly to Renarde. "The other Valpuri sisters released some kind of shadow creatures using Armas. We don't know the details, but they've overrun a good part of the keep and they've taken Armas captive. Once we find them, we can stop this and get Armas back to safety."

Renarde's face scrunched up as she closed her right eye and tilted her head that same way. "Well, that's not right. I mean, it wasn't the sisters, but I can see how they might be a pain about it."

"Wait," Mathilda stepped beside Sigrid, "what do you mean it wasn't my sisters. You were outside. We are telling you what happened."

"Well, yeah, I was outside," Renarde rolled her eyes, "but I wasn't outside before I was outside. I was inside then. And I was there, I know who opened the cabinet and let them all out."

"Yes, it was Armas," Mathilda said. "Wasn't it?"

"Oh yeah!" Renarde smiled and nodded voraciously. "But it was Sebastian who tricked him into doing it."

"Sebastian?" Mathilda raised an eyebrow.

"Sebastian!" Re-gripping her sword, Sigrid bared her teeth and narrowed her eyes.

"Yeah, Sebastian." Playing her tongue over her fangs, Renarde laid her ears back against her head. "I have a feeling about him."

"Well, you're wrong. I've known Sebastian for years, and he's a decent man. A little eccentric, yes, but not a monster." Mathilda shook her head defiantly.

"Uh, I kinda watched him do it. I snuck in that room and watched what happened. He tricked Armas into opening up the door, the shadow thingies came out, he got all mean and evil, and then he made Jam-bar take Armas away." Her ears perked back up and her tail swung freely behind her.

"Hjalmar. Yes, Sebastian said he took Armas. Do you know where?" Sigrid asked.

Nodding, Renarde smiled, but said nothing.

"Where?" Sigrid took a half step forward, her eyes glazing for a moment. "Please tell me where."

The floors and walls shook. Bits of the ceiling fell around them, adding to the littered floor.

"We will rescue him, Sigrid." Mathilda stated sternly. "You have my word. Right now, however, we have to save this place. I still think that means finding my sisters."

"Yeah, she's right. We have to find her sisters," Renarde said. "But I think I can guess where they are, too, from what I'm hearing."

"What you're hearing?" Mathilda asked.

"Oh yeah. I've got really good ears." As if to demonstrate, she turned her ears, first together, and then one at a time. "They're downstairs."

"Then let's go!" Mathilda turned and started to walk off.

She was stopped by a sharp whistle. Renarde stood there, shaking her head slowly. "Not yet. We still have a couple of things to do, actually. Like go over the plan and other stuff."

"Plan? You have a plan?" Her jaw dropped, but she kept her mouth closed, so her whole head fell down to her chest. "That... that seems unlikely."

Pulling back her head, the corners of Renarde's lips curled down. "Hey! I can plan!"

"Of course you can." With a nod, Mathilda straightened herself upright once more. "And what was the other...stuff...you wanted to go over?"

"Well, there is really only one thing. And I gotta say," she turned and gave a short whistle, "I've really been looking forward to seeing this."

A rope fell down to the window where Renarde stood. It twitched, moved from above. Slowly, a figure crept down into view, sliding down the rope and into the room to join everyone else. He stood up and look over at the women across from him.

Sigrid blinked. "A-Armas?"

"Sigrid?" Light seemed to wash over his face like a newborn morning.

He ran towards her, moving past Renarde without a second glance. She ran towards him, dropping her sword with a clatter onto the floor. By the time they embraced, both of their faces were wet with tears. Neither of them moved or said a word. With all of their being they clung to each other, instantly oblivious to everything around them, content in only knowing each other for this one moment.

Renarde stood there, left arm across her body and right elbow resting on that, her hand on her cheek. "Awwww…."

"Touching." The word dripped off of Mathilda's tongue. "It doesn't help, though."

"Sure it does!" Renarde bounced towards her. "Because that gets us all together, and we need that before the whole house crumbles apart."

"Crumbles apart?" Mathilda mused. "What do you know?"

"Wow. That's gonna take a long time to answer. I'm not sure this is the best time to—"

"About what is happening!" Mathilda interrupted.

"Oh. Well," Renarde's eyes went around in a big circle, "don't see many shadows right now, do you?"

They all glanced around as the realization sank in.

"Where did they go?" Mathilda asked.

"Into the building," Renarde said. "I watched them. They sorta blended into the actual shadows and didn't come back out. I'm guessing that's what's making the house rumble and stuff."

"We have to get out of here." They turned to see Sigrid, hand-in-hand with Armas, staring at them. "Let the house fall. Who cares? Let's get out of here."

"No." Armas pulled far enough away to look at her. "We can't. I...I can't. I have to stay."

"Why?" Sigrid pleaded.

He reached out and touched her face. "Because, this is all my fault. I have to try to stop it."

"And we need to get Olav out," Mathilda said. "We can't just leave him."

"Olav?" Renarde's voice raised up. "Olav's here?"

"Yes, he helped me get inside," Sigrid admitted. "And now he's trapped inside that room with Sebastian. We told him to stay there to keep him safe and watched Sebastian seal the door with both of them inside."

"That's great!" Renarde bounced up and down, her tail swinging wildly behind her. "Perfect!"

They all turned to look at her.

"What? You didn't think I was gonna do this all by myself, did you?"

* * * * * * *

It was easy to become confused in the golden light of the hall, especially considering the pandemonium that lay beyond it.

A cacophony of chaos constantly crashing on a thin barrier separating these two men from the witches beyond.

Olav shuddered involuntarily.

"Disquieting?" Sebastian asked.

With a slight jerk to his head, Olav turned towards Sebastian. He staggered backwards, putting some space between himself and the surprisingly close man.

"Yes, of course it is. You heard them. Between the sisters outside and the shadows beyond them, this keep has become a nightmare. You've seen them," he answered.

"Indeed I have," Sebastian answered. "The very definition of fear, I would think."

"Not far from it. If it wasn't for Sigrid and Mathilda I...." His words trailed off as he took another step back. "Sebastian, how did you survive being attacked? You said that Oikea and Vasen attacked you, and that you've seen the shadows, but you didn't tell us how you got past them."

"Hmm. I suppose I didn't, did I? Well, it doesn't matter, does it?" He looked over at Olav. "What is your name, by the way? I don't believe we've met."

"Olav. Olav Karhu," he answered methodically. "And we met years ago."

"Oh, did we? I'm sorry. It must have slipped my mind." Sebastian shook his head. "Forgive an old man, won't you?"

"Of course." Olav stepped backwards until he was near the wall, watching as Sebastian moved towards the doors.

"Are you familiar with this room, Olav?" Sebastian asked. "I find it very fascinating."

"How so?" Olav's voice wavered softly.

"It is the most secure room in the keep, all because of," he reached the door, "this door. Once it is locked from the inside, you cannot unlock it from the outside." He turned and looked at Olav. "We are effectively trapped inside."

"Which is what we want, right?" Olav asked, swallowing back growing fears.

Sebastian turned. The light from the hall fell short of illuminating his face, casting him in an unexpected shadow.

"Without a doubt. Anything to keep those damn Valpuri out of this room. I doubt they can affect the cabinet, but why take a chance. It won't matter in a few minutes, anyway." His voice was deeper, darker.

"Who are you? What are you talking about?" Olav barely spoke above a whisper.

"I'm talking about me destroying Valpuri Keep. It seems the easiest way to insure those pests are gone for good, don't you think?" The light in the room seemed to dim, drawn in towards Sebastian.

A tremor shook the building.

• • • • • • •

Laces of energy streamed from their fingers, covering the door and the surrounding wall like a massive web from an unseen spider. It danced over the surface, skimming it and sparking off of it, but like a drop of water on a hot skillet it never was able to settle.

Only a few seconds after it began, the magic disappeared.

"Are you even trying?" Vasen turned to Oikea. "We have to get this door open, you know."

"Darling, I was trying to do just that. I'm not entirely sure what you were doing, though," she answered with a smile.

"Obviously I was trying to compensate for your shortcomings, but even I have my limits," Vasen said with a small nod.

They turned together to face each other.

"I thought you understood the construction of this door, darling?" Oikea asked with her mouth pulled tight into a thin grin.

"Oh, I assure you that I do. I wanted to make sure I could keep you out," Vasen answered. "It seems I was successful."

The building shook once more, jerking heads around.

"What is that?" Vasen asked. "Are you doing that?"

"Shut up!" Oikea snapped around to her. "I'm sure it's Sebastian doing something. If you hadn't been so naive and recognized him for what he was, then—"

"Mind your tongue, or else you will be carrying it on a necklace," Vasen growled.

"Well, let me use it to say this at least. I'm glad you saw to it this door could keep me out. Obviously doing that was enough to keep us both out as well, as adding your power to mine doesn't do much," Oikea said casually. "I'm sure you can't help it though, darling."

As Vasen yanked her hand free, the magic pouring from them faded and then died, leaving the barrier before them scarred, but standing strong. Both of them rubbed their hands in a quick massage. Stalking away, Vasen's body stiffened and then turned back. She was smiling.

"Oikea, dear, our enemy lies beyond that door. We mustn't bicker outside when we have much more important things to do." Vasen stepped back towards her sister. "It is only together that we will be able to get through that door."

"Oh, darling." Oikea met her sister and took her hands. Gracefully she leaned in and kissed her gently on the cheek. A motion that her sister returned. "I will always stand by your side. There are no two closer people in Elan than us."

"So true." She looked past her at the door. "That door is an obstacle, nothing more. A misplaced step that we will soon correct."

Oikea turned and stood beside Vasen. "It's not even that, is it? Soon we will be inside and then—" She stopped, turning her head. "Did you hear that?"

"Hear what?" Darting her eyes around the hall, Vasen tried to locate the sound she had missed.

"It sounded like…laughing. A giggle. Followed by an odd clicking sound," she said.

"Laughing?" Vasen's voice sharpened to a point. "That will not be tolerated."

Grasping her sister's hand once more, Vasen stepped towards the door, pulling her sister along. She looked over and nodded once. "This time, it cannot stand."

A spark traveled over Oikea's skin. "No, it will not."

The hallway was once again awash in the deafening color of their magical assault.

• • • • • • •

"Why am I still alive?" Olav's voice trembled. He sat still on the floor, leaning against a bare patch of the gold-tinted wall. "You could kill me, couldn't you? So why haven't you?"

Sebastian let his head fall over to one side. "So there is a witness." He smiled. "I have no desire to live in anonymity. I want all of Elan to know what happened here. Where this started. A name and a face to put with their nightmares."

His head slowly started to shake back and forth. "You must be joking."

"Oh no," Sebastian answered. "I assure you I am very serious. In fact, I should give you some background, so you can properly explain it."

Treading lightly, one foot in front of the other, Sebastian began to pace in front of Olav, his eyes watching the floor, looking for the right place to start.

"Do you know what evil is, Olav?" He stopped walking for a moment and looked at the seated man. "No need to actually answer, it was a rhetorical question. Still, I want to answer it for you." He began to pace once more. "Evil is exactly what someone tells you it is. That is to say that what you say is evil, is just that— it is evil. The thing that many don't consider is that what you call evil is standing on the other side, looking back at you, and quite possibly calling you evil in return."

Sebastian took a deep breath and turned, walking the other direction. His eyes were now focused at head level, but seemed to be on no one thing in particular.

"That is to say, you are evil by someone's description. Everyone in this keep is evil according to some soul out there—likely Armas and his wife, actually." With every step his hands moved, trying to enhance his description. "Yet, I'm guessing that the people in this castle would be looking at Sigrid and you raiding this place and thinking of you as evil, in your own way."

Once more he stopped, turning completely to look at Sebastian. "So, you see, evil is subjective. It is only the person telling the tale who dictates what is and what isn't evil. Which is to say, basically, that I am not evil."

There was a long pause, and Olav eventually filled it weakly. "That's...good. Then we all have nothing to fear."

"Ah!" Sebastian raised a finger. "Don't jump to conclusions. You see, since I am not evil, then all of those who think me and my kind should be destroyed are evil—at least to us. What is it that gives you more right to exist than we have? Nothing. It is simply a matter of perspective. So, to that end, the monsters that caged my brothers hundreds and hundreds of years ago, and, much more recently, the false deities who subjugate Elan and force them into worship just so they may feel superior, now those are evil. To us. And we will see evil driven from the face of Elan so the proper order of things may be established."

"The proper order?" Olav asked.

"Yes. Far too long we have been cast aside or caged because it was decided that we did not deserve to live, and that is only because someone else came along and said that it was to be so. We existed first. This is our world, not yours." Sebastian's head looked around in a wide arc, his arms following to complete a circle. "All of this life was put here for us." He looked back. "And it will be again. Now that I have begun to free my brothers."

"That's not the first time you've called them your brothers. Were you trapped in the thing in the mountain?" Olav asked, his eyes looking at Sebastian in a new light.

"Me? Oh no. Those are my...my older brothers. They came about in a much earlier era. I'm still something of a newborn, actually. I came here from Harmonia," Sebastian said. "I was traveling and I sensed the power of this place—I was drawn to it. When I arrived, I saw the retention chamber—that large white edifice in the heart of the mountain—and…well, I am fortunate that I am of a different era. While it pains me to be near it, it doesn't cause the same absolute discomfort that my brethren suffer. So, when Sebastian—the actual Sebastian—was down there, we met and he told me a great many things about what he had learned. That only made me want to learn more, though, so I borrowed his body from him, so that I might find out more of what was happening in the keep. I found the cabinet, and was able to speak with my brothers through it, and learned even more. And then…. Well, I'm guessing you can figure out the rest, actually."

"What happened to Sebastian?" Olav asked.

"I told you. I borrowed his body. That's why you humans exist. You are vessels for us to drain and shape ourselves. I drained his life and shaped myself to look like he once did. One day you will understand, and come to appreciate us, and to worship the lady Dissonance properly," he explained. "And that, actually, is what I want you to tell people. That they serve us, and need to pay homage to The Dark Lady, as they should."

A tremor ran through the room. His jaw opened and closed, but Olav found nothing coming out. His breath was unable to push past his lips, afraid of leaving his body. Fortunately, he didn't have to say anything.

"Wow. You are really, really crazy, you know that?"

Olav's eyes shifted, and Sebastian spun around. Resting casually on top of the empty cabinet sat Renarde, shaking her head slowly.

"I mean, seriously, how is anyone supposed to think you aren't evil? You plan on using everybody as a bottle to store yourself in or something, and you think they aren't gonna think you're the bad guy? That's just horribly messed up." She sat up straight, staring down at him.

"Ah, the spawn of Serenade. I would ask how you got in here, but frankly I don't care. Personally, I was hoping to find you myself and not see you expire in the collapse of the keep." He took a deep breath and rolled his neck.

"Oh. Oh no. I am so scared. Please, do not hurt me." There was no expression in her words or on her face.

Sebastian's eyebrow raised. "Are you mocking me?"

"Nope!" She hopped off the cabinet and landed on the floor. Her tail immediately began swishing behind her and a gigantic smile crossed her face. "I'm making fun of you. If I was mocking you I would say something like," her chest puffed out and her voice dropped down a couple of octaves, "'behold me and my bad excuse for not being evil' or something."

Sebastian's eyes turned solid black and closed to slits, and fire burned through the air as he stared at her. "I will enjoy seeing your body wither and die beneath me."

"Let me guess, you have to say that to all your lovers, too, right?" Renarde bounced on the balls of her feet.

He rushed at her, but she sprang up and to her right, moving her deeper into the golden chamber, well before he was near enough to touch her. Crouching down, she stared up from him, her face low to the ground and her tail high in the air.

"You are fast, beast, but eventually you will run out of places to hide. When I touch you, I will drain the life from you completely." His voice became a ragged grate as the room shook violently. "I will harvest your flesh and soul."

"Ooh, harvest is such a cheery word! And here you claim you aren't the evil one," Renarde said from the back of the room.

"Is that any different from the Valpuri's harvesting humans for their purposes?" he asked.

Renarde popped up, her ears twisting around to the side. "Well, no. I never said they were good people. It's not like it's an all or nothing situation. See, that's the thing. Good is what you do, not what your called. Same with evil."

He stalked back into the room, hands out, tracking her. "And you see with limited vision."

"Actually, I'd say that's you. Me, I'm open." She bounced to the side, once again dropping low to the ground. "I'm not the one lumping everyone into a group."

Breaking into a sprint, he dashed towards her, only to once more find empty air. Jumping backwards, she sprang off the wall, landing far to his right.

"Stop running! Stand and fight you little monster!" he spat, turning towards her.

A slight gasp came from her as she stood up, eyes wide. "Little monster? What? That is just not nice." Her eyes looked skyward for a moment. "Though I guess it's better than always going straight to demon."

"Well, what would you call yourself?" He walked towards her once again.

"Oh! Yeah, sorry. We haven't been introduced. I'm Renarde, and I believe your name is Scum Spawn-Shadow, right?" She extended her hand towards him, and then yanked it back. "Oh yeah, shaking hands is a bad idea."

"Is this how you intended to defeat me? By talking me to death? Are you not even going to attempt to hit me?" He grew closer to her.

"Oh, heck no! I'm a lover, not a fighter. I have no intention of doing anything to you." Her smile grew from ear to ear. She pointed past him. "That's why they're here."

At the front of the golden chamber, Olav stood beside the massive door he had just opened. Beyond him stood Oikea and Vasen Valpuri, their eyes crackling with power.

"Olav, darling, what are you doing here?" Oikea asked. "Do tell me that you are not a part of Sebastian's overture?"

"No! No, I'm not. I came here…." his voice trailed off.

"For what? To apologize? To ask forgiveness?" Oikea prodded as Olav shrank away from her, falling to the ground and pushing himself backwards.

"In a moment, dear." Vasen said coldly. "Let's deal with one husband at a time, shall we?"

"Yes," she hissed. "Yes, I agree."

They stepped past Olav, slowly crossing the room.

"Sepi, I don't think we should be together any longer," Vasen said, her voice rumbling up from the depths of her being.

"Yes, darling, I must agree with my sister. I do think your relationship has become just the slightest bit poisonous," Oikea's voice was dripping.

"Vasen. Oikea." He grew a crooked smile. "We still have a chance to make the very best of this. Join us. You will have a place of untold power in the new world."

"Yeah!" Renarde shouted. "Just remember to…. What was it you said? Oh yeah! Pay homage to the Duck Lady!"

Sebastian blinked slowly, but kept his face towards the Valpuri twins. "I…didn't say that. She's lying."

"He's right actually, I did lie." Her voice was right behind him, and he glanced to look at her—just in time to see the board smack him in the face. In a desperate dance, Sebastian's feet attempted to rally underneath his torso as his momentum carried him backwards, only to fail miserably as he hit the floor with an unceremonious flop. Renarde took a small step forward, putting a narrow plank of wood over her shoulder. "I really did want to hit you."

"You…you…BEAST!" he shouted at her, his hands grasping at his nose as blood began leaking from it. His hands stopped moving as he sensed two figures looming above him. With a scowl he looked up at the Valpuri twins. "Fine. Destroy me. It will do you no good. Your keep is lost and so is your world!"

"Renarde! Come here! Now!" Vasen shouted. Immediately, she scurried over and crouched down behind her, staring out towards Sebastian.

"Darling," Oikea glanced down at him, "we aren't going to kill you. Where did you get such a silly idea?"

"What?" Sebastian's word was echoed at the same time by Olav on the far side of the room.

"You are far too valuable." Vasen gestured towards the cabinet. "You are, after all, the only one who truly understands how that wonderful device works. We want you to serve us."

"What do you say?" Oikea asked just as another tremor shook the room, sending a wide crack up the wall of the chamber. "And do be quick about it."

"I serve Dissonance and no other, as will both of you in time," Sebastian stated, raising his head up, displaying the line of blood that ran from his nose and down his chin.

A ticking noise preceded Oikea's words. "No, it is you who will learn to serve us in time, but right now we need immediate action, so do try to be understanding, darling."

He said nothing.

An arc of energy crossed the space between Vasen's hand and Sebastian's body, joined a moment later by a similar action from Oikea. The room filled with the smell of burning flesh and the sound of crackling energy and screams.

"Swear fealty to us and the pain will stop," Vasen spoke with a sound of inevitability in her voice.

"N-never!" he growled. "You can slay this body, but my essence will go on. I'm not as frail as the shadows I freed. Soon enough, all of Elan will bow before me and my mistress."

"You're partially right, darling. Elan will soon be ruled by someone here, just not you." Another wave of energy crackled from Oikea's hands, searing the flesh on his body. "And we can certainly keep you from dying from this, as well. The pain, however, can last a very, very long time."

"What are you doing?!"

The sudden shout caught all of their attention, causing a momentary delay in the assault on Sebastian. He crumpled to the ground, motionless, as the sisters turned to see Mathilda, Armas, and a woman they didn't recognize at the doorway.

"You…you're throwing energy at him and…." Mathilda's expression fell, and the tone of her voice dropped even further. "You killed mother that way. The two of you…you're…."

"You didn't know?" Sigrid asked her.

"I knew about the potions and the artifacts, but…." she shook her head.

"They're witches. Pure and simple," Sigrid explained.

"I had no idea," Mathilda whispered.

"And who exactly are you?" Vasen inquired to Sigrid.

Standing tall, she looked at the sisters directly. "I am Sigrid Elsker, daughter of Brinna, and second swordmistress of Kyla. I am wife to Armas, and I have come to return him to our home."

Many times Sigrid had gone over those words in her head before today, hoping one day to say them to the person or persons holding her husband. Each time she thought of a different response she might receive. She never once considered the one that happened.

The sisters laughed.

"That's adorable," Vasen stated.

"Yes, darling, you are very amusing, but," she gestured to Sebastian, who was slowly regaining himself, "we have someone else to take care of first. We still have to bring him under control."

Turning back, energy once more surrounded Sebastian, filling the hall with screams once more.

"You...you can't be serious," Mathilda stepped forward, stammering. "He just told us that he intends to subjugate all of Elan. This is no time to play your little power games!"

A sudden burst of air slapped Mathilda, causing her to take a half step backwards. Vasen spoke without looking at her, "Tilly, dear, please never tell us what to do. Family or not, we can't tolerate that sort of behavior."

Oikea did turn to her sister. "We realize that you cannot hope to have any true ambition, but if you just obey us, we will care for you as best we can. We do love you, after all."

"You're insane," Mathilda muttered. "You're both insane."

With a sigh, Vasen gestured towards Mathilda and Sigrid. "Renarde, deal with them. Subdue them without hurting them if you can, but if you have to...."

Immediately Renarde acted, taking one small jump before clearing the rest of the distance in an impressive leap—where she landed behind the trio and stood up to look at the sisters.

"Y'know, after thinking about it," Renarde grasped the collar around her neck, "I kinda like them more." A single sharp tug freed the metal band from her throat, and she then tossed it over to land at Vasen's feet.

"What? How did you…?" Vasen asked.

"A friendly white outline told me how to turn it off. I didn't want to tell you about that, though, since you might try to zap me like you're doing to him. So, I waited for backup." She gestured to Sigrid and Mathilda. "Now we can get on with things."

"I agree completely," Oikea stated as another torrent of energy tore across Sebastian, causing him to drop to the ground motionless. "Give us a moment and we'll be finished here."

Renarde smiled at Armas. "So, you ready?"

"R-ready?" Armas stammered. "Ready for what?"

"To do your thing!" A moment later she winced and flattened her ears at the sound of a particularly sharp scream. "We better hurry."

"For what? What are you doing?" Sigrid looked from Armas to Renarde.

"He's gotta go use the cabinet. He's an Auntiedeclanden," Renarde said quickly. The room fell silent suddenly, and Renarde glanced over her shoulder to see Oikea and Vasen circling a collapsed Sebastian with vulture's eyes. "And we really better hurry. Seriously."

"She means Antediluvian," Armas answered the expression on Sigrid's face. "And I think I have to try. We can't just do nothing."

Sigrid put her hand on the side of his face. "No, we can't. Go. I will always love you."

As she turned away, Armas' hand followed her, but she was gone too quickly.

"You!" Sigrid shouted to the twins, stepping beside Mathilda. "You kidnap my husband, you hold this land in a grip of fear, and now you threaten all of Dula Koarr? I will not tolerate this!"

Shooting her a look, Mathilda scowled, "This is not wise, Sigrid."

Both of the twins looked her way. Vasen spoke, "It is rare for me to say this, but Mathilda is correct. What insanity has possessed you to do this?"

"Yes, darling, please do go away. We will deal with your petty complaints later," Oikea added.

"Petty?" The corner of Sigrid's mouth curled up. "You couldn't be more wrong."

Her feet moved at the same speed as her arm, creating a seemingly effortless arc over her head, with her sword speeding down towards Oikea.

Striking firmly, it buried deep, cleaving a line straight through between her neck and right shoulder.

With a sharp grimace, Oikea glanced down at the weapon lodged in her upper chest. She looked to Sigrid, standing next to her and raised an eyebrow.

An explosion of energy erupted from Oikea, sending Sigrid flying and catching Mathilda in its wake, causing her to tumble down and land beside Sigrid in a heap. Disoriented and disheveled, Sigrid shook her head, turning around until she saw the two sisters pacing towards her.

"Do you really think we would leave ourselves open to physical attack?" Vasen stated. "That was one of the first guards we put up, dear."

"Everything…has weakness." Sigrid's hands fumbled around until she felt the cold steel of her blade. Tracing along, she directed them to the grip and took hold of it firmly, raising the tip in front of her as she climbed to her feet.

"It's a shame, darling. I was thinking we could keep you around to entertain Armas when we didn't need him," Oikea sighed. "Ah well. Goodbye."

The ground trembled once more as the sisters raised their hands, pointing them at Sigrid.

"No!" Mathilda leapt in front of her, splaying her arms wide. "Stand down!"

Their hands dropped slightly as Oikea and Vasen glanced at each other. Together they shrugged their shoulders and brought their hands back up, pointing at their sister and her companion. The magic left their hands, arcing towards the two women, each of whom jumped desperately for their lives.

Sigrid felt her hair rise up, and the unmistakable smell of it scorching surrounded her as she dove for safety. Her tumbling stopped against a table, rattling and toppling a few objects resting on top of it. Her eyes locked across the room on Mathilda, who was also regaining her feet. A quick nod propelled them towards the sisters, Sigrid at Oikea and Mathilda towards Vasen.

The air in front of the twins suddenly filled with shards of stone. They twisted and turned, each motion matching the movements of their fingers. By the time Mathilda and Sigrid reached them, the shards had reshaped into stone swords, dancing in front of the twins.

"I will try not to kill you, Tilly," Vasen said as her stone sword sparked against Mathilda's steel, "but I make no promises."

"Wow. Those two really are horrible," Renarde said in amazement from where she stood beside the cabinet. "And I've met Dissonance, so I know horrible." A conflict ran through her. In her heart, she knew that it was her duty to stay and protect Armas. To make sure he was safe. That made it no less difficult to take no action of her own as Sigrid and Mathilda were attacked. She looked at Armas. "So, you got this?"

"What? It's…it's a box. A cabinet. What am I supposed to do?" He turned to her, opening his hands pleadingly.

"I don't know," Renarde said softly. "I do know that you can do it, though. You opened this box. I was there. I saw it. I know that you can close it again." She put a hand on his shoulder. "Trust yourself."

"I…." He filled his lungs. "Okay. I'll see what I can do." Armas moved to the cabinet and began to examine it closely.

Sigrid allowed herself a brief glance towards her beloved, but she dare not take a single moment more. Flashing steel, she battered against the stone foe separating her from Oikea Valpuri.

"You wield that well," Oikea stated. "I do wonder what you hope to accomplish, though? You've already seen the effect it has on me."

"Yes, it seemed to hurt you." A slash, a step, and a shove against the stone sword moved her closer.

Oikea's chest rose out and slowly receded. "Oh, it does hurt. I'll show you how much shortly."

Mathilda heard her sister's threat towards Sigrid, but had too much to deal with herself to react. Vasen's sword battered against her own, trying—and succeeding—in pushing her back slowly.

"Why are you doing this, Tilly? We're blood. You should be helping us," Vasen said calmly.

The corner of Mathilda's mouth twitched the moment before she spun to her right and slipped past the stone sword. She closed the distance instantly, driving her fist into Vasen's face. The stone sword clattered to the ground as she staggered back a step. Vasen brought her hand to her nose and moved it back to look at the trace of red on her fingers.

"How long would it be before you decided I was in your way?" Mathilda asked. "Would you give me a chance to defend myself, or slaughter me in my sleep like you did Mother?"

Vasen's tongue traced over her upper lip, finding the coppery taste she expected. "It doesn't matter now, does it? You've drawn first blood." Her voice turned to a growl. "I can't let you get away with that."

Energy arced from Vasen's hands once more. Mathilda felt her body spasm, reacting to some unusual force. It wasn't until she felt her back impact against the floor that she realized how far she had flown through the air. The familiar sound of metal clattering on a hard surface drew her attention to her sword. Her fingers wrapped around it as she forced herself back to her feet, and then moved forward to meet her oncoming sister.

Renarde watched, bouncing on her toes constantly. A groaning sound pulled her attention briefly, and she saw Sebastian stirring. "Uh, you might want to hurry." She looked back towards Armas. He was running his fingers over the seams of the cabinet carefully, searching with something other than his eyes.

"I'm trying!" he snapped back at her. "It's just…. This is a cabinet! That's all it is!" Turning around he faced Renarde. The corner of his eye held back a tear. "It's…it's well made. Amazingly so. I can't tell how the joints were crafted or what's holding them together."

"Okay," Renarde nodded, "that's good, right? It means you learned something."

"Nothing useful! I can't even tell what kind of wood this is! I've never seen anything else made out of…." His words trailed off, leaving his mouth slightly open.

"What?" Renarde asked. "What is it?"

He turned to his left, staring at the object resting a few feet away from the cabinet. A perfect sphere of black on a pedestal.

"Why would they do that?" he asked to no one.

Renarde answered him anyway. "Because it impressed the ladies? What are we talking about?"

Blinking, he turned back to her. "Why create a special item that would just test someone? They would already know who should be able to use it? And they wouldn't want to find more people randomly." He spun and ran to the sphere. "This isn't a test. It's a control."

"A what?" Renarde didn't get the answer she expected.

For an instant, the hall filled with a rainbow of colors. An almost physical sensation of iridescence raced over everyone when Armas touched the orb. As he picked it up, each person in the room turned to look at him silently, despite any attempt at making noise. No sound traveled in the chamber at all. They all could see one thing, however: Armas' eyes were glowing white.

"Innihalda."

For one heartbeat after Armas spoke, there was nothing. The next heartbeat, Sebastian pulled himself up and whispered, "No."

Everyone smelled something not unlike the odor of lilacs. And then there was chaos. A storm unlike anything any of them had ever considered whipped around them, circling and penetrating each of them, chilling some to the core and comforting others. A torrent of air whistled past them all, directed at the cabinet.

Armas stood there, his hands holding tightly to the orb. The first shadow that passed him came up from the ground, yanked from its place by an unstoppable force, and then disappearing inside the cabinet. It was soon joined by another. And then two. Then six. Then more than could visibly be counted as a steady stream of darkness flew past him into the cabinet.

"No!" Sebastian stood and rushed towards Armas, his hands outstretched, desperate to simply touch him.

Instead, he found a hand holding him by the throat. Renarde's icy blue eyes stared at him, and in that single moment Sebastian saw something more than just a playful fox.

"Yes," she growled, baring a fang.

His hands beat against her, grabbing her arm and pulling out fistfuls of fur. It was the fingers on his left hand that went first, dissolving into shadow and pulling past her and beyond Armas and into the cabinet. All of his extremities went next, shifting and sliding past her and beyond, until she was left holding only an echo of the man, and then that, too, left and disappeared beyond her.

She smiled and let out a quick sigh.

"Armas," Vasen purred, "you've figured it out."

"Yes, darling. That's wonderful. I cannot wait to use what you've learned," Oikea added. "Soon all of Dula Koarr will be ours, thanks to you."

"No!" The scream struck her ears as hard as Sigrid struck her body. Rushing into and then on with her, Sigrid contacted and carried Oikea towards the cabinet. With a tumble they both fell into the box, landing hard against the wooden interior. Only one of them stood up.

Sigrid staggered backwards, staring at Oikea who thrashed from side to side.

"I…. This is intolerable!" Oikea shouted. "I cannot…stand up."

A sudden jolt of energy ravaged through Sigrid, catapulting her several feet away. Her head struck a display, shifting her body unnaturally to the side where she lay motionless.

"It's a good thing you have me here, then," Vasen chuckled to her sister as she reached out, grasping Oikea's left hand with her right.

A faint whisper of sound was heard when their flesh met. Reflexively, Vasen tried to yank her hand away, but it remained firmly attached to Oikea.

"What…what is happening?" Vasen asked.

Renarde stared at them and blinked a few times. Long slivers of shadow were trailing out of Vasen and Oikea, flowing into the cabinet slowly. Sparks of energy surrounded Oikea's hands, only to be lost in the growing pull and slipping behind her into the cabinet.

"What did you do?!" A look of daggers shot from Oikea to her sister.

"Me? This must be something you did!" Vasen spat back. "All of your tinkering with the box and the orb. You foolish idiot!"

"I will not be insulted by someone like you!" Oikea's right hand reached out, but no magic obeyed her. A more primal urge took over and she grabbed Vasen by the throat, squeezing as hard as she could.

"You…have always been…less than me!" Vasen met her grip, circling Oikea's throat with her left hand.

"I will…destroy you!" Oikea screamed hoarsely as her lower body began to wisp away to shadow, absorbed into the cabinet.

Moving upwards, shards of darkness broke away, transforming into a thick inky shadow, draining out and away, swirling to an unknown destination. The pattern worked slowly upwards, eating away at them until it reached their throats and then their heads, each of them fixated on the other as they trailed away, leaving only the memory of their hate behind.

"Innsigli."

The moment Armas spoke everything returned to normal. The orb slipped from his hands and bounced against the floor, rolling to lay against the wall. Falling back, he stumbled into Renarde's arms, who held him up until he regained his feet. The doors on the cabinet moved, sliding out, up, and then towards each other until they connected. The sound of rushing air accompanied them as they fell into place, a line of white tracing the seams of the cabinet before disappearing into the depths of the wood.

"Armas?" Shifting on the floor, Sigrid pushed herself up with her hands. Her knees slowly gathered under her, letting her stand on her own. "Armas!" Sigrid rushed forward, pulling him from Renarde and holding him tight against her own body. His hand pulled up to her back, returning the embrace.

It was at that moment the tears began to flow.

end chapter eight

EPILOGUE

"So, you have no idea what you said?"

He shook his head, smiling. "Not a clue. The word just…came to me."

It had been over a day since Armas and Sigrid set foot outside of their room. They had taken time to order some food up to their room, but other than those few minutes with the person who brought the food, the entire time had been spent together, alone.

"And how did you know that the orb would control the box?" The tone of her voice raised considerably at the end of her sentence.

"Instinct again." The two of them lay next to each other in bed, naked limbs entwined leisurely. "Supposedly it's because I'm Antediluvian. Which I still don't believe."

"Your mother never mentioned anything about that?" She gently ran her hand across his chest.

"The concept that I might be part of a race of people long thought dead who once ruled the world? No, Mother never brought that up. Neither did Father. And it's not like I can go ask them now. I think I just got lucky," he laughed.

"Well, you did activate that cabinet somehow," Sigrid said, nestling in closer to him. "Besides, I always knew you were special."

"You're biased," he laughed.

"Yes, I am." Moving her head up she gave him a light peck on the cheek before returning her head to his chest.

The knock on the door barely preceded it opening and Renarde bounding into the room, shutting it behind her.

"Hi!" she blurted as she jumped onto the bed, sitting down on the end of it, legs crossed.

Covers flew wildly as the couple tried to cover themselves from view.

"Renarde!" Sigrid shouted. "You can't just barge into a room like that!"

She looked over at the door and then back at Sigrid. Pointing over her shoulder she said, "Yeah I can. I just did. Weren't you watching?"

"That's…." Sigrid closed her eyes and took a deep breath. When she spoke again, her tone was much softer. "That's not what I meant."

"Besides, I've already seen him naked!" Renarde waved her hand towards them. She then turned her head and flattened down her ears. "He, uh, he did tell you about that, right?"

"I did," Armas stated.

"Yes, and he said that neither of you were in control of your actions," Sigrid added, "so there is no issue of concern there."

"Good! And besides, I don't mind naked." She pointed vaguely at Sigrid. "You look good naked from what I just saw. You should

walk around naked. I walk around naked all the time—literally."
She shrugged her shoulders.

"That's…. I never thought about that, but yes, I guess that's true,"
Sigrid said.

"See!" Renarde sat there smiling at them, her tail trashing back
and forth against the bed.

They stared at each for several seconds.

"Renarde?" Sigrid asked.

"Yep!" she answered back.

"Why are you here?"

"Oh!" She popped up, somehow jumping backwards from a
cross-legged position and landing beside the bed. "Mathilda
wants to see you guys. And me, too, actually, but she sent
someone to come get me, and then they were going to come find
you, but I told them that I would come find you instead since I
hadn't seen you guys in forever—it's been over a day, you know—
and I got really excited by the idea, and somehow that scared him
off, so I thought that meant he thought it was okay that I came
here." She took a breath. "So, I came here."

The words settled into place in both of their minds. Sigrid was
the first to respond. "Why does Mathilda want to see us? Did
something happen?"

"I dunno. I didn't do anything." Her eyes rolled up as she stared at
the ceiling for a moment, and then back down to them. "Nope. I
didn't do anything."

"Then I suppose that we should go see her," Sigrid sighed as she
shifted under the covers.

"That's what I thought, too!" Renarde nodded.

"So, we need to get ready," Sigrid explained gently.

"Yep." Renarde's head hadn't stopped nodding yet.

Taking in a deep breath, Sigrid held in for a moment before letting it out slowly. "That means you need to leave the room, Renarde."

"Oh! Okay." She pointed over her shoulder in the general direction of the door. "I'll just wait outside I guess. In the hall."

"Thank you," Sigrid stated.

Renarde took a long, leisure look around the room just bouncing on her feet. "You guys have a nice room."

"Renarde! Get out!" Sigrid pointed at the door.

"Geez! Fine." She turned and walked to the door, her tail hanging slightly low. "I'll be in the hall."

The moment the door clicked shut Armas turned to his wife. "Is she always like that?"

Nodding, Sigrid stated, "Unfortunately, yes, she is. Aggravating, isn't it?"

"I can hear you!" Renarde shouted through the door.

"I know!" Sigrid answered. Leaning over, she gave Armas a light kiss and stood up from the bed. At the end of a long stretch she caught a glimpse of her husband staring at her, bringing a wide grin to her face. "Thanks." His eyes moved up to hers just as a deep blush covered his cheeks.

"You're welcome." His voice had the soft embarrassment of having your hand caught in the cookie jar.

"C'mon, let's get dressed," she laughed.

• • • • • • •

Far above the city, Valpuri Keep clung precariously to the mountainside. Mathilda stood on the balcony of her current office, staring up at it, considering possibilities. Below her, people busied themselves on the street, going about their daily business. Every once in a while she would hear a faint utterance of her name, or see someone stop and look up.

"Madam Valpuri?" The soft voice belonged to her new aide. She still couldn't remember the woman's name. "Your guests are here."

With a wave of her hand, she sent the woman away. Beyond her, inside her office, she could hear the unmistakable voice of Renarde talking endlessly. She took a moment to enjoy the brisk feel of the cold on her face before turning and walking back inside.

Armas sat in a chair, Sigrid standing behind him with one hand on his shoulder. Over at a bookcase, Renarde was poking through items with no apparent plan or order, and Mathilda was suddenly grateful that she had no personal effects here. There was some incoherent mumbling coming from Renarde, and she was content to let it remain a mystery.

Walking past her desk and over towards the shelves where Renarde stood, Mathilda stopped at a small table holding a crystal cruet and several glasses. The stopper came free with the faint ringing tone identifying the container's construction material. Bringing the decanter just below her nose, she took a deep breath, measuring the aroma carefully. With practiced precision she poured four glasses, one of them slightly more full than the others. With one glass in hand she stepped towards Renarde and offered it.

Sensing Mathilda's approach, Renarde turned to see an outreached hand holding a familiar brown liquid. "Ah! Whipskey!" Grabbing her tail, Renarde retreated, doing her best to hide behind her own fur.

With a sigh and a shrug Mathilda moved past her and, taking a moment to pick up a second glass, headed to Armas and Sigrid, offering each of them a glass. They accepted with only slight hesitation.

Mathilda returned to pick up her own glass and then looked around the room. She held the glass high. "To the future and Dula Koarr."

As Armas and Sigrid raised their glasses, Mathilda brought hers to her lips. A second later her glass was empty, while both Sigrid and Armas sat theirs down on the table nearby without a sip being taken.

"Isn't it a little early for drinking?" Sigrid asked.

"Probably," Mathilda answered and set her empty glass down on the table beside the full one. She walked behind her new desk, clasped her hands behind her back, and stood, chin high and eyes forward.

"Now, to the matter at hand." She was staring at Sigrid, after a glance at Armas. "I trust you are well rested?"

"Yes, Mathilda, thank you," Armas answered.

Looking down at him, she smiled weakly. "For reference, you should address me as either Lady Valpuri or Madam Valpuri. As the new Ranee of this Hundred, I have to establish myself and my place. It wouldn't be proper for commoners to address me with familiarity."

"Um, sorry," Armas replied. "That is, um, my apologies, Lady Valpuri."

Her smile grew warmer. "In private it's not as important, but still, thank you."

"What did you want, Valpuri?" Sigrid asked bluntly.

Her eyes traveled back up to Sigrid. "Madam Valpuri." She turned and took a step to the side. "I want to discuss reparations."

"Oh, well…good," Sigrid replied, her tone softening.

"What's a reparation?" Renarde bounced over to stand beside Sigrid. Barely visible in her grip was a small fetich of an animal. "Oh, and I found a bear. I want to take this to Porter. Is that okay?"

"That's…fine," Mathilda answered. "And reparations are what you must pay for the damages done to my home."

"Wait, what?" Sigrid blinked multiple times. "We have to pay? You? Are you joking? You're joking."

Mathilda took another deep breath and let it out slowly. "Do I seem to you like the type who jokes casually?"

"You do make snide remarks sometimes," Armas stated.

She opened her mouth, paused, and then slowly closed it. With a single nod of her head she continued speaking, "True. You make a valid point, Armas."

"Y'know, you're a lot nicer to him than you are her," Renarde commented, gesturing towards Armas and Sigrid respectfully. Mathilda glared at her, causing Renarde to shrink back slightly. "I'm just saying…."

"She hates me," Sigrid said. "I stole her favorite new boy toy from her."

It was visibly obvious that Mathilda was repressing a laugh. "No. No, that's not it." A short cough cleared the tickle from her throat and she continued. "In fact, you assaulted Valpuri Keep, killed several guards, and attempted to kill not only myself but my sisters. This puts you in violation of not only local, but the noble laws of Dula Koarr."

The expression on Sigrid's face tightened, closing her eyes halfway as she stared at Mathilda. "That's ridiculous. You know exactly why I was there. And if it wasn't for my 'assault' then you and your sisters would be dead and this city, and possibly all of Dula Koarr would be in jeopardy, since I was the one that brought Renarde to this place!"

"It's true, she did." Renarde raised her hand.

"And besides, you fought your sisters, too! Right beside me!" Sigrid's voice grew slowly louder with each word.

"As a member of the Valpuri household, that was my right. I was defending my mother's honor," she explained.

"Defending your…. What do you think I was doing?" She pointed at Armas. "I was rescuing him!"

The door opened, interrupting the conversation for a moment, and Olav walked in quickly, somewhat out of breath. "Sorry. So sorry. I had a patient. I got here as quickly as I could." He looked at Armas and Sigrid and their dire expressions. He also looked at Renarde, but she just smiled at him and waved. "What's going on?"

"Ah, Olav. I'm glad you are here. I was just discussing with Sigrid the reparations that she needed to consider for her assault on my home and family," Mathilda explained. "Please, have a seat."

"And I was just explaining that she could stick her reparations up her—"

"Sigrid," Armas interrupted. "Let's wait and hear what she has to say." He nodded up at her, pleading. She took a deep breath and relaxed slightly.

"As I was saying," Mathilda started again, "due to your assault, reparations are in order. The standard penalty for your crime is, of course, death. Considering the…extenuating circumstances of this situation however, I believe the penalty can be reduced."

"Yay! Reduced penalty!" Renarde cheered.

"You are not helping," Sigrid growled.

"You do have another option," Mathilda moved her hands, placing one on her sword. "You can challenge me openly to have all of your crimes rescinded, but considering that we both know how our last duel would have ended, I do not advise it."

Her hand playing around her own sword, Sigrid stepped to the side of Armas' chair. A gentle touch from Olav held her back.

"Wouldn't you prefer to have her sword when you go to deal with that demon I told you about?" he asked.

"I have more than enough to deal with it. I've already sent troops to handle the situation, in fact," Mathilda said with a grin.

"Good enough," Olav answered, "but there are still other things that the Ranee has to answer for."

"Such as?" She raised an eyebrow.

"What about the Harvest?" Olav asked.

She looked over to him. "What about it? It's gone. There is no need for it as the mine itself is going to be collapsed after the thaw."

"Collapsed? But…but what about all of the artifacts?" Armas asked. "There are still so many things down there."

"Which is where they are going to remain. Forever," she said. "Valpuri Keep is also to be destroyed. It's virtually destroyed already. Repairing it would just bring back too many bad memories. My family has lived above this place for far too long.

It's time we became a part of it—a part of our land. The Seat of this Hundred will be moved into the city. I will build my home here."

"Perfect. Then I know exactly where to find you," Sigrid said with a cold smile.

"Ah yes, about that…." Mathilda returned the smile in earnest.

•   •   •   •   •   •   •

"Exile!" She stomped down the snowy road, her feet compacting the already pressed snow even further. "I still can't believe it!"

"Sigrid, we've been over this. Mathilda had no choice. She can't break the law with her first ruling as Ranee, or she will be seen as weak." Armas stopped to shift the duffle on his shoulder and then rushed up to walk beside his wife again. "It wasn't personal."

"Ha!" she blurted. "It was entirely personal, Armas. She hates me, but that's fine, the feeling is mutual."

"She doesn't hate you," Armas said.

"You weren't there for our duel."

The road stretched on into the distance, providing a slightly better avenue for them to follow as they traveled. Already the sun was getting low in the sky, and the city was a faint echo in the distance behind them. They both wore thick and warm clothing and coats, with ample supplies to get them to their destination. A new home.

Looking off to her right, Sigrid squinted out the excess light of the dying day to watch Renarde as she bounded up and down, leaping through the heavy snow with playful ease. The image brought a smile to Sigrid's face despite herself.

"At least we have someplace to go," Sigrid muttered.

Armas followed Sigrid's eyes. "True. Renarde says that we'll be welcome in Harmonia, and I trust her on that."

"No reason not to. She's never lied to me once," Sigrid stated. She turned back to Armas and sighed. "We'll be okay. I know that. It doesn't mean I have to like that witch." She motioned her head the direction they had come.

"I don't think that Mathilda is a witch. You're confusing her for her sisters," Armas chuckled.

"And you're forgetting that there is more than one kind of witch." She raised a single finger in emphasis.

Looking past his wife he saw Renarde standing in the snow, ears back and tail high. Slowly, she crouched down and her butt began to wiggle. A second later she was in the middle of a high arc, gracefully leaping above the snow in a powerful bound. The next second she was half buried in the snow, only her legs, tail, and butt visible above the snow. Without meaning to, Armas giggled. Sigrid followed his eyes to the slightly familiar image.

"Is she always like this?" he asked.

"Like I told you yesterday, yes," she answered, smiling over at her husband.

"Do you think that the others in Harmonia are like her? I mean those other three she told us about, not the normal people," he asked.

Snow went flying as Renarde stood, and then scattered further as she shook her head to clear it. "Nope! I'm only me, no one else. And besides, I have one thing on all those others—not to say that Thibaan isn't really sexy—but I'm—"

"Ah!" Sigrid turned to her, cutting her off. "I've got this." Looking back at Armas she smiled. "Haven't you noticed? Renarde is super cute."

"Yes! Confirmation!" In a series of small jumps, Renarde moved back to the road to walk next to the couple. "I knew that you guys would see it my way."

Sigrid felt Renarde's tail hitting the back of her legs with every alternate step, and glanced back to see the snow still falling off of it from where she had been in the deep drifts.

"Renarde, you do remember that you can run on top of the snow, right? You don't have to run through it like you were." Sigrid looked over at her, watching her face.

"Well sure," Renarde smiled back at her, a bright twinkle dancing across her eyes, "but where's the fun in that?"

Sigrid huffed a half laugh. "Good point. Very good point."

The three of them continued down their path, heading south.

•   •   •   •   •   •   •

"I can't believe that we're just supposed to seal this up." He laid another brick in place, looking past it into the gold-lined walls of the deep, narrow chamber.

"Seal it up, and then they are going to bring the whole keep down is what I hear." The other man laid a brick next to the first.

"I don't get it. I just don't. Look at all that stuff." He shook his head, but didn't hesitate putting the next brick in place.

"Yeah, yeah. What do we know?"

The bricks lay down, one after another, gradually cutting out the light entering the room. Even the brilliant sheen of the walls wasn't enough to maintain any level of brightness. The shadows grew, moving from the ground up, slowly covering everything inside the room.

The standing cabinet, black with swirling shades of red and blue slowly disappeared in the darkness, swallowed up and becoming another lost item in the depths of room.

Darkness only broken by the occasional spark of energy arcing from one side to the other, lying just below the surface of the veneer, trying again and again to leap out of the cabinet under it's own power.

A bolt of lightning captured in a moment—for now.

THE END